THIS BOOK
BELONGS TO

_____

_____

VINTAGE CLASSICS

OTHER BOOKS BY LEWIS CARROLL

Lewis Carroll

Alice's Adventures in Wonderland

and

Through the Looking Glass

VINTAGE BOOKS
London

Published by Vintage 2012

2 4 6 8 10 9 7 5 3 1

Alice's Adventures in Wonderland was first published in 1865
Through the Looking-Glass was first published in 1871

Illustrations by John Tenniel

Vintage
Random House, 20 Vauxhall Bridge Road,
London SW1V 2SA

www.vintage-classics.info

Addresses for companies within The Random House Group Limited can
be found at: www.randomhouse.co.uk/offices.htm

The Random House Group Limited Reg. No. 954009

A CIP catalogue record for this book
is available from the British Library

ISBN 9780099572923

The Random House Group Limited supports The Forest Stewardship
Council (FSC®), the leading international forest certification organisation.
Our books carrying the FSC label are printed on FSC® certified paper.
FSC is the only forest certification scheme endorsed by the leading
environmental organisations, including Greenpeace. Our paper
procurement policy can be found at
www.randomhouse.co.uk/environment

Printed and bound in Great Britain by
CPI Group (UK) Ltd, Croydon, CR0 4YY

Contents

Alice's Adventures in Wonderland

Contents

Alice's Adventures in Wonderland

All in the golden afternoon
    Full leisurely we glide;
For both our oars, with little skill,
    By little arms are plied,
While little hands make vain pretence
    Our wanderings to guide.

Ah, cruel Three! In such an hour,
    Beneath such dreamy weather,
To beg a tale of breath too weak
    To stir the tiniest feather!
Yet what can one poor voice avail
    Against three tongues together?

Imperious Prima flashes forth
    Her edict 'to begin it' –
In gentler tone Secunda hopes
    'There will be nonsense in it!'
While Tertia interrupts the tale
    Not *more* than once a minute.

Anon, to sudden silence won,
    In fancy they pursue
The dream-child moving through a land
    Of wonders wild and new,
In friendly chat with bird or beast –
    And half believe it true.

And ever, as the story drained
   The wells of fancy dry,
And faintly strove that weary one
   To put the subject by,
'The rest next time –' 'It *is* next time!'
   The happy voices cry.

Thus grew the tale of Wonderland:
   Thus slowly, one by one,
Its quaint events were hammered out –
   And now the tale is done,
And home we steer, a merry crew,
   Beneath the setting sun.

Alice! a childish story take,
   And with a gentle hand
Lay it where Childhood's dreams are twined
   In Memory's mystic band,
Like pilgrim's wither'd wreath of flowers
   Pluck'd in a far-off land.

1

Down the Rabbit-Hole

ALICE was beginning to get very tired of sitting by her sister on the bank, and of having nothing to do: once or twice she had peeped into the book her sister was reading, but it had no pictures or conversations in it, 'and what is the use of a book,' thought Alice, 'without pictures or conversation?'

So she was considering in her own mind (as well as she could, for the hot day made her feel very sleepy and stupid), whether the pleasure of making a daisy-chain would be worth the trouble of getting up and picking the daisies, when suddenly a White Rabbit with pink eyes ran close by her.

There was nothing so *very* remarkable in that; nor did Alice think it so *very* much out of the way to hear the Rabbit say to itself, 'Oh dear! Oh dear! I shall be too late!' (when she thought it over afterwards, it occurred to her that she ought to have wondered at this, but at the time it all seemed quite natural); but when the Rabbit actually *took a watch out of its waistcoat-pocket*, and looked at it, and then hurried on, Alice started to her feet, for it flashed across her mind that she had never before seen a rabbit with either waistcoat-pocket, or a watch to take out of it, and burning with curiosity, she ran across the field after it, and fortunately was just in time to see it pop down a large rabbit-hole under the hedge.

In another moment down went Alice after it, never once considering how in the world she was to get out again.

The rabbit-hole went straight on like a tunnel for some way, and then dipped suddenly down, so suddenly that Alice had not a moment to think about stopping herself before she found herself falling down a very deep well.

Either the well was very deep or she fell very slowly, for she had plenty of time as she went down to look about her, and to wonder what was going to happen next. First, she tried to look down and make out what she was coming to, but it was too dark to see anything; then she looked at the sides of the well, and noticed that they were filled with cupboards and pictures hung upon pegs. She took down a jar from one of the shelves as she passed; it was labelled 'orange marmalade', but to her great disappointment it was empty: she did not like to drop the jar for fear of killing somebody, so managed to put it into one of the cupboards as she fell past it.

'Well!' thought Alice to herself, 'after such a fall as this, I shall think nothing of tumbling down stairs! How brave they'll all think me at home! Why, I wouldn't say anything about it, even if I fell off the top of the house!' (Which was very likely true.)

Down, down, down. Would the fall *never* come to an end! 'I wonder how many miles I've fallen by this time?' she said aloud. 'I must be getting somewhere near the centre of the earth. Let me see: that would be four thousand miles down, I think –' (for, you see, Alice had learnt several things of this sort in her lessons in the schoolroom, and though this was not a *very* good opportunity for showing off her knowledge, as there was no one to listen to her, still it was good practice to say it over) '– yes, that's about the right distance – but then I wonder what Latitude or Longitude I've got to?' (Alice had no idea what Latitude was, or Longitude either, but thought they were nice grand words to say.)

Presently she began again. 'I wonder if I shall fall right *through* the earth! How funny it'll seem to come out among the people that walk with their heads downwards! The Antipathies, I think –' (she was rather glad there *was* no one listening, this time, as it didn't sound at all the right word) '– but I shall have to ask them what the name of the country is, you know. Please, Ma'am, is this New Zealand or Australia?' (and she tried to curtsey as she spoke – fancy *curtseying* as you're falling through the air! Do you think you could manage it!) 'And what an ignorant little girl she'll think me for asking! No, it'll never do to ask: perhaps I shall see it written up somewhere.'

Down, down, down. There was nothing else to do, so Alice soon began talking again. 'Dinah'll miss me very much to-night, I should think!' (Dinah was the cat.) 'I hope they'll remember her saucer of milk at tea-time. Dinah, my dear! I wish you were down here with me! There are no mice in the air, I'm afraid, but you might catch a bat, and that's very like a mouse, you know. But do cats eat bats, I wonder?' And here Alice began to get rather sleepy, and went on saying to herself, in a dreamy sort of way, 'Do cats eat bats? Do cats eat bats?' and sometimes, 'Do bats eat cats?' for, you see, as she couldn't answer either question, it didn't much matter which way she put it. She felt that she was dozing off, and had just begun to dream that she was walking hand in hand with Dinah, and saying to her very earnestly, 'Now, Dinah, tell me the truth: did you ever eat a bat?' when suddenly, thump! thump! down she came upon a heap of sticks and dry leaves, and the fall was over.

Alice was not a bit hurt, and she jumped up on to her feet in a moment: she looked up, but it was all dark overhead; before her was another long passage, and the White Rabbit was still in sight, hurrying down it. There was not a moment to be lost: away went Alice like the wind, and was just in time to hear it say, as it turned a corner, 'Oh my ears and whiskers, how late it's getting!' She was close behind it when she turned the corner, but the Rabbit was no longer to be seen: she found herself in a long, low hall, which was lit up by a row of lamps hanging from the roof.

There were doors all round the hall, but they were all locked; and when Alice had been all the way down one side and up the other, trying every door, she walked sadly down the middle, wondering how she was ever to get out again.

Suddenly she came upon a little three-legged table, all made of solid glass; there was nothing on it except a tiny golden key, and Alice's first thought was that it might belong to one of the doors of the hall; but, alas! either the locks were too large, or the key was too small, but at any rate it would not open any of them. However, on the second time round, she came upon a low curtain she had not noticed before, and behind it was a little door about fifteen inches high: she tried the little golden key in the lock, and to her great delight it fitted!

Alice opened the door and found that it led into a small passage, not much larger than a rat-hole: she knelt down and looked along the passage into the loveliest garden you ever saw.

How she longed to get out of that dark hall, and wander about among those beds of bright flowers and those cool fountains, but she could not even get her head through the doorway; 'and even if my head would go through,' thought poor Alice, 'it would be of very little use without my shoulders. Oh, how I wish I could shut up like a telescope! I think I could, if I only knew how to begin.' For, you see, so many out-of-the-way things had happened lately, that Alice had begun to think that very few things indeed were really impossible.

There seemed to be no use in waiting by the little door, so she went back to the table, half hoping she might find another key on it, or at any rate a book of rules for shutting people up like telescopes: this time she found a little bottle on it, ('which certainly was not here before,' said Alice,) and round the neck of the bottle was a paper label, with the words 'DRINK ME' beautifully printed on it in large letters.

It was all very well to say 'Drink me,' but the wise little Alice was not going to do *that* in a hurry. 'No, I'll look first,' she said, 'and see whether it's marked "*poison*" or not'; for she had read several nice little histories about children who had got burnt, and eaten up by wild beasts and other unpleasant things, all because they *would* not remember the simple rules their friends had taught them: such as, that a red-hot poker will burn you if

you hold it too
long; and that
if you cut your
finger *very*
deeply with a
knife, it usually
bleeds; and
she had never
forgotten that,
if you drink
much from a
bottle marked
'poison,' it is
almost certain
to disagree with
you, sooner or
later.

However, the bottle was *not* marked 'poison,' so Alice ventured to taste it, and finding it very nice, (it had, in fact, a sort of mixed flavour of cherry-tart, custard, pineapple, roast turkey, toffee, and hot buttered toast,) she very soon finished it off.

*   *   *   *   *

*   *   *   *

*   *   *   *   *

'What a curious feeling!' said Alice; 'I must be shutting up like a telescope.'

And so it was indeed: she was now only ten inches high, and her face brightened up at the thought that she was now the right size for going through the little door into that lovely garden. First, however, she waited for a few minutes to see if she was going to shrink any further: she felt a little nervous about this; 'for it might end, you know,' said Alice to herself, 'in my going out altogether, like a candle. I wonder what I should be like then?' And she tried to fancy what the flame of a candle is like after the candle is blown out, for she could not remember ever having seen such a thing.

After a while, finding that nothing more happened, she decided on going into the garden at once; but, alas for poor Alice! when she got to the door, she found she had forgotten the little golden key, and when she went back to the table for it, she found she could not possibly reach it: she could see it quite plainly through the glass, and she tried her best to climb up one of the legs of the table, but it was too slippery; and when she had tired herself out with trying, the poor little thing sat down and cried.

'Come, there's no use in crying like that!' said Alice to herself, rather sharply; 'I advise you to leave off this minute!' She generally gave herself very good advice, (though she very seldom followed it), and sometimes she scolded herself so severely as to bring tears into her eyes; and once she remembered trying to box her own ears for having cheated herself in a game of croquet she was playing against herself, for this curious child was very fond of pretending to be two people. 'But it's no use now,' thought poor Alice, 'to pretend to be two people! Why, there's hardly enough of me left to make *one* respectable person!'

Soon her eye fell on a little glass box that was lying under the table: she opened it, and found in it a very small cake, on which the words 'eat me' were beautifully marked in currants. 'Well, I'll eat it,' said Alice, 'and if it makes me grow larger, I can reach the key; and if it makes me grow smaller, I can creep under the door; so either way I'll get into the garden, and I don't care which happens!'

She ate a little bit, and said anxiously to herself, 'Which way? Which way?' holding her hand on the top of her head to feel which way it was growing, and she was quite surprised to find that she remained the same size: to be sure, this generally happens when one eats cake, but Alice had got so much into the way of expecting nothing but out-of-the-way things to happen, that it seemed quite dull and stupid for life to go on in the common way.

So she set to work, and very soon finished off the cake.

        *   *   *   *
            *   *   *
        *   *   *   *

2

The Pool of Tears

'CURIOUSER and curiouser!' cried Alice (she was so much surprised, that for the moment she quite forgot how to speak good English); 'now I'm opening out like the largest telescope that ever was! Good-bye, feet!' (for when she looked down at her feet, they seemed to be almost out of sight, they were getting so far off). 'Oh, my poor little feet, I wonder who will put on your shoes and stockings for you now, dears? I'm sure *I* shan't be able! I shall be a great deal too far off to trouble myself about you: you must manage the best way you can; – but I must be kind to them,' thought Alice, 'or perhaps they won't walk the way I want to go! Let me see: I'll give them a new pair of boots every Christmas.'

And she went on planning to herself how she would manage it. 'They must go by the carrier,' she thought; 'and how funny it'll seem, sending presents to one's own feet! And how odd the directions will look!

> *Alice's Right Foot, Esq.*
> *Hearthrug,*
> *near the Fender,*
> *(with Alice's love).*

O dear, what nonsense I'm talking!'

Just then her head struck against the roof of the hall: in fact she was now more than nine feet high, and she at once took up the little golden key and hurried off to the garden door.

Poor Alice! It was as much as she could do, lying down on one side, to look through into the garden with one eye; but to get through was more hopeless than ever: she sat down and began to cry again.

'You ought to be ashamed of yourself,' said Alice, 'a great girl like you,' (she might well say this), 'to go on crying in this way! Stop this moment, I tell you!' But she

went on all the same, shedding gallons of tears, until there was a large pool all round her, about four inches deep and reaching half down the hall.

After a time she heard a little pattering of feet in the distance, and she hastily dried her eyes to see what was coming. It was the White Rabbit returning, splendidly dressed, with a pair of white kid gloves in one hand and a large fan in the other: he came trotting along in a great hurry, muttering to himself as he came, 'Oh! the Duchess, the Duchess! Oh! won't she be savage if I've kept her waiting!' Alice felt so desperate that she was ready to ask help of any one; so, when the Rabbit came near her, she began, in a low, timid voice, 'If you please, sir –' The Rabbit started violently, dropped the white kid gloves and the fan, and skurried away into the darkness as hard as he could go.

Alice took up the fan and gloves, and, as the hall was very hot, she kept fanning herself all the time she went on talking: 'Dear, dear! How queer everything is today! And yesterday things went on just as usual. I wonder if I've been changed in the night? Let me think: was I the same when I got up this morning? I almost think I can remember feeling a little different. But if I'm not the same, the next question is, Who in the world am I? Ah *that's* the great puzzle!' And she began thinking over all the children she knew that were of the same age as herself, to see if she could have been changed for any of them.

'I'm sure I'm not Ada,' she said, 'for her hair goes in such long ringlets, and mine doesn't go in ringlets at all; and I'm sure I can't be Mabel, for I know all sorts of things, and she, oh! she knows such a very little! Besides, *she's* she, and *I'm* I, and – oh dear, how puzzling it all is! I'll try if I know all the things I used to know. Let me see: four times five is twelve, and four times six is thirteen, and four times seven is – oh dear! I shall never get to twenty at that rate! However, the Multiplication Table doesn't signify: let's try Geography. London is the capital of Paris, and Paris is the capital of Rome, and Rome – no, *that's* all wrong, I'm certain! I must have been changed for Mabel! I'll try and say "*How doth the little –*"' and she crossed her hands on her lap as if she were saying lessons, and began to repeat it, but her voice sounded hoarse and strange, and the words did not come the same as they used to do:

> '*How doth the little crocodile*
> *Improve his shining tail,*
> *And pour the waters of the Nile*
> *On every golden scale!*

> '*How cheerfully he seems to grin,*
> *How neatly spread his claws,*

And welcome little fishes in
With gently smiling jaws!'

'I'm sure those are not the right words,' said poor Alice, and her eyes filled with tears again as she went on, 'I must be Mabel after all, and I shall have to go and live in that poky little house, and have next to no toys to play with, and oh! ever so many lessons to learn! No, I've made up my mind about it; if I'm Mabel, I'll stay down here! It'll be no use their putting their heads down and saying "Come up again, dear!" I shall only look up and say "Who am I then? Tell me that first, and then, if I like being that person, I'll come up: if not, I'll stay down here till I'm somebody else" – but, oh dear!' cried Alice, with a sudden burst of tears, 'I do wish they *would* put their heads down! I am so *very* tired of being all alone here!'

As she said this she looked down at her hands, and was surprised to see that she had put on one of the Rabbit's little white kid gloves while she was talking. 'How *can* I have done that?' she thought. 'I must be growing small again.' She got up and went to the table to measure herself by it, and found that, as nearly as she could guess, she was now about two feet high, and was going on shrinking rapidly: she soon found out that the cause of this was the fan she was holding, and she

dropped it hastily, just in time to avoid shrinking away altogether.

'That *was* a narrow escape!' said Alice, a good deal frightened at the sudden change, but very glad to find herself still in existence; 'and now for the garden!' and she ran with all speed back to the little door: but, alas! the little door was shut again, and the little golden key was lying on the glass table as before, 'and things are worse than ever,' thought the poor child, 'for I never was so small as this before, never! And I declare it's too bad, that it is!'

As she said these words her foot slipped, and in another moment, splash! she was up to her chin in salt water. Her first idea was that she had somehow fallen into the sea, 'and in that case I can go back by railway,' she said to herself. (Alice had been to the seaside once in her life, and had come to the general conclusion, that wherever you go to on the English coast you find a number of bathing machines in the sea, some children digging in the sand with wooden spades, then a row of lodging houses, and behind them a railway station.) However, she soon made out that she was in the pool of tears which she had wept when she was nine feet high.

'I wish I hadn't cried so much!' said Alice, as she swam about, trying to find her way out. 'I shall be punished for it now, I suppose, by being drowned in my own tears! That *will* be a queer thing, to be sure! However, everything is queer today.'

Just then she heard something splashing about in the pool a little way off, and she swam nearer to make out what it was: at first she thought it must be a walrus or hippopotamus, but then she remembered how small she was now, and she soon made out that it was only a mouse that had slipped in like herself.

'Would it be of any use, now,' thought Alice, 'to speak to this mouse? Everything is so out-of-the-way down here, that I should think very likely it can talk: at any rate, there's no harm in trying.' So she began: 'O Mouse, do you know the way out of this pool? I am very tired of swimming about here, O Mouse!' (Alice thought this must be the right way of speaking to a mouse: she had never done such a thing before, but she remembered having seen in her brother's Latin Grammar, 'A mouse – of a mouse – to a mouse – a mouse – O mouse!') The Mouse looked at her rather inquisitively, and seemed to her to wink with one of its little eyes, but it said nothing.

'Perhaps it doesn't understand English,' thought Alice; 'I daresay it's a French mouse, come over with William the Conqueror.' (For, with all her knowledge of history, Alice had no very clear notion how long ago anything had happened.) So she began again: 'Où est ma chatte?' which was the first sentence in her French lesson-book. The Mouse gave a sudden leap out of the water, and seemed to quiver all over with fright. 'Oh, I beg your pardon!' cried Alice hastily, afraid that she had hurt the poor animal's feelings. 'I quite forgot you didn't like cats.'

'Not like cats!' cried the Mouse, in a shrill, passionate voice. 'Would you like cats if you were me?'

'Well, perhaps not,' said Alice in a soothing tone: 'don't be angry about it. And yet I wish I could show you our cat Dinah: I think you'd take a fancy to cats if you could only see her. She is such a dear quiet thing,' Alice went on, half to herself, as she swam lazily about in the pool, 'and she sits purring so nicely by the fire, licking her paws and washing her face – and she is such

a nice soft thing to nurse and she's such a capital one for catching mice – oh, I beg your pardon!' cried Alice again, for this time the Mouse was bristling all over, and she felt certain it must be really offended. 'We won't talk about her any more if you'd rather not.'

'We, indeed!' cried the Mouse, who was trembling down to the end of his tail. As if *I* would talk on such a subject! Our family always *hated* cats: nasty, low, vulgar things! Don't let me hear the name again!'

'I won't indeed!' said Alice, in a great hurry to change the subject of conversation. 'Are you – are you fond – of – of dogs?' The Mouse did not answer, so Alice went on eagerly: 'There is such a nice little dog near our house I should like to show you! A little bright-eyed terrier, you know, with oh, such long curly brown hair! And it'll fetch things when you throw them, and it'll sit up and beg for its dinner, and all sorts of things – I can't remember half of them – and it belongs to a farmer, you know, and he says it's so useful, it's worth a hundred pounds! He says it kills all the rats and – oh dear!' cried Alice in a sorrowful tone, 'I'm afraid I've offended it again!' For the Mouse was swimming away from her as hard as it could go, and making quite a commotion in the pool as it went.

So she called softly after it, 'Mouse dear! Do come back again, and we won't talk about cats or dogs either, if you don't like them!' When the Mouse heard this, it turned round and swam slowly back to her: its face was quite pale (with passion, Alice thought), and it said in a low trembling voice, 'Let us get to the shore, and then I'll tell you my history, and you'll understand why it is I hate cats and dogs.'

It was high time to go, for the pool was getting quite crowded with the birds and animals that had fallen into it: there were a Duck and a Dodo, a Lory and an Eaglet, and several other curious creatures. Alice led the way, and the whole party swam to the shore.

3

A Caucus-race and a Long Tale

THEY were indeed a queer-looking party that assembled on the bank – the birds with draggled feathers, the animals with their fur clinging close to them, and all dripping wet, cross, and uncomfortable.

The first question of course was, how to get dry again: they had a consultation about this, and after a few minutes it seemed quite natural to Alice to find herself talking familiarly with them, as if she had known them all her life. Indeed, she had quite a long argument with the Lory, who at last turned sulky, and would only say, 'I am older than you, and must know better'; and this Alice would not allow without knowing how old it was, and, as the Lory positively refused to tell its age, there was no more to be said.

At last the Mouse, who seemed to be a person of authority among them, called out, 'Sit down, all of you, and listen to me! *I'll* soon make you dry enough!' They all sat down at once, in a large ring, with the Mouse in the middle. Alice kept her eyes anxiously fixed on it, for she felt sure she would catch a bad cold if she did not get dry very soon.

'Ahem!' said the Mouse with an important air, 'are you all ready? This is the driest thing I know. Silence all round, if you please! "William the Conqueror, whose cause was favoured by the pope, was soon submitted to by the English, who wanted leaders, and had been of late much accustomed to usurpation and conquest. Edwin and Morcar, the earls of Mercia and Northumbria –"'

'Ugh!' said the Lory, with a shiver.

'I beg your pardon!' said the Mouse, frowning, but very politely: 'Did you speak?'

'Not I!' said the Lory hastily.

'I thought you did,' said the Mouse. '– I proceed. "Edwin and Morcar, the earls of Mercia and Northumbria, declared for him, and even Stigand, the patriotic archbishop of Canterbury, found it advisable –"'

'Found *what*?' said the Duck.

'Found *it*,' the Mouse replied rather crossly: 'of course you know what "it" means.'

'I know what "it" means well enough, when *I* find a

thing,' said the Duck: 'it's generally a frog or a worm. The question is, what did the archbishop find?'

The Mouse did not notice this question, but hurriedly went on, '"– found it advisable to go with Edgar Atheling to meet William and offer him the crown. William's conduct at first was moderate. But the insolence of his Normans –" How are you getting on now, my dear?' it continued, turning to Alice as it spoke.

'As wet as ever,' said Alice in a melancholy tone: 'it doesn't seem to dry me at all.'

'In that case,' said the Dodo solemnly, rising to its feet, 'I move that the meeting adjourn, for the immediate adoption of more energetic remedies –'

'Speak English!' said the Eaglet. 'I don't know the meaning of half those long words, and, what's more, I don't believe you do either!' And the Eaglet bent down its head to hide a smile: some of the other birds tittered audibly.

'What I was going to say,' said the Dodo in an offended tone, 'was, that the best thing to get us dry would be a Caucus-race.'

'What *is* a Caucus-race?' said Alice; not that she wanted much to know, but the Dodo had paused as if it thought that *somebody* ought to speak, and no one else seemed inclined to say anything.

'Why,' said the Dodo, 'the best way to explain it is to do it.' (And, as you might like to try the thing yourself, some winter day, I will tell you how the Dodo managed it.)

First it marked out a race-course, in a sort of circle, ('the exact shape doesn't matter,' it said,) and then all the party were placed along the course, here and there. There was no 'One, two, three, and away,' but they began running when they liked, and left off when they liked, so that it was not easy to know when the race was over. However, when they had been running half an hour or so, and were quite dry again, the Dodo suddenly called out 'The race is over!' and they all crowded round it, panting, and asking, 'But who has won?'

This question the Dodo could not answer without a great deal of thought, and it sat for a long time with one finger pressed upon its forehead (the position in which you usually see Shakespeare, in the pictures of him), while the rest waited in silence. At last the Dodo said, '*Everybody* has won, and all must have prizes.'

'But who is to give the prizes?' quite a chorus of voices asked.

'Why, *she*, of course,' said the Dodo, pointing to Alice with one finger; and the whole party at once crowded round her, calling out in a confused way, 'Prizes! Prizes!'

Alice had no idea what to do, and in despair she put her hand in her pocket, and pulled out a box of comfits, (luckily the salt water had not got into it), and handed them round as prizes. There was exactly one a-piece all round.

'But she must have a prize herself, you know,' said the Mouse.

'Of course,' the Dodo replied very gravely. 'What else have you got in your pocket?' he went on, turning to Alice.

'Only a thimble,' said Alice sadly.

'Hand it over here,' said the Dodo.

Then they all crowded round her once more, while the Dodo solemnly presented the thimble, saying 'We beg your acceptance of this elegant thimble'; and, when it had finished this short speech, they all cheered.

Alice thought the whole thing very absurd, but they all looked so grave that she did not dare to laugh; and, as she could not think of anything to say, she simply bowed, and took the thimble, looking as solemn as she could.

The next thing was to eat the comfits: this caused some noise and confusion, as the large birds complained that they could not taste theirs, and the small ones choked and had to be patted on the back. However, it

was over at last, and they sat down again in a ring, and begged the Mouse to tell them something more.

'You promised to tell me your history, you know,' said Alice, 'and why it is you hate – C and D,' she added in a whisper, half afraid that it would be offended again.

'Mine is a long and a sad tale!' said the Mouse, turning to Alice, and sighing.

'It *is* a long tail, certainly,' said Alice, looking down with wonder at the Mouse's tail; 'but why do you call it sad?' And she kept on puzzling about it while the Mouse was speaking, so that her idea of the tale was something like this:–

              'Fury said to a
              mouse, That he
            met in the
          house,
        "Let us
        both go to
        law: *I* will
          prosecute
              you. – Come,
                  I'll take no
                      denial; We
                        must have a
                        trial: For
                        really this
                        morning I've
                        nothing
                        to do."
                      Said the
                        mouse to the
                      cur, "Such
                    a trial,
                  dear Sir,
              With
            no jury
          or judge,
        would be
        wasting
        our
          breath."
              "I'll be
                judge, I'll
                    be jury "
                    Said
                      cunning
                      old Fury:
                      "I'll
                      try the
                      whole
                      cause,
                    and
                  condemn
                you
                to
                death."

'You are not attending!' said the Mouse to Alice
severely. 'What are you thinking of?'

34

'I beg your pardon,' said Alice very humbly: 'you had got to the fifth bend, I think?'

'I had *not*!' cried the Mouse, sharply and very angrily. 'A knot!' said Alice, always ready to make herself useful, and looking anxiously about her, 'Oh, do let me help to undo it!'

'I shall do nothing of the sort,' said the Mouse, getting up and walking away. 'You insult me by talking such nonsense!'

'I didn't mean it!' pleaded poor Alice. 'But you're so easily offended, you know!'

The Mouse only growled in reply.

'Please come back and finish your story!' Alice called after it; and the others all joined in chorus, 'Yes, please do!' but the Mouse only shook its head impatiently, and walked a little quicker.

'What a pity it wouldn't stay!' sighed the Lory, as soon as it was quite out of sight; and an old Crab took the opportunity of saying to her daughter 'Ah, my dear! Let this be a lesson to you never to lose *your* temper!' 'Hold your tongue, Ma!' said the young Crab, a little snappishly. 'You're enough to try the patience of an oyster!'

'I wish I had our Dinah here, I know I do!' said Alice aloud, addressing nobody in particular. 'She'd soon fetch it back!'

'And who is Dinah, if I might venture to ask the question?' said the Lory.

Alice replied eagerly, for she was always ready to talk about her pet: 'Dinah's our cat. And she's such a capital one for catching mice you can't think! And oh, I wish you could see her after the birds! Why, she'll eat a little bird as soon as look at it!'

This speech caused a remarkable sensation among the party. Some of the birds hurried off at once: one old Magpie began wrapping itself up very carefully, remarking, 'I really must be getting home; the night-air doesn't suit my throat!' and a Canary called out in a trembling voice to its children, 'Come away, my dears! It's high time you were all in bed!' On various pretexts they all moved off, and Alice was soon left alone.

'I wish I hadn't mentioned Dinah!' she said to herself in a melancholy tone. 'Nobody seems to like her, down here, and I'm sure she's the best cat in the world! Oh, my dear Dinah! I wonder if I shall ever see you any more!' And here poor Alice began to cry again, for she felt very lonely and low-spirited. In a little while, however, she again heard a little pattering of footsteps in the distnce, and she looked up eagerly, half hoping that the Mouse had changed his mind, and was coming back to finish his story.

4
The Rabbit Sends in a Little Bill

IT was the White Rabbit, trotting slowly back again, and looking anxiously about as it went, as if it had lost something; and she heard it muttering to itself 'The Duchess! The Duchess! Oh my dear paws! Oh my fur and whiskers! She'll get me executed, as sure as ferrets are ferrets! Where *can* I have dropped them, I wonder?' Alice guessed in a moment that it was looking for the fan and the pair of white kid gloves, and she very good-naturedly began hunting about for them, but they were nowhere to be seen – everything seemed to have changed since her swim in the pool, and the great hall, with the glass table and the little door, had vanished completely.

Very soon the Rabbit noticed Alice, as she went hunting about, and called out to her in an angry tone,

'Why, Mary Ann, what *are* you doing out here? Run home this moment, and fetch me a pair of gloves and a fan! Quick, now!' And Alice was so much frightened that she ran off at once in the direction it pointed to, without trying to explain the mistake it had made.

'He took me for his housemaid,' she said to herself as she ran. 'How surprised he'll be when he finds out who I am! But I'd better take him his fan and gloves – that is, if I can find them.' As she said this, she came upon a neat little house, on the door of which was a bright brass plate with the name 'w. RABBIT' engraved upon it. She went in without knocking, and hurried upstairs, in great fear lest she should meet the real Mary Ann, and be turned out of the house before she had found the fan and gloves.

'How queer it seems,' Alice said to herself, 'to be going messages for a rabbit! I suppose Dinah'll be sending me on messages next!' And she began fancying the sort of thing that would happen: '"Miss Alice! Come here directly, and get ready for your walk!" "Coming in a minute, nurse! But I've got to watch this mouse-hole till Dinah comes back, and see that the mouse doesn't get out." Only I don't think,' Alice went on, 'that they'd let Dinah stop in the house if it began ordering people about like that!'

By this time she had found her way into a tidy little

room with a table in the window, and on it (as she had hoped) a fan and two or three pairs of tiny white kid gloves: she took up the fan and a pair of the gloves, and was just going to leave the room, when her eye fell upon a little bottle that stood near the looking-glass. There was no label this time with the words 'DRINK ME,' but nevertheless she uncorked it and put it to her lips. 'I know *something* interesting is sure to happen,' she said to herself, 'whenever I eat or drink anything; so I'll just see what this bottles does. I do hope it'll make me grow large again, for really I'm quite tired of being such a tiny little thing!'

It did so indeed, and much sooner than she had expected: before she had drunk half the bottle, she found her head pressing against the ceiling, and had to stoop to save her neck from being broken. She hastily put down the bottle, saying to herself 'That's quite enough – I hope I shan't grow any more – As it is, I can't get out at the door – I do wish I hadn't drunk quite so much!'

Alas! It was too late to wish that! She went on growing, and growing, and very soon had to kneel down on the floor: in another minute there was not even room for this, and she tried the effect of lying down with one elbow against the door, and the other arm curled round her head. Still she went on growing, and as a last resource, she put one arm out of the window, and one foot up the chimney, and said to herself 'Now I can do no more, whatever happens. What *will* become of me?'

Luckily for Alice, the little magic bottle had now had its full effect, and she grew no larger: still it was very uncomfortable, and, as there seemed to be no sort of chance of her ever getting out of the room again, no wonder she felt unhappy.

'It was much pleasanter at home,' thought poor Alice, 'when one wasn't always growing larger and smaller, and being ordered about by mice and rabbits. I almost wish I hadn't gone down that rabbit-hole – and yet – and yet – it's rather curious, you know, this sort of life! I do

wonder what *can* have happened to me! When I used to read fairytales, I fancied that kind of thing never happened, and now here I am in the middle of one! There ought to be a book written about me, that there ought! And when I grow up, I'll write one – but I'm grown up now,' she added in a sorrowful tone; 'at least there's no room to grow up any more *here*.'

'But then,' thought Alice, 'shall I *never* get any older than I am now? That'll be a comfort, one way – never to be an old woman – but then – always to have lessons to learn! Oh, I shouldn't like *that*!'

'Oh, you foolish Alice!' she answered herself. 'How can you learn lessons in here? Why, there's hardly room for *you*, and no room at all for any lesson-books!'

And so she went on, taking first one side and then the other, and making quite a conversation of it altogether; but after a few minutes she heard a voice outside, and stopped to listen.

'Mary Ann! Mary Ann!' said the voice. 'Fetch me my gloves this moment!' Then came a little pattering of feet on the stairs. Alice knew it was the Rabbit coming to look for her, and she trembled till she shook the house, quite forgetting that she was now about a thousand times as large as the Rabbit, and had no reason to be afraid of it.

Presently the Rabbit came up to the door, and tried

to open it; but, as the door opened inwards, and Alice's elbow was pressed hard against it, that attempt proved a failure. Alice heard it say to itself 'Then I'll go round and get in at the window.'

'*That* you won't!' thought Alice, and, after waiting till she fancied she heard the Rabbit just under the window, she suddenly spread out her hand, and made a snatch in the air. She did not get hold of anything, but she heard a little shriek and a fall, and a crash of broken glass, from which she concluded that it was just possible it

had fallen into a cucumber-frame, or something of the sort.

Next came an angry voice – the Rabbit's – 'Pat! Pat! Where are you?' And then a voice she had never heard before, 'Sure then I'm here! Digging for apples, yer honour!'

'Digging for apples, indeed!' said the Rabbit angrily. 'Here! Come and help me out of *this*!' (Sounds of more broken glass.)

'Now tell me, Pat, what's that in the window?'

'Sure, it's an arm, yer honour!' (He pronounced it 'arrum.')

'An arm, you goose! Who ever saw one that size? Why, it fills the whole window!'

'Sure, it does, yer honour: but it's an arm for all that.'

'Well, it's got no business there, at any rate: go and take it away!'

There was a long silence after this, and Alice could only hear whispers now and then; such as, 'Sure, I don't like it, yer honour, at all, at all!' 'Do as I tell you, you coward!' and at last she spread out her hand again, and made another snatch in the air. This time there were *two* little shrieks, and more sounds of broken glass. 'What a number of cucumber-frames there must be!' thought Alice. 'I wonder what they'll do next! As for pulling me out of the window, I only wish they *could*! I'm sure *I* don't want to stay in here any longer!'

She waited for some time without hearing anything more: at last came a rumbling of little cartwheels, and the sound of a good many voices all talking together: she made out the words: 'Where's the other ladder? – Why, I hadn't to bring but one; Bill's got the other – Bill! fetch it here, lad! – Here, put 'em up at this corner – No, tie 'em together first – they don't reach half high enough yet – Oh! they'll do well enough; don't be particular – Here, Bill! catch hold of this rope – Will the roof bear? – Mind that loose slate – Oh, it's coming down! Heads below!' (a loud crash) – 'Now, who did that? – It was Bill, I fancy – Who's to go down the chimney? – Nay, *I* shan't! *You* do it! – *That* I won't, then! – Bill's to go down – Here, Bill! the master says you're to go down the chimney!'

'Oh! So Bill's got to come down the chimney, has he?' said Alice to herself. 'Why, they seem to put everything upon Bill! I wouldn't be in Bill's place for a good deal: this fireplace is narrow, to be sure; but I *think* I can kick a little!'

She drew her foot as far down the chimney as she could, and waited till she heard a little animal (she couldn't guess of what sort it was) scratching and scrambling about in the chimney close above her: then, saying to herself 'This is Bill,' she gave one sharp kick, and waited

to see what would
happen next.

The first thing she
heard was a general
chorus of 'There goes
Bill!' then the Rabbit's
voice alone – 'Catch
him, you by the
hedge!' then silence,
and then another
confusion of voices
– 'Hold up his head –
Brandy now – Don't
choke him – How was
it, old fellow? What
happened to you? Tell
us all about it!'

Last came a little
feeble, squeaking
voice, ('That's Bill,'
thought Alice,) 'Well,
I hardly know – No
more, thank ye; I'm
better now – but I'm
a deal too flustered to
tell you – all I know is,

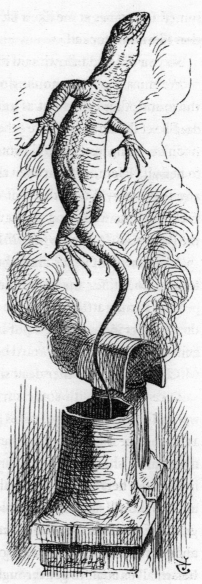

something comes at me like a Jack-in-the-box, and up I goes like a sky-rocket!'

'So you did, old fellow!' said the others.

'We must burn the house down!' said the Rabbit's voice; and Alice called out as loud as she could, 'If you do, I'll set Dinah at you!'

There was a dead silence instantly, and Alice thought to herself, 'I wonder what they *will* do next! If they had any sense, they'd take the roof off.' After a minute or two, they began moving about again, and Alice heard the Rabbit say, 'A barrowful will do, to begin with.'

'A barrowful of *what*?' thought Alice; but she had not long to doubt, for the next moment a shower of little pebbles came rattling in at the window, and some of them hit her in the face. 'I'll put a stop to this,' she said to herself, and shouted out, 'You'd better not do that again!' which produced another dead silence.

Alice noticed with some surprise that the pebbles were all turning into little cakes as they lay on the floor, and a bright idea came into her head. 'If I eat one of these cakes,' she thought, 'it's sure to make *some* change in my size; and as it can't possibly make me larger, it must make me smaller, I suppose.'

So she swallowed one of the cakes, and was delighted to find that she began shrinking directly. As soon as she was small enough to get through the door, she ran out of the house, and found quite a crowd of little animals and birds waiting outside. The poor little Lizard, Bill, was in the middle, being held up by two guinea-pigs, who were giving it something out of a bottle. They all made a rush at Alice the moment she appeared; but she ran off as hard as she could, and soon found herself safe in a thick wood.

'The first thing I've got to do,' said Alice to herself, as she wandered about in the wood, 'is to grow to my right size again; and the second thing is to find my way into that lovely garden. I think that will be the best plan.'

It sounded an excellent plan, no doubt, and very neatly and simply arranged; the only difficulty was, that she had not the smallest idea how to set about it; and while she was peering about anxiously among the trees, a little sharp bark just over her head made her look up in a great hurry.

An enormous puppy was looking down at her with large round eyes, and feebly stretching out one paw, trying to touch her. 'Poor little thing!' said Alice, in a coaxing tone, and she tried hard to whistle to it; but she was terribly frightened all the time at the thought that it might be hungry, in which case it would be very likely to eat her up in spite of all her coaxing.

Hardly knowing what she did, she picked up a little bit of stick, and held it out to the puppy; whereupon

the puppy jumped into the air off all its feet at once, with a yelp of delight, and rushed at the stick, and made believe to worry it; then Alice dodged behind a great thistle, to keep herself from being run over; and the moment she appeared on the other side, the puppy made another rush at the stick, and tumbled head over heels in its hurry to get hold of it; then Alice, thinking it was very like having a game of play with a cart-horse, and expecting every moment to be trampled under its feet, ran round the thistle again; then the puppy began a series of short charges at the stick, running a very little way forwards each time and a long way back, and barking hoarsely all the while, till at last it sat down a good way off, panting, with its tongue hanging out of its mouth, and its great eyes half shut.

This seemed to Alice a good opportunity for making her escape; so she set off at once, and ran till she was quite tired and out of breath, and till the puppy's bark sounded quite faint in the distance.

'And yet what a dear little puppy it was!' said Alice, as she leant against a buttercup to rest herself, and fanned herself with one of the leaves: 'I should have liked teaching it tricks very much, if – if I'd only been the right size to do it! Oh dear! I'd nearly forgotten that I've got to grow up again! Let me see – how is it to be managed? I suppose I ought to eat or drink something or other; but the great question is, what?'

The great question certainly was, what? Alice looked all round her at the flowers and the blades of grass, but she could not see anything that looked like the right thing to eat or drink under the circumstances. There was a large mushroom growing near her, about the same height as herself; and when she had looked under it, and on both sides of it, and behind it, it occurred to her that she might as well look and see what was on top of it.

She stretched herself up on tiptoe, and peeped over the edge of the mushroom, and her eyes immediately met those of a large blue caterpillar, that was sitting on the top with its arms folded, quietly smoking a long hookah, and taking not the smallest notice of her or anything else.

5

Advice from a Caterpillar

THE Caterpillar and Alice looked at each other for some time in silence: at last the Caterpillar took the hookah out of its mouth, and addressed her in a languid, sleepy voice.

'Who are *you*?' said the Caterpillar.

This was not an encouraging opening for a conversation. Alice replied, rather shyly, 'I-I hardly know, sir, just at present – at least I know who I *was* when I got up this morning, but I think I must have been changed several times since then.'

'What do you mean by that?' said the Caterpillar sternly. 'Explain yourself!'

'I can't explain *myself*, I'm afraid, sir,' said Alice, 'because I'm not myself, you see.'

'I don't see,' said the Caterpillar.

'I'm afraid I can't put it more clearly,' Alice replied very politely, 'for I can't understand it myself to begin with; and being so many different sizes in a day is very confusing.'

'It isn't,' said the Caterpillar.

'Well, perhaps you haven't found it so yet,' said Alice; 'but when you have to turn into a chrysalis – you will some day, you know – and then after that into a butterfly, I should think you'll feel it a little queer, won't you?'

'Not a bit,' said the Caterpillar.

'Well, perhaps your feelings may be different,' said Alice; 'all I know is, it would feel very queer to *me*.'

'You!' said the Caterpillar contemptuously. 'Who are *you*?'

Which brought them back again to the beginning

of the conversation. Alice felt a little irritated at the Caterpillar's making such *very* short remarks, and she drew herself up and said, very gravely, 'I think you ought to tell me who *you* are, first.'

'Why?' said the Caterpillar.

Here was another puzzling question; and as Alice could not think of any good reason, and as the Caterpillar seemed to be in a *very* unpleasant state of mind, she turned away.

'Come back!' the Caterpillar called after her. 'I've something important to say!'

This sounded promising, certainly: Alice turned and came back again.

'Keep your temper,' said the Caterpillar.

'Is that all?' said Alice, swallowing down her anger as well as she could.

'No,' said the Caterpillar.

Alice thought she might as well wait, as she had nothing else to do, and perhaps after all it might tell her something worth hearing. For some minutes it puffed away without speaking, but at last it unfolded its arms, took the hookah out of its mouth again, and said, 'So you think you're changed, do you?'

'I'm afraid I am, sir,' said Alice; 'I can't remember things as I used – and I don't keep the same size for ten minutes together!'

'Can't remember *what* things?' said the Caterpillar.

'Well, I've tried to say "*How doth the little busy bee*," but it all came different!' Alice replied in a very melancholy voice.

'Repeat, "*You are old, Father William*,"' said the Caterpillar.

Alice folded her hands, and began:–

'You are old, Father William,' the young man said,
'And your hair has become very white;
And yet you incessantly stand on your head –
Do you think, at your age, it is right?'

'In my youth,' Father William replied to his son,
'I feared it might injure the brain;
But, now that I'm perfectly sure I have none,
Why, I do it again and again.'

'You are old, said the youth, 'as I mentioned before,
And have grown most uncommonly fat;
Yet you turned a back-somersault in at the door –
Pray, what is the reason of that?'

'In my youth,' said the sage, as he shook his grey locks,
'I kept all my limbs very supple
By the use of this ointment – one shilling the box –
Allow me to sell you a couple?'

'You are old,' said the youth, 'and your jaws are too weak
For anything tougher than suet;
Yet you finished the goose, with the bones and the beak –
Pray how did you manage to do it?'

'In my youth,' said his father, 'I took to the law,
And argued each case with my wife;
And the muscular strength, which it gave to my jaw,
Has lasted the rest of my life.'

'You are old,' said the youth, 'one would hardly suppose
That your eye was as steady as ever;
Yet you balanced an eel on the end of your nose –
What made you so awfully clever?'

'I have answered three questions, and that is enough,'
Said his father; 'don't give yourself airs!
Do you think I can listen all day to such stuff?
Be off, or I'll kick you down stairs!'

'That is not said right,' said the Caterpillar.

'Not *quite* right, I'm afraid,' said Alice, timidly; 'some of the words have got altered.'

'It is wrong from beginning to end,' said the Caterpillar decidedly, and there was silence for some minutes.

The Caterpillar was the first to speak.

'What size do you want to be?' it asked.

'Oh, I'm not particular as to size,' Alice hastily replied; 'only one doesn't like changing so often, you know.'

'I *don't* know,' said the Caterpillar.

Alice said nothing: she had never been so much contradicted in all her life before, and she felt that she was losing her temper.

'Are you content now?' said the Caterpillar.

'Well, I should like to be a *little* larger, sir, if you wouldn't mind,' said Alice: 'three inches is such a wretched height to be.'

'It is a very good height indeed!' said the Caterpillar angrily, rearing itself upright as it spoke (it was exactly three inches high).

'But I'm not used to it!' pleaded poor Alice in a piteous tone. And she thought to herself, 'I wish the creatures wouldn't be so easily offended!'

'You'll get used to it in time,' said the Caterpillar; and put the hookah into its mouth and began smoking again.

This time Alice waited patiently until it chose to speak again. In a minute or two the Caterpillar took the hookah out of its mouth and yawned once or twice, and shook itself. Then it got down off the mushroom, and crawled away into the grass, merely remarking as it went, 'One side will make you grow taller, and the other side will make you grow shorter.'

'One side of *what*? The other side of *what*?' thought Alice to herself.

'Of the mushroom,' said the Caterpillar, just as if she had asked it aloud; and in another moment it was out of sight.

Alice remained looking thoughtfully at the mushroom for a minute, trying to make out which were the two sides of it; and as it was perfectly round, she found this a very difficult question. However, at last she stretched her arms round it as far as they would go, and broke off a bit of the edge with each hand.

'And now which is which?' she said to herself, and nibbled a little of the right-hand bit to try the effect: the next moment she felt a violent blow underneath her chin: it had struck her foot!

She was a good deal frightened by this very sudden change, but she felt that there was no time to be lost, as she was shrinking rapidly; so she set to work at once to eat some of the other bit. Her chin was pressed so closely against her foot, that there was hardly room to open her mouth; but she did it at last, and managed to swallow a morsel of the left-hand bit.

*　　　*　　　*　　　*

　　*　　　*　　　*

　　*　　　*　　　*　　　*

'Come, my head's free at last!' said Alice in a tone of delight, which changed into alarm in another moment, when she found that her shoulders were nowhere to be found: all she could see, when she looked down, was an immense length of neck, which seemed to rise like a stalk out of a sea of green leaves that lay far below her.

'What *can* all that green stuff be?' said Alice. 'And where *have* my shoulders got to? And oh, my poor hands, how is it I can't see you?' She was moving them about as she spoke, but no result seemed to follow, except a little shaking among the distant green leaves.

As there seemed to be no chance of getting her hands up to her head, she tried to get her head down to them, and was delighted to find that her neck would bend about easily in any direction, like a serpent. She had just succeeded in curving it down into a graceful zigzag, and was going to dive in among the leaves, which she found to be nothing but the tops of the trees under which she had been wandering, when a sharp hiss made her draw back in a hurry: a large pigeon had flown into her face, and was beating her violently with its wings.

'Serpent!' screamed the Pigeon.

'I'm *not* a serpent!' said Alice indignantly. 'Let me alone!'

'Serpent, I say again!' repeated the Pigeon, but in a more subdued tone, and added with a kind of sob, 'I've tried every way, and nothing seems to suit them!'

'I haven't the least idea what you're talking about,' said Alice.

'I've tried the roots of trees, and I've tried banks, and I've tried hedges,' the Pigeon went on without attending to her; 'but those serpents! There's no pleasing them!'

Alice was more and more puzzled, but she thought there was no use in saying anything more till the Pigeon had finished.

'As if it wasn't trouble enough hatching the eggs,' said the Pigeon; 'but I must be on the look-out for serpents night and day! Why, I haven't had a wink of sleep these three weeks!'

'I'm very sorry you've been annoyed,' said Alice, who was beginning to see its meaning.

'And just as I'd taken the highest tree in the wood,' continued the Pigeon, raising its voice to a shriek, 'and just as I was thinking I should be free of them at last, they must needs come wriggling down from the sky! Ugh, Serpent!'

'But I'm *not* a serpent, I tell you!' said Alice. 'I'm a – I'm a –'

'Well, *what* are you?' said the Pigeon. 'I can see you're trying to invent something!'

'I-I'm a little girl,' said Alice, rather doubtfully, as

she remembered the number of changes she had gone through that day.

'A likely story indeed!' said the Pigeon in a tone of the deepest contempt. 'I've seen a good many little girls in my time, but never *one* with such a neck as that! No, no! You're a serpent; and there's no use denying it. I suppose you'll be telling me next that you never tasted an egg!'

'I *have* tasted eggs, certainly,' said Alice, who was a very truthful child; 'but little girls eat eggs quite as much as serpents do, you know.'

'I don't believe it,' said the Pigeon; 'but if they do, why then they're a kind of serpent, that's all I can say.'

This was such a new idea to Alice, that she was quite silent for a minute or two, which gave the Pigeon the opportunity of adding, 'You're looking for eggs, I know *that* well enough; and what does it matter to me whether you're a little girl or a serpent?'

'It matters a good deal to *me*,' said Alice hastily; 'but I'm not looking for eggs, as it happens; and if I was, I shouldn't want *yours*: I don't like them raw.'

'Well, be off, then!' said the Pigeon in a sulky tone, as it settled down again into its nest. Alice crouched down among the trees as well as she could, for her neck kept getting entangled among the branches, and every now and then she had to stop and untwist it. After a while she remembered that she still held the pieces of mushroom in her hands, and she set to work very carefully, nibbling first at one and then at the other, and growing sometimes taller and sometimes shorter, until she had succeeded in bringing heself down to her usual height.

It was so long since she had been anything near the right size, that it felt quite strange at first; bur she got used to it in a few minutes, and began talking to herself, as usual. 'Come, there's half my plan done now! How puzzling all these changes are! I'm never sure what I'm going to be, from one minute to another! However, I've got back to my right size: the next thing is, to get into that beautiful garden – how *is* that to be done, I wonder?' As she said this, she came suddenly upon an open place, with a little house in it about four feet high. 'Whoever lives there,' thought Alice, 'it'll never do to come upon them *this* size: why, I should frighten them out of their wits!' So she began nibbling at the right-hand bit again, and did not venture to go near the house till she had brought herself down to nine inches high.

6

Pig and Pepper

FOR a minute or two she stood looking at the house, and wondering what to do next, when suddenly a footman in livery came running out of the wood – (she considered him to be a footman because he was in livery: otherwise, judging by his face only, she would have called him a fish) – and rapped loudly at the door with his knuckles. It was opened by another footman in livery, with a round face, and large eyes like a frog; and both footmen, Alice noticed, had powdered hair that curled all over their heads. She felt very curious to know what it was all about, and crept a little way out of the wood to listen.

The Fish-Footman began by producing from under his arm a great letter, nearly as large as himself, and this he handed over to the other, saying, in a solemn tone,

'For the Duchess. An invitation from the Queen to play croquet.' The Frog-Footman repeated, in the same solemn tone, only changing the order of the words a little, 'From the Queen. An invitation for the Duchess to play croquet.'

Then they both bowed low, and their curls got entangled together.

Alice laughed so much as this, that she had to run back into the wood for fear of their hearing her; and when she next peeped out the Fish-Footman was gone, and the other was sitting on the ground near the door, staring stupidly up into the sky.

Alice went timidly up to the door, and knocked.

'There's no sort of use in knocking,' said the Footman, 'and that for two reasons. First, because I'm on the same side of the door as you are; secondly, because they're making such a noise inside, no one could possibly hear you.' And certainly there was a most extraordinary noise going on within – a constant howling and sneezing, and every now and then a great crash, as if a dish or kettle had been broken to pieces.

'Please, then,' said Alice, 'how am I to get in?'

'There might be some sense in your knocking,' the Footman went on without attending to her, 'if we had the door between us. For instance, if you were *inside*, you might knock, and I could let you out, you know.' He was looking up into the sky all the time he was speaking, and this Alice thought decidedly uncivil. 'But perhaps he can't help it,' she said to herself; 'his eyes are so *very* nearly at the top of his head. But at any rate he might answer questions. – How am I to get in?' she repeated, aloud.

'I shall sit here,' the Footman remarked, 'till

tomorrow –'

At this moment the door of the house opened, and a large plate came skimming out, straight at the Footman's head: it just grazed his nose, and broke to pieces against one of the trees behind him.

'– or next day, maybe,' the Footman continued in the same tone, exactly as if nothing had happened.

'How am I to get in?' asked Alice again, in a louder tone.

'*Are* you to get in at all?' said the Footman. 'That's the first question, you know.'

It was, no doubt: only Alice did not like to be told so. 'It's really dreadful,' she muttered to herself, 'the way all the creatures argue. It's enough to drive one crazy!'

The Footman seemed to think this a good opportunity for repeating his remark, with variations. 'I shall sit here,' he said, 'on and off, for days and days.'

'But what am *I* to do?' said Alice.

'Anything you like,' said the Footman, and began whistling.

'Oh, there's no use in talking to him,' said Alice desperately: 'he's perfectly idiotic!' And she opened the door and went in.

The door led right into a large kitchen, which was full of smoke from one end to the other: the Duchess was sitting on a three-legged stool in the middle, nursing a baby; the cook was leaning over the fire, stirring a large cauldron which seemed to be full of soup.

'There's certainly too much pepper in that soup!' Alice said to herself, as well as she could for sneezing.

There was certainly too much of it in the air. Even the Duchess sneezed occasionally; and as for the baby, it was sneezing and howling alternately without a moment's pause. The only things in the kitchen that did not sneeze, were the cook, and a large cat which was sitting on the hearth and grinning from ear to ear.

'Please would you tell me,' said Alice, a little timidly, for she was not quite sure whether it was good manners for her to speak first, 'why your cat grins like that?'

'It's a Cheshire cat,' said the Duchess, 'and that's why. Pig!'

She said the last word with such sudden violence that Alice quite jumped; but she saw in another moment that it was addressed to the baby, and not to her, so she took courage, and went on again:—

'I didn't know that Cheshire cats always grinned; in fact, I didn't know that cats *could* grin.'

'They all can,' said the Duchess; 'and most of 'em do.'

'I don't know of any that do,' Alice said very politely, feeling quite pleased to have got into a conversation.

'You don't know much,' said the Duchess; 'and that's a fact.'

Alice did not at all like the tone of this remark, and thought it would be as well to introduce some other subject of conversation. While she was trying to fix on one, the cook took the cauldron of soup off the fire, and at once set to work throwing everything within her reach at the Duchess and the baby – the fire-irons came first; then followed a shower of saucepans, plates, and dishes. The Duchess took no notice of them even when they hit her; and the baby was howling so much already, that it was quite impossible to say whether the blows hurt it or not.

'Oh, *please* mind what you're doing!' cried Alice, jumping up and down in an agony of terror. 'Oh, there goes his *precious* nose'; as an unusually large saucepan flew close by it, and very nearly carried it off.

'If everybody minded their own business,' the Duchess said in a hoarse growl, 'the world would go round a deal faster than it does.'

'Which would *not* be an advantage,' said Alice, who felt very glad to get an opportunity of showing off a little of her knowledge. 'Just think of what work it would make with the day and night! You see the earth takes twenty-four hours to turn round on its axis –'

'Talking of axes,' said the Duchess, 'chop off her head!'

Alice glanced rather anxiously at the cook, to see if she meant to take the hint; but the cook was busily stirring the soup, and seemed not to be listening, so she went on again: 'Twenty-four hours, I *think*; or is it twelve? I –'

'Oh, don't bother *me*,' said the Duchess; 'I never could abide figures!' And with that she began nursing her child again, singing a sort of lullaby to it as she did so, and giving it a violent shake at the end of every line:

> '*Speak roughly to your little boy,*
> *And beat him when he sneezes:*

70

He only does it to annoy,
Because he knows it teases.'

CHORUS

(in which the cook and the baby joined):–
'Wow! wow! wow!'

While the Duchess sang the second verse of the song, she kept tossing the baby violently up and down, and the poor little thing howled so, that Alice could hardly hear the words:–

'I speak severely to my boy,
I beat him when he sneezes;
For he can thoroughly enjoy
The pepper when he pleases!'

CHORUS

'Wow! wow! wow!'

'Here! you may nurse it a bit, if you like!' the Duchess said to Alice, flinging the baby at her as she spoke. 'I must go and get ready to play croquet with the Queen,' and she hurried out of the room. The cook threw a frying-pan after her as she went out, but it just missed her.

Alice caught the baby with some difficulty, as it was a queer-shaped little creature, and held out its arms and legs in all directions, 'just like a star-fish,' thought Alice. The poor little thing was snorting like a steam-engine when she caught it, and kept doubling itself up and straightening itself out again, so that altogether, for the first minute or two, it was as much as she could do to hold it.

As soon as she had made out the proper way of nursing it, (which was to twist it up into a sort of knot, and then keep tight hold of its right ear and left foot, so as to prevent its undoing itself,) she carried it out into the open air. 'If I don't take this child away with me,' thought Alice, 'they're sure to kill it in a day or two: wouldn't it be murder to leave it behind?' She said the last words out loud, and the little thing grunted in reply (it had left off sneezing by this time). 'Don't grunt,' said Alice; 'that's not at all a proper way of expressing yourself.'

The baby grunted again, and Alice looked very anxiously into its face to see what was the matter with it. There could be no doubt that it had a *very* turn-up nose, much more like a snout than a real baby: altogether Alice did not like the look of the thing at all. 'But perhaps it was only sobbing,' she thought, and looked into its eyes again, to see if there were any tears.

No, there were no tears. 'If you're going to turn into

a pig, my dear,' said Alice, seriously, 'I'll have nothing more to do with you. Mind now!' The poor little thing sobbed again (or grunted, it was impossible to say which), and they went on for some while in silence.

Alice was just beginning to think to herself, 'Now, what am I to do with this creature when I get it home?' when it grunted again, so violently, that she looked down into its face in some alarm. This time there could be *no* mistake about it: it was neither more nor less than a pig, and she felt that it would be quite absurd for her to carry it any further.

So she set the little creature down, and felt quite relieved to see it trot away quietly into the wood. 'If it had grown up,' she said to herself, 'it would have made a dreadfully ugly child: but it makes rather a handsome pig, I think.' And she began thinking over other children she knew, who might do very well as pigs, and was just saying to herself, 'if one only knew the right way to change them –' when she was a little startled by seeing the Cheshire Cat sitting on a bough of a tree a few yards off.

The Cat only grinned when it saw Alice. It looked good-natured, she thought: still it had *very* long claws and a great many teeth, so she felt that it ought to be treated with respect.

'Cheshire Puss,' she began, rather timidly, as she did not at all know whether it would like the name: however, it only grinned a little wider. 'Come, it's pleased so far,' thought Alice, and she went on. 'Would you tell me, please, which way I ought to go from here?'

'That depends a good deal on where you want to get to,' said the Cat.

'I don't much care where –' said Alice.

'Then it doesn't matter which way you go,' said the Cat.

'– so long as I get *somewhere*,' Alice added as an explanation.

'Oh, you're sure to do that,' said the Cat, 'if you only walk long enough.'

Alice felt this could not be denied, so she tried another question. 'What sort of people live about here?'

'In *that* direction,' the Cat said, waving its right paw round, 'lives a Hatter: and in *that* direction,' waving the other paw, 'lives a March Hare. Visit either you like: they're both mad.'

'But I don't want to go among mad people,' Alice remarked.

'Oh, you can't help that,' said the Cat: 'we're all mad here. I'm mad. You're mad.'

'How do you know I'm mad?' said Alice.

'You must be,' said the Cat, 'or you wouldn't have come here.'

Alice didn't think that proved it at all; however, she went on 'And how do you know that you're mad?'

'To begin with,' said the Cat, 'a dog's not mad. You grant that?'

'I suppose so,' said Alice.

'Well, then,' the Cat went on, 'you see, a dog growls when it's angry, and wags its tail when it's pleased. Now *I* growl when I'm pleased, and wag my tail when I'm angry. Therefore I'm mad.'

'*I* call it purring, not growling,' said Alice.

'Call it what you like,' said the Cat. 'Do you play

croquet with the Queen today?'

'I should like it very much,' said Alice, 'but I haven't been invited yet.'

'You'll see me there,' said the Cat, and vanished.

Alice was not much surprised at this, she was getting so used to queer things happening. While she was looking at the place where it had been, it suddenly appeared again.

'By-the-bye, what became of the baby?' said the Cat. 'I'd nearly forgotten to ask.'

'It turned into a pig,' Alice quietly said, just as if it had come back in a natural way.

'I thought it would,' said the Cat, and vanished again.

Alice waited a little, half expecting to see it again, but it did not appear, and after a minute or two she walked on in the direction in which the March Hare was said to live. 'I've seen hatters before,' she said to herself; 'the March Hare will be much the most interesting, and perhaps as this is May it won't be raving mad – at least not so mad as it was in March.' As she said this, she looked up, and there was the Cat again, sitting on a branch of a tree.

'Did you say pig, or fig?' said the Cat.

'I said pig,' replied Alice; 'and I wish you wouldn't keep appearing and vanishing so suddenly: you

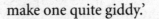

make one quite giddy.'

'All right,' said the Cat; and this time it vanished quite slowly, beginning with the end of the tail, and ending with the grin, which remained some time after the rest of it had gone.

'Well! I've often seen a cat without a grin,' thought Alice; 'but a grin without a cat! It's the most curious

thing I ever saw in all my life!'

She had not gone much farther before she came in sight of the house of the March Hare: she thought it must be the right house, because the chimneys were shaped like ears and the roof was thatched with fur. It was so large a house, that she did not like to go nearer till she had nibbled some more of the left-hand bit of mushroom, and raised herself to about two feet high: even then she walked up towards it rather timidly, saying to herself 'Suppose it should be raving mad after all! I almost wish I'd gone to see the Hatter instead!'

7

A Mad Tea-Party

THERE was a table set out under a tree in front of the house, and the March Hare and the Hatter were having tea at it: a Dormouse was sitting between them, fast asleep, and the other two were using it as a cushion, resting their elbows on it, and talking over its head. 'Very uncomfortable for the Dormouse,' thought Alice; 'only, as it's asleep, I suppose it doesn't mind.'

The table was a large one, but the three were all crowded together at one corner of it: 'No room! No room!' they cried out when they saw Alice coming. 'There's *plenty* of room!' said Alice indignantly, and she sat down in a large arm-chair at one end of the table.

'Have some wine,' the March Hare said in an encouraging rone.

Alice looked all round the table, but there was nothing on it but tea. 'I don't see any wine,' she remarked.

'There isn't any,' said the March Hare.

'Then it wasn't very civil of you to offer it,' said Alice angrily.

'It wasn't very civil of you to sit down without being invited,' said the March Hare.

'I didn't know it was *your* table,' said Alice; 'it's laid for a great many more than three.'

'Your hair wants cutting,' said the Hatter. He had been looking at Alice for some time with great curiosity, and this was his first speech.

'You should learn not to make personal remarks,' Alice said with some severity; 'it's very rude.'

The Hatter opened his eyes very wide on hearing this; but all he *said* was, 'Why is a raven like a writing-desk?'

'Come, we shall have some fun now!' thought Alice. 'I'm glad they've begun asking riddles. – I believe I can guess that,' she added aloud.

'Do you mean that you think you can find out the answer to it?' said the March Hare.

'Exactly so,' said Alice.

'Then you should say what you mean,' the March Hare went on.

'I do,' Alice hastily replied; 'at least – at least I mean what I say – that's the same thing, you know.'

'Not the same thing a bit!' said the Hatter. 'You might just as well say that "I see what I eat" is the same thing as "I eat what I see"!'

'You might just as well say,' added the March Hare, 'that "I like what I get" is the same thing as "I get what I like"!'

'You might just as well say,' added the Dormouse, who seemed to be talking in his sleep, 'that "I breathe when I sleep" is the same thing as "I sleep when I breathe"!'

'It *is* the same thing with you,' said the Hatter, and here the conversation dropped, and the party sat silent for a minute, while Alice thought over all she could remember about ravens and writing-desks, which wasn't much.

The Hatter was the first to break the silence.

'What day of the month is it?' he said, turning to Alice: he had taken his watch out of his pocket, and was looking at it uneasily, shaking it every now and then, and holding it to his ear.

Alice considered a little, and then said 'The fourth.'

'Two days wrong!' sighed the Hatter. 'I told you butter wouldn't suit the works!' he added, looking angrily at the March Hare.

'It was the *best* butter,' the March Hare meekly replied.

'Yes, but some crumbs must have got in as well,' the Hatter grumbled: 'you shouldn't have put it in with the bread-knife.'

The March Hare took the watch and looked at it gloomily: then he dipped it into his cup of tea, and looked at it again: but he could think of nothing better to say than his first remark, 'It was the *best* butter, you know.'

Alice had been looking over his shoulder with some curiosity. 'What a funny watch!' she remarked. 'It tells the day of the month, and doesn't tell what o'clock it is!'

'Why should it?' muttered the Hatter. 'Does *your* watch tell you what year it is?'

'Of course not,' Alice replied very readily: 'but that's because it stays the same year for such a long time together.'

'Which is just the case with *mine*,' said the Hatter.

Alice felt dreadfully puzzled. The Hatter's remark seemed to have no sort of meaning in it, and yet it was certainly English. 'I don't quite understand you,' she said, as politely as she could.

'The Dormouse is asleep again,' said the Hatter, and he poured a little hot tea upon its nose.

The Dormouse shook its head impatiently, and said, without opening its eyes, 'Of course, of course; just what I was going to remark myself.'

'Have you guessed the riddle yet?' the Hatter said, turning to Alice again.

'No, I give it up,' Alice replied: 'what's the answer?'

'I haven't the slightest idea,' said the Hatter.

'Nor I,' said the March Hare.

Alice sighed wearily. 'I think you might do something better with the time,' she said, 'than waste it in asking riddles that have no answers.'

'If you knew Time as well as I do,' said the Hatter, 'you wouldn't talk about wasting *it*. It's *him*.'

'I don't know what you mean,' said Alice.

'Of course you don't!' the Hatter said, tossing his head contemptuously. 'I dare say you never even spoke to Time!'

'Perhaps not,' Alice cautiously replied: 'but I know I have to beat time when I learn music.'

'Ah! that accounts for it,' said the Hatter. 'He won't stand beating. Now, if you only kept on good terms with him, he'd do almost anything you liked with the clock. For instance, suppose it were nine o'clock in the morning, just time to begin lessons: you'd only have to whisper a hint to Time, and round goes the clock in a twinkling! Half-past one, time for dinner!'

('I only wish it was,' the March Hare said to itself in a whisper.)

'That would be grand, certainly,' said Alice thoughtfully: 'but then – I shouldn't be hungry for it, you know.'

'Not at first, perhaps,' said the Hatter: 'but you could keep it to half-past one as long as you liked.'

'Is that the way *you* manage?' Alice asked.

The Hatter shook his head mournfully. 'Not I!' he replied. 'We quarrelled last March – just before *he* went mad, you know –' (pointing with his teaspoon at the March Hare,) '– it was at the great concert given by the Queen of Hearts, and I had to sing

> *"Twinkle, twinkle, little bat!*
> *How I wonder what you're at!"*

You know the song, perhaps?'

'I've heard something like it,' said Alice.

'It goes on, you know,' the Hatter continued, 'in this way:–

> *"Up above the world you fly,*
> *Like a tea-tray in the sky.*
> *Twinkle, twinkle –"'*

Here the Dormouse shook itself, and began singing in its sleep '*Twinkle, twinkle, twinkle, twinkle –*' and went on so long that they had to pinch it to make it stop.

'Well, I'd hardly finished the first verse,' said the Hatter, 'when the Queen jumped up and bawled out, "He's murdering the time! Off with his head!"'

'How dreadfully savage!' exclaimed Alice.

'And ever since that,' the Hatter went on in a mournful tone, 'he won't do a thing I ask! It's always six o'clock now.'

A bright idea came into Alice's head. 'Is that the reason so many tea-things are put out here?' she asked.

'Yes, that's it,' said the Hatter with a sigh: 'it's always tea-time, and we've no time to wash the things between whiles.'

'Then you keep moving round, I suppose?' said Alice.

'Exactly so,' said the Hatter: 'as the things get used up.'

'But what happens when you come to the beginning again?' Alice ventured to ask.

'Suppose we change the subject,' the March Hare interrupted, yawning. 'I'm getting tired of this. I vote the young lady tells us a story.'

'I'm afraid I don't know one,' said Alice, rather alarmed at the proposal.

'Then the Dormouse shall!' they both cried. 'Wake up, Dormouse!' And they pinched it on both sides at once.

The Dormouse slowly opened his eyes. 'I wasn't asleep,' he said in a hoarse, feeble voice: 'I heard every word you fellows were saying.'

'Tell us a story!' said the March Hare.

'Yes, please do!' pleaded Alice.

'And be quick about it,' added the Hatter, 'or you'll be asleep again before it's done.'

'Once upon a time there were three little sisters,' the Dormouse began in a great hurry; 'and their names were Elsie, Lacie, and Tillie; and they lived at the bottom of a well –'

'What did they live on?' said Alice, who always took a great interest in questions of eating and drinking.

'They lived on treacle,' said the Dormouse, after thinking a minute or two.

'They couldn't have done that, you know,' Alice gently remarked; 'they'd have been ill.'

'So they were,' said the Dormouse; '*very* ill.'

Alice tried to fancy to herself what such an extraordinary way of living would be like, but it puzzled her too much, so she went on: 'But why did they live at the bottom of a well?'

'Take some more tea,' the March Hare said to Alice, very earnestly.

'I've had nothing yet,' Alice replied in an offended tone, 'so I can't take more.'

'You mean you can't take *less*,' said the Hatter: 'it's very easy to take *more* than nothing.'

'Nobody asked *your* opinion,' said Alice.

'Who's making personal remarks now?' the Hatter asked triumphantly.

Alice did not quite know what to say to this: so she helped herself to some tea and bread-and-butter, and then turned to the Dormouse, and repeated her question. 'Why did they live at the bottom of a well?'

The Dormouse again took a minute or two to think about it, and then said, 'It was a treacle-well.'

'There's no such thing!' Alice was beginning very angrily, but the Hatter and the March Hare went 'Sh! sh!' and the Dormouse sulkily remarked, 'If you can't be civil, you'd better finish the story for yourself.'

'No, please go on!' Alice said very humbly: 'I won't interrupt again. I dare say there may be *one*.'

'One, indeed!' said the Dormouse indignantly. However, he consented to go on. 'And so these three little sisters – they were learning to draw, you know –'

'What did they draw?' said Alice, quite forgetting her promise.

'Treacle,' said the Dormouse, without considering at all this time.

'I want a clean cup,' interrupted the Hatter: 'let's all move one place on.'

He moved on as he spoke, and the Dormouse followed him: the March Hare moved into the Dormouse's place, and Alice rather unwillingly took the place of the March Hare. The Hatter was the only one who got any advantage from the change: and Alice was a good deal worse off than before, as the March Hare had just upset the milk-jug into his plate.

Alice did not wish to offend the Dormouse again, so she began very cautiously: 'But I don't understand. Where did they draw the treacle from?'

'You can draw water out of a water-well,' said the Hatter; 'so I should think you could draw treacle out of a treacle-well – eh, stupid?'

'But they were *in* the well,' Alice said to the Dormouse, not choosing to notice this last remark.

'Of course they were,' said the Dormouse; '– well in.'

This answer so confused poor Alice, that she let the Dormouse go on for some time without interrupting it.

'They were learning to draw,' the Dormouse went on, yawning and rubbing its eyes, for it was getting very sleepy; 'and they drew all manner of things – everything that begins with an M –'

'Why with an M?' said Alice.

'Why not?' said the March Hare.

Alice was silent.

The Dormouse had closed its eyes by this time, and was going off into a doze; but, on being pinched by the Hatter, it woke up again with a little shriek, and went on: '– that begins with an M, such as mouse-traps, and the moon, and memory, and muchness – you know you say things are "much of a muchness" – did you ever see such a thing as a drawing of a muchness?'

'Really, now you ask me,' said Alice, very much confused, 'I don't think –'

'Then you shouldn't talk,' said the Hatter.

This piece of rudeness was more than Alice could bear: she got up in great disgust, and walked off; the Dormouse fell asleep instantly, and neither of the others took the least notice of her going, though she looked back once or twice, half hoping that they would call after her: the last time she saw them, they were trying to put the Dormouse into the teapot.

At any rate I'll never go *there* again!' said Alice as she picked her way through the wood. 'It's the stupidest tea-party I ever was at in all my life!'

Just as she said this, she noticed that one of the trees had a door leading right into it. 'That's very curious!' she thought. 'But everything's curious today. I think I may as well go in at once.' And in she went.

Once more she found herself in the long hall, and close to the little glass table. 'Now, I'll manage better this time,' she said to herself, and began by taking the little golden key, and unlocking the door that led into the garden. Then she set to work nibbling at the mushroom (she had kept a piece of it in her pocket) till she was about a foot high: then she walked down the little passage: and *then* – she found herself at last in the beautiful garden, among the bright flower-beds and the cool fountains.

8

The Queen's Croquet-Ground

A LARGE rose-tree stood near the entrance of the garden: the roses growing on it were white, but there were three gardeners at it, busily painting them red. Alice thought this a very curious thing, and she went nearer to watch them, and just as she came up to them she heard one of them say, 'Look out now, Five! Don't go splashing paint over me like that!'

'I couldn't help it,' said Five in a sulky tone; 'Seven jogged my elbow.'

On which Seven looked up and said, 'That's right, Five! Always lay the blame on others!'

'*You'd* better not talk!' said Five. 'I heard the Queen say only yesterday you deserved to be beheaded!'

'What for?' said the one who had spoken first.

'That's none of *your* business, Two!' said Seven.

'Yes it *is* his business!' said Five, 'and I'll tell him – it was for bringing the cook tulip-roots instead of onions.'

Seven flung down his brush, and had just begun 'Well, of all the unjust things –' when his eye chanced to fall upon Alice, as she stood watching them, and he checked himself suddenly: the others looked round also, and all of them bowed low.

'Would you tell me,' said Alice, a little timidly 'why you are painting those roses?'

Five and Seven said nothing, but looked at Two. Two began in a low voice, 'Why the fact is, you see, Miss, this here ought to have been a *red* rose-tree, and we put a white one in by mistake; and if the Queen was to find out, we should all have our heads cut off, you know. So you see, Miss, we're doing our best, afore she comes, to –' At this moment Five, who had been anxiously looking across the garden, called out 'The Queen! The Queen!' and the three gardeners instantly threw themselves flat upon their faces. There was a sound of many footsteps, and Alice looked round, eager to see the Queen.

First came ten soldiers carrying clubs; these were all shaped like the three gardeners, oblong and flat, with their hands and feet at the corners: next the ten courtiers; these were ornamented all over with diamonds, and walked two and two, as the soldiers did. After these came the royal children; there were ten of them, and the little dears came jumping merrily along hand in hand, in couples: they were all ornamented with hearts. Next came the guests, mostly Kings and Queens, and among them Alice recognised the White Rabbit: it was talking in a hurried nervous manner, smiling at everything that was said, and went by without noticing her. Then followed the Knave of Hearts, carrying the King's crown on a crimson velvet cushion; and, last of all this procession, came THE KING AND QUEEN OF HEARTS.

Alice was rather doubtful whether she ought not to lie down on her face like the three gardeners, but she could not remember ever having heard of such a rule at processions; 'and besides, what would be the use of a procession,' thought she, 'if people had all to lie down upon their faces, so that they couldn't see it?' So she stood still where she was, and waited.

When the procession came opposite to Alice, they all stopped and looked at her, and the Queen said severely 'Who is this?' She said it to the Knave of Hearts, who only bowed and smiled in reply.

'Idiot!' said the Queen, tossing her head impatiently; and, turning to Alice, she went on, 'What's your name, child?'

'My name is Alice, so please your Majesty,' said Alice very politely; but she added, to herself, 'Why, they're only a pack of cards, after all. I needn't be afraid of them!'

'And who are *these*?' said the Queen, pointing to the three gardeners who were lying round the rose-tree; for, you see, as they were lying on their faces, and the pattern on their backs was the same as the rest of the pack, she could not tell whether they were gardeners, or soldiers, or courtiers, or three of her own children.

'How should *I* know?' said Alice, surprised at her own courage. 'It's no business of *mine*.'

The Queen turned crimson with fury, and, after glaring at her for a moment like a wild beast, screamed 'Off with her head! Off –'

'Nonsense!' said Alice, very loudly and decidedly, and the Queen was silent.

The King laid his hand upon her arm, and timidly said 'Consider, my dear: she is only a child!'

The Queen turned angrily away from him, and said to the Knave 'Turn them over!'

The Knave did so, very carefully, with one foot.

'Get up!' said the Queen, in a shrill, loud voice, and the three gardeners instantly jumped up, and began bowing to the King, the Queen, the royal children, and everybody else.

'Leave off that!' screamed the Queen. 'You make me giddy.' And then, turning to the rose-tree, she went on, 'What *have* you been doing here?'

'May it please your Majesty,' said Two, in a very humble tone, going down on one knee as he spoke, 'we were trying –'

'*I* see!' said the Queen, who had meanwhile been examining the roses. 'Off with their heads!' and the procession moved on, three of the soldiers remaining behind to execute the unfortunate gardeners, who

ran to Alice for protection.

'You shan't be beheaded!' said Alice, and she put them into a large flower-pot that stood near. The three soldiers wandered about for a minute or two, looking for them, and then quietly marched off after the others.

'Are their heads off?' shouted the Queen.

'Their heads are gone, if it please your Majesty!' the soldiers shouted in reply.

'That's right!' shouted the Queen. 'Can you play croquet?'

The soldiers were silent, and looked at Alice, as the question was evidently meant for her.

'Yes!' shouted Alice.

'Come on, then!' roared the Queen, and Alice joined the procession, wondering very much what would happen next.

'It's – it's a very fine day!' said a timid voice at her side. She was walking by the White Rabbit, who was peeping anxiously into her face.

'Very,' said Alice: '– where's the Duchess?'

'Hush! Hush!' said the Rabbit in a low, hurried tone. He looked anxiously over his shoulder as he spoke, and then raised himself upon tiptoe, put his mouth close to her ear, and whispered 'She's under sentence of execution.'

'What for?' said Alice.

'Did you say "What a pity!"?' the Rabbit asked.

'No, I didn't,' said Alice: 'I don't think it's at all a pity. I said "What for?"'

'She boxed the Queen's ears –' the Rabbit began. Alice gave a little scream of laughter. 'Oh, hush!' the Rabbit whispered in a frightened tone. 'The Queen will hear you! You see, she came rather late, and the Queen said –'

'Get to your places!' shouted the Queen in a voice of thunder, and people began running about in all directions, tumbling up against each other; however, they got settled down in a minute or two, and the game began. Alice thought she had never seen such a curious croquet-ground in all her life; it was all ridges and furrows; the balls were live hedgehogs, the mallets live flamingoes, and the soldiers had to double themselves up and to stand on their hands and feet, to make the arches.

The chief difficulty Alice found at first was in managing her flamingo: she succeeded in getting its body tucked away, comfortably enough, under her arm, with its legs hanging down, but generally, just as she had got its neck nicely straightened out, and was going to give the hedgehog a blow with its head, it *would* twist itself round and look up in her face, with such a puzzled expression that she could not help bursting out laughing: and when she had got its head down, and was going to begin again, it was very provoking to find that the hedgehog had unrolled itself, and was in the act of crawling away: besides all this, there was generally a ridge or furrow in the way wherever she wanted to send the hedgehog to, and, as the doubled-up soldiers were

always getting up and walking off to other parts of the ground, Alice soon came to the conclusion that it was a very difficult game indeed.

The players all played at once without waiting for turns, quarrelling all the while, and fighting for the hedgehogs; and in a very short time the Queen was in a furious passion, and went stamping about, and shouting 'Off with his head!' or 'Off with her head!' about once in a minute.

Alice began to feel very uneasy: to be sure, she had not as yet had any dispute with the Queen, but she knew that it might happen any minute, 'and then,' thought she, 'what would become of me? They're dreadfully fond of beheading people here; the great wonder is, that there's any one left alive!'

She was looking about for some way of escape, and wondering whether she could get away without being seen, when she noticed a curious appearance in the air: it puzzled her very much at first, but, after watching it a minute or two, she made it out to be a grin, and she said to herself 'It's the Cheshire Cat: now I shall have somebody to talk to.'

'How are you getting on?' said the Cat, as soon as there was mouth enough for it to speak with.

Alice waited till the eyes appeared, and then nodded. 'It's no use speaking to it,' she thought, 'till its ears have come, or at least one of them.' In another minute the whole head appeared, and then Alice put down her flamingo, and began an account of the game, feeling very glad she had someone to listen to her. The Cat seemed to think that there was enough of it now in sight, and no more of it appeared.

'I don't think they play at all fairly,' Alice began, in rather a complaining tone, 'and they all quarrel so dreadfully one can't hear oneself speak – and they don't seem to have any rules in particular; at least, if there are, nobody attends to them – and you've no idea how confusing it is all the things being alive; for instance, there's the arch I've got to go through next walking about at the other end of the ground – and I should have croqueted the Queen's hedgehog just now, only it ran away when it saw mine coming!'

'How do you like the Queen?' said the Cat in a low voice.

'Not at all, 'said Alice: 'she's so extremely –' Just then she noticed that the Queen was close behind her, listening: so she went on, '– likely to win, that it's hardly worth while finishing the game.'

The Queen smiled and passed on.

'Who *are* you talking to?' said the King, coming up to Alice, and looking at the Cat's head with great curiosity.

'It's a friend of mine – a Cheshire Cat,' said Alice: 'allow me to introduce it.'

'I don't like the look of it at all,' said the King: 'however, it may kiss my hand if it likes.'

'I'd rather not,' the Cat remarked.

'Don't be impertinent,' said the King, 'and don't look at me like that!' He got behind Alice as he spoke.

'A cat may look at a king,' said Alice. 'I've read that in some book, but I don't remember where.'

'Well, it must be removed,' said the King very decidedly, and he called to the Queen, who was passing at the moment, 'My dear! I wish you would have this cat removed!'

The Queen had only one way of settling all difficulties, great or small. 'Off with his head!' she said, without even looking round.

'I'll fetch the executioner myself,' said the King eagerly, and he hurried off.

Alice thought she might as well go back, and see how the game was going on, as she heard the Queen's voice in the distance, screaming with passion. She had already heard her sentence three of the players to be executed for having missed their turns, and she did not like the look of things at all, as the game was in such confusion that she never knew whether it was her turn or not. She she went in search of her hedgehog.

The hedgehog was engaged in a fight with another hedgehog, which seemed to Alice an excellent opportunity for croqueting one of them with the other: the only difficulty was, that her flamingo was gone across to the other side of the garden, where Alice could see it trying in a helpless sort of way to fly up into a tree.

By the time she had caught the flamingo and brought it back, the fight was over, and both the hedgehogs were out of sight: 'but it doesn't matter much,' thought Alice, 'as all the arches are gone from this side of the

ground.' So she tucked it away under her arm, that it might not escape again, and went back for a little more conversation with her friend.

When she got back to the Cheshire Cat, she was surprised to find quite a large crowd collected round it:

there was a dispute going on between the executioner, the King, and the Queen, who were all talking at once, while all the rest were quite silent, and looked very uncomfortable.

The moment Alice appeared, she was appealed to by all three to settle the question, and they repeated their arguments to her, though, as they all spoke at once, she found it very hard indeed to make out exactly what they said.

The executioner's argument was, that you couldn't cut off a head unless there was a body to cut it off from: that he had never had to do such a thing before, and he wasn't going to begin at *his* time of life.

The King's argument was, that anything that had a head could be beheaded, and that you weren't to talk nonsense.

The Queen's argument was, that if something wasn't done about it in less than no time she'd have everybody executed, all round. (It was this last remark that had made the whole party look so grave and anxious.)

Alice could think of nothing else to say but 'It belongs to the Duchess: you'd better ask *her* about it.'

'She's in prison,' the Queen said to the executioner: 'fetch her here.' And the executioner went off like an arrow.

The Cat's head began fading away the moment he was gone, and, by the time he had come back with the Duchess, it had entirely disappeared; so the King and the executioner ran wildly up and down looking for it, while the rest of the party went back to the game.

9

The Mock Turtle's Story

'YOU can't think how glad I am to see you again, you dear old thing!' said the Duchess, as she tucked her arm affectionately into Alice's, and they walked off together.

Alice was very glad to find her in such a pleasant temper, and thought to herself that perhaps it was only the pepper that had made her so savage when they met in the kitchen.

'When *I'm* a Duchess,' she said to herself, (not in a very hopeful tone though), 'I won't have any pepper in my kitchen *at all*. Soup does very well without – Maybe it's always pepper that makes people hot-tempered,' she went on, very much pleased at having found out a new kind of rule, 'and vinegar that makes them sour – and camomile that makes them bitter – and – and barley-sugar and such things that make children sweet-tempered. I only wish people knew *that*: then they wouldn't be so stingy about it, you know –'

She had quite forgotten the Duchess by this time, and was a little startled when she heard her voice close to her ear. 'You're thinking about something, my dear, and that makes you forget to talk. I can't tell you just now what the moral of that is, but I shall remember it in a bit.'

'Perhaps it hasn't one,' Alice ventured to remark.

'Tut, tut, child!' said the Duchess. 'Everything's got a moral, if only you can find it.' And she squeezed herself up closer to Alice's side as she spoke.

Alice did not much like keeping so close to her: first, because the Duchess was *very* ugly; and secondly, because she was exactly the right height to rest her chin upon Alice's shoulder, and it was an uncomfortably sharp chin. However, she did not like to be rude, so she bore it as well as she could.

'The game's going on rather better now,' she said, by way of keeping up the conversation a little.

''Tis so,' said the Duchess: 'and the moral of that is – "Oh, 'tis love, 'tis love, that makes the world go round!"'

'Somebody said,' Alice whispered, 'that it's done by everybody minding their own business!'

'Ah, well! It means much the same thing,' said the Duchess, digging her sharp little chin into Alice's shoulder as she added, 'and the moral of *that* is – "Take care of the sense, and the sounds will take care of themselves."'

'How fond she is of finding morals in things!' Alice thought to herself.

'I dare say you're wondering why I don't put my arm round your waist,' the Duchess said after a pause: 'the reason is, that I'm doubtful about the temper of your flamingo. Shall I try the experiment?'

'He might bite,' Alice cautiously replied, not feeling at all anxious to have the experiment tried.

'Very true,' said the Duchess: 'flamingoes and mustard both bite. And the moral of that is – "Birds of a feather flock together."'

'Only mustard isn't a bird,' Alice remarked.

'Right, as usual,' said the Duchess: 'what a clear way you have of putting things!'

'It's a mineral, I *think*,' said Alice.

'Of course it is,' said the Duchess, who seemed ready to agree to everything that Alice said; 'there's a large mustard-mine near here. And the moral of that is – "The more there is of mine, the less there is of yours."'

'Oh, I know!' exclaimed Alice, who had not attended to this last remark, 'it's a vegetable. It doesn't look like one, but it is.'

'I quite agree with you,' said the Duchess; 'and the moral of that is – "Be what you would seem to be" – or if you'd like it put more simply – "Never imagine yourself not to be otherwise than what it might appear to others that what you were or might have been was not otherwise than what you had been would have appeared to them to be otherwise."'

'I think I should understand that better,' Alice said very politely, 'if I had it written down: but I can't quite follow it as you say it.'

'That's nothing to what I could say if I chose,' the Duchess replied, in a pleased tone.

'Pray don't trouble yourself to say it any longer than that,' said Alice.

'Oh, don't talk about trouble!' said the Duchess. 'I make you a present of everything I've said as yet.'

'A cheap sort of present!' thought Alice. 'I'm glad they don't give birthday presents like that!' But she did not venture to say it out loud.

'Thinking again?' the Duchess asked, with another dig of her sharp little chin.

'I've a right to think,' said Alice sharply, for she was beginning to feel a little worried.

'Just about as much right,' said the Duchess, 'as pigs have to fly; and the m —'

But here, to Alice's great surprise, the Duchess's voice died away, even in the middle of her favourite word 'moral,' and the arm that was linked into hers began to tremble. Alice looked up, and there stood the Queen in front of them, with her arms folded, frowning like a thunderstorm.

'A fine day, your Majesty!' the Duchess began in a low, weak voice.

'Now, I give you fair warning,' shouted the Queen, stamping on the ground as she spoke; 'either you or your head must be off, and that in about half no time! Take your choice!'

The Duchess took her choice, and was gone in a moment.

'Let's go on with the game,' the Queen said to Alice; and Alice was too much frightened to say a word, but slowly followed her back to the croquet-ground.

The other guests had taken advantage of the Queen's absence, and were resting in the shade: however, the moment they saw her, they hurried back to the game, the Queen merely remarking that a moment's delay would cost them their lives.

All the time they were playing the Queen never left off quarrelling with the other players, and shouting 'Off with his head!' or 'Off with her head!' Those whom she sentenced were taken into custody by the soldiers, who of course had to leave off being arches to do this, so that by the end of half an hour or so there were no arches left, and all the players, except the King, the Queen, and Alice, were in custody and under sentence of execution.

Then the Queen left off, quite out of breath, and said to Alice, 'Have you seen the Mock Turtle yet?'

'No,' said Alice. 'I don't even know what a Mock Turtle is.'

'It's the thing Mock Turtle Soup is made from,' said the Queen.

'I never saw one, or heard of one,' said Alice.

'Come on, then,' said the Queen, 'and he shall tell you his history.'

As they walked off together, Alice heard the King say in a low voice, to the company generally, 'You are all pardoned.' 'Come, *that's* a good thing!' she said to herself, for she had felt quite unhappy at the number of executions the Queen had ordered.

They very soon came upon a Gryphon, lying fast asleep in the sun. (If you don't know what a Gryphon is, look at the picture.) 'Up, lazy thing!' said the Queen, 'and take this young lady to see the Mock Turtle, and to hear his history. I must go back and see after some executions I have ordered'; and she walked off, leaving Alice alone with the Gryphon. Alice did not quite like the look of the creature, but on the whole she thought it would be quite as safe to stay with it as to go after that savage Queen: so she waited.

The Gryphon sat up and rubbed its eyes: then it watched the Queen till she was out of sight: then it chuckled. 'What fun!' said the Gryphon, half to itself, half to Alice.

'What *is* the fun?' said Alice.

'Why, *she*,' said the Gryphon. 'It's all her fancy, that: they never executes nobody, you know. Come on!'

'Everybody says "come on!" here,' thought Alice, as she went slowly after it: 'I never was so ordered about in all my life, never!'

They had not gone far before they saw the Mock Turtle in the distance, sitting sad and lonely on a little ledge of rock, and, as they came nearer, Alice could hear him sighing as if his heart would break. She pitied him deeply. 'What is his sorrow?' she asked the Gryphon, and the Gryphon answered, very nearly in the same words as before, 'It's all his fancy, that: he hasn't got no sorrow, you know. Come on!'

So they went up to the Mock Turtle, who looked at them with large eyes full of tears, but said nothing.

'This here young lady,' said the Gryphon, 'she wants for to know your history, she do.'

'I'll tell it her,' said the Mock Turtle in a deep, hollow

tone: 'sit down, both of you, and don't speak a word till I've finished.'

So they sat down, and nobody spoke for some minutes. Alice thought to herself, 'I don't see how he can *ever* finish, if he doesn't begin.' But she waited patiently.

'Once,' said the Mock Turtle at last, with a deep sigh, 'I was a real Turtle.'

These words were followed by a very long silence, broken only by an occasional exclamation of 'Hjckrrh!' from the Gryphon, and the constant heavy sobbing of the Mock Turtle. Alice was very nearly getting up and saying, 'Thank you, sir, for your interesting story,' but she could not help thinking there must be more to come, so she sat still and said nothing.

'When we were little,' the Mock Turtle went on at last, more calmly, though still sobbing a little now and then, 'we went to school in the sea. The master was an old Turtle – we used to call him Tortoise –'

'Why did you call him Tortoise, if he wasn't one?' Alice asked.

'We called him Tortoise because he taught us,' said the Mock Turtle angrily: 'really you are very dull!'

'You ought to be ashamed of yourself for asking such a simple question,' added the Gryphon; and then they both sat silent and looked at poor Alice, who felt ready to sink into the earth. At last the Gryphon said to the Mock

Turtle, 'Drive on, old fellow! Don't be all day about it!'
and he went on in these words:

'Yes, we went to school in the sea, though you mayn't
believe it –'

'I never said I didn't!' interrupted Alice.

'You did,' said the Mock Turtle.

'Hold your tongue!' added the Gryphon, before Alice could speak again. The Mock Turtle went on.

'We had the best of educations – in fact, we went to school every day –'

'*I've* been to a day-school, too,' said Alice; 'you needn't be so proud as all that.'

'With extras?' asked the Mock Turtle a little anxiously.

'Yes,' said Alice, 'we learned French and music.'

'And washing?' said the Mock Turtle.

'Certainly not!' said Alice indignantly.

'Ah! then yours wasn't a really good school,' said the Mock Turtle in a tone of great relief. 'Now at *ours* they had at the end of the bill, "French, music, *and washing* – extra."'

'You couldn't have wanted it much,' said Alice; 'living at the bottom of the sea.'

'I couldn't afford to learn it,' said the Mock Turtle with a sigh. 'I only took the regular course.'

'What was that?' inquired Alice.

'Reeling and Writhing, of course, to begin with,' the Mock Turtle replied; 'and then the different branches of Arithmetic – Ambition, Distraction, Uglification, and Derision.'

'I never heard of "Uglification,"' Alice ventured to say. 'What is it?'

The Gryphon lifted up both its paws in surprise. 'What! Never heard of uglifying!' it exclaimed. 'You know what to beautify is, I suppose?'

'Yes,' said Alice doubtfully: 'it means – to – make – anything – prettier.'

'Well, then,' the Gryphon went on, 'if you don't know what to uglify is, you *are* a simpleton.'

Alice did not feel encouraged to ask any more questions about it, so she turned to the Mock Turtle, and said 'What else had you to learn?'

'Well, there was Mystery,' the Mock Turtle replied, counting off the subjects on his flappers, '– Mystery, ancient and modern, with Seaography: then Drawling – the Drawling-master was an old conger-eel, that used to come once a week: *he* taught us Drawling, Stretching, and Fainting in Coils.'

'What was *that* like?' said Alice.

'Well, I can't show it you myself,' the Mock Turtle said: 'I'm too stiff. And the Gryphon never learnt it.'

'Hadn't time,' said the Gryphon: 'I went to the Classical master, though. He was an old crab, *he* was.'

'I never went to him,' the Mock Turtle said with a sigh: 'he taught Laughing and Grief, they used to say.'

'So he did, so he did,' said the Gryphon, sighing in his turn; and both creatures hid their faces in their paws.

'And how many hours a day did you do lessons?' said Alice, in a hurry to change the subject.

'Ten hours the first day,' said the Mock Turtle: 'nine the next, and so on.'

'What a curious plan!' exclaimed Alice.

'That's the reason they're called lessons,' the Gryphon remarked: 'because they lessen from day to day.'

This was quite a new idea to Alice, and she thought it over a little before she made her next remark. 'Then the eleventh day must have been a holiday?'

'Of course it was,' said the Mock Turtle.

'And how did you manage on the twelfth?' Alice went on eagerly.

'That's enough about lessons,' the Gryphon interrupted in a very decided tone: 'tell her something about the games now.'

10

The Lobster Quadrille

THE Mock Turtle sighed deeply, and drew the back of one flapper across his eyes. He looked at Alice, and tried to speak, but for a minute or two sobs choked his voice. 'Same as if he had a bone in his throat,' said the Gryphon: and it set to work shaking him and punching him in the back. At last the Mock Turtle recovered his voice, and, with tears running down his cheeks, he went on again:–

'You may not have lived much under the sea –' ('I haven't,' said Alice) – 'and perhaps you were never even introduced to a lobster –' (Alice began to say 'I once tasted –' but checked herself hastily, and said 'No, never') '– so you can have no idea what a delightful thing a Lobster Quadrille is!'

'No, indeed,' said Alice. 'What sort of a dance is it?'

'Why,' said the Gryphon, 'you first form into a line along the sea-shore –'

'Two lines!' cried the Mock Turtle. 'Seals, turtles, salmon, and so on; then, when you've cleared all the jellyfish out of the way –'

'*That* generally takes some time,' interrupted the Gryphon.

'– you advance twice –'

'Each with a lobster as a partner!' cried the Gryphon.

'Of course,' the Mock Turtle said: 'advance twice, set to partners –'

'– change lobsters, and retire in same order,' continued the Gryphon.

'Then, you know,' the Mock Turtle went on, 'you throw the –'

'The lobsters!' shouted the Gryphon, with a bound into the air.

'– as far out to sea as you can –'

'Swim after them!' screamed the Gryphon.

'Turn a somersault in the sea!' cried the Mock Turtle, capering wildly about.

'Change lobsters again!' yelled the Gryphon.

'Back to land again, and that's all the first figure,' said the Mock Turtle, suddenly dropping his voice; and the two creatures, who had been jumping about like mad things all this time. sat down again very sadly and quietly, and looked at Alice.

'It must be a very pretty dance,' said Alice timidly.

'Would you like to see a little of it?' said the Mock Turtle.

'Very much indeed,' said Alice.

'Come, let's try the first figure!' said the Mock Turtle to the Gryphon. 'We can do without lobsters, you know. Which shall sing?'

'Oh, *you* sing,' said the Gryphon. 'I've forgotten the words.'

So they began solemnly dancing round and round Alice, every now and then treading on her toes when they passed too close, and waving their forepaws to mark the time, while the Mock Turtle sang this, very slowly and sadly:

'"*Will you walk a little faster?" said a whiting to a snail.*
"There's a porpoise close behind us, and he's treading on my tail.
See how eagerly the lobsters and the turtles all advance!
They are waiting on the shingle – will you come and join the dance?
Will you, won't you, will you, won't you, will you join the dance?
Will you, won't you, will you, won't you, won't you join the dance?

'"*You can really have no notion how delightful it will be*
When they take us up and throw us, with the lobsters, out to sea!"

But the snail replied "Too far, too far!" and gave a
   look askance –
Said he thanked the whiting kindly, but he would not
   join the dance.
Would not, could not, would not, could not, would
   not join the dance.
Would not, could not, would not, could not, could not
   join the dance.

""What matters it how far we go?" his scaly friend
   replied.
"There is another shore, you know, upon the other
   side.
The further off from England the nearer is to
   France –
Then turn not pale, beloved snail, but come and join
   the dance.
Will you, won't you, will you, won't you, will you join
   the dance?
Will you, won't you, will you, won't you, won't you
   join the dance?"'

'Thank you, it's a very interesting dance to watch,' said
Alice, feeling very glad that it was over at last: 'and I do
so like that curious song about the whiting!'

'Oh, as to the whiting,' said the Mock Turtle, 'they –

you've seen them, of course?'

'Yes,' said Alice, 'I've often seen them at dinn –' she checked herself hastily.

'I don't know where Dinn may be,' said the Mock Turtle, 'but if you've seen them so often, of course you know what they're like.'

'I believe so,' Alice replied thoughtfully. 'They have their tails in their mouths – and they're all over crumbs.'

'You're wrong about the crumbs,' said the Mock Turtle: 'crumbs would all wash off in the sea. But they *have* their tails in their mouths; and the reason is –' here the Mock Turtle yawned and shut his eyes. – 'Tell her about the reason and all that,' he said to the Gryphon.

'The reason is,' said the Gryphon, 'that they *would* go with the lobsters to the dance. So they got thrown out to sea. So they had to fall a long way. So they got their tails fast in their mouths. So they couldn't get them out again. That's all.'

'Thank you,' said Alice, 'it's very interesting. I never knew so much about a whiting before.'

'I can tell you more than that, if you like,' said the Gryphon. 'Do you know why it's called a whiting?'

'I never thought about it,' said Alice. 'Why?'

'*It does the boots and shoes*,' the Gryphon replied very solemnly.

Alice was thoroughly puzzled. 'Does the boots and shoes!' she repeated in a wondering tone.

'Why, what are *your* shoes done with?' said the Gryphon. 'I mean what makes them so shiny?'

Alice looked down at them, and considered a little before she gave her answer. 'They're done with blacking, I believe.'

'Boots and shoes under the sea,' the Gryphon went on in a deep voice, 'are done with whiting. Now you know.'

'And what are they made of?' Alice asked in a tone of great curiosity.

'Soles and eels, of course,' the Gryphon replied rather impatiently: 'any shrimp could have told you that.'

'If I'd been the whiting,' said Alice, whose thoughts were still running on the song, 'I'd have said to the porpoise, "Keep back, please: we don't want *you* with us!"'

'They were obliged to have him with them,' the Mock Turtle said: 'no wise fish would go anywhere without a porpoise.'

'Wouldn't it really?' said Alice in a tone of great surprise.

'Of course not,' said the Mock Turtle: 'why, if a fish came to *me*, and told me he was going a journey, I should say "With what porpoise?"'

'Don't you mean "purpose"?' said Alice.

'I mean what I say,' the Mock Turtle replied in an offended tone. And the Gryphon added 'Come, let's hear some of *your* adventures.'

'I could tell you my adventures – beginning from this morning,' said Alice a little timidly: 'but it's no use going back to yesterday, because I was a different person then.'

'Explain all that,' said the Mock Turtle.

'No, no! The adventures first,' said the Gryphon in an impatient tone: 'explanations take such a dreadful time.'

So Alice began telling them her adventures from the time when she first saw the White Rabbit. She was a little nervous about it just at first, the two creatures got so close to her, one on each side, and opened their eyes and mouths so *very* wide, but she gained courage as she went on. Her listeners were perfectly quiet till she got to the part about her repeating '*You are old, Father William,*' to the Caterpillar, and the words all coming different, and then the Mock Turtle drew a long breath, and said 'That's very curious.'

'It's all about as curious as it can be,' said the Gryphon.

'It all came different!' the Mock Turtle repeated thoughtfully. 'I should like to hear her try and repeat something now. Tell her to begin.' He looked at the Gryphon as if he thought it had some kind of authority over Alice.

'Stand up and repeat '"*Tis the voice of the sluggard*,"' said the Gryphon.

'How the creatures order one about, and make one repeat lessons!' thought Alice; 'I might as well be at school at once.' However, she got up, and began to repeat it, but her head was so full of the Lobster Quadrille, that she hardly knew what she was saying, and the words came very queer indeed:–

'Tis the voice of the Lobster; I heard him declare,
"You have baked me too brown, I must sugar my hair."
As a duck with its eyelids, so he with his nose
Trims his belt and his buttons, and turns out his toes.'

'That's different from what *I* used to say when I was a child,' said the Gryphon.

'Well, I never heard it before,' said the Mock Turtle; 'but it sounds uncommon nonsense.'

Alice said nothing; she had sat down with her face in her hands, wondering if anything would *ever* happen in a natural way again.

'I should like to have it explained,' said the Mock Turtle.

'She can't explain it,' said the Gryphon hastily. 'Go on with the next verse.'

'But about his toes?' the Mock Turtle persisted. 'How *could* he turn them out with his nose, you know?'

'It's the first position in dancing,' Alice said; but was dreadfully puzzled by the whole thing, and longed to change the subject.

'Go on with the next verse,' the Gryphon repeated impatiently: 'it begins "*I passed by his garden.*"'

Alice did not dare to disobey, though she felt sure it would all come wrong, and she went on in a trembling voice:–

> *'I passed by his garden, and marked, with one eye,*
> *How the Owl and the Panther were sharing a pie –'*

'What *is* the use of repeating all that stuff,' the Mock Turtle interrupted, 'if you don't explain it as you go on? It's by far the most confusing thing *I* ever heard!'

'Yes, I think you'd better leave off,' said the Gryphon: and Alice was only too glad to do so.

'Shall we try another figure of the Lobster Quadrille?' the Gryphon went on. 'Or would you like the Mock Turtle to sing you a song?'

'Oh, a song, please, if the Mock Turtle would be so kind,' Alice replied, so eagerly that the Gryphon said, in a rather offended tone, 'Hm! No accounting for tastes! Sing her "*Turtle Soup*," will you, old fellow?'

The Mock Turtle sighed deeply, and began, in a voice sometimes choked with sobs, to sing this:–

> *'Beautiful Soup, so rich and green,*
> *Waiting in a hot tureen!*

Who for such dainties would not stoop?
Soup of the evening, beautiful Soup!
Soup of the evening, beautiful Soup!
    Beau – ootiful Soo – oop!
    Beau – ootiful Soo – oop!
Soo – oop of the e – e – evening,
    Beautiful, beautiful Soup!

'Beautiful Soup! Who cares for fish,
Game, or any other dish?
Who would not give all else for two p
ennyworth only of beautiful Soup?
Pennyworth only of beautiful Soup?
    Beau – ootiful Soo – oop!
    Beau – ootiful Soo – oop!
Soo – oop of the e – e – evening,
    Beautiful, beauti – FUL SOUP!'

'Chorus again!' cried the Gryphon, and the Mock Turtle had just begun to repeat it, when a cry of 'The trial's beginning!' was heard in the distance.

'Come on!' cried the Gryphon, and, taking Alice by the hand, it hurried off, without waiting for the end of the song.

'What trial is it?' Alice panted as she ran; but the Gryphon only answered 'Come on!' and ran the faster, while more and more faintly came, carried on the breeze that followed them, the melancholy words:–

> '*Soo – oop of the e – e – evening,*
> *Beautiful, beautiful Soup!*'

Who Stole the Tarts?

THE King and Queen of Hearts were seated on their throne when they arrived, with a great crowd assembled about them – all sorts of little birds and beasts, as well as the whole pack of cards: the Knave was standing before them, in chains, with a soldier on each side to guard him; and near the King was the White Rabbit, with a trumpet in one hand, and a scroll of parchment in the other. In the very middle of the court was a table, with a large dish of tarts upon it: they looked so good, that it made Alice quite hungry to look at them – 'I wish they'd get the trial done,' she thought, 'and hand round the refreshments!' But there seemed to be no chance of this, so she began looking at everything about her, to pass away the time.

Alice had never been in a court of justice before,

but she had read about them in books, and she was quite pleased to find that she knew the name of nearly everything there. 'That's the judge,' she said to herself, 'because of his great wig.'

The judge, by the way, was the King; and as he wore his crown over the wig, (look at the frontispiece if you want to see how he did it,) he did not look at all comfortable, and it was certainly not becoming.

'And that's the jury-box,' thought Alice, 'and those twelve creatures,' (she was obliged to say 'creatures' you see, because some of them were animals, and some were birds,) 'I suppose they are the jurors.' She said this last word two or three times over to herself, being rather proud of it: for she thought and rightly too, that very few little girls of her age knew the meaning of it at all. However, 'jury-men' would have done just as well.

The twelve jurors were all writing very busily on slates. 'What are they doing?' Alice whispered to the Gryphon. 'They can't have anything to put down yet, before the trial's begun.'

'They're putting down their names,' the Gryphon whispered in reply, 'for fear they should forget them before the end of the trial.'

'Stupid things!' Alice began in a loud, indignant voice, but she stopped hastily, for the White Rabbit cried out, 'Silence in the court!' and the King put on his spectacles and looked anxiously round, to make out who was talking.

Alice could see, as well as if she were looking over their shoulders, that all the jurors were writing down 'stupid things!' on their slates, and she could even make out that one of them didn't know how to spell 'stupid,' and that he had to ask his neighbour to tell him. 'A nice muddle their slates'll be in before the trial's over!' thought Alice.

One of the jurors had a pencil that squeaked. This of course, Alice could *not* stand, and she went round the court and got behind him, and very soon found an opportunity of taking it away. She did it so quickly that the poor little juror (it was Bill, the Lizard) could not make out at all what had become of it; so, after hunting all about for it, he was obliged to write with one finger for the rest of the day; and this was of very little use, as it left no mark on the slate.

'Herald, read the accusation!' said the King.

On this the White Rabbit blew three blasts on the trumpet, and then unrolled the parchment scroll, and read as follows:–

> *'The Queen of Hearts, she made some tarts,*
> *All on a summer day:*
> *The Knave of Hearts, he stole those tarts,*
> *And took them quite away!'*

'Consider your verdict,' the King said to the jury.

'Not yet, not yet!' the Rabbit hastily interrupted. 'There's a great deal to come before that!'

'Call the first witness,' said the King; and the White Rabbit blew three blasts on the trumpet, and called out, 'First witness!'

The first witness was the Hatter. He came in with a

teacup in one hand and a piece of bread-and-butter in the other. 'I beg pardon, your Majesty,' he began, 'for bringing these in: but I hadn't quite finished my tea when I was sent for.'

'You ought to have finished,' said the King. 'When did you begin?'

The Hatter looked at the March Hare, who had followed him into the court, arm-in-arm with the Dormouse. 'Fourteenth of March, I *think* it was,' he said.

'Fifteenth,' said the March Hare.

'Sixteenth,' added the Dormouse.

'Write that down,' the King said to the jury, and the jury eagerly wrote down all three dates on their slates, and then added them up, and reduced the answer to shillings and pence.

'Take off your hat,' the King said to the Hatter.

'It isn't mine,' said the Hatter.

'*Stolen!*' the King exclaimed, turning to the jury, who instantly made a memorandum of the fact.

'I keep them to sell,' the Hatter added as an explanation: 'I've none of my own. I'm a hatter.'

Here the Queen put on her spectacles, and began staring at the Hatter, who turned pale and fidgeted.

'Give your evidence,' said the King; 'and don't be nervous, or I'll have you executed on the spot.'

This did not seem to encourage the witness at all: he kept shifting from one foot to the other, looking uneasily at the Queen, and in his confusion he bit a large piece out of his teacup instead of the bread-and-butter.

Just at this moment Alice felt a very curious sensation, which puzzled her a good deal until she made out what it was: she was beginning to grow larger again, and she thought at first she would get up and leave the court; but on second thoughts she decided to remain where she was as long as there was room for her.

'I wish you wouldn't squeeze so,' said the Dormouse, who was sitting next to her. 'I can hardly breathe.'

'I can't help it,' said Alice very meekly: 'I'm growing.'

'You have no right to grow *here*,' said the Dormouse.

'Don't talk nonsense,' said Alice more boldly: 'you know you're growing too.'

'Yes, but I grow at a reasonable pace,' said the Dormouse: 'not in that ridiculous fashion.' And he got up very sulkily and crossed over to the other side of the court.

All this time the Queen had never left off staring at the Hatter, and, just as the Dormouse crossed the court, she said to one of the officers of the court, 'Bring me the list of the singers in the last concert!' on which the wretched Hatter trembled so, that he shook both his shoes off.

'Give your evidence,' the King repeated angrily, 'or I'll have you executed. whether you're nervous or not.'

'I'm a poor man, your Majesty,' the Hatter began, in a trembling voice, '– and I hadn't begun my tea – not above a week or so – and what with the bread-and-butter getting so thin – and the twinkling of the tea –'

'The twinkling of the *what*?' said the King.

'It *began* with the tea,' the Hatter replied.

'Of course twinkling begins with a T!' said the King sharply. 'Do you take me for a dunce? Go on!'

'I'm a poor man,' the Hatter went on, 'and most things twinkled after that – only the March Hare said –'

'I didn't!' the March Hare interrupted in a great hurry.

'You did!' said the Hatter.

'I deny it!' said the March Hare.

'He denies it,' said the King: 'leave out that part.'

'Well, at any rate, the Dormouse said –' the Hatter went on, looking anxiously round to see if he would deny it too: but the Dormouse denied nothing, being fast asleep.

'After that,' continued the Hatter, 'I cut some more bread-and-butter –'

'But what did the Dormouse say?' one of the jury asked.

'That I can't remember,' said the Hatter.

'You *must* remember,' remarked the King, 'or I'll have you executed.'

The miserable Hatter dropped his teacup and bread-and-butter, and went down on one knee. 'I'm a poor man, your Majesty,' he began.

'You're a *very* poor *speaker*,' said the King.

Here one of the guinea-pigs cheered, and was immediately suppressed by the officers of the court. (As that is rather a hard word, I will just explain to you how it was done. They had a large canvas bag, which tied up at the mouth with strings: into this they slipped the guinea-pig, head first, and then sat upon it.)

'I'm glad I've seen that done,' thought Alice. 'I've so often read in the newspapers, at the end of trials, "There was some attempt at applause, which was immediately suppressed by the officers of the court," and I never understood what it meant till now.'

'If that's all you know about it, you may stand down,' continued the King.

'I can't go no lower,' said the Hatter: 'I'm on the floor as it is.'

'Then you may *sit* down,' the King replied.

Here the other guinea-pig cheered, and was suppressed.

'Come, that finishes the guinea-pigs!' thought Alice. 'Now we shall get on better.'

'I'd rather finish my tea,' said the Hatter, with an anxious look at the Queen, who was reading the list of singers.

'You may go,' said the King, and the Hatter hurriedly left the court, without even waiting to put his shoes on.

'– and just take his head off outside,' the Queen added to one of the officers: but the Hatter was out of sight before the officer could get to the door.

'Call the next witness!' said the King.

The next witness was the Duchess's cook. She carried the pepper-box in her hand, and Alice guessed who it was, even before she got into the court, by the way people near the door began sneezing all at once.

'Give your evidence,' said the King.

'Shan't,' said the cook.

The King looked anxiously at the White Rabbit, who said in a low voice, 'Your Majesty must cross-examine *this* witness.'

'Well, if I must, I must,' the King said, with a melancholy air, and, after folding his arms and frowning at the cook till his eyes were nearly out of sight, he said in a deep voice, 'What are tarts made of?'

'Pepper, mostly,' said the cook.

'Treacle,' said a sleepy voice behind her.

'Collar that Dormouse,' the Queen shrieked out. 'Behead that Dormouse! Turn that Dormouse out of court! Suppress him! Pinch him! Off with his whiskers!'

For some minutes the whole court was in confusion, getting the Dormouse turned out, and, by the time they had settled down again, the cook had disappeared.

'Never mind!' said the King, with an air of great relief. 'Call the next witness.' And he added in an undertone to the Queen, 'Really, my dear, *you* must cross-examine the next witness. It quite makes my forehead ache!'

Alice watched the White Rabbit as he fumbled over the list, feeling very curious to see what the next witness would be like, '– for they haven't got much evidence *yet*,' she said to herself. Imagine her surprise, when the White Rabbit read out, at the top of his shrill little voice, the name 'Alice!'

12

Alice's Evidence

'HERE!' cried Alice, quite forgetting in the flurry of the moment how large she had grown in the last few minutes, and she jumped up in such a hurry that she tipped over the jury-box with the edge of her skirt, upsetting all the jurymen on to the heads of the crowd below, and there they lay sprawling about, reminding her very much of a globe of goldfish she had accidentally upset the week before.

'Oh, I *beg* your pardon!' she exclaimed in a tone of great dismay, and began picking them up again as quickly as she could, for the accident of the goldfish kept running in her head, and she had a vague sort of idea that they must be collected at once and put back into the jury-box, or they would die.

'The trial cannot proceed,' said the King in a very

grave voice, 'until all the jurymen are back in their proper places – *all*,' he repeated with great emphasis, looking hard at Alice as he said so.

Alice looked at the jury-box, and saw that, in her haste,

she had put the Lizard in head downwards, and the poor little thing was waving its tail about in a melancholy way, being quite unable to move. She soon got it out again, and put it right; 'not that it signifies much,' she said to herself; 'I should think it would be *quite* as much use in the trial one way up as the other.'

As soon as the jury had a little recovered from the shock of being upset, and their slates and pencils had been found and handed back to them, they set to work very diligently to write out a history of the accident, all except the Lizard, who seemed too much overcome to do anything but sit with its mouth open, gazing up into the roof of the court.

'What do you know about this business?' the King said to Alice.

'Nothing,' said Alice.

'Nothing *whatever*?' persisted the King.

'Nothing whatever,' said Alice.

'That's very important,' the King said, turning to the jury. They were just beginning to write this down on their slates, when the White Rabbit interrupted: '*Un*important, your Majesty means, of course,' he said in a very respectful tone, but frowning and making faces at him as he spoke.

'*Un*important, of course, I meant,' the King hastily said, and went on to himself in an undertone, 'important

– unimportant – unimportant – important –' as if he were trying which word sounded best.

Some of the jury wrote it down 'important,' and some 'unimportant.' Alice could see this, as she was near enough to look over their slates; 'but it doesn't matter a bit,' she thought to herself.

At this moment the King, who had been for some time busily writing in his note-book, called out 'Silence!' and read out from his book, 'Rule Forty-two. *All persons more than a mile high to leave the court.*'

Everybody looked at Alice.

'*I'm* not a mile high,' said Alice.

'You are,' said the King.

'Nearly two miles high,' added the Queen.

'Well, I shan't go, at any rate,' said Alice: 'besides, that's not a regular rule: you invented it just now.'

'It's the oldest rule in the book,' said the King.

'Then it ought to be Number One,' said Alice.

The King turned pale, and shut his note-book hastily. 'Consider your verdict,' he said to the jury, in a low trembling voice.

'There's more evidence to come yet, please your Majesty,' said the White Rabbit, jumping up in a great hurry; 'this paper has just been picked up.'

'What's in it?' said the Queen.

'I haven't opened it yet,' said the White Rabbit, 'but

it seems to be a letter, written by the prisoner to – to somebody.'

'It must have been that,' said the King, 'unless it was written to nobody, which isn't usual, you know.'

'Who is it directed to?' said one of the jurymen.

'It isn't directed at all,' said the White Rabbit; 'in fact, there's nothing written on the *outside*.' He unfolded the paper as he spoke, and added 'It isn't a letter, after all: it's a set of verses.'

'Are they in the prisoner's handwriting?' asked another of the jurymen.

'No, they're not,' said the White Rabbit, 'and that's the queerest thing about it.' (The jury all looked puzzled.)

'He must have imitated somebody else's hand,' said the King. (The jury all brightened up again.)

'Please your Majesty,' said the Knave; 'I didn't write it, and they can't prove I did: there's no name signed at the end.'

'If you didn't sign it,' said the King, 'that only makes the matter worse. You *must* have meant some mischief, or else you'd have signed your name like an honest man.'

There was a general clapping of hands at this: it was the first really clever thing the King had said that day.

'That *proves* his guilt,' said the Queen.

'It proves nothing of the sort!' said Alice. 'Why, you don't even know what they're about!'

'Read them,' said the King.

The White Rabbit put on his spectacles. 'Where shall I begin, please your Majesty?' he asked.

'Begin at the beginning,' the King said gravely, 'and go on till you come to the end: then stop.'

These were the verses the White Rabbit read:–

> '*They told me you had been to her,*
> *And mentioned me to him:*
> *She gave me a good character,*
> *But said I could not swim.*
>
> *He sent them word I had not gone*
> *(We know it to be true):*
> *If she should push the matter on,*
> *What would become of you?*
>
> *I gave her one, they gave him two,*
> *You gave us three or more;*
> *They all returned from him to you,*
> *Though they were mine before.*

If I or she should chance to be
Involved in this affair,
He trusts to you to set them free,
Exactly as we were.

My notion was that you had been
(Before she had this fit)
An obstacle that came between
Him, and ourselves, and it.

Don't let him know she liked them best,
For this must ever be
A secret, kept from all the rest,
Between yourself and me.'

'That's the most important piece of evidence we've heard yet,' said the King, rubbing his hands; 'so now let the jury –'

'If any one of them can explain it,' said Alice, (she had grown so large in the last few minutes that she wasn't a bit afraid of interrupting him,) 'I'll give him sixpence. *I* don't believe there's an atom of meaning in it.'

The jury all wrote down on their slates, '*She* doesn't believe there's an atom of meaning in it,' but none of them attempted to explain the paper.

'If there's no meaning in it,' said the King, 'that

saves a world of trouble, you know, as we needn't try to find any. And yet I don't know,' he went on, spreading out the verses on his knee, and looking at them with one eye; 'I seem to see some meaning in them, after all. "– *said I could not swim* –" you can't swim, can you?' he added, turning to the Knave.

The Knave shook his head sadly. 'Do I look like it?' he said. (Which he certainly did *not*, being made entirely of cardboard.)

'All right, so far,' said the King, and he went on muttering over the verses to himself: '"*We know it to be true* –" that's the jury, of course – "*I gave her one, they gave him two* –" why, that must be what he did with the tarts, you know –'

'But, it goes on "*they all returned from him to you*,"' said Alice.

'Why, there they are!' said the King triumphantly, pointing to the tarts on the table. 'Nothing can be clearer than *that*. Then again – "*before she had this fit* –" you never had fits, my dear, I think?' he said to the Queen.

'Never!' said the Queen furiously, throwing an inkstand at the Lizard as she spoke. (The unfortunate little Bill had left off writing on his slate with one finger, as he found it made no mark; but he now hastily began again, using the ink, that was trickling down his face, as long as it lasted.)

'Then the words don't *fit* you,' said the King, looking round the court with a smile. There was a dead silence.

'It's a pun!' the King added in an offended tone, and everybody laughed. 'Let the jury consider their verdict,' the King said, for about the twentieth time that day.

'No, no!' said the Queen. 'Sentence first – verdict afterwards.'

'Stuff and nonsense!' said Alice loudly. 'The idea of having the sentence first!'

'Hold your tongue!' said the Queen, turning purple.

'I won't!' said Alice.

'Off with her head!' the Queen shouted at the top of her voice. Nobody moved.

'Who cares for you?' said Alice, (she had grown to her full size by this time.) 'You're nothing but a pack of cards!'

At this the whole pack rose up into the air, and came flying down upon her: she gave a little scream, half of fright and half of anger, and tried to beat them off, and found herself lying on the bank, with her head in the lap of her sister, who was gently brushing away some dead leaves that had fluttered down from the trees upon her face.

'Wake up, Alice dear!' said her sister; 'Why, what a long sleep you've had!'

'Oh, I've had such a curious dream!' said Alice, and she told her sister, as well as she could remember them, all these strange Adventures of hers that you have just been reading about; and when she had finished, her sister kissed her, and said, 'It *was* a curious dream, dear, certainly: but now run in to your tea; it's getting late.' So Alice got up and ran off, thinking while she ran, as well she might, what a wonderful dream it had been.

But her sister sat still just as she left her, leaning her head on her hand, watching the setting sun, and thinking of little Alice and all her wonderful Adventures, till she too began dreaming after a fashion, and this was her dream:—

First, she dreamed of little Alice herself, and once again the tiny hands were clasped upon her knee, and the bright eager eyes were looking up into hers – she could hear the very tones of her voice, and see that queer little toss of her head to keep back the wandering hair that *would* always get into her eyes – and still as she listened, or seemed to listen, the whole place around her became alive with the strange creatures of her little sister's dream.

The long grass rustled at her feet as the White Rabbit hurried by – the frightened Mouse splashed his way through the neighbouring pool – she could hear the rattle of the teacups as the March Hare and his friends shared their never-ending meal, and the shrill voice of the Queen ordering off her unfortunate guests to execution – once more the pig-baby was sneezing on the Duchess's knee, while plates and dishes crashed around it – once more the shriek of the Gryphon, the squeaking of the Lizard's slate-pencil, and the choking of the suppressed guinea-pigs, filled the air, mixed up with the distant sobs of the miserable Mock Turtle.

So she sat on, with closed eyes, and half believed herself in Wonderland, though she knew she had but to open them again, and all would change to dull reality – the grass would be only rustling in the wind, and the pool rippling to the waving of the reeds – the rattling teacups would change to tinkling sheep-bells, and the Queen's shrill cries to the voice of the shepherd boy – and the sneeze of the baby, the shriek of the Gryphon, and all the other queer noises, would change (she knew) to the confused clamours of the busy farm-yard – while the lowing of the cattle in the distance would take the place of the Mock Turtle's heavy sobs.

Lastly, she pictured to herself how this same little sister of hers would, in the after-time, be herself a grown woman; and how she would keep, through all her riper years, the simple and loving heart of her childhood: and how she would gather about her other little children, and make their eyes bright and eager with many a strange tale, perhaps even with the dream of Wonderland of long ago: and how she would feel with all their simple sorrows, and find a pleasure in all their simple joys, remembering her own child-life, and the happy summer days.

THE END

13

An Easter Greeting
to
Every Child Who Loves
Alice

DEAR CHILD

Please to fancy, if you can, that you are reading a real letter, from a real friend whom you have seen, and whose voice you can seem to yourself to hear wishing you, as I do now with all my heart, a happy Easter.

Do you know that delicious dreamy feeling when one first wakes on a summer morning, with the twitter of birds in the air, and the fresh breeze coming in at the open window – when, lying lazily with eyes half-shut, one sees as in a dream green boughs waving, or waters rippling in a golden light? It is a pleasure very near to sadness, bringing tears to one's eyes like a beautiful picture or poem. And is not that a Mother's gentle hand that undraws your curtains, and a Mother's sweet voice that summons you to rise? To rise and forget, in the bright sunlight, the ugly dreams that frightened you so when all was dark – to rise and enjoy another happy day, first kneeling to thank that unseen Friend, who sends you the beautiful sun?

Are these strange words from a writer of such tales as 'Alice'? And is this a strange letter to find in a book of nonsense? It may be so. Some perhaps may blame me for thus mixing together things grave and gay; others may smile and think it odd that any one should speak of solemn things at all, except in church and on a Sunday: but I think – nay, I am sure – that some children will read this gently and lovingly, and in the spirit in which I have written it.

For I do not believe God means us thus to divide life into two halves – to wear a grave face on Sunday, and to think it out-of-place to even so much as mention Him on a week-day. Do you think He cares to see only kneeling figures, and to hear only tones of prayer – and that He does not also love to see the lambs leaping in the sunlight, and to hear the merry voices of the children, as they roll among the hay? Surely their innocent laughter is as sweet in His ears as the grandest anthem that ever rolled up from the 'dim religious light' of some solemn cathedral?

And if I have written anything to add to those stories of innocent and healthy amusement that are laid up in books for the children I love so well, it is surely something I may hope to look back upon without shame and sorrow (as how much of life must then be recalled!) when my turn comes to walk through the valley of shadows.

This Easter sun will rise on you, dear child, feeling your 'life in every limb', and eager to rush out into the fresh morning air – and many an Easter-day will come and go, before it finds you feeble and gray-headed, creeping wearily out to bask once more in the sunlight – but it is good, even now, to think sometimes of that great morning when the 'Sun of Righteousness shall arise with healing in his wings'.

Surely your gladness need not be the less for the thought that you will one day see a brighter dawn than this – when lovelier sights will meet your eyes than any waving trees or rippling waters – when angel-hands shall undraw your curtains, and sweeter tones than ever loving Mother breathed shall wake you to a new and glorious day – and when all the sadness, and the sin, that darkened life on this little earth, shall be forgotten like the dreams of a night that is past!

Your affectionate friend,
LEWIS CARROLL

Easter, 1876

14

Christmas Greetings
From a Fairy to a Child

LADY dear, if Fairies may
    For a moment lay aside
Cunning tricks and elfish play,
    'Tis at happy Christmas-tide.

We have heard the children say –
    Gentle children, whom we love –
Long ago, on Christmas Day,
    Came a message from above.

Still, as Christmas-tide comes round,
    They remember it again –
Echo still the joyful sound,
    'Peace on earth, good-will to men.'

Yet the hearts must child-like be
 Where such heavenly guests abide.
Unto children, in their glee,
 All the year is Christmas-tide.

Thus, forgetting tricks and play
 For a moment, Lady dear,
We would wish you, if we may,
 Merry Christmas, glad New Year.

Christmas, 1887

Through the
Looking-Glass
and what Alice found there

DRAMATIS PERSONÆ

(As arranged before commencement of game)

WHITE		RED	
PIECES	**PAWNS**	**PAWNS**	**PIECES**
Tweedledee	Daisy	Daisy	Humpty Dumpty
Unicorn	Haigha	Messenger	Carpenter
Sheep	Oyster	Oyster	Walrus
W.Queen	'Lily'	Tiger-lily	R.Queen
W.King	Fawn	Rose	R.King
Aged man	Oyster	Oyster	Crow
W.Knight	Hatta	Frog	R.Knight
Tweedledum	Daisy	Daisy	Lion

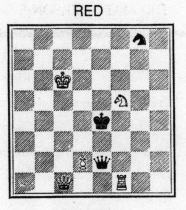

WHITE

White Pawn (Alice) to play, and win in eleven moves

Preface

As the chess-problem, given on a previous page, has puzzled some of my readers, it may be well to explain that it is correctly worked out, so far as the *moves* are concerned. The *alternation* of Red and White is perhaps not so strictly observed as it might be, and the 'castling' of the three Queens is merely a way of saying that they entered the palace: but the 'check' of the White King at move 6, the capture of the Red Knight at move 7, and the final 'checkmate' of the Red King, will be found, by any one who will take the trouble to set the pieces and play the moves as directed, to be strictly in accordance with the laws of the game.

The new words, in the poem *Jabberwocky* (see p. 186), have given rise to some differences of opinion as to their pronunciation: so it may be well to give instructions on *that* point also. Pronounce 'slithy' as if it were the two words 'sly, the': make the 'g' *hard* in 'gyre' and 'gimble': and pronounce 'rath' to rhyme with 'bath.'

Child of the pure unclouded brow
And dreaming eyes of wonder!
Though time be fleet, and I and thou
Are half a life asunder,
Thy loving smile will surely hail
The love-gift of a fairy-tale.

I have not seen thy sunny face,
Nor heard thy silver laughter;
No thought of me shall find a place
In thy young life's hereafter –
Enough that now thou wilt not fail
To listen to my fairy-tale.

A tale begun in other days,
When summer suns were glowing –
A simple chime, that served to time
The rhythm of our rowing –
Whose echoes live in memory yet,
Though envious years would say 'forget.'

Come, hearken then, ere voice of dread,
With bitter tidings laden,
Shall summon to unwelcome bed
A melancholy maiden!
We are but older children, dear,
Who fret to find our bedtime near.

Without, the frost, the blinding snow,
The storm-wind's moody madness –
Within, the firelight's ruddy glow,
And childhood's nest of gladness.
The magic words shall hold thee fast:
Thou shalt not heed the raving blast.

And though the shadow of a sigh
May tremble through the story,
For 'happy summer days' gone by,
And vanish'd summer glory –
It shall not touch with breath of bale
The pleasance of our fairy-tale.

1

Looking-Glass House

ONE thing was certain, that the *white* kitten had had nothing to do with it: – it was the black kitten's fault entirely. For the white kitten had been having its face washed by the old cat for the last quarter of an hour (and bearing it pretty well, considering); so you see that it *couldn't* have had any hand in the mischief.

The way Dinah washed her children's faces was this: first she held the poor thing down by its ear with one paw, and then with the other paw she rubbed its face all over, the wrong way, beginning at the nose: and just now, as I said, she was hard at work on the white kitten, which was lying quite still and trying to purr – no doubt feeling that it was all meant for its good.

But the black kitten had been finished with earlier in the afternoon, and so, while Alice was sitting curled up in a corner of the great arm-chair, half talking to herself and half asleep, the kitten had been having a grand game of romps with the ball of worsted Alice had been trying to wind up, and had been rolling it up and down till it had all come undone again; and there it was, spread over the hearth-rug, all knots and tangles, with the kitten running after its own tail in the middle.

'Oh, you wicked wicked little thing!' cried Alice, catching up the kitten, and giving it a little kiss to make it understand that it was in disgrace. 'Really, Dinah ought to have taught you better manners! You *ought*, Dinah, you know you ought!' she added, looking reproachfully at the old cat, and speaking in as cross a voice as she could manage – and then she scrambled back into the arm-chair, taking the kitten and the worsted with her, and began winding up the ball again. But she didn't get on very fast, as she was talking all the time, sometimes to the kitten, and sometimes to herself. Kitty sat very demurely on her knee, pretending to watch the progress of the winding, and now and then putting out one paw and gently touching the ball, as if it would be glad to help if it might.

'Do you know what tomorrow is, Kitty?' Alice began. 'You'd have guessed if you'd been up in the window with me – only Dinah was making you tidy, so you couldn't. I was watching the boys getting in sticks for the bonfire – and it wants plenty of sticks, Kitty! Only it got so cold, and it snowed so, they had to leave off. Never mind, Kitty, we'll go and see the bonfire tomorrow.' Here Alice wound two or three turns of the worsted round the kitten's neck, just to see how it would look: this led to a scramble, in which the ball rolled down upon the floor, and yards and yards of it got unwound again.

'Do you know, I was so angry, Kitty,' Alice went on as soon as they were comfortably settled again, 'when I saw all the mischief you had been doing, I was very nearly opening the window, and putting you out into the snow! And you'd have deserved it, you little mischievous darling! What have you got to say for yourself? Now don't interrupt me!' she went on, holding up one finger. 'I'm going to tell you all your faults. Number one: you squeaked twice while Dinah was washing your face this morning. Now you can't deny it, Kitty: I heard you! What's that you say?' (pretending that the kitten was speaking.) 'Her paw went into your eye? Well, that's *your* fault, for keeping your eyes open – if you'd shut them tight up, it wouldn't have happened. Now don't make any more excuses, but listen! Number two: you pulled Snowdrop away by the tail just as I had put down the saucer of milk before her! What, you were thirsty, were you? How do you know she wasn't thirsty too? Now for Number three: you unwound every bit of the worsted while I wasn't looking!

'That's three faults, Kitty, and you've not been punished for any of them yet. You know I'm saving up all your punishments for Wednesday week – Suppose they had saved up all *my* punishments!' she went on, talking more to herself than the kitten. 'What *would* they do at the end of the year? I should be sent to prison, I suppose, when the day came. Or – let me see – suppose each punishment was to be going without a dinner: then, when the miserable day came, I should have to go without fifty dinners at once! Well, I shouldn't mind *that* much! I'd far rather go without them than eat them!

'Do you hear the snow against the window-panes, Kitty? How nice and soft it sounds! Just as if some one was kissing the window all over outside. I wonder if the

snow *loves* the trees and fields, that it kisses them so gently? And then it covers them up snug, you know, with a white quilt; and perhaps it says, "Go to sleep, darlings, till the summer comes again." And when they wake up in the summer, Kitty, they dress themselves all in green, and dance about – whenever the wind blows – oh, that's very pretty!' cried Alice, dropping the ball of worsted to clap her hands. 'And I do so *wish* it was true! I'm sure the woods look sleepy in the autumn, when the leaves are getting brown.

'Kitty, can you play chess? Now, don't smile, my dear, I'm asking it seriously. Because, when we were playing just now, you watched just as if you understood it: and when I said "Check!" you purred! Well, it *was* a nice check, Kitty, and really I might have won, if it hadn't been for that nasty Knight, that came wriggling down among my pieces. Kitty, dear, let's pretend –' And here I wish I could tell you half the things Alice used to say, beginning with her favourite phrase 'Let's pretend.' She had had quite a long argument with her sister only the day before – all because Alice had begun with 'Let's pretend we're kings and queens;' and her sister, who liked being very exact, had argued that they couldn't, because there were only two of them, and Alice had been reduced at last to say, 'Well, *you* can be one of them then, and *I'll* be all the rest.' And once she had really frightened her old nurse by shouting suddenly in her ear, 'Nurse! Do let's pretend that I'm a hungry hyæna, and you're a bone!'

But this is taking us away from Alice's speech to the kitten. 'Let's pretend that you're the Red Queen, Kitty! Do you know, I think if you sat up and folded your arms, you'd look exactly like her. Now do try, there's a dear!' And Alice got the Red Queen off the table, and set it up before the kitten as a model for it to imitate: however, the thing didn't succeed, principally, Alice said, because the kitten wouldn't fold its arms properly. So, to punish it, she held it up to the Looking-glass, that it might see how sulky it was – 'and if you're not good directly,' she added, 'I'll put you through the Looking-glass House. How would you like *that*?

'Now, if you'll only attend, Kitty, and not talk so much, I'll tell you all my ideas about Looking-glass House. First, there's the room you can see through the glass – that's just the same as our drawing-room, only the things go the other way. I can see all of it when I get upon a chair – all but the bit just behind the fireplace. Oh! I do so wish I could see *that* bit! I want so much to know whether they've a fire in the winter: you never *can* tell, you know, unless our fire smokes, and then smoke comes up in that room too – but that may be only pretence, just to make it look as if they had a fire. Well then, the books are something like our books, only the words go the wrong way; I know that, because I've held up one of our books to the glass, and then they hold up one in the other room.

'How would you like to live in Looking-glass House, Kitty? I wonder if they'd give you milk in there? Perhaps

Looking-glass milk isn't good to drink – But oh, Kitty! now we come to the passage. You can just see a little *peep* of the passage in Looking-glass House, if you leave the door of our drawing-room wide open: and it's very

like our passage as far as you can see, only you know it may be quite different on beyond. Oh, Kitty! how nice it would be if we could only get through into Looking-glass House! I'm sure it's got, oh! such beautiful things in it! Let's pretend there's a way of getting through into it, somehow, Kitty. Let's pretend the glass has got all soft like gauze, so that we can get through. Why, it's turning into a sort of mist now, I declare! It'll be easy enough to get through –' She was up on the chimney-piece while she said this, though she hardly knew how she had got there. And certainly the glass was beginning to melt away, just like a bright silvery mist.

In another moment Alice was through the glass, and had jumped lightly down into the Looking-glass room. The very first thing she did was to look whether there was a fire in the fireplace, and she was quite pleased to find that there was a real one, blazing away as brightly as the one she had left behind. 'So I shall be as warm here as I was in the old room,' thought Alice: 'warmer, in fact, because there'll be no one here to scold me away from the fire. Oh, what fun it'll be, when they see me through the glass in here, and can't get at me!'

Then she began looking about and noticed that what could be seen from the old room was quite common and uninteresting, but that all the rest was as different as possible. For instance, the pictures on the wall next the fire seemed to be all alive, and the very clock on the chimney-piece (you know you can only see the back of it in the Looking-glass) had got the face of a little old man, and grinned at her.

'They don't keep this room so tidy as the other,' Alice thought to herself, as she noticed several of the chessmen down in the hearth among the cinders: but in another moment, with a little 'Oh!' of surprise, she was down on her hands and knees watching them. The chessmen were walking about, two and two!

'Here are the Red King and the Red Queen,' Alice said (in a whisper, for fear of frightening them), 'and there are the White King and the White Queen sitting on the edge of the shovel – and here are two Castles walking arm in arm – I don't think they can hear me,' she went on, as she put her head closer down, 'and I'm nearly sure they can't see me. I feel somehow as if I were invisible –'

Here something began squeaking on the table behind Alice, and made her turn her head just in time to see one of the White Pawns roll over and begin kicking: she watched it with great curiosity to see what would happen next.

'It is the voice of my child!' the White Queen cried out as she rushed past the King, so violently that she knocked him over among the cinders. 'My precious Lily! My imperial kitten!' and she began scrambling wildly up the side of the fender.

'Imperial fiddlestick!' said the King, rubbing his nose, which had been hurt by the fall. He had a right to be a *little* annoyed with the Queen, for he was covered with ashes from head to foot.

Alice was very anxious to be of use, and, as the poor little Lily was nearly screaming herself into a fit, she hastily picked up the Queen and set her on the table by the side of her noisy little daughter.

The Queen gasped, and sat down: the rapid journey through the air had quite taken away her breath and for a minute or two she could do nothing but hug the little Lily in silence. As soon as she had recovered her breath a little, she called out to the White King, who was sitting sulkily among the ashes, 'Mind the volcano!'

'What volcano?' said the King, looking up anxiously

into the fire, as if he thought that was the most likely place to find one.

'Blew – me – up,' panted the Queen, who was still a little out of breath. 'Mind you come up – the regular way – don't get blown up!'

Alice watched the White King as he slowly struggled up from bar to bar, till at last she said, 'Why, you'll be hours and hours getting to the table, at that rate. I'd far better help you, hadn't I?' But the King took no notice of the question: it was quite clear that he could neither hear her nor see her.

So Alice picked him up very gently, and lifted him across more slowly than she had lifted the Queen, that she mightn't take his breath away: but, before she put him on the table, she thought she might as well dust him a little, he was so covered in ashes.

She said afterwards that she had never seen in all her life such a face as the King made, when he found himself held in the air by an invisible hand, and being dusted: he was far too much astonished to cry out, but his eyes and mouth went on getting larger and larger, and rounder and rounder, till her hand shook so with laughing that she nearly let him drop upon the floor.

'Oh! *please* don't make such faces, my dear!' she cried out, quite forgetting that the King couldn't hear her. 'You make me laugh so that I can hardly hold you! And don't keep your mouth so wide open! All the ashes will get into it – there, now I think you're tidy enough!' she added, as she smoothed his hair, and set him upon the table near the Queen.

The King immediately fell flat on his back, and lay perfectly still: and Alice was a little alarmed at what she had done, and went round the room to see if she could find any water to throw over him. However, she could find nothing but a bottle of ink, and when she got back with it she found he had recovered, and he and the Queen were talking together in a frightened whisper – so low, that Alice could hardly hear what they said.

The King was saying, 'I assure you, my dear, I turned cold to the very ends of my whiskers!'

To which the Queen replied, 'You haven't got any whiskers.'

'The horror of that moment,' the King went on, 'I shall never, *never* forget!'

'You will, though,' the Queen said, 'if you don't make a memorandum of it.'

Alice looked on with great interest as the King took an enormous memorandum-book out of his pocket, and began writing. A sudden thought struck her, and she took hold of the end of the pencil, which came some way over his shoulder, and began writing for him.

The poor King looked puzzled and unhappy, and struggled with the pencil for some time without saying anything; but Alice was too strong for him, and at last he panted out, 'My dear! I really *must* get a thinner pencil. I can't manage this one a bit; it writes all manner of things that I don't intend —'

'What manner of things?' said the Queen, looking over the book (in which Alice had put '*The White Knight is sliding down the poker. He balances very badly*'). 'That's not a memorandum of *your* feelings!'

There was a book lying near Alice on the table, and while she sat watching the White King (for she was still

a little anxious about him, and had the ink all ready to throw over him, in case he fainted again), she turned over the leaves, to find some part that she could read, '– for it's all in some language I don't know,' she said to herself.

It was like this.

JABBERWOCKY

'Twas brillig, and the slithy toves
Did gyre and gimble in the wabe;
All mimsy were the borogoves,
And the mome raths outgrabe

She puzzled over this for some time, but at last a bright thought struck her. 'Why, it's a Looking-glass book, of course! And if I hold it up to a glass, the words will all go the right way again.'

This was the poem that Alice read.

JABBERWOCKY

'Twas brillig, and the slithy toves
    Did gyre and gimble in the wabe;
All mimsy were the borogoves,
    And the mome raths outgrabe.

'Beware the Jabberwock, my son!
The jaws that bite, the claws that catch!
Beware the Jubjub bird, and shun
The frumious Bandersnatch!'

He took his vorpal sword in hand:
Long time the manxome foe he sought —
So rested he by the Tumtum tree,
And stood awhile in thought.

And as in uffish thought he stood,
The Jabberwock, with eyes of flame,
Came whiffling through the tulgey wood,
And burbled as it came!

One, two! One, two! And through and through
The vorpal blade went snicker-snack!
He left it dead, and with its head
He went galumphing back.

'And has thou slain the Jabberwock?
Come to my arms, my beamish boy!
A frabjous day! Callooh! Callay!'
He chortled in his joy.

'Twas brillig, and the slithy toves
Did gyre and gimble in the wabe;
All mimsy were the borogoves,
And the mome raths outgrabe.

'It seems very pretty,' she said when she had finished it, 'but it's *rather* hard to understand!' (You see she didn't like to confess, even to herself, that she couldn't make it out at all.) 'Somehow it seems to fill my head with ideas – only I don't exactly know what they are! However, *somebody* killed *something*: that's clear, at any rate –'

'But oh!' thought Alice, suddenly jumping up, 'if I don't make haste I shall have to go back through the Looking-glass, before I've seen what the rest of the house is like! Let's have a look at the garden first!' She was out of the room in a moment, and ran down stairs –

or, at least, it wasn't exactly running, but a new invention for getting down stairs quickly and easily, as Alice said to herself. She just kept the tips of her fingers on the hand-rail, and floated gently down without even touching the stairs with her feet; then she floated on through the hall, and would have gone straight out at the door in the same way, if she hadn't caught hold of the door-post. She was getting a little giddy with so much floating in the air, and was rather glad to find herself walking again in the natural way.

2

The Garden of Live Flowers

'I SHOULD see the garden far better,' said Alice to herself, 'if I could get to the top of that hill: and here's a path that leads straight to it – at least, no, it doesn't do that –' (after going a few yards along the path, and turning several sharp corners), 'but I suppose it will at last. But how curiously it twists! It's more like a corkscrew than a path! Well, *this* turn goes to the hill, I suppose – no, it doesn't! This goes straight back to the house! Well then, I'll try it the other way.'

And so she did: wandering up and down, and trying turn after turn, but always coming back to the house, do what she would. Indeed, once, when she turned a corner rather more quickly than usual, she ran against it before she could stop herself.

'It's no use talking about it,' Alice said, looking up at the house and pretending it was arguing with her. 'I'm not going in again yet. I know I should have to get through the Looking-glass again – back into the old room – and there'd be an end of all my adventures!'

So, resolutely turning her back upon the house, she set out once more down the path, determined to keep straight on till she got to the hill. For a few minutes all went on well, and she was just saying, 'I really *shall* do it this time –' when the path gave a sudden twist and shook itself (as she described it afterwards), and the next moment she found herself actually walking in at the door.

'Oh, it's too bad!' she cried. 'I never saw such a house for getting in the way! Never!'

However, there was the hill full in sight, so there was nothing to be done but start again. This time she came upon a large flower-bed, with a border of daisies, and a willow-tree growing in the middle.

'O Tiger-lily,' said Alice, addressing herself to one that was waving gracefully about in the wind, 'I *wish* you could talk!'

'We *can* talk,' said the Tiger-lily: 'when there's anybody worth talking to.'

Alice was so astonished that she could not speak for a minute: it quite seemed to take her breath away. At length, as the Tiger-lily only went on waving about, she spoke again, in a timid voice – almost in a whisper. 'And can *all* the flowers talk?'

'As well as *you* can,' said the Tiger-lily. 'And a great deal louder.'

'It isn't manners for us to begin, you know,' said the Rose, 'and I really was wondering when you'd speak! Said

I to myself, "Her face has got *some* sense in it, though it's not a clever one!" Still, you're the right colour, and that goes a long way.'

'I don't care about the colour,' the Tiger-lily remarked. 'If only her petals curled up a little more, she'd be all right.'

Alice didn't like being criticised, so she began asking questions. 'Aren't you sometimes frightened at being planted out here, with nobody to take care of you?'

'There's the tree in the middle,' said the Rose: 'what else is it good for?'

'But what could it do, if any danger came?' Alice asked.

'It could bark,' said the Rose.

'It says "Bough-wough!"' cried a Daisy: 'that's why its branches are called boughs!'

'Didn't you know *that*?' cried another Daisy, and here they all began shouting together, till the air seemed quite full of little shrill voices. 'Silence, every one of you!' cried the Tiger-lily, waving itself passionately from side to side, and trembling with excitement. 'They know I can't get at them!' it panted, bending its quivering head towards Alice, 'or they wouldn't dare to do it!'

'Never mind!' Alice said in a soothing tone, and stooping down to the daisies, who were just beginning again, she whispered, 'If you don't hold your tongues, I'll pick you!'

There was silence in a moment, and several of the pink daisies turned white.

'That's right!' said the Tiger-lily. 'The daisies are worst of all. When one speaks, they all begin together, and it's enough to make one wither to hear the way they go on!'

'How is it you can all talk so nicely?' Alice said, hoping to get it into a better temper by a compliment. 'I've been in many gardens before, but none of the flowers could talk.'

'Put your hand down, and feel the ground,' said the Tiger-lily. 'Then you'll know why.'

Alice did so. 'It's very hard,' she said, 'but I don't see what that has to do with it.'

'In most gardens,' the Tiger-lily said, 'they make the beds too soft – so that the flowers are always asleep.'

This sounded a very good reason, and Alice was quite pleased to know it. 'I never thought of that before!' she said.

'It's *my* opinion that you never think *at all*,' the Rose said in a rather severe tone.

'I never saw anybody looked stupider,' a Violet said, so suddenly, that Alice quite jumped; for it hadn't spoken before.

'Hold *your* tongue!' cried the Tiger-lily. 'As if *you* ever saw anybody! You keep your head under the leaves, and snore away there, till you know no more what's going on in the world, than if you were a bud!'

'Are there any more people in the garden besides me?' Alice said, not choosing to notice the Rose's last remark.

'There's one other flower in the garden that can move about like you,' said the Rose. 'I wonder how you do it –' ('You're always wondering,' said the Tiger-lily), 'but she's more bushy than you are.'

'Is she like me?' Alice asked eagerly, for the thought crossed her mind, 'There's another little girl in the garden, somewhere!'

'Well, she has the same awkward shape as you,' the Rose said, 'but she's redder – and her petals are shorter, I think.'

'Her petals are done up close, almost like a dahlia,' the Tiger-lily interrupted: 'not tumbled about anyhow, like yours.'

'But that's not *your* fault,' the Rose added kindly: 'you're beginning to fade, you know – and then one can't help one's petals getting a little untidy.'

Alice didn't like this idea at all: so, to change the subject, she asked 'Does she ever come out here?'

'I daresay you'll see her soon,' said the Rose. 'She's

one of the thorny kind.'

'Where does she wear the thorns?' Alice asked with some curiosity.

'Why, all round her head, of course,' the Rose replied. 'I was wondering *you* hadn't got some too. I thought it was the regular rule.'

'She's coming!' cried the Larkspur. 'I hear her footstep, thump, thump, along the gravel-walk!'

Alice looked round eagerly, and found that it was the Red Queen. 'She's grown a good deal!' was her first remark. She had indeed: when Alice first found her in the ashes, she had been only three inches high – and here she was, half a head taller than Alice herself!

'It's the fresh air that does it,' said the Rose: 'wonderfully fine air it is, out here.'

'I think I'll go and meet her,' said Alice, for though the flowers were interesting enough, she felt that it would be far grander to have a talk with a real Queen.

'You can't possibly do that,' said the Rose, '*I* should advise you to walk the other way.'

This sounded nonsense to Alice, so she said nothing, but set off at once towards the Red Queen. To her surprise, she lost sight of her in a moment, and found herself walking in at the front-door again.

A little provoked, she drew back, and after looking everywhere for the Queen (whom she spied out at last, a long way off), she thought she would try the plan, this time, of walking in the opposite direction.

It succeeded beautifully. She had not been walking a minute before she found herself face to face with the Red Queen, and full in sight of the hill she had been so long aiming at.

'Where do you come from?' said the Red Queen. 'And where are you going? Look up, speak nicely, and don't twiddle your fingers all the time.'

Alice attended to all these directions, and explained, as well as she could, that she had lost her way.

'I don't know what you mean by *your* way,' said the Queen: 'all the ways about here belong to *me* – but why did you come out here at all?' she added in a kinder tone. 'Curtsey while you're thinking what to say, it saves time.'

Alice wondered a little at this, but she was too much in awe of the Queen to disbelieve it. 'I'll try it when I go home,' she thought to herself, 'the next time I'm a little late for dinner.'

'It's time for you to answer now,' the Queen said, looking at her watch: 'open your mouth a *little* wider when you speak, and always say "your Majesty."'

'I only wanted to see what the garden was like, your Majesty –'

'That's right,' said the Queen, patting her on the head,

which Alice didn't like at all, 'though, when you say
"garden," – *I've* seen gardens, compared with which this
would be a wilderness.'

Alice didn't dare to argue the point, but went on:
'– and I thought I'd try and find my way to the top of
that hill –'

'When you say "hill,"' the Queen interrupted, '*I* could show you hills, in comparison with which you'd call that a valley.'

'No, I couldn't,' said Alice, surprised into contradicting her at last: 'a hill *can't* be a valley, you know. That would be nonsense —'

The Red Queen shook her head. 'You may call it "nonsense" if you like,' she said, 'but *I've* heard nonsense, compared with which that would be as sensible as a dictionary!'

Alice curtseyed again, as she was afraid from the Queen's tone that she was a *little* offended: and they walked on in silence till they got to the top of the little hill.

For some minutes Alice stood without speaking, looking out in all directions over the country – and a most curious country it was. There were a number of tiny little brooks running straight across it from side to side, and the ground between was divided up into squares by a number of little green hedges, that reached from brook to brook.

'I declare it's marked out just like a large chessboard!' Alice said at last. 'There ought to be some men moving about somewhere – and so there are!' she added in a tone of delight, and her heart began to beat quick with excitement as she went on. 'It's a great huge game of

chess that's being played – all over the world – if this is the world at all, you know. Oh, what fun it is! How I *wish* I was one of them! I wouldn't mind being a Pawn, if only I might join – though of course I should *like* to be a Queen, best.'

She glanced rather shyly at the real Queen as she said this, but her companion only smiled pleasantly, and said, 'That's easily managed. You can be the White Queen's Pawn, if you like, as Lily's too young to play: and you're in the Second Square to begin with: when you get to the Eighth Square you'll be a Queen –' Just at this moment, somehow or other, they began to run.

Alice never could quite make out, in thinking it over afterwards, how it was that they began: all she remembers is, that they were running hand in hand, and the Queen went so fast that it was all she could do to keep up with her: and still the Queen kept crying 'Faster! Faster!' but Alice felt she *could not* go faster, though she had no breath left to say so.

The most curious part of the thing was, that the trees and other things round them never changed their places at all: however fast they went, they never seemed to pass anything. 'I wonder if all the things move along with us?' thought poor puzzled Alice. And the Queen seemed to guess her thoughts, for she cried, 'Faster! Don't try to talk!'

Not that Alice had any idea of doing *that*. She felt as if she would never be able to talk again, she was getting so much out of breath: and still the Queen cried 'Faster!

Faster!' and dragged her along. 'Are we nearly there?' Alice managed to pant out at last.

'Nearly there!' the Queen repeated. 'Why, we passed it ten minutes ago! Faster!' And they ran on for a time in silence, with the wind whistling in Alice's ears, and almost blowing her hair off her head, she fancied.

'Now! Now!' cried the Queen. 'Faster! Faster!' And they went so fast that at last they seemed to skim through the air, hardly touching the ground with their feet, till suddenly, just as Alice was getting quite exhausted, they stopped, and she found herself sitting on the ground, breathless and giddy.

The Queen propped her up against a tree, and said kindly, 'You may rest a little now.'

Alice looked round her in great surprise. 'Why, I do believe we've been under this tree the whole time! Everything's just as it was!'

'Of course it is,' said the Queen: 'what would you have it?'

'Well, in *our* country,' said Alice, still panting a little, 'you'd generally get to somewhere else – if you ran very fast for a long time, as we've been doing.'

'A slow sort of country!' said the Queen. 'Now, *here*, you see, it takes all the running *you* can do, to keep in the same place. If you want to get somewhere else, you must run at least twice as fast as that!'

'I'd rather not try, please!' said Alice. 'I'm quite content to stay here – only I *am* so hot and thirsty!'

'I know what *you'd* like!' the Queen said good-naturedly, taking a little box out of her pocket. 'Have a biscuit?'

Alice thought it would not be civil to say 'No,' though it wasn't at all what she wanted. So she took it, and ate it as well as she could: and it was *very* dry; and she thought she had never been so nearly choked in all her life.

'While you're refreshing yourself,' said the Queen, 'I'll just take the measurements.' And she took a ribbon out of her pocket, marked in inches, and began measuring the ground, and sticking little pegs in here and there.

'At the end of two yards,' she said, putting in a peg to mark the distance, 'I shall give you your directions – have another biscuit?'

'No, thank you,' said Alice: 'one's *quite* enough!'

'Thirst quenched, I hope?' said the Queen.

Alice did not know what to say to this, but luckily the Queen did not wait for an answer, but went on. 'At the end of *three* yards I shall repeat them – for fear of your forgetting them. At the end of *four*, I shall say good-bye. And at the end of *five*, I shall go!'

She had got all the pegs put in by this time, and Alice looked on with great interest as she returned to the tree, and then began slowly walking down the row.

At the two-yard peg she faced round, and said, 'A pawn goes two squares in its first move, you know. So you'll go *very* quickly through the Third Square – by railway, I should think – and you'll find yourself in the Fourth Square in no time. Well, *that* square belongs to Tweedledum and Tweedledee – the Fifth is mostly water – the Sixth belongs to Humpty Dumpty – But you make no remark?'

'I – I didn't know I had to make one – just then,' Alice faltered out.

'You *should* have said,' the Queen went on in a tone of grave reproof, '"It's extremely kind of you to tell me all this" – however, we'll suppose it said – the Seventh Square is all forest – however, one of the Knights will show you the way – and in the Eighth Square we shall be Queens together, and it's all feasting and fun!' Alice got up and curtseyed, and sat down again.

At the next peg the Queen turned again, and this time she said, 'Speak in French when you can't think of the English for a thing – turn out your toes as you walk – and remember who you are!' She did not wait for Alice to curtsey this time, but walked on quickly to the next peg, where she turned for a moment to say 'good-bye,' and then hurried on to the last.

How it happened, Alice never knew, but exactly as she came to the last peg, she was gone. Whether she vanished into the air, or whether she ran quickly into the wood ('and she *can* run very fast!' thought Alice), there was no way of guessing, but she was gone, and Alice began to remember that she was a Pawn, and that it would soon be time for her to move.

3

Looking-Glass Insects

O F course the first thing to do was to make a grand survey of the country she was going to travel through. 'It's something very like learning geography,' thought Alice, as she stood on tiptoe in hopes of being able to see a little further. 'Principal rivers – there *are* none. Principal mountains – I'm on the only one, but I don't think it's got any name. Principal towns – why, what *are* those creatures, making honey down there? They can't be bees – nobody ever saw bees a mile off, you know –' and for some time she stood silent, watching one of them that was bustling about among the flowers, poking its proboscis into them, 'just as if it was a regular bee,' thought Alice.

However, this was anything but a regular bee: in fact, it was an elephant – as Alice soon found out, though the idea quite took her breath away at first. 'And what enormous flowers they must be!' was her next idea. 'Something like cottages with the roofs taken off, and stalks put to them – and what quantities of honey they must make! I think I'll go down and – no, I won't go *just* yet,' she went on, checking herself just as she was beginning to run down the hill, and trying to find some excuse for turning shy so suddenly. 'It'll never do to go down among them without a good long branch to brush them away – and what fun it'll be when they ask me how I liked my walk. I shall say – "Oh, I liked it well enough –"' (here came the favourite little toss of the head), '"only it was so dusty and hot, and the elephants did tease so!"'

'I think I'll go down the other way,' she said after a pause: 'and perhaps I may visit the elephants later on. Besides, I do so want to get into the Third Square!'

So with this excuse she ran down the hill and jumped over the first of the six little brooks.

*   *   *   *

*   *   *

*   *   *   *

'Tickets, please!' said the Guard, putting his head in at the window. In a moment everybody was holding out a ticket: they were about the same size as the people, and quite seemed to fill the carriage.

'Now then! Show your ticket, child!' the Guard went on, looking angrily at Alice. And a great many voices all said together ('like the chorus of a song,' thought Alice), 'Don't keep him waiting, child! Why, his time is worth a thousand pounds a minute!'

'I'm afraid I haven't got one,' Alice said in a frightened tone: 'there wasn't a ticket-office where I came from.' And again the chorus of voices went on. 'There wasn't room for one where she came from. The land there is worth a thousand pounds an inch!'

'Don't make excuses,' said the Guard: 'you should have bought one from the engine-driver.' And once more the chorus of voices went on with 'The man that drives the engine. Why, the smoke alone is worth a thousand pounds a puff!'

Alice thought to herself, 'Then there's no use in speaking.' The voices didn't join in this time, as she hadn't spoken, but, to her great surprise, they all *thought* in chorus (I hope you understand what *thinking in chorus* means – for I must confess that *I* don't), 'Better say nothing at all. Language is worth a thousand pounds a word!'

'I shall dream about a thousand pounds to-night, I know I shall!' thought Alice.

All this time the Guard was looking at her, first through a telescope, then through a microscope, and then through an opera-glass. At last he said, 'You're travelling the wrong way,' and shut up the window and went away.

'So young a child,' said the gentleman sitting opposite to her (he was dressed in white paper), 'ought to know which way she's going, even if she doesn't know her own name!'

A Goat, that was sitting next to the gentleman in white, shut his eyes and said in a loud voice, 'She ought to know her way to the ticket-office, even if she doesn't know her alphabet!'

There was a Beetle sitting next the Goat (it was a very queer carriage-full of passengers altogether), and, as the rule seemed to be that they should all speak in turn, *he* went on with 'She'll have to go back from here as luggage!'

Alice couldn't see who was sitting beyond the Beetle, but a hoarse voice spoke next. 'Change engines –' it said, and there it choked and was obliged to leave off.

'It sounds like a horse,' Alice thought to herself. And an extremely small voice, close to her ear, said,

'You might make a joke on that – something about "horse" and "hoarse," you know.'

Then a very gentle voice in the distance said, 'She must be labelled "Lass, with care," you know –'

And after that other voices went on ('What a number of people there are in the carriage!' thought Alice), saying, 'She must go by post, as she's got a head on her –' 'She must be sent as a message by the telegraph –' 'She must draw the train herself the rest of the way –,' and so on.

But the gentleman dressed in white paper leaned forwards and whispered in her ear, 'Never mind what they all say, my dear, but take a return-ticket every time the train stops.'

'Indeed I shan't!' Alice said rather impatiently. 'I don't

belong to this railway journey at all – I was in a wood just now – and I wish I could get back there!'

'You might make a joke on *that*,' said the little voice close to her ear: 'something about "you *would* if you could," you know.'

'Don't tease so,' said Alice, looking about in vain to see where the voice came from; 'if you're so anxious to have a joke made, why don't you make one yourself?'

The little voice sighed deeply: it was *very* unhappy, evidently, and Alice would have said something pitying to comfort it, 'if it would only sigh like other people!' she thought. But this was such a wonderfully small sigh, that she wouldn't have heard it at all, if it hadn't come *quite* close to her ear. The consequence of this was that it tickled her ear very much, and quite took off her thoughts from the unhappiness of the poor little creature.

'I know you are a friend,' the little voice went on; 'a dear friend, and an old friend. And you won't hurt me, though I *am* an insect.'

'What kind of insect?' Alice inquired a little anxiously. What she really wanted to know was, whether it could sting or not, but she thought this wouldn't be quite a civil question to ask.

'What, then you don't –' the little voice began, when it was drowned by a shrill scream from the engine, and everybody jumped up in alarm, Alice among the rest.

The Horse, who had put his head out of the window, quietly drew it in and said, 'It's only a brook we have to jump over.' Everybody seemed satisfied with this, though Alice felt a little nervous at the idea of trains jumping at all. 'However, it'll take us into the Fourth Square, that's some comfort!' she said to herself. In another moment she felt the carriage rise straight up into the air, and in her fright she caught at the thing nearest to her hand, which happened to be the Goat's beard.

*   *   *   *

*   *   *

*   *   *   *

But the beard seemed to melt away as she touched it, and she found herself sitting quietly under a tree – while the Gnat (for that was the insect she had been talking to) was balancing itself on a twig just over her head, and fanning her with its wings.

It certainly was a *very* large Gnat: 'about the size of a chicken,' Alice thought. Still, she couldn't feel nervous with it, after they had been talking together so long.

'– then you don't like all insects?' the Gnat went on, as quietly as if nothing had happened.

'I like them when they can talk,' Alice said. 'None of them ever talk, where *I* come from.'

'What sort of insects do you rejoice in, where *you* come from?' the Gnat inquired.

'I don't *rejoice* in insects at all,' Alice explained, 'because I'm rather afraid of them – at least the large kinds. But I can tell you the names of some of them.'

'Of course they answer to their names?' the Gnat remarked carelessly.

'I never knew them do it.'

'What's the use of their having names,' the Gnat said, 'if they won't answer to them?'

'No use to *them*,' said Alice; 'but it's useful to the people that name them, I suppose. If not, why do things have names at all?'

'I can't say,' the Gnat replied. 'Further on, in the wood down there, they've got no names – however, go on with your list of insects: you're wasting time.'

'Well, there's the Horse-fly,' Alice began, counting off the names on her fingers.

'All right,' said the Gnat: 'half way up that bush, you'll see a Rocking-horse-fly, if you look. It's made entirely of wood, and gets about by swinging itself from branch to branch.'

'What does it live on?' Alice asked, with great curiosity.

'Sap and sawdust,' said the Gnat. 'Go on with the list.'

Alice looked at the Rocking-horse-fly with great interest, and made up her mind that it must have been

just repainted, it looked so bright and sticky; and then she went on.

'And there's the Dragon-fly.'

'Look on the branch above your head,' said the Gnat, 'and there you'll find a Snap-dragan-fly. Its body is made of plum-pudding, its wings of holly-leaves, and its head is a raisin burning in brandy.'

'And what does it live on?' Alice asked, as before.

'Frumenty and mince-pie,' the Gnat replied; 'and it makes its nest in a Christmas-box.'

'And then there's the Butterfly,' Alice went on, after she had taken a good look at the insect with its head on fire, and had thought to herself, 'I wonder if that's the reason insects are so fond of flying into candles – because they want to turn into Snap-dragon-flies!'

'Crawling at your feet,' said the Gnat (Alice drew her feet back in some alarm), 'you may observe a Bread-and-Butterfly. Its wings are thin slices of Bread-and-butter, its body is a crust, and its head is a lump of sugar.'

'And what does *it* live on?'

'Weak tea with cream in it.'

A new difficulty came into Alice's head. 'Supposing it couldn't find any?' she suggested.

'Then it would die, of course.'

'But that must happen very often,' Alice remarked thoughtfully.

'It always happens,' said the Gnat.

After this, Alice was silent for a minute or two, pondering. The Gnat amused itself meanwhile by humming round and round her head: at last it settled again and remarked, 'I suppose you don't want to lose your name?'

'No, indeed,' Alice said, a little anxiously.

'And yet I don't know,' the Gnat went on in a careless tone: 'only think how convenient it would be if you could manage to go home without it! For instance, if the governess wanted to call you to your lessons, she would call out "Come here –," and there she would have to leave off, because there wouldn't be any name for her to call, and of course you wouldn't have to go, you know.'

'That would never do, I'm sure,' said Alice: 'the governess would never think of excusing me lessons for that. If she couldn't remember my name, she'd call me "Miss!" as the servants do.'

'Well, if she said "Miss," and didn't say anything more,' the Gnat remarked, 'of course you'd miss your lessons. That's a joke. I wish *you* had made it.'

'Why do you wish *I* had made it?' Alice asked. 'It's a very bad one.'

But the Gnat only sighed deeply, while two large tears came rolling down its cheeks.

'You shouldn't make jokes,' Alice said, 'if it makes you so unhappy.'

Then came another of those melancholy little sighs, and this time the poor Gnat really seemed to have sighed itself away, for, when Alice looked up, there was nothing whatever to be seen on the twig, and, as she was getting quite chilly with sitting still so long, she got up and walked on.

She very soon came to an open field, with a wood on the other side of it: it looked much darker than the last wood, and Alice felt a *little* timid about going into it. However, on second thoughts, she made up her mind to go on: 'for I certainly won't go *back*,' she thought to herself, and this was the only way to the Eighth Square.

'This must be the wood,' she said thoughtfully to herself, 'where things have no names. I wonder what'll become of *my* name when I go in? I shouldn't like to lose it at all – because they'd have to give me another, and it would be almost certain to be an ugly one. But then the fun would be, trying to find the creature that had got my old name! That's just like the advertisements, you know, when people lose dogs – "*answers to the name of 'Dash:'* *had on a brass collar*" – just fancy calling everything you met "Alice," till one of them answered! Only they wouldn't answer at all, if they were wise.'

She was rambling on in this way when she reached the wood: it looked very cool and shady. 'Well, at any rate it's a great comfort,' she said as she stepped under the trees, 'after being so hot, to get into the – into the – into *what*?' she went on, rather surprised at not being able to think of the word. 'I mean to get under the – under the – under *this*, you know!' putting her hand on the trunk of the tree. 'What *does* it call itself, I wonder? I do believe it's got no name – why, to be sure it hasn't!'

She stood silent for a minute, thinking: then she suddenly began again. 'Then it really *has* happened, after all! And now, who am I? I *will* remember, if I can! I'm determined to do it!' But being determined didn't help her much, and all she could say, after a great deal of puzzling, was, 'L, I *know* it begins with L!'

Just then a Fawn came wandering by: it looked at Alice with its large gentle eyes, but didn't seem at all frightened. 'Here then! Here then!' Alice said, as she held out her hand and tried to stroke it; but it only started back a little, and then stood looking at her again.

'What do you call yourself?' the Fawn said at last. Such a soft sweet voice it had!

'I wish I knew!' thought poor Alice. She answered, rather sadly, 'Nothing, just now.'

'Think again,' it said: 'that won't do.'

Alice thought, but nothing came of it. 'Please, would you tell me what *you* call yourself?' she said timidly. 'I think that might help a little.'

'I'll tell you, if you'll come a little further on,' the Fawn said. 'I can't remember here.'

So they walked on together through the wood, Alice with her arms clasped lovingly round the soft neck of the Fawn, till they came out into another open field, and here the Fawn gave a sudden bound into the air, and shook itself free from Alice's arms. 'I'm a Fawn!' it cried out in a voice of delight, 'and, dear me! you're a human child!' A sudden look of alarm came into its beautiful brown eyes, and in another moment it had darted away at full speed.

Alice stood looking after it, almost ready to cry with vexation at having lost her dear little fellow-traveller so suddenly. 'However, I know my name now,' she said, 'that's *some* comfort. Alice – Alice – I won't forget it again. And now, which of these finger-posts ought I to follow, I wonder?'

It was not a very difficult question to answer, as there was only one road through the wood, and the two fingerposts both pointed along it. 'I'll settle it,' Alice said to herself, 'when the road divides and they point different ways.'

But this did not seem likely to happen. She went on and on, a long way, but wherever the road divided there were sure to be two finger-posts pointing the same way, one marked 'TO TWEEDLEDUM'S HOUSE, and the other 'TO THE HOUSE OF TWEEDLEDEE.'

'I do believe,' said Alice at last, 'that they live in the

same house! I wonder I never thought of that before – But I can't stay there long. I'll just call and say "How d'you do?" and ask them the way out of the wood. If I could only get to the Eighth Square before it gets dark!' So she wandered on, talking to herself as she went, till, on turning a sharp corner, she came upon two fat little men, so suddenly that she could not help starting back, but in another moment she recovered herself, feeling sure that they must be

4

Tweedledum and Tweedledee

THEY were standing under a tree, each with an arm
round the other's neck, and Alice knew which was
which in a moment, because one of them had 'DUM'
embroidered on his collar, and the other 'DEE.' 'I suppose

they've each got "TWEEDLE" round at the back of the collar,' she said to herself.

They stood so still that she quite forgot they were alive, and she was just looking round to see if the word 'TWEEDLE' was written at the back of each collar, when she was startled by a voice coming from the one marked 'DUM.'

'If you think we're wax-works,' he said, 'you ought to pay, you know. Wax-works weren't made to be looked at for nothing. Nohow!'

'Contrariwise,' added the one marked 'DEE,' 'if you think we're alive, you ought to speak.'

'I'm sure I'm very sorry,' was all Alice could say; for the words of the old song kept ringing through her head like the ticking of a clock, and she could hardly help saying them out loud:–

> 'Tweedledum and Tweedledee
>   Agreed to have a battle;
> For Tweedledum said Tweedledee
>   Had spoiled his nice new rattle.
>
> Just then flew down a monstrous crow,
>   As black as a tar-barrel;
> Which frightened both the heroes so,
>   They quite forgot their quarrel.'

'I know what you're thinking about,' said Tweedledum: 'but it isn't so, nohow.'

'Contrariwise,' continued Tweedledee, 'if it was so, it might be; and if it were so, it would be; but as it isn't, it ain't. That's logic.'

'I was thinking,' Alice said very politely, 'which is the best way out of this wood: it's getting so dark. Would you tell me, please?'

But the fat little men only looked at each other and grinned.

They looked so exactly like a couple of great schoolboys, that Alice couldn't help pointing her finger at Tweedledum, and saying 'First Boy!'

'Nohow!' Tweedledum cried out briskly, and shut his mouth up again with a snap.

'Next Boy!' said Alice, passing on to Tweedledee, though she felt quite certain he would only shout out 'Contrariwise!' and so he did.

'You've begun wrong!' cried Tweedledum. 'The first thing in a visit is to say "How d'ye do?" and shake hands!' And here the two brothers gave each other a hug, and then they held out the two hands that were free, to shake hands with her.

Alice did not like shaking hands with either of them first, for fear of hurting the other one's feelings; so, as the best way out of the difficulty, she took hold of both hands at once: the next moment they were dancing round in a ring. This seemed quite natural (she remembered afterwards), and she was not even surprised to hear music playing: it seemed to come from the tree under which they were dancing and it was done (as well as she could make it out) by the branches rubbing one across the other, like fiddles and fiddle-sticks.

'But it certainly *was* funny,' (Alice said afterwards, when she was telling her sister the history of all this,) 'to find myself singing "*Here we go round the mulberry bush.*" I don't know when I began it, bur somehow I felt as if I'd been singing it a long long time!'

The other two dancers were fat, and very soon out of breath. 'Four times round is enough for one dance,' Tweedledum panted out, and they left off dancing as suddenly as they had begun: the music stopped at the same moment.

Then they let go of Alice's hands, and stood looking at her for a minute: there was a rather awkward pause, as Alice didn't know how to begin a conversation with people she had just been dancing with. 'It would never do to say "How d'ye do?" *now*,' she said to herself: 'we seem to have got beyond that, somehow!'

'I hope you're not much tired?' she said at last.

'Nohow. And thank you *very* much for asking,' said Tweedledum.

'So *much* obliged!' added Tweedledee. 'You like poetry?'

'Ye-es, pretty well – *some* poetry,' Alice said doubtfully. 'Would you tell me which road leads out of the wood?'

'What shall I repeat to her?' said Tweedledee, looking round at Tweedledum with great solemn eyes, and not noticing Alice's question.

'"*The Walrus and the Carpenter*" is the longest,' Tweedledum replied, giving his brother an affectionate hug.

Tweedledee began instantly:

> '*The sun was shining* –'

Here Alice ventured to interrupt him. 'If it's *very* long,' she said, as politely as she could, 'would you please tell me first which road –'

Tweedledee smiled gently, and began again:

> '*The sun was shining on the sea,*
> *Shining with all his might:*
> *He did his very best to make*
> *The billows smooth and bright –*
> *And this was odd, because it was*
> *The middle of the night.*

The moon was shining sulkily,
  Because she thought the sun
Had got no business to be there
  After the day was done –
"It's very rude of him," she said,
  "To come and spoil the fun!"

The sea was wet as wet could be,
  The sands were dry as dry.
You could not see a cloud, because
  No cloud was in the sky:
No birds were flying overhead -
  There were no birds to fly.

The Walrus and the Carpenter
  Were walking close at hand;
They wept like anything to see
  Such quantities of sand:
"If this were only cleared away,"
  They said, "it would be grand!"

"If seven maids with seven mops
  Swept it for half a year,
Do you suppose," the Walrus said,
  "That they could get it clear?"

"I doubt it," said the Carpenter,
  And shed a bitter tear.

"O Oysters, come and walk with us!"
  The Walrus did beseech.
"A pleasant walk, a pleasant talk,
  Along the briny beach:
We cannot do with more than four,
  To give a hand to each."

The eldest Oyster looked at him.
  But never a word he said:
The eldest Oyster winked his eye,
  And shook his heavy head –

Meaning to say he did not choose
    To leave the oyster-bed.

But four young oysters hurried up,
    All eager for the treat:
Their coats were brushed, their faces washed,
    Their shoes were clean and neat –
And this was odd, because, you know,
    They hadn't any feet.

Four other Oysters followed them,
    And yet another four;
And thick and fast they came at last,
    And more, and more, and more –
All hopping through the frothy waves,
    And scrambling to the shore.

The Walrus and the Carpenter
    Walked on a mile or so,
And then they rested on a rock
    Conveniently low:
And all the little Oysters stood
    And waited in a row.

"The time has come," the Walrus said,
    "To talk of many things:

Of shoes – and ships – and sealing wax –
  Of cabbages – and kings –
And why the sea is boiling hot –
  And whether pigs have wings."

"But wait a bit," the Oysters cried,
  "Before we have our chat;
For some of us are out of breath,
  And all of us are fat!"
"No hurry!" said the Carpenter.
  They thanked him much for that.

"A loaf of bread," the Walrus said,
  "Is what we chiefly need:

Pepper and vinegar besides
    Are very good indeed –
Now if you're ready, Oysters dear,
    We can begin to feed."

"But not on us!" the Oysters cried,
    Turning a little blue,
"After such kindness, that would be
    A dismal thing to do!"
"The night is fine," the Walrus said.
    "Do you admire the view?"

"It was so kind of you to come!
    And you are very nice!"
The Carpenter said nothing but
    "Cut us another slice:
I wish you were not quite so deaf –
    I've had to ask you twice!"

"It seems a shame," the Walrus said,
    "To play them such a trick,
After we've brought them out so far,
    And made them trot so quick!"
The Carpenter said nothing but
    "The butter's spread too thick!"

'I weep for you,' the Walrus said,
    'I deeply sympathize.'
With sobs and tears he sorted out
    Those of the largest size,
Holding his pocket-handkerchief
    Before his streaming eyes.

'O Oysters,' said the Carpenter.
    'You've had a pleasant run!
Shall we be trotting home again?'
    But answer came there none –
And this was scarcely odd, because
    They'd eaten every one.'

'I like the Walrus best,' said Alice: 'because you see he was a *little* sorry for the poor oysters.'

'He ate more than the Carpenter, though,' said Tweedledee. 'You see he held his handkerchief in front, so that the Carpenter couldn't count how many he took: contrariwise.'

'That was mean!' Alice said indignantly. 'Then I like the Carpenter best – if he didn't eat so many as the Walrus.'

'But he ate as many as he could get,' said Tweedledum.

This was a puzzler. After a pause, Alice began, 'Well! They were *both* very unpleasant characters –' Here she checked herself in some alarm, at hearing something that sounded to her like the puffing of a large steam-engine in the wood near them, though she feared it was more likely to be a wild beast. 'Are there any lions or tigers about here?' she asked timidly.

'It's only the Red King snoring,' said Tweedledee.

'Come and look at him!' the brothers cried, and they took each one of Alice's hands, and led her up to where the King was sleeping.

'Isn't he a *lovely* sight?' said Tweedledum.

Alice couldn't say honestly that he was. He had a tall red night-cap on, with a tassel, and he was lying crumpled up into a sort of untidy heap, and snoring loud

– 'fit to snore his head off!' as Tweedledum remarked.

'I'm afraid he'll catch cold with lying on the damp grass,' said Alice, who was a very thoughtful little girl.

'He's dreaming now,' said Tweedledee: 'and what do you think he's dreaming about?'

Alice said 'Nobody can guess that.'

'Why, about *you*!' Tweedledee exclaimed, clapping his hands triumphantly. 'And if he left off dreaming about you, where do you suppose you'd be?'

'Where I am now, of course,' said Alice.

'Not you!' Tweedledee retorted contemptuously. 'You'd be nowhere. Why, you're only a sort of thing in his dream!'

'If that there King was to wake,' added Tweedledum, 'you'd go out – bang! – just like a candle!'

'I shouldn't!' Alice exclaimed indignantly. 'Besides, if *I'm* only a sort of thing in his dream, what are *you*, I should like to know?'

'Ditto,' said Tweedledum.

'Ditto, ditto!' cried Tweedledee.

He shouted this so loud that Alice couldn't help saying, 'Hush! You'll be waking him, I'm afraid, if you make so much noise.'

'Well, it's no use *your* talking about waking him,' said Tweedledum, 'when you're only one of the things in his dream. You know very well you're not real.'

'I *am* real!' said Alice, and began to cry.

'You won't make yourself a bit realler by crying,' Tweedledee remarked: 'there's nothing to cry about.'

'If I wasn't real,' Alice said – half-laughing through her tears, it all seemed so ridiculous – 'I shouldn't be able to cry.'

'I hope you don't suppose those are real tears?' Tweedledum interrupted in a tone of great contempt.

'I know they're talking nonsense,' Alice thought to herself: 'and it's foolish to cry about it.' So she brushed away her tears, and went on as cheerfully as she could, 'At any rate I'd better be getting out of the wood, for really it's coming on very dark. Do you think it's going to rain?'

Tweedledum spread a large umbrella over himself

and his brother, and looked up into it. 'No, I don't think it is,' he said: 'at least – not under *here*. Nohow.'

'But it may rain *outside*?'

'It may – if it chooses,' said Tweedledee: 'we've no objection. Contrariwise.'

'Selfish things!' thought Alice, and she was just going to say 'Good-night' and leave them, when Tweedledum sprang out from under the umbrella, and seized her by the wrist.

'Do you see *that*?' he said, in a voice choking with passion, and his eyes grew large and yellow all in a moment, as he pointed with a trembling finger at a small white thing lying under the tree.

'It's only a rattle,' Alice said, after a careful examination of the little white thing. 'Not a rattle-*snake*, you know,' she added hastily, thinking that he was frightened: 'only an old rattle – quite old and broken.'

'I knew it was!' cried Tweedledum, beginning to stamp about wildly and tear his hair. 'It's spoilt, of course!' Here he looked at Tweedledee, who immediately sat down on the ground, and tried to hide himself under the umbrella.

Alice laid her hand upon his arm, and said in a soothing tone, 'You needn't be so angry about an old rattle.'

'But it isn't old!' Tweedledum cried, in a greater fury

than ever. 'It's new, I tell you – I bought it yesterday –
my nice new RATTLE!' and his voice rose to a perfect
scream.

All this time Tweedledee was trying his best to fold
up the umbrella, with himself in it: which was such an
extraordinary thing to do, that it quite took off Alice's
attention from the angry brother. But he couldn't quite
succeed, and it ended in his rolling over, bundled up
in the umbrella, with only his head out: and there he
lay, opening and shutting his mouth and his large eyes
– 'looking more like a fish than anything else,' Alice
thought.

'Of course you agree to have a battle?' Tweedledum
said in a calmer tone.

'I suppose so,' the other sulkily replied, as he crawled out of the umbrella: 'only *she* must help us to dress up, you know.'

So the two brothers went off hand-in-hand into the wood, and returned in a minute with their arms full of things – such as bolsters, blankets, hearth-rugs, table-cloths, dish-covers and coal-scuttles. 'I hope you're a good hand at pinning and tying strings?' Tweedledum remarked. 'Every one of these things has got to go on, somehow or other.'

Alice said afterwards she had never seen such a fuss made about anything in all her life – the way those two bustled about – and the quantity of things they put on – and the trouble they gave her in tying strings and fastening buttons – 'Really they'll be more like bundles of old clothes than anything else, by the time they're ready!' she said to herself, as she arranged a bolster round the neck of Tweedledee, 'to keep his head from being cut off,' as he said.

'You know,' he added very gravely, 'it's one of the most serious things that can possibly happen to one in a battle – to get one's head cut off.'

Alice laughed loud: but she managed to turn it into a cough, for fear of hurting his feelings.

'Do I look very pale?' said Tweedledum, coming up to have his helmet tied on. (He *called* it a helmet, though it certainly looked much more like a saucepan.)

'Well – yes – a *little*,' Alice replied gently.

'I'm very brave generally,' he went on in a low voice: 'only today I happen to have a headache.'

'And *I've* got a toothache!' said Tweedledee, who had overheard the remark. 'I'm far worse than you!'

'Then you'd better not fight today,' said Alice thinking it a good opportunity to make peace.

'We *must* have a bit of a fight, but I don't care about going on long,' said Tweedledum. 'What's the time now?'

Tweedledee looked at his watch, and said 'Half-past four.'

'Let's fight till six, and then have dinner,' said Tweedledum.

'Very well,' the other said, rather sadly: 'and *she* can watch us – only you'd better not come *very* close,' he added: 'I generally hit everything I can see – when I get really excited.'

'And *I* hit everything within reach,' cried Tweedledum, 'whether I can see it or not.'

Alice laughed. 'You must hit the *trees* pretty often, I should think,' she said.

Tweedledum looked round him with a satisfied smile. 'I don't suppose,' he said, 'there'll be a tree left standing, for ever so far round, by the time we've finished!'

'And all about a rattle!' said Alice still hoping to make them a *little* ashamed of fighting for such a trifle.

'I shouldn't have minded it so much,' said Tweedledum, 'if it hadn't been a new one.'

'I wish the monstrous crow would come!' thought Alice.

'There's only one sword, you know,' Tweedledum said to his brother: 'but you can have the umbrella – it's quite as sharp. Only we must begin quick. It's getting as dark as it can.'

'And darker,' said Tweedledee.

It was getting dark so suddenly that Alice thought there must be a thunderstorm coming on. 'What a thick black cloud that is!' she said. 'And how fast it comes! Why, I do believe it's got wings!'

'It's the crow!' Tweedledum cried out in a shrill voice of alarm: and the two brothers took to their heels and were out of sight in a moment.

Alice ran a little way into the wood, and stopped under a large tree. 'It can never get at me *here*,' she thought: 'it's far too large to squeeze itself in among the trees. But I wish it wouldn't flap its wings so – it makes quite a hurricane in the wood – here's somebody's shawl being blown away!'

5
Wool and Water

S HE caught the shawl as she spoke, and looked about for the owner: in another moment the White Queen came running wildly through the wood, with both arms stretched out wide, as if she were flying, and Alice very civilly went to meet her with the shawl.

'I'm very glad I happened to be in the way,' Alice said, as she helped her to put on her shawl again.

The White Queen only looked at her in a helpless frightened sort of way, and kept repeating something in a whisper to herself that sounded like 'Bread-and-butter, bread-and butter,' and Alice felt that if there was to be any conversation at all, she must manage it herself. So she began rather timidly: 'Am I addressing the White Queen?'

'Well, yes, if you call that a-dressing,' the Queen said.

'It isn't *my* notion of the thing, at all.'

Alice thought it would never do to have an argument at the very beginning of their conversation, so she smiled and said, 'If your Majesty will only tell me the right way to begin, I'll do it as well as I can.'

'But I don't want it done at all!' groaned the poor Queen. 'I've been a-dressing myself for the last two hours.'

It would have been all the better, as it seemed to Alice, if she had got some one else to dress her, she was so dreadfully untidy. 'Every single thing's crooked,' Alice thought to herself, 'and she's all over pins! – May I put your shawl straight for you?' she added aloud.

'I don't know what's the matter with it!' the Queen said, in a melancholy voice. 'It's out of temper, I think. I've pinned it here, and I've pinned it there, but there's no pleasing it!'

'It *can't* go straight, you know, if you pin it all on one side,' Alice said, as she gently put it right for her; 'and, dear me, what a state your hair is in!'

'The brush has got entangled in it!' the Queen said with a sigh. 'And I lost the comb yesterday.'

Alice carefully released the brush, and did her best to get the hair into order. 'Come, you look rather better now!' she said, after altering most of the pins. 'But really you should have a lady's-maid!'

'I'm sure I'll take you with pleasure!' the Queen said. 'Twopence a week, and jam every other day.'

Alice couldn't help laughing, as she said, 'I don't want you to hire *me* – and I don't care for jam.'

'It's very good jam,' said the Queen.

'Well, I don't want any *today*, at any rate.'

'You couldn't have if it you *did* want it,' the Queen said. 'The rule is, jam tomorrow and jam yesterday – but never jam today.'

'It *must* come sometimes to "jam today,"' Alice objected.

'No, it can't,' said the Queen. 'It's jam every other day: today isn't any *other* day, you know.'

'I don't understand you,' said Alice. 'It's dreadfully confusing!'

'That's the effect of living backwards,' the Queen said kindly: 'it always makes one a little giddy at first –'

'Living backwards!' Alice repeated in great astonishment. 'I never heard of such a thing!'

'– but there's one great advantage in it, that one's memory works both ways.'

'I'm sure *mine* only works one way,' Alice remarked. 'I can't remember things before they happen.'

'It's a poor sort of memory that only works backwards,' the Queen remarked.

'What sorts of things do *you* remember best?' Alice ventured to ask.

'Oh, things that happened the week after next,' the Queen replied in a careless tone. 'For instance, now,' she went on, sticking a large piece of plaster on her finger as she spoke, 'there's the King's Messenger. He's in prison now, being punished; and the trial doesn't even begin till next Wednesday: and of course the crime comes last of all.'

'Suppose he never commits the crime?' said Alice.

'That would be all the better, wouldn't it?' the Queen
said, as she bound the plaster round her finger with a bit
of ribbon.

Alice felt there was no denying *that*. 'Of course it
would be all the better,' she said: 'but it wouldn't be all
the better his being punished.'

'You're wrong *there*, at any rate,' said the Queen: 'were
you ever punished?'

'Only for faults,' said Alice.

'And you were all the better for it, I know!' the Queen said triumphantly.

'Yes, but then I *had* done the things I was punished for,' said Alice: 'that makes all the difference.'

'But if you *hadn't* done them,' the Queen said, 'that would have been better still; better, and better, and better!' Her voice went higher with each 'better,' till it got quite to a squeak at last.

Alice was just beginning to say 'There's a mistake somewhere –', when the Queen began screaming so loud that she had to leave the sentence unfinished. 'Oh, oh, oh!' shouted the Queen, shaking her hand about as if she wanted to shake it off. 'My finger's bleeding! Oh, oh, oh, oh!'

Her screams were so exactly like the whistle of a steam-engine, that Alice had to hold both her hands over her ears.

'What is the matter?' she said, as soon as there was a chance of making herself heard. 'Have you pricked your finger?'

'I haven't pricked it *yet*,' the Queen said, 'but I soon shall – oh, oh, oh!'

'When do you expect to do it?' Alice asked, feeling very much inclined to laugh.

'When I fasten my shawl again,' the poor Queen groaned out: 'the brooch will come undone directly. Oh, oh!' As she said the words the brooch flew open, and the Queen clutched wildly at it, and tried to clasp it again.

'Take care!' cried Alice. 'You're holding it all crooked!' And she caught at the brooch: but it was too late: the pin had slipped, and the Queen had pricked her finger.

'That accounts for the bleeding, you see,' she said to Alice with a smile. 'Now you understand the way things happen here.'

'But why don't you scream now?' Alice asked, holding her hands ready to put over her ears again.

'Why, I've done all the screaming already,' said the Queen. 'What would be the good of having it all over again?'

By this time it was getting light. 'The crow must have flown away, I think,' said Alice: 'I'm so glad it's gone. I thought it was the night coming on.'

'I wish *I* could manage to be glad!' the Queen said. 'Only I never can remember the rule. You must be very happy, living in this wood, and being glad whenever you like!'

'Only it is so *very* lonely here!' Alice said in a melancholy voice; and at the thought of her loneliness two large tears came rolling down her cheeks.

'Oh, don't go on like that!' cried the poor Queen, wringing her hands in despair. 'Consider what a great girl you are. Consider what a long way you've come today. Consider what o'clock it is. Consider anything, only don't cry!'

Alice could not help laughing at this, even in the midst of her tears. 'Can *you* keep from crying by considering things?' she asked.

'That's the way it's done,' the Queen said with great decision: 'nobody can do two things at once, you know. Let's consider your age to begin with – how old are you?'

'I'm seven and a half exactly.'

'You needn't say "exactually,"' the Queen remarked: 'I can believe it without that. Now I'll give *you* something to believe. I'm just one hundred and one, five months and a day.'

'I can't believe *that!*' said Alice.

'Can't you?' the Queen said in a pitying tone. 'Try again: draw a long breath, and shut your eyes.'

Alice laughed. 'There's no use trying,' she said: 'one *can't* believe impossible things.'

'I daresay you haven't had much practice,' said the Queen. 'When I was your age, I always did it for half-an-hour a day. Why, sometimes I've believed as many as six impossible things before breakfast. There goes the shawl again!'

The brooch had come undone as she spoke, and a sudden gust of wind blew the Queen's shawl across a little brook. The Queen spread out her arms again, and went flying after it, and this time she succeeded in catching it for herself. 'I've got it!' she cried in a triumphant tone. 'Now you shall see me pin it on again, all by myself!'

'Then I hope your finger is better now?' Alice said very politely, as she crossed the little brook after the Queen.

*   *   *   *
  *   *   *
*   *   *   *

'Oh, much better!' cried the Queen, her voice rising into a squeak as she went on. 'Much be-etter! Be-etter! Be-e-e-etter! Be-e-ehh!' The last word ended in a long bleat, so like a sheep that Alice quite started.

She looked at the Queen, who seemed to have suddenly wrapped herself up in wool. Alice rubbed her eyes, and looked again. She couldn't make out what had happened at all. Was she in a shop? And was that really – was it really a *sheep* that was sitting on the other side of the counter? Rub as she would, she could make nothing more of it: she was in a little dark shop, leaning with her elbows on the counter, and opposite to her was an old Sheep, sitting in an arm-chair knitting, and every now and then leaving off to look at her through a great pair of spectacles.

'What is it you want to buy?' the Sheep said at last,
looking up for a moment from her knitting.

'I don't *quite* know yet,' Alice said, very gently. 'I
should like to look all round me first, if I might.'

'You may look in front of you, and on both sides, if
you like,' said the Sheep: 'but you can't look *all* round
you – unless you've got eyes at the back of your head.'

But these, as it happened, Alice had *not* got: so she contented herself with turning round, looking at the shelves as she came to them.

The shop seemed to be full of all manner of curious things – but the oddest part of it all was, that whenever she looked hard at any shelf, to make out exactly what it had on it, that particular shelf was always quite empty: though the others round it were crowded as full as they could hold.

'Things flow about so here!' she said at last in a plaintive tone, after she had spent a minute or so in vainly pursuing a large bright thing, that looked sometimes like a doll and sometimes like a work-box, and was always in the shelf next above the one she was looking at. 'And this one is the most provoking of all – but I'll tell you what –' she added, as a sudden thought struck her, 'I'll follow it up to the very top shelf of all. It'll puzzle it to go through the ceiling, I expect!'

But even this plan failed: the 'thing' went through the ceiling as quietly as possible, as if it were quite used to it.

'Are you a child or a teetotum?' the Sheep said, as she took up another pair of needles. 'You'll make me giddy soon, if you go on turning round like that.' She was now working with fourteen pairs at once, and Alice couldn't help looking at her in great astonishment.

'How *can* she knit with so many?' the puzzled child thought to herself. 'She gets more and more like a porcupine every minute!'

'Can you row?' the Sheep asked, handing her a pair of knitting-needles as she spoke.

'Yes, a little – but not on land – and not with needles –' Alice was beginning to say, when suddenly the needles turned into oars in her hands, and she found they were in a little boat, gliding along between banks: so there was nothing for it but to do her best.

'Feather!' cried the Sheep, as she took up another pair of needles.

This didn't sound like a remark that needed any answer, so Alice said nothing, but pulled away. There was something very queer about the water, she thought, as every now and then the oars got fast in it, and would hardly come out again.

'Feather! Feather!' the Sheep cried again, taking more needles. 'You'll be catching a crab directly.'

'A dear little crab!' thought Alice. 'I should like that.'

'Didn't you hear me say "Feather"?' the Sheep cried angrily, taking up quite a bunch of needles.

'Indeed I did,' said Alice: 'you've said it very often – and very loud. Please, where *are* the crabs?'

'In the water, of course!' said the Sheep, sticking

some of the needles into her hair, as her hands were full. 'Feather, I say!'

'*Why* do you say "Feather" so often?' Alice asked at last, rather vexed. 'I'm not a bird!'

'You are,' said the Sheep: 'You're a little goose.'

This offended Alice a little, so there was no more conversation for a minute or two, while the boat glided gently on, sometimes among beds of weeds (which made the oars stick fast in the water, worse than ever), and sometimes under trees, but always with the same tall riverbanks frowning over their heads.

'Oh, please! There are some scented rushes!' Alice cried in a sudden transport of delight. 'There really are – and *such* beauties!'

'You needn't say "please" to *me* about 'em,' the Sheep said, without looking up from her knitting: 'I didn't put 'em there, and I'm not going to take 'em away.'

'No, but I meant – please, may we wait and pick some?' Alice pleaded. 'If you don't mind stopping the boat for a minute.'

'How am *I* to stop it?' said the Sheep. 'If you leave off rowing, it'll stop of itself.'

So the boat was left to drift down the stream as it would, till it glided gently in among the waving rushes. And then the little sleeves were carefully rolled up, and the little arms were plunged in elbow-deep, to get hold

of the rushes a good long way down before breaking them off – and for a while Alice forgot all about the Sheep and the knitting, as she bent over the side of the boat, with just the ends of her tangled hair dipping in the water – while with bright eager eyes she caught at one bunch after another of the darling scented rushes.

'I only hope the boat won't tipple over!' she said to

herself. 'Oh, *what* a lovely one! Only I couldn't quite reach it.' And it certainly *did* seem a little provoking ('almost as if it happened on purpose,' she thought) that, though she managed to pick plenty of beautiful rushes as the boat glided by, there was always a more lovely one that she couldn't reach.

'The prettiest are always further!' she said at last, with a sigh at the obstinacy of the rushes in growing so far off, as, with flushed cheeks and dripping hair and hands, she scrambled back into her place, and began to arrange her new-found treasures.

What mattered it to her just then that the rushes had begun to fade, and to lose all their scent and beauty, from the very moment that she picked them? Even real scented rushes, you know, last only a very little while – and these, being dream-rushes, melted away almost like snow, as they lay in heaps at her feet – but Alice hardly noticed this, there were so many other curious things to think about.

They hadn't gone much farther before the blade of one of the oars got fast in the water and *wouldn't* come out again (so Alice explained it afterwards), and the consequence was that the handle of it caught her under the chin, and, in spite of a series of little shrieks of 'Oh, oh, oh!' from poor Alice, it swept her straight off the seat, and down among the heap of rushes.

However, she wasn't a bit hurt, and was soon up again: the Sheep went on with her knitting all the while, just as if nothing had happened. 'That was a nice crab you caught!' she remarked, as Alice got back into her place, very much relieved to find herself still in the boat.

'Was it? I didn't see it,' said Alice, peeping cautiously over the side of the boat into the dark water. 'I wish it hadn't let go – I should so like a little crab to take home with me!' But the Sheep only laughed scornfully, and went on with her knitting.

'Are there many crabs here?' said Alice.

'Crabs, and all sorts of things,' said the Sheep: 'plenty of choice, only make up your mind. Now, what *do* you want to buy?'

'To buy!' Alice echoed in a tone that was half astonished and half frightened – for the oars, and the boat, and the river, had vanished all in a moment, and she was back again in the little dark shop.

'I should like to buy an egg, please,' she said timidly. 'How do you sell them?'

'Fivepence farthing for one – twopence for two,' the Sheep replied.

'Then two are cheaper than one?' Alice said in a surprised tone, taking out her purse.

'Only you *must* eat them both, if you buy two,' said the Sheep.

'Then I'll have *one* please,' said Alice, as she put the money down on the counter. For she thought to herself, 'They mightn't be at all nice, you know.'

The Sheep took the money, and put it away in a box: then she said 'I never put things into people's hands – that would never do – you must get it for yourself.' And so saying, she went off to the other end of the shop, and set the egg upright on a shelf.

'I wonder *why* it wouldn't do?' thought Alice, as she groped her way among the tables and chairs, for the shop was very dark towards the end. 'The egg seems to get further away the more I walk towards it. Let me see, is this a chair? Why, it's got branches, I declare! How very odd to find trees growing here! And actually here's a little brook! Well, this is the very queerest shop I ever saw!'

* * * * *

* * *

* * * *

So she went on, wondering more and more at every step, as everything turned into a tree the moment she came up to it, and she quite expected the egg to do the same.

6

Humpty Dumpty

HOWEVER, the egg only got larger and larger, and more and more human: when she had come within a few yards of it, she saw that it had eyes and a nose and mouth; and when she had come close to it, she saw clearly that it was HUMPTY DUMPTY himself. 'It can't be anybody else!' she said to herself. 'I'm as certain of it, as if his name were written all over his face.'

It might have been written a hundred times, easily, on that enormous face. Humpty Dumpty was sitting with his legs crossed, like a lurk, on the top of a high wall – such a narrow one that Alice quite wondered how he could keep his balance – and, as his eyes were steadily fixed in the opposite direction, and he didn't take the least notice of her, she thought he must be a stuffed figure after all.

'And how exactly like an egg he is!' she said aloud, standing with her hands ready to catch him, for she was every moment expecting him to fall.

'It's *very* provoking,' Humpty Dumpty said after a long silence, looking away from Alice as he spoke, 'to be called an egg – *very!*'

'I said you *looked* like an egg, Sir,' Alice gently explained. 'And some eggs are very pretty, you know,' she added, hoping to turn her remark into a sort of compliment.

'Some people,' said Humpty Dumpty, looking away from her as usual, 'have no more sense than a baby!'

Alice didn't know what to say to this: it wasn't at all like conversation, she thought, as he never said anything to *her*; in fact, his last remark was evidently addressed to a tree – so she stood and softly repeated to herself:–

'Humpty Dumpty sat on a wall:
Humpty Dumpty had a great fall.
All the King's horses and all the King's men
Couldn't put Humpty Dumpty in his place again.'

'That last line is much too long for the poetry,' she added, almost out loud, forgetting that Humpty Dumpty would hear her.

'Don't stand chattering to yourself like that,' Humpty

Dumpty said, looking at her for the first time, 'but tell me your name and your business.'

'My *name* is Alice, but –'

'It's a stupid name enough!' Humpty Dumpty interrupted impatiently. 'What does it mean?'

'*Must* a name mean something?' Alice asked doubtfully.

'Of course it must,' Humpty Dumpty said with a short laugh: '*my* name means the shape I am – and a good handsome shape it is, too. With a name like yours, you might be any shape, almost.'

'Why do you sit out here all alone?' said Alice, not wishing to begin an argument.

'Why, because there's nobody with me!' cried Humpty Dumpty. 'Did you think I didn't know the answer to *that*? Ask another.'

'Don't you think you'd be safer down on the ground?' Alice went on, not with any idea of making another riddle, but simply in her good-natured anxiety for the queer creature. 'That wall is so *very* narrow!'

'What tremendously easy riddles you ask!' Humpty Dumpty growled out. 'Of course I don't think so! Why, if ever I *did* fall off – which there's no chance of – but *if* I did –' Here he pursed up his lips and looked so solemn and grand that Alice could hardly help laughing. '*If* I did fall,' he went on, '*the King has promised me* – ah, you may

turn pale, if you like! You didn't think I was going to say that, did you? *The King has promised me – with his very own mouth* to – to –'

'To send all his horses and all his men,' Alice interrupted, rather unwisely.

'Now I declare that's too bad!' Humpty Dumpty cried, breaking into a sudden passion. 'You've been listening at doors – and behind trees – and down chimneys – or you couldn't have known it!'

'I haven't, indeed!' Alice said very gently. 'It's in a book.'

'Ah, well! They may write such things in a *book*,' Humpty Dumpty said in a calmer tone. 'That's what you call a History of England, that is. Now, take a good look at me! I'm one that has spoken to a King, *I* am: mayhap you'll never see such another: and to show you I'm not proud, you may shake hands with me!' And he grinned almost from ear to ear, as he leant forwards (and as nearly as possible fell off the wall in doing so) and offered Alice his hand. She watched him a little anxiously as she took it. 'If he smiled much more, the ends of his mouth might meet behind,' she thought: 'and then I don't know what would happen to his head! I'm afraid it would come off!'

'Yes, all his horses and all his men,' Humpty Dumpty went on. 'They'd pick me up again in a minute, *they* would! However, this conversation is going on a little too fast: let's go back to the last remark but one.'

'I'm afraid I can't quite remember it,' Alice said very politely.

'In that case we start fresh,' said Humpty Dumpty, 'and it's my turn to choose a subject –' ('He talks about it just as if it was a game!' thought Alice.) 'So here's a question for you. How old did you say you were?'

Alice made a short calculation, and said 'Seven years and six months.'

'Wrong!' Humpty Dumpty exclaimed triumphantly. 'You never said a word like it!'

'I thought you meant "How old *are* you?"' Alice explained.

'If I'd meant that, I'd have said it,' said Humpty Dumpty.

Alice didn't want to begin another argument, so she said nothing.

'Seven years and six months!' Humpty Dumpty repeated thoughtfully. 'An uncomfortable sort of age. Now if you'd asked *my* advice, I'd have said "Leave off at seven" – but it's too late now.'

'I never ask advice about growing,' Alice said indignantly.

'Too proud?' the other enquired.

Alice felt even more indignant at this suggestion. 'I mean,' she said, 'that one can't help growing older.'

'*One* can't, perhaps,' said Humpty Dumpty, 'but *two* can. With proper assistance, you might have left off at seven.'

'What a beautiful belt you've got on!' Alice suddenly remarked. (They had had quite enough of the subject of age, she thought: and if they really were to take turns in choosing subjects, it was her turn now.) 'At least,' she corrected herself on second thoughts, 'a beautiful cravat, I should have said – no, a belt, I mean – I beg your pardon!' she added in dismay, for Humpty Dumpty looked thoroughly offended, and she began to wish she hadn't chosen that subject. 'If only I knew,' she thought to herself, 'which was neck and which was waist!'

Evidently Humpty Dumpty was very angry, though he said nothing for a minute or two. When he *did* speak again, it was in a deep growl.

'It is a – *most* – *provoking* – thing,' he said at last, 'when a person doesn't know a cravat from a belt!'

'I know it's very ignorant of me,' Alice said, in so humble a tone that Humpty Dumpty relented.

'It's a cravat, child, and a beautiful one, as you say. It's a present from the White King and Queen. There now!'

'Is it really?' said Alice, quite pleased to find that she *had* chosen a good subject, after all.

'They gave it me,' Humpty Dumpty continued thoughtfully, as he crossed one knee over the other and clasped his hands round it, 'they gave it me – for an un-birthday present.'

'I beg your pardon?' Alice said with a puzzled air.

'I'm not offended,' said Humpty Dumpty.

'I mean, what *is* an un-birthday present?'

'A present given when it isn't your birthday, of course.'

Alice considered a little. 'I like birthday presents best,' she said at last.

'You don't know what you're talking about!' cried Humpty Dumpty. 'How many days are there in a year?'

'Three hundred and sixty-five,' said Alice.

'And how many birthdays have you?'

'One.'

'And if you take one from three hundred and sixty-five, what remains?'

'Three hundred and sixty-four, of course.'

Humpty Dumpty looked doubtful. 'I'd rather see that done on paper,' he said.

Alice couldn't help smiling as she took out her memorandum-book, and worked the sum for him:

$$
\begin{array}{r}
365 \\
1 \\
\hline
364
\end{array}
$$

Humpty Dumpty took the book, and looked at it carefully. 'That seems to be done right –' he began.

'You're holding it upside down!' Alice interrupted.

'To be sure I was!' Humpty Dumpty said gaily, as she turned it round for him. 'I thought it looked a little queer. As I was saying, that *seems* to be done right –

though I haven't time to look it over thoroughly just now – and that shows that there are three hundred and sixty-four days when you might get un-birthday presents –'

'Certainly,' said Alice.

'And only *one* for birthday presents, you know. There's glory for you!'

'I don't know what you mean by "glory,"' Alice said.

Humpty Dumpty smiled contemptuously. 'Of course you don't – till I tell you. I meant "there's a nice knock-down argument for you!"'

'But "glory" doesn't mean "a nice knock-down argument,"' Alice objected.

'When *I* use a word,' Humpty Dumpty said in rather a scornful tone, 'it means just what I choose it to mean – neither more nor less.'

'The question is,' said Alice, 'whether you *can* make words mean so many different things.'

'The question is,' said Humpty Dumpty, 'which is to be master – that's all.'

Alice was too much puzzled to say anything, so after a minute Humpty Dumpty began again. 'They've a temper, some of them – particularly verbs, they're the proudest – adjectives you can do anything with, but not verbs – however, *I* can manage the whole lot of them! Impenetrability! That's what *I* say!'

'Would you tell me, please,' said Alice, 'what that means?'

'Now you talk like a reasonable child,' said Humpty Dumpty, looking very much pleased. 'I meant by "impenetrability" that we've had enough of that subject, and it would be just as well if you'd mention what you mean to do next, as I suppose you don't mean to stop here all the rest of your life.'

'That's a great deal to make one word mean,' Alice said in a thoughtful tone.

'When I make a word do a lot of work like that,' said Humpty Dumpty, 'I always pay it extra.'

'Oh!' said Alice. She was too much puzzled to make any other remark.

'Ah, you should see 'em come round me of a Saturday night,' Humpty Dumpty went on, wagging his head gravely from side to side: 'for to get their wages, you know.'

(Alice didn't venture to ask what he paid them with; and so you see I can't tell *you*.)

'You seem very clever at explaining words, Sir,' said Alice. 'Would you kindly tell me the meaning of the poem called "Jabberwocky"?'

'Let's hear it,' said Humpty Dumpty. 'I can explain all the poems that ever were invented – and a good many that haven't been invented just yet.'

This sounded very hopeful, so Alice repeated the first verse:

> *''Twas brillig, and the slithy toves*
> *Did gyre and gimble in the wabe:*
> *All mimsy were the borogoves,*
> *And the mome raths outgrabe.'*

'That's enough to begin with,' Humpty Dumpty interrupted: 'there are plenty of hard words there. "*Brillig*" means four o'clock in the afternoon – the time when you begin *broiling* things for dinner.'

'That'll do very well,' said Alice: 'and "*slithy*"?'

'Well, "*slithy*" means "lithe and slimy." "Lithe" is the same as "active." You see it's like a portmanteau – there are two meanings packed up into one word.'

'I see it now,' Alice remarked thoughtfully: 'and what are "*toves*"?'

'Well, "toves" are something like badgers – they're something like lizards – and they're something like corkscrews.'

'They must be very curious-looking creatures.'

'They are that,' said Humpty Dumpty: 'also they make their nests under sun-dials – also they live on cheese.'

'And what's to "*gyre*" and to "*gimble*"?'

'To "*gyre*" is to go round and round like a gyroscope.
To "*gimble*" is to make holes like a gimblet.'

'And "*the wabe*" is the grass-plot round a sun-dial I
suppose?' said Alice, surprised at her own ingenuity.

'Of course it is. It's called "*wabe*" you know, because
it goes a long way before it, and a long way behind it –'

'And a long way beyond it on each side,' Alice added.

'Exactly so. Well then, "*mimsy*" is "flimsy and miserable" (there's another portmanteau for you). And a "*borogove*" is a thin shabby-looking bird with its feathers sticking out all round – something like a live mop.'

'And then "*mome raths*"?' said Alice. 'I'm afraid I'm giving you a great deal of trouble.'

'Well, a "*rath*" is a sort of green pig: but "*mome*" I'm not certain about. I think it's short for "from home" – meaning that they'd lost their way, you know.'

'And what does "*outgrabe*" mean?'

'Well, "*outgribing*" is something between bellowing and whistling, with a kind of sneeze in the middle: however, you'll hear it done, maybe – down in the wood yonder – and when you've once heard it you'll be *quite* content. Who's been repeating all that hard stuff to you?'

'I read it in a book,' said Alice. 'But I had some poetry repeated to me, much easier than that, by – Tweedledee, I think it was.'

'As to poetry, you know,' said Humpty Dumpty, stretching out one of his great hands, '*I* can repeat poetry as well as other folk, if it comes to that –'

'Oh, it needn't come to that!' Alice hastily said, hoping to keep him from beginning.

'The piece I'm going to repeat,' he went on without noticing her remark, 'was written entirely for your amusement.'

Alice felt that in that case she really *ought* to listen to it, so she sat down, and said 'Thank you' rather sadly.

> *'In winter, when the fields are white,*
> *I sing this song for your delight –*

only I don't sing it,' he added, as an explanation.

'I see you don't,' said Alice.

'If you can *see* whether I'm singing or not, you've sharper eyes than most,' Humpty Dumpty remarked severely. Alice was silent.

> *'In spring, when woods are getting green,*
> *I'll try and tell you what I mean.'*

'Thank you very much,' said Alice.

> *'In summer, when the days are long;*
> *Perhaps you'll understand the song:*
>
> *In autumn, when the leaves are brown,*
> *Take pen and ink, and write it down.*

'I will, if I can remember it so long,' said Alice.

'You needn't go on making remarks like that,' Humpty Dumpty said: 'they're not sensible, and they put me out.

> *'I sent a message to the fish:*
> *I told them "This is what I wish."*
>
> *The little fishes of the sea,*
> *They sent an answer back to me.*
>
> *The little fishes' answer was*
> *"We cannot do it, Sir, because –"'*

'I'm afraid I don't quite understand,' said Alice.

'It gets easier further on,' Humpty Dumpty replied.

> *'I sent to them again to say*
> *"It will be better to obey."*
>
> *The fishes answered with a grin,*
> *"Why, what a temper you are in!"*
>
> *I told them once, I told them twice:*
> *They would not listen to advice.*

I took a kettle large and new,
Fit for the deed I had to do.

My heart went hop, my heart went thump;
I filled the kettle at the pump.

Then some one came to me and said,
"The little fishes are in bed."

I said to him, I said it plain,
"Then you must wake them up again."

I said it very loud and clear;
I went and shouted in his ear.'

Humpty Dumpty raised his voice almost to a scream as he repeated this verse, and Alice thought with a shudder, 'I wouldn't have been the messenger for anything!'

'But he was very stiff and proud;
He said "You needn't shout so loud!"

And he was very proud and stiff;
He said "I'd go and wake them, if—"

I took a corkscrew from the shelf:
I went to wake them up myself.

And when I found the door was locked,
I pulled and pushed and kicked and knocked.

And when I found the door was shut,
I tried to turn the handle, but —'

There was a long pause,
'Is that all?' Alice timidly asked.
'That's all,' said Humpty Dumpty. 'Good-bye.'
This was rather sudden, Alice thought: but, after such

a *very* strong hint that she ought to be going, she felt that it would hardly be civil to stay. So she got up, and held out her hand. 'Good-bye, till we meet again!' she said as cheerfully as she could.

'I shouldn't know you again if we *did* meet,' Humpty Dumpty replied in a discontented tone, giving her one of his fingers to shake; 'you're so exactly like other people.'

'The face is what one goes by, generally,' Alice remarked in a thoughtful tone.

'That's just what I complain of,' said Humpty Dumpty. 'Your face is the same as everybody has – the two eyes, so –' (marking their places in the air with his thumb) 'nose in the middle, mouth under. It's always the same. Now if you had the two eyes on the same side of the nose, for instance – or the mouth at the top – that would be *some* help.'

'It wouldn't look nice,' Alice objected. But Humpty Dumpty only shut his eyes and said 'Wait till you've tried.'

Alice waited a minute to see if he would speak again, but as he never opened his eyes or took any further notice of her, she said 'Good-bye!' once more, and, getting no answer to this, she quietly walked away: but she couldn't help saying to herself as she went, 'Of all the unsatisfactory –' (she repeated this aloud, as it was a great comfort to have such a long word to say) 'of all the unsatisfactory people I *ever* met –' She never finished the sentence, for at this moment a heavy crash shook the forest from end to end.

7

The Lion and the Unicorn

THE next moment soldiers came running through the wood, at first in twos and threes, then ten or twenty together, and at last in such crowds that they seemed to fill the whole forest. Alice got behind a tree, for fear of being run over, and watched them go by.

She thought that in all her life she had never seen soldiers so uncertain on their feet: they were always tripping over something or other, and whenever one went down, several more always fell over him, so that the ground was soon covered with little heaps of men.

Then came the horses. Having four feet, these managed rather better than the foot-soldiers: but even *they* stumbled now and then; and it seemed to be a regular rule that, whenever a horse stumbled, the rider fell off instantly. The confusion got worse every moment, and Alice was very glad to get out of the wood into an open place, where she found the White King seated on the ground, busily writing in his memorandum-book.

'I've sent them all!' the King cried in a tone of delight, on seeing Alice. 'Did you happen to meet any soldiers, my dear, as you came through the wood?'

'Yes, I did,' said Alice: 'several thousand, I should think.'

'Four thousand two hundred and seven, that's the exact number,' the King said, referring to his book. 'I couldn't send all the horses, you know, because two of them are wanted in the game. And I haven't sent the two Messengers, either. They're both gone to the town. Just look along the road, and tell me if you can see either of them.'

'I see nobody on the road,' said Alice.

'I only wish *I* had such eyes,' the King remarked in a fretful tone. 'To be able to see Nobody! And at that distance too! Why, it's as much as *I* can do to see real people, by this light!'

All this was lost on Alice, who was still looking intently along the road, shading her eyes with one hand. 'I see somebody now!' she exclaimed at last. 'But he's coming very slowly – and what curious attitudes he goes into!' (For the Messenger kept skipping up and down, and wriggling like an eel, as he came along, with his great hands spread out like fans on each side.)

'Not at all,' said the King. 'He's an Anglo-Saxon Messenger – and those are Anglo-Saxon attitudes. He only does them when he's happy. His name is Haigha.' (He pronounced it so as to rhyme with 'mayor.')

'I love my love with an H,' Alice couldn't help

beginning, 'because he is Happy. I hate him with an H, because he is Hideous. I fed him with – with – with Ham sandwiches and Hay. His name is Haigha, and he lives –'

'He lives on the Hill,' the King remarked simply, without the least idea that he was joining in the game, while Alice was still hesitating for the name of a town beginning with H. 'The other Messenger's called Hatta. I must have *two*, you know – to come and go. One to come, and one to go.'

'I beg your pardon?' said Alice.

'It isn't respectable to beg,' said the King.

'I only meant that I didn't understand,' said Alice. 'Why one to come and one to go?'

'Don't I tell you?' the King repeated impatiently. 'I must have *two* – to fetch and carry. One to fetch, and one to carry.'

At this moment the Messenger arrived: he was far too much out of breath to say a word, and could only wave his hands about, and make the most fearful faces at the poor King.

'This young lady loves you with an H,' the King said, introducing Alice in the hope of turning off the Messenger's attention from himself – but it was no use – the Anglo-Saxon attitudes only got more extraordinary every moment, while the great eyes rolled wildly from side to side.

'You alarm me!' said the King. 'I feel faint – Give me a ham sandwich!'

On which the Messenger, to Alice's great amusement, opened a bag that hung round his neck, and handed a sandwich to the King, who devoured it greedily.

'Another sandwich!' said the King.

'There's nothing but hay left now,' the Messenger said, peeping into the bag.

'Hay, then,' the King murmured in a faint whisper.

Alice was glad to see that it revived him a good deal. 'There's nothing like eating hay when you're faint,' he remarked to her, as he munched away.

'I should think throwing cold water over you would be better,' Alice suggested: '– or some sal-volatile.'

'I didn't say there was nothing *better*,' the King replied. 'I said there was nothing *like* it.' Which Alice did not venture to deny.

'Who did you pass on the road?' the King went on, holding out his hand to the Messenger for some more hay.

'Nobody,' said the Messenger.

'Quite right,' said the King: 'this young lady saw him too. So of course Nobody walks slower than you.'

'I do my best,' the Messenger said in a sulky tone. 'I'm sure Nobody walks much faster than I do!'

'He can't do that,' said the King, 'or else he'd have been here first. However, now you've got your breath, you may tell us what's happened in the town.

'I'll whisper it,' said the Messenger, putting his hands to his mouth in the shape of a trumpet, and stooping so as to get close to the King's ear. Alice was sorry for this, as she wanted to hear the news too. However, instead of whispering, he simply shouted at the top of his voice 'They're at it again!'

'Do you call *that* a whisper?' cried the poor King, jumping up and shaking himself. 'If you do such a thing again, I'll have you buttered! It went through and through my head like an earthquake!'

'It would have to be a very tiny earthquake!' thought Alice. 'Who are at it again?' she ventured to ask.

'Why, the Lion and the Unicorn, of course,' said the King.

'Fighting for the crown?'

'Yes, to be sure,' said the King: 'and the best of the joke is, that it's *my* crown all the while! Let's run and see them.' And they trotted off, Alice repeating to herself, as she ran, the words of the old song:

'The Lion and the Unicorn were fighting for the crown:
The Lion beat the Unicorn all round the town.

Some gave them white bread, some gave them brown;
Some gave them plum-cake and drummed them out of town.'

'Does – the one – that wins – get the crown?' she asked, as well as she could, for the run was putting her quite out of breath.

'Dear me, no!' said the King. 'What an idea!'

'Would you – be good enough,' Alice panted out, after running a little further, 'to stop a minute – just to get – one's breath again?'

'I'm *good* enough,' the King said, 'only I'm not strong

enough. You see, a minute goes by so fearfully quick. You might as well try to stop a Bandersnatch!'

Alice had no more breath for talking, so they trotted on in silence, till they came in sight of a great crowd, in the middle of which the Lion and Unicorn were fighting. They were in such a cloud of dust, that at first Alice could not make out which was which: but she soon managed to distinguish the Unicorn by his horn.

They placed themselves close to where Hatta, the other Messenger, was standing watching the fight, with a cup of tea in one hand and a piece of bread-and-butter in the other.

'He's only just out of prison, and he hadn't finished his tea when he was sent in,' Haigha whispered to Alice: 'and they only give them oyster-shells in there – so you see he's very hungry and thirsty. How are you, dear child?' he went on, putting his arm affectionately round Hatta's neck.

Hatta looked round and nodded, and went on with his bread-and-butter.

'Were you happy in prison, dear child?' said Haigha.

Hatta looked round once more, and this time a tear or two trickled down his cheek: but not a word would he say.

'Speak, can't you!' Haigha cried impatiently. But Hatta only munched away, and drank some more tea.

'Speak, won't you!' cried the King. 'How are they getting on with the fight?'

Hatta made a desperate effort, and swallowed a large piece of bread-and-butter. 'They're getting on very well,' he said in a choking voice: 'each of them has been down about eighty-seven times.'

'Then I suppose they'll soon bring the white bread and the brown?' Alice ventured to remark.

'It's waiting for 'em now,' said Hatta: 'This is a bit of it as I'm eating.'

There was a pause in the fight just then, and the Lion and the Unicorn sat down, panting, while the King called out 'Ten minutes allowed for refreshments!' Haigha and

Hatta set to work at once, carrying round trays of white and brown bread. Alice took a piece to taste, but it was *very* dry.

'I don't think they'll fight any more today,' the King said to Hatta: 'go and order the drums to begin.' And Hatta went bounding away like a grasshopper.

For a minute or two Alice stood silent, watching him. Suddenly she brightened up. 'Look, look!' she cried, pointing eagerly. 'There's the White Queen running across the country! She came flying out of the wood over yonder – How fast those Queens *can* run!'

'There's some enemy after her, no doubt,' the King said, without even looking round. 'That wood's full of them.'

'But aren't you going to run and help her?' Alice asked, very much surprised at his taking it so quietly.

'No use, no use!' said the King. 'She runs so fearfully quick. You might as well try to catch a Bandersnatch! But I'll make a memorandum about her, if you like – She's a dear good creature,' he repeated softly to himself, as he opened his memorandum-book. 'Do you spell "creature" with a double "e"?'

At this moment the Unicorn sauntered by them, with his hands in his pockets. 'I had the best of it this time?' he said to the King, just glancing at him as he passed.

'A little – a little,' the King replied, rather nervously. 'You shouldn't have run him through with your horn, you know.'

'It didn't hurt him,' the Unicorn said carelessly, and he was going on, when his eye happened to fall upon Alice: he turned round instantly, and stood for some time looking at her with an air of the deepest disgust.

'What – is – this?' he said at last.

'This is a child!' Haigha replied eagerly, coming in front of Alice to introduce her, and spreading out both his hands towards her in an Anglo-Saxon attitude. 'We only found it today. It's as large as life, and twice as natural!'

'I always thought they were fabulous monsters!' said the Unicorn. 'Is it alive?'

'It can talk,' said Haigha, solemnly.

The Unicorn looked dreamily at Alice, and said 'Talk, child.'

Alice could not help her lips curling up into a smile as she began: 'Do you know, I always thought Unicorns were fabulous monsters, too! I never saw one alive before!'

'Well, now that we *have* seen each other,' said the Unicorn, 'if you'll believe in me, I'll believe in you. Is that a bargain?'

'Yes, if you like,' said Alice.

'Come, fetch out the plum-cake, old man!' the Unicorn went on, turning from her to the King. 'None of your brown bread for me!'

'Certainly – certainly!' the King muttered, and beckoned to Haigha. 'Open the bag!' he whispered. 'Quick! Not that one – that's full of hay!'

Haigha took a large cake out of the bag, and gave it to Alice to hold, while he got out a dish and carving-knife. How they all came out of it Alice couldn't guess. It was just like a conjuring-trick, she thought.

The Lion had joined them while this was going on: he looked very tired and sleepy, and his eyes were half shut. 'What's this!' he said, blinking lazily at Alice, and speaking in a deep hollow tone that sounded like the tolling of a great bell.

'Ah, what *is* it, now?' the Unicorn cried eagerly. 'You'll never guess! *I* couldn't.'

The Lion looked at Alice wearily. 'Are you animal – or vegetable – or mineral?' he said, yawning at every other word.

'It's a fabulous monster!' the Unicorn cried out, before Alice could reply.

'Then hand round the plum-cake, Monster,' the Lion said, lying down and putting his chin on his paws. 'And sit down, both of you,' (to the King and the Unicorn): 'fair play with the cake, you know!'

The King was evidently very uncomfortable at having to sit down between the two great creatures; but there was no other place for him.

'What a fight we might have for the crown, now!' the Unicorn said, looking slyly up at the crown, which the poor King was nearly shaking off his head, he trembled so much.

'I should win easy,' said the Lion.

'I'm not so sure of that,' said the Unicorn.

'Why, I beat you all round the town, you chicken!' the Lion replied angrily, half getting up as he spoke.

Here the King interrupted, to prevent the quarrel going on: he was very nervous, and his voice quite

quivered. 'All round the town?' he said. 'That's a good long way. Did you go by the old bridge, or the market-place? You get the best view by the old bridge.'

'I'm sure I don't know,' the Lion growled out as he lay down again. 'There was too much dust to see anything. What a time the Monster is, cutting up that cake!'

Alice had seated herself on the bank of a little brook, with the great dish on her knees, and was sawing very diligently with the knife. 'It's very provoking!' she said, in reply to the Lion (she was getting quite used to being called 'the Monster'). 'I've cut several slices already, but they always join on again!'

'You don't know how to manage Looking-glass cakes,' the Unicorn remarked. 'Hand it round first, and cut it afterwards.'

This sounded nonsense, but Alice very obediently got up, and carried the dish round, and the cake divided itself into three pieces as she did so. '*Now* cut it up,' said the Lion, as she returned to her place with the empty dish.

'I say, this isn't fair!' cried the Unicorn, as Alice sat with the knife in her hand, very much puzzled how to begin. 'The Monster has given the Lion twice as much as me.'

'She's kept none for herself, anyhow,' said the Lion. 'Do you like plum-cake, Monster?'

But before Alice could answer him, the drums began.

Where the noise came from, she couldn't make out: the air seemed full of it, and it rang through and through her head till she felt quite deafened. She started to her feet and sprang across the little brook in terror,

*   *   *   *

*   *   *

*   *   *   *

and had just time to see the Lion and the Unicorn rise to their feet, with angry looks at being interrupted in their feast, before she dropped to her knees, and put her hands over her ears, vainly trying to shut out the dreadful uproar.

'If *that* doesn't "drum them out of town,"' she thought to herself, 'nothing ever will!'

8

'It's My Own Invention'

AFTER a while the noise seemed gradually to die away, till all was dead silence, and Alice lifted up her head in some alarm. There was no one to be seen, and her first thought was that she must have been dreaming about the Lion and the Unicorn and those queer Anglo-Saxon Messengers. However, there was the great dish still lying at her feet, on which she had tried to cut the plum-cake, 'So I wasn't dreaming, after all,' she said to herself, 'unless – unless we're all part of the same dream. Only I do hope it's *my* dream, and not the Red King's! I don't like belonging to another person's dream,' she went on in a rather complaining tone: 'I've a great mind to go and wake him, and see what happens!'

At this moment her thoughts were interrupted by a loud shouting of 'Ahoy! Ahoy! Check!' and a Knight, dressed in crimson armour, came galloping down upon her, brandishing a great club. Just as he reached her, the horse stopped suddenly: 'You're my prisoner!' the Knight cried, as he tumbled off his horse.

Startled as she was, Alice was more frightened for him than for herself at the moment, and watched him with some anxiety as he mounted again. As soon as he was comfortably in the saddle, he began once more 'You're my –' but here another voice broke in 'Ahoy! Ahoy! Check!' and Alice looked round in some surprise for the new enemy.

This time it was a White Knight. He drew up at Alice's side, and tumbled off his horse just as the Red Knight had done: then he got on again, and the two Knights sat and looked at each other for some time without speaking. Alice looked from one to the other in some bewilderment.

'She's *my* prisoner, you know!' the Red Knight said at last.

'Yes, but then *I* came and rescued her!' the White Knight replied.

'Well, we must fight for her, then,' said the Red Knight, as he took up his helmet (which hung from the saddle, and was something the shape of a horse's head), and put it on.

'You will observe the Rules of Battle, of course?' the

White Knight remarked, putting on his helmet too.

'I always do,' said the Red Knight, and they began banging away at each other with such fury that Alice got behind a tree to be out of the way of the blows.

'I wonder, now, what the Rules of Battle are,' she said to herself, as she watched the fight, timidly peeping out from her hiding-place: 'one Rule seems to be, that if one Knight hits the other, he knocks him off his horse, and if he misses, he tumbles off himself – and another Rule seems to be that they hold their clubs with their arms, as if they were Punch and Judy – What a noise they make when they tumble! Just like a whole set of fire-irons falling into the fender! And how quiet the horses are! They let them get on and off them just as if they were tables!'

Another Rule of Battle, that Alice had not noticed, seemed to be that they always fell on their heads, and the battle ended with their both falling off in this way, side by side: when they got up again, they shook hands, and then the Red Knight mounted and galloped off.

'It was a glorious victory, wasn't it?' said the White Knight, as he came up panting.

'I don't know,' Alice said doubtfully. 'I don't want to be anybody's prisoner. I want to be a Queen.'

'So you will, when you've crossed the next brook,' said the White Knight. 'I'll see you safe to the end of the

wood – and then I must go back, you know. That's the
end of my move.'

'Thank you very much,' said Alice. May I help you off
with your helmet?' It was evidently more than he could
manage by himself; however, she managed to shake him
out of it at last.

'Now one can breathe more easily,' said the Knight,
putting back his shaggy hair with both hands, and
turning his gentle face and large mild eyes to Alice.

She thought she had never seen such a strange-looking soldier in all her life.

He was dressed in tin armour, which seemed to fit him very badly, and he had a queer-shaped little deal box fastened across his shoulders, upside-down, and with the lid hanging open. Alice looked at it with great curiosity.

'I see you're admiring my little box,' the Knight said in a friendly tone. 'It's my own invention – to keep clothes and sandwiches in. You see I carry it upside-down, so that the rain can't get in.'

'But the things can get *out*', Alice gently remarked. 'Do you know the lid's open?'

'I didn't know it,' the Knight said, a shade of vexation passing over his face. 'Then all the things must have fallen out! And the box is no use without them.' He unfastened it as he spoke, and was just going to throw it into the bushes, when a sudden thought seemed to strike him, and he hung it carefully on a tree. 'Can you guess why I did that?' he said to Alice.

Alice shook her head.

'I hope some bees may make a nest in it – then I should get the honey.'

'But you've got a bee-hive – or something like one – fastened to the saddle,' said Alice.

'Yes, it's a very good bee-hive,' the Knight said in a

discontented tone, 'one of the best kind. But not a single bee has come near it yet. And the other thing is a mouse-trap. I suppose the mice keep the bees out – or the bees keep the mice out, I don't know which.'

'I was wondering what the mouse-trap was for,' said Alice. 'It isn't very likely there would be any mice on the horse's back.'

'Not very likely, perhaps,' said the Knight; 'but if they *do* come, I don't choose to have them running all about.'

'You see,' he went on after a pause, 'it's as well to be provided for *everything*. That's the reason the horse has all those anklets round his feet.'

'But what are they for?' Alice asked in a tone of great curiosity.

'To guard against the bites of sharks,' the Knight replied. 'It's an invention of my own. And now help me on. I'll go with you to the end of the wood – What's that dish for?'

'It's meant for plum-cake,' said Alice.

'We'd better take it with us,' the Knight said. 'It'll come in handy if we find any plum-cake. Help me to get it into this bag.'

This took a long time to manage, though Alice held the bag open very carefully, because the Knight was so *very* awkward in putting in the dish: the first two or three times that he tried he fell in himself instead. 'It's rather a tight fit, you see,' he said, as they got it in at last; 'there are so many candlesticks in the bag.' And he hung it to the saddle, which was already loaded with bunches of carrots, and fire-irons, and many other things.

'I hope you've got your hair well fastened on?' he continued, as they set off.

'Only in the usual way,' Alice said, smiling.

'That's hardly enough,' he said, anxiously. 'You see the wind is so *very* strong here. It's as strong as soup.'

'Have you invented a plan for keeping the hair from being blown off?' Alice enquired.

'Not yet,' said the Knight. 'But I've got a plan for keeping it from *falling* off.'

'I should like to hear it, very much.'

'First you take an upright stick,' said the Knight. 'Then you make your hair creep up it, like a fruit-tree. Now the reason hair falls off is because it hangs *down* – things never fall *upward*, you know. It's a plan of my own invention. You may try it if you like.'

It didn't sound a comfortable plan, Alice thought, and for a few minutes she walked on in silence, puzzling over the idea, and every now and then stopping to help the poor Knight, who certainly was *not* a good rider.

Whenever the horse stopped (which it did very often), he fell off in front; and whenever it went on again (which

it generally did rather suddenly), he fell off behind. Otherwise he kept on pretty well, except that he had a habit of now and then falling off sideways; and as he generally did this on the side on which Alice was walking, she soon found that it was the best plan not to walk *quite* so close to the horse.

'I'm afraid you've not had much practice in riding,' she ventured to say, as she was helping him up from his fifth tumble.

The Knight looked very much surprised, and a little offended at the remark. 'What makes you say that?' he asked, as he scrambled back into the saddle, keeping hold of Alice's hair with one hand, to save himself from falling over on the other side.

'Because people don't fall off quite so often, when they've had much practice.'

'I've had plenty of practice,' the Knight said very gravely: 'plenty of practice!'

Alice could think of nothing better to say than 'Indeed?' but she said it as heartily as she could. They went on a little way in silence after this, the Knight with his eyes shut, muttering to himself, and Alice watching anxiously for the next tumble.

'The great art of riding,' the Knight suddenly began in a loud voice, waving his right arm as he spoke, 'is to keep –' Here the sentence ended as suddenly as it had begun, as the Knight fell heavily on the top of his head exactly in the path where Alice was walking. She was quite frightened this time, and said in an anxious tone, as she picked him up, 'I hope no bones are broken?'

'None to speak of,' the Knight said, as if he didn't mind breaking two or three of them. 'The great art of riding, as I was saying, is – to keep your balance properly. Like this, you know –'

He let go the bridle, and stretched out both his arms to show Alice what he meant, and this time he fell flat on his back, right under the horse's feet.

'Plenty of practice!' he went on repeating, all the time that Alice was getting him on his feet again. 'Plenty of practice!'

'It's too ridiculous!' cried Alice, losing all her patience this time. 'You ought to have a wooden horse on wheels, that you ought!'

'Does that kind go smoothly?' the Knight asked in a tone of great interest, clasping his arms round the horse's neck as he spoke, just in time to save himself from tumbling off again.

'Much more smoothly than a live horse,' Alice said, with a little scream of laughter, in spite of all she could do to prevent it.

'I'll get one,' the Knight said thoughtfully to himself. 'One or two – several.'

There was a short silence after this, and then the Knight went on again. 'I'm a great hand at inventing things. Now, I daresay you noticed, the last time you picked me up, that I was looking rather thoughtful?'

'You *were* a little grave,' said Alice.

'Well, just then I was inventing a new way of getting

over a gate – would you like to hear it?'

'Very much indeed,' Alice said politely.

'I'll tell you how I came to think of it,' said the Knight. 'You see, I said to myself, "The only difficulty is with the feet: the *head* is high enough already." Now, first I put my head on the top of the gate – then the head's high enough – then I stand on my head – then the feet are high enough, you see – then I'm over, you see.'

'Yes, I suppose you'd be over when that was done,' Alice said thoughtfully: 'but don't you think it would be rather hard?'

'I haven't tried it yet,' the Knight said, gravely: 'so I can't tell for certain – but I'm afraid it *would* be a little hard.'

He looked so vexed at the idea, that Alice changed the subject hastily. 'What a curious helmet you've got!' she said cheerfully. 'Is that your invention too?'

The Knight looked down proudly at his helmet, which hung from the saddle. 'Yes,' he said, 'but I've invented a better one than that – like a sugar-loaf. When I used to wear it, if I fell off the horse, it always touched the ground directly. So I had a *very* little way to fall, you see – But there *was* the danger of falling *into* it, to be sure. That happened to me once – and the worst of it was, before I could get out again, the other White Knight came and put it on. He thought it was his own helmet.

The Knight looked so solemn about it that Alice did not dare to laugh. 'I'm afraid you must have hurt him,' she said in a trembling voice, 'being on the top of his head.'

'I had to kick him, of course,' the Knight said, very seriously. 'And then he took the helmet off again – but it took hours and hours to get me out. I was as fast as – as lightning, you know.'

'But that's a different kind of fastness,' Alice objected.

The Knight shook his head. 'It was all kinds of fastness with me, I can assure you!' he said. He raised his hands in some excitemem as he said this, and instantly rolled out of the saddle, and fell headlong into a deep ditch.

Alice ran to the side of the ditch to look for him. She was rather startled by the fall, as for some time he had kept on very well, and she was afraid that he really *was* hurt this time. However, though she could see nothing but the soles of his feet, she was much relieved to hear that he was talking on in his usual tone. 'All kinds of fastness,' he repeated: 'but it was careless of him to put another man's helmet on – with the man in it, too.'

'How *can* you go on talking so quietly, head downwards?' Alice asked, as she dragged him out by the feet, and laid him in a heap on the bank.

The Knight looked surprised at the question. 'What does it matter where my body happens to be?' he said. 'My mind goes on working all the same. In fact, the more head downwards I am, the more I keep inventing new things.'

'Now the cleverest thing of the sort that I ever did,' he went on after a pause, 'was inventing a new pudding during the meat-course.'

'In time to have it cooked for the next course?' said Alice. 'Well, that *was* quick work, certainly!'

'Well, not the *next* course,' the Knight said in a slow thoughtful tone: 'no, certainly not the next *course*.'

'Then it would have to be the next day. I suppose you wouldn't have two pudding-courses in one dinner?'

'Well, not the *next* day,' the Knight repeated as before: 'not the next *day*. In fact,' he went on, holding his head down, and his voice getting lower and lower, 'I don't believe that pudding ever *was* cooked! In fact, I don't believe that pudding ever *will* be cooked! And yet it was a very clever pudding to invent.'

'What did you mean it to be made of?' Alice asked, hoping to cheer him up, for the poor Knight seemed quite low-spirited about it.

'It began with blotting-paper,' the Knight answered with a groan.

'That wouldn't be very nice, I'm afraid –'

'Not very nice *alone*,' he interrupted, quite eagerly: 'but you've no idea what a difference it makes mixing it with other things – such as gun-powder and sealing-wax. And here I must leave you.' They had just come to the end of the wood.

Alice could only look puzzled: she was thinking of the pudding.

'You are sad,' the Knight said in an anxious tone: 'let me sing you a song to comfort you.'

'Is it very long?' Alice asked, for she had heard a good deal of poetry that day.

'It's long,' said the Knight, 'but it's very, *very* beautiful. Everybody that hears me sing it – either it brings the *tears* into their eyes, or else –'

'Or else what?' said Alice, for the Knight had made a sudden pause.

'Or else it doesn't, you know. The name of the song is called "*Haddocks' Eyes*."'

'Oh, that's the name of the song, is it?' Alice said, trying to feel interested.

'No, you don't understand,' the Knight said, looking a little vexed. 'That's what the name is *called*. The name really *is* "*The Aged Aged Man*."'

'Then I ought to have said "That's what the *song* is called"?' Alice corrected herself.

'No, you oughtn't: that's quite another thing! The *song* is called "*Ways and Means*": but that's only what it's *called*, you know!'

'Well, what *is* the song, then?' said Alice, who was by this time completely bewildered.

'I was coming to that,' the Knight said. 'The song really *is* "*A-sitting On A Gate*": and the tune's my own invention.'

So saying, he stopped his horse and let the reins fall on its neck: then, slowly beating time with one hand, and with a faint smile lighting up his gentle foolish face, as if he enjoyed the music of his song, he began.

Of all the strange things that Alice saw in her journey Through The Looking-Glass, this was the one that she always remembered most clearly. Years afterwards she could bring the whole scene back again, as if it had been only yesterday – the mild blue eyes and kindly smile of the Knight – the setting sun gleaming through his hair, and shining on his armour in a blaze of light that quite dazzled her – the horse quietly moving about. with the reins hanging loose on his neck, cropping the grass at her feet – and the black shadows of the forest behind – all this she took in like a picture, as, with one hand shading her eyes, she leant against a tree, watching the strange pair, and listening, in a half dream, to the melancholy music of the song.

'But the tune *isn't* his own invention,' she said to herself: 'it's "*I give thee all, I can no more.*"' She stood and listened very attentively, but no tears came into her eyes.

> 'I'll tell thee everything I can;
>   There's little to relate.
> I saw an aged aged man,
>   A-sitting on a gate.
> "Who are you, aged man?" I said.
>   "And how is it you live?"
> And his answer trickled through my head
>   Like water through a sieve.

He said "I look for butterflies
   That sleep among the wheat:
I make them into mutton-pies,
   And sell them in the street.
I sell them unto men," he said,
   "Who sail on stormy seas;
And that's the way I get my bread –
   A trifle, if you please."

But I was thinking of a plan
   To dye one's whiskers green,
And always use so large a fan
   That they could not be seen.
So, having no reply to give
   To what the old man said,

I cried, "Come, tell me how you live!"
  And thumped him on the head.

His accent, mild took up the tale:
  He said "I go my ways,
And when I find a mountain-rill,
  I set it in a blaze;
And thence they make a stuff they call
  Rowlands' Macassar Oil –
Yet twopence-halfpenny is all
  They give me for my toil."

But I was thinking of a way
  To feed oneself on batter,
And so go on from day to day
  Getting a little fatter.
I shook him well from side to side,
  Until his face was blue:
"Come, tell me how you live," I cried,
  "And what it is you do!"

He said "I hunt for haddocks' eyes
  Among the heather bright,
And work them into waistcoat-buttons
  In the silent night.
And these I do not sell for gold

Or coin of silvery shine,
But for a copper halfpenny,
    And that will purchase nine.

"I sometimes dig for buttered rolls,
    Or set limed twigs for crabs;
I sometimes search the grassy knolls
    For wheels of Hansom-cabs.
And that's the way" (he gave a wink)
    "By which I get my wealth —
And very gladly will I drink
    Your Honour's noble health."

I heard him then, for I had just
    Completed my design
To keep the Menai bridge from rust
    By boiling it in wine.
I thanked him much for telling me
    The way he got his wealth,
But chiefly for his wish that he
    Might drink my noble health.

And now, if e'er by chance I put
    My fingers into glue,
Or madly squeeze a right-hand foot
    Into a left-hand shoe

Or if I drop upon my toe
  A very heavy weight,
I weep, for it reminds me so,
Of that old man I used to know –

Whose look was mild, whose speech was slow,
Whose hair was whiter than the snow,
Whose face was very like a crow,
With eyes, like cinders, all aglow,
Who seemed distracted with his woe,
Who rocked his body to and fro,
And muttered mumblingly and low,
As if his mouth were full of dough,
Who snorted like a buffalo –
That summer evening, long ago,
  A-sitting on a gate.'

As the Knight sang the last words of the ballad, he gathered up the reins, and turned his horse's head along the road by which they had come. 'You've only a few yards to go,' he said, 'down the hill and over that little brook, and then you'll be a Queen – But you'll stay and see me off first?' he added as Alice turned with an eager look in the direction to which he pointed. 'I shan't be long. You'll wait and wave your handkerchief when I get to that turn in the road? I think it'll encourage me, you see.'

'Of course I'll wait,' said Alice: 'and thank you very much for coming so far – and for the song – I liked it very much.'

'I hope so,' the Knight said doubtfully: 'but you didn't cry so much as I thought you would.'

So they shook hands, and then the Knight rode slowly away into the forest. 'It won't take long to see him *off*, I expect,' Alice said to herself, as she stood watching him. 'There he goes! Right on his head as usual! However, he gets on again pretty easily – that comes of having so many things hung round the horse –' So she went on talking to herself, as she watched the horse walking leisurely along the road, and the Knight tumbling off, first on one side and then on the other. After the fourth or fifth tumble he reached the turn, and then she waved her handkerchief to him, and waited till he was out of sight.

'I hope it encouraged him,' she said, as she turned to run down the hill: 'and now for the last brook, and to he a Queen! How grand it sounds!' A very few steps brought her to the edge of the brook. 'The Eighth Square at last!' she cried as she bounded across,

* * * *

* * *

* * * *

and threw herself down to rest on a lawn as soft as moss, with little flower-beds dotted about it here and there. 'Oh, how glad I am to get here! And what is this on my head?' she exclaimed in a tone of dismay, as she put her hands up to something very heavy, that fitted tight all round her head.

'But how *can* it have got there without my knowing it?' she said to herself, as she lifted it off, and set it on her lap to make out what it could possibly be.

It was a golden crown.

9

Queen Alice

'WELL, this *is* grand!' said Alice. 'I never expected I should be a Queen so soon – and I'll tell you what it is, your Majesty,' she went on in a severe tone (she was always rather fond of scolding herself), 'it'll never do for you to be lolling about on the grass like that! Queens have to be dignified, you know.'

So she got up and walked about – rather stiffly just at first, as she was afraid that the crown might come off: but she comforted herself with the thought that there was nobody to see her, 'and if I really am a Queen,' she said as she sat down again, 'I shall be able to manage it quite well in time.'

Everything was happening so oddly that she didn't feel a bit surprised at finding the Red Queen and the White Queen sitting close to her, one on each side: she

would have liked very much to ask them how they came there, but she feared it would not be quite civil. However, there would be no harm, she thought, in asking if the game was over. 'Please would you tell me –' she began, looking timidly at the Red Queen.

'Speak when you're spoken to!' the Queen sharply interrupted her.

'But if everybody obeyed that rule,' said Alice, who was always ready for a little argument, 'and if you only spoke when you were spoken to, and the other persons always waited for *you* to begin, you see nobody would ever say anything, so that –'

'Ridiculous!' cried the Queen. 'Why, don't you see, child –' here she broke off with a frown, and, after thinking for a minute; suddenly changed the subject of the conversation. 'What do you mean by "If you really are a Queen"? What right have you to call yourself so? You can't be a Queen, you know, till you've passed the proper examination, and the sooner we begin it, the better.'

'I only said "if"!' poor Alice pleaded in a piteous tone.

The two Queens looked at each other, and the Red Queen remarked, with a little shudder, 'She says she only said "if" –'

'But she said a great deal more than that!' the White

Queen moaned, wringing her hands. 'Oh, ever so much more than that!'

'So you did, you know,' the Red Queen said to Alice. 'Always speak the truth – think before you speak – and write it down afterwards.'

'I'm sure I didn't mean –' Alice was beginning, but the Red Queen interrupted her impatiently.

'That's just what I complain of! You *should* have meant! What do you suppose is the use of a child without any meaning? Even a joke should have some meaning – and a child's more important than a joke, I hope. You couldn't deny that, even if you tried with both hands.'

'I don't deny things with my *hands*,' Alice objected.

'Nobody said you did,' said the Red Queen. 'I said you couldn't if you tried.'

'She's in that state of mind,' said the White Queen, 'that she wants to deny *something* – only she doesn't know what to deny!'

'A nasty, vicious temper,' the Red Queen remarked; and then there was an uncomfortable silence for a minute or two.

The Red Queen broke the silence by saying to the White Queen, 'I invite you to Alice's dinner-party this afternoon.'

The White Queen smiled feebly, and said 'And I invite *you*.'

'I didn't know I was to have a party at all,' said Alice; 'but if there is to be one, I think I ought to invite the guests.'

'We gave you the opportunity of doing it,' the Red Queen remarked: 'but I daresay you've not had many lessons in manners yet?'

'Manners are not taught in lessons,' said Alice. 'Lessons teach you to do sums, and things of that sort.'

'Can you do Addition?' the White Queen asked. 'What's one and one and one and one and one and one and one and one and one and one?'

'I don't know,' said Alice. 'I lost count.'

'She can't do Addition,' the Red Queen interrupted. 'Can you do Subtraction? Take nine from eight.'

'Nine from eight I can't, you know,' Alice replied very readily: 'but –'

'She can't do Subtraction,' said the White Queen. 'Can you do Division? Divide a loaf by a knife – what's the answer to that?'

'I suppose –' Alice was beginning, but the Red Queen answered for her. 'Bread-and-butter, another Subtraction sum. Take a bone from a dog: what remains?'

Alice considered. 'The bone wouldn't remain, of course, if I took it – and the dog wouldn't remain; it would come to bite me – and I'm sure *I* shouldn't remain!'

'Then you think nothing would remain?' said the Red Queen.

'I think that's the answer.'

'Wrong, as usual,' said the Red Queen: 'the dog's temper would remain.'

'But I don't see how –'

'Why, look here!' the Red Queen cried. 'The dog would lose its temper, wouldn't it!'

'Perhaps it would,' Alice replied cautiously.

'Then if the dog went away, its temper would remain!' the Queen exclaimed triumphantly.

Alice said, as gravely as she could, 'They might go different ways.' But she couldn't help thinking to herself, 'What dreadful nonsense we *are* talking!'

'She can't do sums a *bit!*' the Queens said together, with great emphasis.

'Can *you* do sums?' Alice said, turning suddenly on the White Queen, for she didn't like being found fault with so much.

The Queen gasped and shut her eyes. 'I can do Addition,' she said, 'if you give me time – but I can't do Subtraction, under *any* circumstances!'

'Of course you know your A B C?' said the Red Queen.

'To be sure I do,' said Alice.

'So do I,' the White Queen whispered: 'we'll often say it over together, dear. And I'll tell you a secret – I can read words of one letter! Isn't *that* grand! However, don't be discouraged. You'll come to it in time.'

Here the Red Queen began again. 'Can you answer useful questions?' she said. 'How is bread made?'

'I know *that!*' Alice cried eagerly. 'You take some flour –'

'Where do you pick the flower?' the White Queen asked. 'In a garden, or in the hedges?'

'Well, it isn't picked at all,' Alice explained: 'it's *ground* –'

'How many acres of ground?' said the White Queen. 'You mustn't leave out so many things.'

'Fan her head!' the Red Queen anxiously interrupted.

'She'll be feverish after so much thinking.' So they set to work and fanned her with bunches of leaves, till she had to beg them to leave off, it blew her hair about so.

'She's all right again now,' said the Red Queen. 'Do you know Languages? What's the French for fiddle-de-dee?'

'Fiddle-de-dee's not English,' Alice replied gravely.

'Who ever said it was?' said the Red Queen.

Alice thought she saw a way out of the difficulty this time. 'If you'll tell me what language "fiddle-de-dee" is, I'll tell you the French for it!' she exclaimed triumphantly.

But the Red Queen drew herself up rather stiffly, and said 'Queens never make bargains.'

'I wish Queens never asked questions', Alice thought to herself.

'Don't let us quarrel,' the White Queen said in an anxious tone. 'What is the cause of lightning?'

'The cause of lightning,' Alice said very decidedly, for she felt quite certain about this, 'is the thunder – no, no!' she hastily corrected herself. 'I meant the other way.'

'It's too late to correct it,' said the Red Queen: 'when you've once said a thing, that fixes it, and you must take the consequences.'

'Which reminds me –' the White Queen said, looking down and nervously clasping and unclasping her hands, 'we had *such* a thunderstorm last Tuesday – I mean one of the last set of Tuesdays, you know.'

Alice was puzzled. 'In *our* country,' she remarked, 'there's only one day at a time.'

The Red Queen said 'That's a poor thin way of doing things. Now *here*, we mostly have days and nights two or three at a time, and sometimes in the winter we take as many as five nights together – for warmth, you know.'

'Are five nights warmer than one night, then?' Alice ventured to ask.

'Five times as warm, of course.'

'But they should be five times as *cold*, by the same rule –'

'Just so!' cried the Red Queen. 'Five times as warm, *and* five times as cold – just as I'm five times as rich as you are, *and* five times as clever!'

Alice sighed and gave it up, 'It's exactly like a riddle with no answer!' she thought.

'Humpty Dumpty saw it too,' the White Queen went on in a low voice, more as if she were talking to herself. 'He came to the door with a corkscrew in his hand –'

'What did he want?' said the Red Queen.

'He said he *would* come in,' the White Queen went on, 'because he was looking for a hippopotamus. Now, as it happened, there wasn't such a thing in the house, that morning.'

'Is there generally?' Alice asked in an astonished tone.

'Well, only on Thursdays,' said the Queen.

'I know what he came for,' said Alice: 'he wanted to punish the fish, because –'

Here the White Queen began again. 'It was *such* a thunderstorm, you can't think!' ('She *never* could you know,' said the Red Queen.) 'And part of the roof came off, and ever so much thunder got in – and it went rolling round the room in great lumps – and knocking over the tables and things – till I was so frightened, I couldn't remember my own name!'

Alice thought to herself, 'I never should *try* to remember my name in the middle of an accident! Where would be the use of it?' but she did not say this aloud, for fear of hurting the poor Queen's feelings.

'Your Majesty must excuse her,' the Red Queen said to Alice, taking one of the White Queen's hands in her own, and gently stroking it: 'she means well, but she can't help saying foolish things, as a general rule.'

The White Queen looked timidly at Alice, who felt she *ought* to say something kind, but really couldn't think of anything at the moment.

'She never was really well brought up,' the Red Queen went on: 'but it's amazing how good-tempered she is! Pat her on the head, and see how pleased she'll be!'

But this was more than Alice had courage to do.

'A little kindness – and putting her hair in papers would do wonders with her –'

The White Queen gave a deep sigh, and laid her head on Alice's shoulder. 'I *am* so sleepy!' she moaned.

'She's tired, poor thing!' said the Red Queen. 'Smooth her hair – lend her your nightcap – and sing her a soothing lullaby.'

'I haven't got a nightcap with me,' said Alice, as she tried to obey the first direction: 'and I don't know any soothing lullabies.'

'I must do it myself, then,' said the Red Queen, and she began:

> '*Hush-a-by lady, in Alice's lap!*
> *Till the feast's ready, we've time for a nap:*
> *When the feast's over, we'll go to the ball –*
> *Red Queen, and White Queen, and Alice, and all!*'

'And now you know the words,' she added, as she put her head down on Alice's other shoulder, 'just sing it through to *me*. I'm getting sleepy, too.' In another moment both Queens were fast asleep, and snoring loud.

'What *am* I to do?' exclaimed Alice, looking about in great perplexity, as first one round head, and then the other, rolled down from her shoulder, and lay like a heavy lump in her lap. 'I don't think it *ever* happened before, that anyone had to take care of two Queens asleep at once! No, not in all the History of England – it couldn't, you know, because there never was more than one Queen at a time. Do wake up, you heavy things!' she went on in an impatient tone; but there was no answer but a gentle snoring.

The snoring got more distinct every minute, and sounded more like a tune: at last she could even make out words, and she listened so eagerly that, when the two great heads suddenly vanished from her lap, she hardly missed them.

She was standing before an arched doorway over which were the words QUEEN ALICE in large letters, and on each side of the arch there was a bell-handle; one was marked 'Visitors' Bell,' and the other 'Servants' Bell.'

'I'll wait till the song's over,' thought Alice, 'and then I'll ring – the – *which* bell must I ring?' she went on, very much puzzled by the names. 'I'm not a visitor, and I'm not a servant. There *ought* to be one marked "Queen" you know –'

Just then the door opened a little way, and a creature with a long beak put its head out for a moment and said 'No admittance till the week after next!' and shut the door again with a bang.

Alice knocked and rang in vain for a long time, but at last a very old Frog, who was sitting under a tree, got up and hobbled slowly towards her: he was dressed in bright yellow, and had enormous boots on.

'What is it, now?' the Frog said in a deep hoarse whisper.

Alice turned round, ready to find fault with anybody. 'Where's the servant whose business it is to answer the door?' she began angrily.

'Which door?' said the Frog.

Alice almost stamped with irritation at the slow drawl in which he spoke. '*This* door, of course!'

The Frog looked at the door with his large dull eyes
for a minute: then he went nearer and rubbed it with
his thumb, as if he were trying whether the paint would
come off; then he looked at Alice.

'To answer the door?' he said. 'What's it been asking of?' He was so hoarse that Alice could scarcely hear him.

'I don't know what you mean,' she said.

'I speaks English, doesn't I?' the Frog went on. 'Or are you deaf? What did it ask you?'

'Nothing!' Alice said impatiently. 'I've been knocking at it!'

'Shouldn't do that – shouldn't do that –' the Frog muttered. 'Wexes it, you know.' Then he went up and gave the door a kick with one of his great feet. 'You let *it* alone,' he panted out, as he hobbled back to his tree, 'and it'll let *you* alone, you know.'

At this moment the door was flung open, and a shrill voice was heard singing:

'To the Looking-Glass world it was Alice that said,
"I've a sceptre, in hand. I've a crown on my head;
Let the Looking-Glass creatures, whatever they be,
Come and dine with the Red Queen, the White Queen, and me!"'

And hundreds of voices joined in the chorus:

'Then fill up the glasses as quick as you can,
And sprinkle the table with buttons and bran:

Put cats in the coffee, and mice in the tea –
And welcome Queen Alice with thirty-times-three!'

Then followed a confused noise of cheering, and Alice thought to herself, 'Thirty times three makes ninety. I wonder if any one's counting?' In a minute there was silence again, and the same shrill voice sang another verse:

'"O Looking-Glass creatures," quoth Alice, "draw near!
'Tis an honour to see me, a favour to hear:
'Tis a privilege high to have dinner and tea
Along with the Red Queen, the White Queen, and me!"'

Then came the chorus again:

'Then fill up the glasses with treacle and ink,
Or anything else that is pleasant to drink;
Mix sand with the cider, and wool with the wine –
And welcome Queen Alice with ninety-times-nine!'

'Ninety times nine!' Alice repeated in despair. 'Oh, that'll never be done! I'd better go in at once –' and in she went, and there was a dead silence the moment she appeared.

Alice glanced nervously along the table, as she walked up the large hall, and noticed that there were about fifty guest, of all kinds: some were animals, some birds, and there were even a few flowers among them. 'I'm glad they've come without waiting to be asked,' she thought: 'I should never have known who were the right people to invite!'

There were three chairs at the head of the table; the Red and White Queens had already taken two of them, bur the middle one was empty. Alice sat down in it, rather uncomfortable at the silence, and longing for some one to speak.

At last the Red Queen began. 'You've missed the soup and fish,' she said. 'Put on the joint!' And the waiters set a leg of mutton before Alice, who looked at it rather anxiously, as she had never had to carve a joint before.

'You look a little shy; let me introduce you to that leg of mutton,' said the Red Queen. 'Alice – Mutton; Mutton – Alice.' The leg of mutton got up in the dish and made a little bow to Alice; and Alice returned the bow, not knowing whether to be frightened or amused.

'May I give you a slice?' she said, taking up the knife and fork, and looking from one Queen to the other.

'Certainly not,' the Red Queen said, very decidedly: 'it isn't etiquette to cut anyone you've been introduced

to. Remove the joint!' And the waiters carried it off, and brought a large plum-pudding in its place.

'I won't be introduced to the pudding, please,' Alice said rather hastily, 'or we shall get no dinner at all. May I give you some?'

But the Red Queen looked sulky, and growled 'Pudding – Alice; Alice – Pudding. Remove the pudding!' and the waiters took it away so quickly that Alice couldn't return its bow.

However, she didn't see why the Red Queen should be the only one to give orders, so, as an experiment, she called out 'Waiter! Bring back the pudding!' and there it was again in a moment, like a conjuring-trick. It was so large that she couldn't help feeling a *little* shy with it, as she had been with the mutton; however, she conquered her shyness by a great effort and cut a slice and handed it to the Red Queen.

'What impertinence!' said the Pudding. 'I wonder how you'd like it, if I were to cut a slice out of *you*, you creature!'

It spoke in a thick, suety sort of voice, and Alice hadn't a word to say in reply: she could only sit and look at it and gasp.

'Make a remark,' said the Red Queen: 'it's ridiculous to leave all the conversation to the pudding!'

'Do you know, I've had such a quantity of poetry repeated to me today,' Alice began, a little frightened at finding that, the moment she opened her lips, there was dead silence, and all eyes were fixed upon her; 'and it's a very curious thing, I think – every poem was about fishes in some way. Do you know why they're so fond of fishes, all about here?'

She spoke to the Red Queen, whose answer was a little wide of the mark. 'As to fishes,' she said, very slowly and solemnly, putting her mouth close to Alice's ear, 'her White Majesty knows a lovely riddle – all in poetry – all about fishes. Shall she repeat it?'

'Her Red Majesty's very kind to mention it,' the White

Queen murmured into Alice's other ear, in a voice like the cooing of a pigeon. 'It would be *such* a treat! May I?'

'Please do,' Alice said very politely.

The White Queen laughed with delight, and stroked Alice's cheek. Then she began:

> *"First, the fish must be caught."*
> *That is easy: a baby, I think, could have caught it.*
> *"Next, the fish must be bought."*
> *That is easy: a penny, I think, would have bought it.*
>
> *"Now cook me the fish!"*
> *That is easy, and will not take more than a minute.*
> *"Let it lie in a dish!"*
> *That is easy, because it already is in it.*
>
> *"Bring it here! Let me sup!"*
> *It is easy to set such a dish on the table.*
> *"Take the dish-cover up!"*
> *Ah, that is so hard that I fear I'm unable!*
>
> *For it holds it like glue –*
> *Holds the lid to the dish, while it lies in the middle:*
> *Which is easiest to do,*
> *Un-dish-cover the fish, or dishcover the riddle?'*

'Take a minute to think about it, and then guess,' said the Red Queen. 'Meanwhile, we'll drink your health – Queen Alice's health!' she screamed at the top of her voice, and all the guests began drinking it directly, and very queerly they managed it: some of them put their glasses upon their heads like extinguishers, and drank all that trickled down their faces – others upset the decanters, and drank the wine as it ran off the edges of the table – and three of them (who looked like kangaroos) scrambled into the dish of roast mutton, and began eagerly lapping up the gravy, 'just like pigs in a trough!' thought Alice.

'You ought to return thanks in a neat speech,' the Red Queen said, frowning at Alice as she spoke.

'We must support you, you know,' the White Queen whispered, as Alice got up to do it, very obediently, but a little frightened.

'Thank you very much,' she whispered in reply, 'but I can do quite well without.'

'That wouldn't be at all the thing,' the Red Queen said very decidedly: so Alice tried to submit to it with a good grace.

('And they *did* push so!' she said afterwards, when she was telling her sister the history of the feast. 'You would have thought they wanted to squeeze me flat!')

In fact it was rather difficult for her to keep in her

place while she made her speech: the two Queens pushed her so, one on each side, that they nearly lifted her up into the air: 'I rise to return thanks –' Alice began: and she really *did* rise as she spoke, several inches; but she got hold of the edge of the table, and managed to pull herself down again.

'Take care of yourself!' screamed the White Queen, seizing Alice's hair with both her hands. 'Something's going to happen!'

And then (as Alice afterwards described it) all sorts of things happened in a moment. The candles all grew up to the ceiling, looking something like a bed of rushes with fireworks at the top. As to the bottles, they each took a pair of plates, which they hastily fitted on as wings, and so, with forks for legs, went fluttering about in all directions: 'and very like birds they look,' Alice thought to herself, as well as she could in the dreadful confusion that was beginning.

At this moment she heard a hoarse laugh at her side, and turned to see what was the matter with the White Queen; but, instead of the Queen, there was the leg of mutton sitting in the chair. 'Here I am!' cried a voice from the soup-tureen, and Alice turned again, just in time to see the Queen's broad good-natured face grinning at her for a moment over the edge of the tureen, before she disappeared into the soup.

There was not a moment to be lost. Already several of the guests were lying down in the dishes, and the soup ladle was walking up the table towards Alice's chair, and beckoning to her impatiently to get out of its way.

'I can't stand this any longer!' she cried as she jumped up and seized the table-cloth with both hands: one good pull, and plates, dishes, guests, and candles came crashing down together in a heap on the floor.

'And as for *you*,' she went on, turning fiercely upon the Red Queen, whom she considered as the cause of all the mischief – but the Queen was no longer at her side – she had suddenly dwindled down to the size of a little doll, and was now on the table, merrily running round and round after her own shawl, which was trailing behind her.

At any other time, Alice would have felt surprised at this, but she was far too much excited to be surprised at anything *now*. 'As for *you*,' she repeated, catching hold of the little creature in the very act of jumping over a bottle which had just lighted upon the table, 'I'll shake you into a kitten, that I will!'

10

Shaking

S HE took her off the table as she spoke, and shook her backwards and forwards with all her might.

The Red Queen made no resistance whatever; only her face grew very small, and her eyes got large and green: and still, as Alice went on shaking her, she kept on growing shorter – and fatter – and softer – and rounder and –

11
Waking

– and it really *was* a kitten, after all.

12

Which Dreamed It?

'YOUR Red Majesty shouldn't purr so loud,' Alice said, rubbing her eyes; and addressing the kitten, respectfully, yet with some severity. 'You woke me out of oh! such a nice dream! And you've been along with me, Kitty – all through the Looking-Glass world. Did you know it, dear?'

It is a very inconvenient habit of kittens (Alice had once made the remark) that, whatever you say to them, they *always* purr. 'If they would only purr for "yes," and mew for "no," or any rule of that sort,' she had said, 'so that one could keep up a conversation! But how *can* you talk with a person if they always say the same thing?'

On this occasion the kitten only purred: and it was impossible to guess whether it meant 'yes' or 'no.'

So Alice hunted among the chessmen on the table

till she had found the Red Queen: then she went down on her knees on the hearth-rug, and put the kitten and the Queen to look at each other. 'Now, Kitty!' she cried, clapping her hands triumphantly. 'Confess that was what you turned into!'

('But it wouldn't look at it,' she said, when she was explaining the thing afterwards to her sister: 'it turned away its head, and pretended not to see it: but it looked

a *little* ashamed of itself, so I think it *must* have been the Red Queen.')

'Sit up a little more stiffly, dear!' Alice cried with a merry laugh. 'And curtsey while you're thinking what to – what to purr. It saves time, remember!' And she caught it up and gave it one little kiss, 'just in honour of its having been a Red Queen.'

'Snowdrop, my pet!' she went on, looking over her shoulder at the White Kitten, which was still patiently undergoing its toilet, 'when *will* Dinah have finished with your White Majesty, I wonder? That must be the reason you were so untidy in my dream – Dinah! Do you know that you're scrubbing a White Queen? Really, it's most disrespectful of you!

'And what did *Dinah* turn to, I wonder?' she prattled on, as she settled comfortably down, with one elbow on the rug, and her chin in her hand, to watch the kittens. 'Tell me, Dinah, did you turn to Humpty Dumpty? I *think* you did – however, you'd better not mention it to your friends just yet, for I'm not sure.

'By the way, Kitty, if only you'd been really with me in my dream, there was one thing you *would* have enjoyed – I had such a quantity of poetry said to me, all about fishes! Tomorrow morning you shall have a real treat. All the time you're eating your breakfast, I'll repeat "The Walrus and the Carpenter" to you; and then you can make believe it's oysters, dear!

'Now, Kitty, let's consider who it was that dreamed it all. This is a serious question, my dear, and you should *not* go on licking your paw like that – as if Dinah hadn't washed you this morning! You see, Kitty, it *must* have been either me or the Red King. He was part of my dream, of course – but then I was part of his dream, too! *Was* it the Red King, Kitty? You were his wife, my dear, so you ought to know – Oh, Kitty, *do* help to settle it! I'm sure your paw can wait!' But the provoking kitten only began on the other paw, and pretended it hadn't heard the question.

Which do you think it was?

A boat beneath a sunny sky,
Lingering onward dreamily
In an evening of July –

Children three that nestle near,
Eager eye and willing ear,
Pleased a simple tale to hear –

Long has paled that sunny sky:
Echoes fade and memories die.
Autumn frosts have slain July.

Still she haunts me, phantomwise,
Alice moving under skies
Never seen by waking eyes.

Children yet, the tale to hear,
Eager eye and willing ear
Lovingly shall nestle near.

In a Wonderland they lie,
Dreaming as the days go by,
Dreaming as the summers die:

Ever drifting down the stream –
Lingering in the golden gleam –
Life, what is it but a dream?

THE END

The Backstory

Test your knowledge of Wonderland and have a go at
making up nonsense verse!

Who's Who in *Alice's Adventures in Wonderland*?

Alice: A curious and polite little girl of seven who loves her pet cat Dinah.

The White Rabbit: A nervous animal in a constant rush, always frantic to please his superiors.

The Caterpillar: A haughty creature who asks puzzling questions. Alice chances upon him reclining on a mushroom smoking a hookah, a type of pipe for flavoured tobacco.

The Duchess: Alice meets the Duchess in the kitchen of her palace, nursing a baby. She is rude and violent towards her baby but later becomes rather too friendly to Alice.

The Cheshire Cat: We first encounter the Cheshire Cat in the Duchess's kitchen. He is known for his distinctive grin and ability to disappear and reappear whenever he likes.

The March Hare: Utterly nutty and full of nonsense, the March Hare spends his time constantly having tea with his friends the Hatter and the Dormouse.

The Hatter: As mad as the March Hare, the Hatter speaks only in riddles. In his world it is always tea-time and he is always attending his own crazy tea party.

The Dormouse: The Dormouse cannot stop falling asleep, no matter how hard he tries, although he is awake for long enough to tell a very strange story about treacle.

The Queen of Hearts: A foul-tempered, croquet-playing monarch, prone to shouting 'Off with their heads!'

The King of Hearts: A gentler ruler than the Queen, the King is no better at logical thinking.

The White King and the White Queen: two living chess pieces. The White Queen explains to Alice how she lives her life backwards.

The Red King and the Red Queen: Also chess pieces, the Red King is asleep throughout the entire story. The Red Queen is very fast runner, although she never seems to get anywhere.

Tweedledum and Tweedledee: A pair of fat twins who recite 'The Walrus and the Carpenter' to Alice and have an absurd fight over a rattle.

Humpty Dumpty: an egg who sits on the top of a high, narrow wall and explains the poem 'Jabberwocky' to Alice.

The Lion and the Unicorn: these characters compete for the White King's crown. They think Alice is a monster.

The White Knight and the Red Knight: These are a pair of very clumsy knights who fight over Alice. When the White Knight wins he sings Alice a long and melancholy song.

How much attention did you pay to the weird and wonderful details of Alice's adventures? Take this quiz to find out how much of a Wonderland expert you are…

Alice's Adventures in Wonderland

1) Who does the White Rabbit mistake Alice for?

2) What kinds of creatures are the comical footmen Alice spots outside the Duchess's house?

3) Why has the Duchess been sentenced to death?

4) In the game of croquet what kinds of animals are used as the bats and balls?

5) According to the King, what rule has Alice broken that requires her to leave the courtroom?

Through the Looking-Glass

6) What are Alice's two kittens called?

7) Can you recite the first line from 'The Jabberwocky'?

8) What kinds of insects does the Gnat point out to Alice?

9) What type of cake does Alice attempt to slice up for the Lion and the Unicorn?

10) Where does the White Queen disappear to at the end of Alice's dinner party?

Answers to the *Wonderland* quiz – how did you do?

1. Mary Ann, his housemaid.
2. A frog and a fish.
3. Because she boxed the queen's ears.
4. The bats are flamingos and the balls are hedgehogs.
5. She has become more than a mile tall.
6. The white kitten is Snowdrop and the black one is called Kitty.
7. ''Twas brillig and the slithy toves'
8. A Rocking-horse-fly, a Snap-dragon-fly and a Bread-and-Butterfly.
9. Plum cake.
10. She dives into the soup-tureen.

Give yourself one point for each correct answer. If you got…

10 points or more: Fiddle-de-dee, you're an Alice whizz!

5 points or more: Your face has got SOME sense in it, but you *could* do some more swotting.

Less than 5 points: Off with your head! As the Duchess says to Alice 'You don't know much, and that's a fact'.

Who was Lewis Carroll?

Lewis Carroll's real name was Charles Lutwidge Dodgson and he was born in 1832, in Cheshire. As a young boy Lewis was excellent at reading and at school he showed himself to be a naturally bright pupil. His gift for numbers led him to study maths at the University of Oxford. He did very well there even though he admitted that he often didn't work hard enough. He suffered from a stammer but he was very good at mimicking people, telling stories and playing charades.

After his degree, Lewis Carroll had a career full of variety. He continued to live in his Oxford college, he taught and wrote books about maths, and he was ordained a church deacon. He also pursued his love of writing stories and photography. As well as the Alice books he wrote many poems, articles and short stories. Although he never married he adored children and spent a lot of time with his young friends, playing with them and taking photographs.

CLASSICS

VINTAGE

Was Alice a real person?

Lewis Carroll certainly knew a little girl called Alice. She was the daughter of a colleague at Oxford University named Henry Liddell. Lewis occasionally took Alice and her sisters out rowing and it was on one of these trips in the summer of 1862 that he invented a story about a character called Alice and her adventures underground. The real Alice begged him to write it down, and when he eventually did, *Alice's Adventures in Wonderland* was published in 1865. If you are very observant you might have spotted the fact that there is an acrostic poem (this means that the first letter of each line spells out a message) at the very end of *Through the Looking-Glass*. 'Alice Pleasance Liddell' is spelled out which suggests that these stories were inspired by her. But Lewis Carroll said that he often dedicated his work to the little girls that he knew.

Stuff and nonsense!

Alice gets pretty tired of listening to the people and animals in Wonderland recite poetry to her. And what strange poetry it is! Lewis Carroll and his contemporary Edward Lear, as well as Dr Seuss and Roald Dahl, are all well-known for writing rhythmic, rhyming and funny poems, known as 'nonsense verse'. Edward Lear wrote 'The Owl and the Pussycat' which is a very famous poem – perhaps you know it? He also wrote many limericks. These are poems which consist of five lines with a strict rhyming pattern, and which normally tell very silly stories. Here's one of Lear's:

There was an Old Man with a beard,
Who said, 'It is just as I feared!
Two Owls and a Hen,
Four Larks and a Wren,
Have all built their nests in my beard!

And another:

> There was a Young Lady of Dorking,
> Who bought a large bonnet for walking;
> But its colour and size,
> So bedazzled her eyes,
> That she very soon went back to Dorking.

Have a go at making up your own limerick – you could be inspired by your home town, your friends and family, or people you see on the street. For instance, if you live in York, and you have a brother, your limerick could begin 'There was a young man from York, who would only ever eat pork'. Get the idea? Off you go!

Twinkle, twinkle, little bat
How I wonder what you're at!
Up above the world you fly
Like a tea-tray in the sky.

Remember the Mad Hatter's version of this famous nursery song? Why don't you get creative with nursery rhymes, and make up your own version of 'Baa Baa Black Sheep', 'Jack and Jill' or 'Three Blind Mice'. Keep the structure but change key words for something completely unexpected.

'Jabberwocky' is one of Lewis Carroll's most famous nonsense poems, and it's wonderful to recite aloud. It's a clever poem, because even though many of the words are made up, you can still understand the story it tells. What do you think the word 'brillig' means? What are the 'mome raths'? What does the 'Jub Jub bird' look like? Make up your own nonsense words and put them together to create a fantastical, atmospheric and exciting poem. Or, if you prefer drawing, why not create your own image of the fearsome Jabberwock!

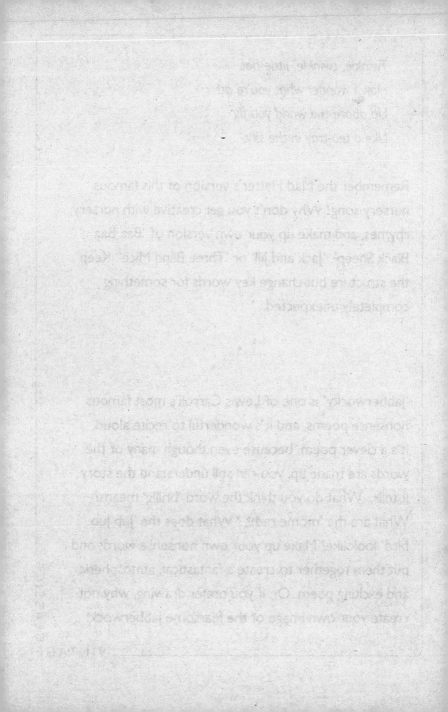

What are the 'tulgey' trees? What does the jub jub

Seize the Day

the

Day

Seven Steps to Achieving the Extraordinary in an Ordinary World

Talents
Knowledge &
Experiend

Conclusions (not in order)

o I am HP — just lost the medium I was swimming in.

o Need to find the medium to swim in ?

o Can I find

Seize the Day

Seven Steps to Achieving the Extraordinary in an Ordinary World

By
Danny Cox and John Hoover

SEIZE THE DAY
ISBN 1-56414-134-9, $21.95
Cover design by Dean Johnson Design, Inc.
Cover photo by Mountain Light Photography Inc.
Printed in the U.S.A. by Book-mart Press

To order this title by mail, please include price as noted above, $2.50 handling per order, and $1.00 for each book ordered. Send to: Career Press, Inc., 180 Fifth Ave., P.O. Box 34, Hawthorne, NJ 07507.

Or call toll-free 1-800-CAREER-1 (Canada: 201-427-0229) to order using VISA or MasterCard, or for further information on books from Career Press.

Library of Congress Cataloging-in-Publication Data

Cox, Danny, 1934-
    Seize the day : seven steps to achieving the extraordinary in an ordinary world / by Danny Cox and John Hoover.
        p.   cm.
    Includes index.
    ISBN 1-56414-134-9 : $21.95
    1. Vocational guidance. 2. Performance standards. 3. Achievement motivation. I. Hoover, John, 1952-   II. Title.
    HF5381.C699   1994
    650.1—dc20
                                                                94-10607
                                                                CIP
Re-print Meridien Marketing
RSA 2001

Dedication/Introduction

Of the many mentors who have helped me "seize the day" I dedicate this to three standouts.

The first is Virgil Cox, my coal miner father. Out of his meager earnings he figured out a way to obtain his private pilot's license. On one of those great Sunday afternoon flights out of the Marion, Illinois airport, he let me fly an airplane for the first time. I was 12 years old. With is unceasing encouragement I progressed from that 90 mph airplane to flying supersonic fighters at 20 miles per minute (1200mph). It was quite an adventure.

The second mentor is Mike Vance, founder and former dean of Disney University where he had also headed up the Idea and People Development Department for Walt Disney. When I heard him speak there in Anaheim I was at a low point in my life. I had just destroyed my employer's top office because I was so bad as a manager. That day I learned people skills that really worked and this profound bit of philosophy:

> *"We do what we are. We are what we think. What we think is determined by what we learn. What we learn is determined by what we experience and what we experience is determined by what we expose ourselves to and what we do with that experience."*

That half-day seminar of Mike's was the turning point in my rebuilding that office into an industry leader.

The third mentor is easily the most interesting person I have ever known. His name is Jim Newton and he is author of *Uncommon Friends,* which chronicles his close friendships with

Thomas Edison, Henry Ford, Harvey Firestone, Charles Lindbergh and Nobel Prize winner Dr. Alexis Carrel. He taught me that his great friends had three things in common:

1. A sense of destiny

2. A spirit of adventure

3. A capacity for growth

He's 89 years old now and he says in this characteristically humorous way, *"I can't say much for my past but my future is spotless."*

As you can see from the loving encouragement of a blue-collar father, to Mickey Mouse, to Thomas Edison, it's been quite a rise— and its not over yet.

"The best is yet to be."

Contents

- No organization can rise above the quality of it's leadership.
- Natural vs self-imposed barriers
- Even if an organization can't rise above the quality of its leadership - the people in it can work to improve their lot & as a consequence lift the whole business.
- Stagnation = when the past seems bigger than the future.
- High performers tend to job hop more than low performers - which is why a lot of businessmen look around them & shake their heads at mediocrity. Low performers don't tend to leave. They stick.
- "Helping preserve the past by postponing the present." PROCRASTINATION
- Freezing at a rung on life's ladder, it doesn't mean no climbing has been done. It means that progress has been stopped.
- When past daydreams accomplishments occupy more daydreams than future visions... every new day starts back in the same old spot.
- Don't get side tracked: Know the difference between interesting & unimportant. Distinguish between URGENT & UNIMPORTANT TASKS.

Foreword

I've spent a professional lifetime seeking out the potential in people. To me, people represent endless possibilities. Within each individual there is tremendous power waiting to be unleashed. I've found nothing more gratifying in my career than to see a man or a woman finally *come into his or her own*. People, possibilities, power: These are among the topics that have inspired me to write scores of books and preach thousands of sermons over the years.

Through those years, I've learned first-hand how it's possible for anyone with a big enough heart to accomplish unbelievable results. The size of your pocketbook, your physical stature and your formal schooling mean very little when it comes to long-term success. It's the ability to place oneself in the future, plan and execute faithfully that makes all the difference. Where the power of human potential is concerned, the sky's the limit.

That's why I'm proud of my good friend Danny Cox. I've watched his career grow. I know what a rich blessing *his* speaking and writing have been to so many people across this great country. Now, Danny has topped himself once again. This time he's carved out a seven-step *high-performance process* that will make the most of your natural abilities, education and experience. Danny weaves an entertaining and informative fabric out of his executive experiences, Air Force test pilot escapades and Ozark country common sense. As usual, he communicates it all in the warm, easy-going, amusing style that's become his trademark on the speaker's platform. Tapping your reservoir of personal potential has never been explained more clearly. Following Danny's time-proven formula will truly enable you to *Seize The Day*.

Dr. Robert H. Schuller

Seize
the
Day

Seven Steps to Achieving the
Extraordinary in an Ordinary World

The High Performance Process

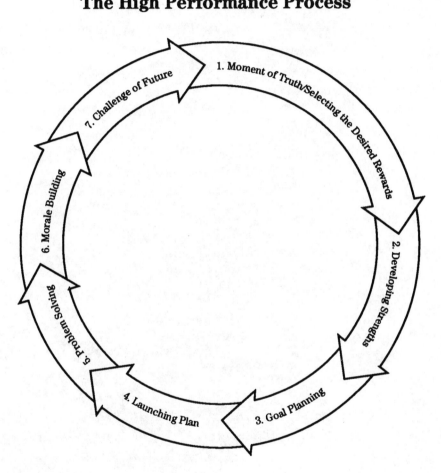

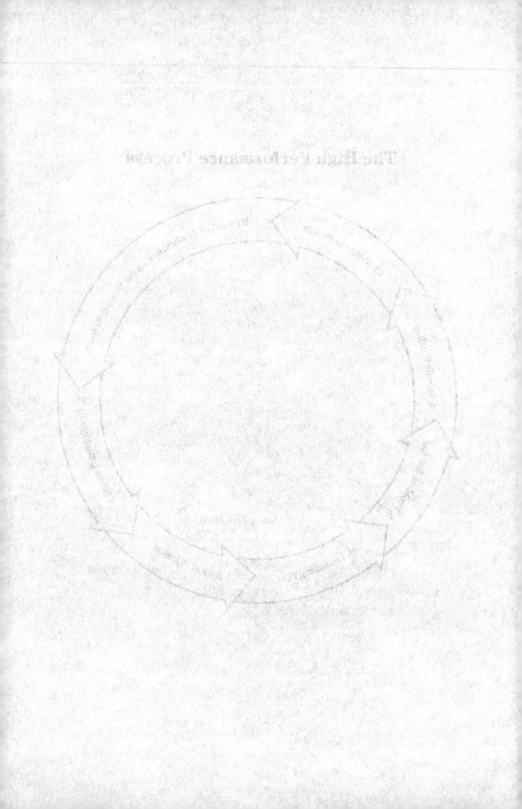

OVERVIEW
Performance Is
Personal

"People are always blaming their circumstances for what they are. I don't believe in circumstances. The people who get on in this world are the people who get up and look for the circumstances they want, and, if they can't find them, make them."

—George Bernard Shaw

Some of my happiest college days were spent spelunking. I mapped many a cave for the geology department at Southern Illinois University. What might look to most people like a pile of rocks in the middle of an Illinois pasture can also be the entrance to an underground adventure.

And so it was the day that three friends and I slid on our stomachs through a narrow crevice and discovered a sizable underground cavern. Following the beams of our flashlights, we ventured deeper into the cave until we came to a ledge. Using the rope we had brought with us, we lowered ourselves down 15 feet or so to the next level.

After exploring a while longer, we decided to head back. When we came to the rope draped over the ledge, we discovered that the moisture in the cave had made it wet and slippery. No matter how hard we tried, none of us could secure a tight enough grip to climb up. As we enthusiastically set out on our adventure earlier that day, we had ignored some of the details that now loomed menacingly before us.

For starters, nobody knew where we were. We hadn't bothered to tell anyone that we were going to explore a specific cave in a specific place. We just sort of stumbled on to the entrance. There was no prominent opening at the mouth of the cave, only a narrow 18-inch gap in a pile of rocks in the middle of a pasture. We were probably the only human beings alive aware that this cave existed.

Our flashlights were getting dim and the air was getting stale. With the urgency of our situation beginning to increase the tension among us, we discussed our options. There didn't seem to be any obvious solution. We weren't aware that we were holding ourselves back with conventional thinking. Our mistake was looking for the *obvious*.

It wasn't until we turned our flashlights off to save the batteries that I began to see possibilities that we hadn't previously considered. In the darkness of the underground cavern, I noticed that the small pieces of driftwood scattered around us were *glowing*. While relying on the beams from our flashlights to illuminate our way, we hadn't noticed the phosphorous properties of the fungus-covered logs that made them glow in the dark.

The glow from the rocks didn't assist us in any practical way. What it did was prick my creativity enough to realize that the solution to our problem was probably close at hand if only we could look at our situation differently. The glowing driftwood made me feel as if the answer had to be there and we just weren't seeing it. As it turned out, I went back to the rope that was too slippery to grip with our hands and realized we might be better off using our *feet*. We tied loops in the rope and climbed up the sheer face of the ledge using the rope as a makeshift ladder.

Different eyes

The necessity for and the rewards that flow from a commitment to personal high performance aren't always obvious. Unless we can mentally switch off the lights and study the glow around us, we probably won't appreciate how important our role is in the scheme of life. In a nutshell, who we are and how we glow in our private lives determines who we are in our professional lives. We just need to sit quietly in the dark long enough to see how we glow. It's in the darkness that our true character shines the brightest.

I've found it universally true that an individual with a high sense of personal ethics and integrity in his or her professional life will have the same ethics and integrity in his or her personal life. The same holds true of enthusiasm, drive, goals and general initiative. Once committed to the *high-performance process,* high-performance people are *always* high-performance people, lights on or lights off.

Different people may demonstrate their performance in different ways, but, in the end, high performance is a way of life. The difference between a high-performance person and a potential high-performance person is the decision to look at life through different eyes and to invest the effort necessary to become a person who makes his or her own circumstances.

Profound thought: No organization can rise above the quality of its leadership.

Performance is everyone's business

The primary thesis of my previous book, *Leadership When The Heat's On,* simply states that *no organization can rise above the quality of its leadership.* That's a valuable idea to hang on the wall opposite your desk at the office, post on your bathroom mirror at home or tattoo on the back of your hand. Some folks miss the point and agree wholeheartedly that leadership is the cause of all their ills. Unfortunately, these people are looking for somewhere else to place the responsibility for their circumstances and aren't accepting their own role in leadership, no matter how obscure.

Everybody is his or her *own* leader, plain and simple. Every person within an organization plays a role in leadership. An organization is a *system.* In a system, the performance of each component has an effect on the performance of the organization as a whole. If you work alone, your commitment to personal high performance will have a more profound impact on your success than the commitment of a single individual at General Motors.

Whether or not you work alone or work for the world's worst boss in a large organization, a personal commitment to high performance influences your circumstances. The greater your commitment to personal high performance, the better the circumstances for you *and* everyone in the organization. Whatever the leaders believe and practice will be reflected throughout the entire organization. *Your* beliefs and values will be reflected in your *performance.*

Nevertheless, the success or failure of individuals within an organization depends largely upon each person's willingness to adopt the vision and commitment of the organization's leadership. One of the primary challenges of leadership is to market its vision to the individuals in the organization and entice them to embrace the vision as their own. At the same time, influence runs the other direction. You might not be the leader, but that doesn't mean leadership isn't important to you. It is.

As individuals within organizations, we all have a professional obligation to keep our leaders honest and focused by working diligently to produce results that reflect leadership's vision. The success of your role in the system is a direct reflection of your commitment to personal high performance.

Give and take

Dedication to personal high performance requires a healthy ability to give selflessly to others and to receive gratefully the rewards of a job well done. Giving and receiving go hand in hand. While it's true that our motivation for giving is not to create indebtedness in others, someone who gives all and accepts nothing in return is fulfilling some sacrificial need in his or her personal agenda.

Conversely, people who want everything given to them without investing something of themselves are seeking a return to infancy and a nurturing, all-providing parent. Either way, what's missing is the balance between giving and receiving that's necessary for a fulfilled life. Even if you work alone at homemaking and/or philanthropy, you will benefit as much or more from a commitment to personal high performance as someone within a large organization. The cornerstone of personal high performance in both cases is to help others and to accept their help in return.

Happy campers, high flyers

The quest for personal high performance can become an ongoing journey and is never an end in itself. The pursuit of personal high performance is the source of tremendous pleasure and gratification. It's the feeling an athlete experiences in victory, the sensation an actor feels during a standing ovation, the satisfaction an artist experiences when his or her music, painting or sculpture makes the statement it was intended to make.

For me it's the way I felt when I broke the sound barrier for the very first of what eventually became almost 800 times during my years as an Air Force test pilot and air show pilot. Even though Chuck Yeager had been the first person to break the sound barrier 11 years earlier in an aircraft designed for supersonic flight, my first supersonic experience was unforgettable.

I was alone at the controls of an F-86D fighter, in a vertical dive at 45,000 feet, full throttle, with my afterburner lit, watching the Okefenoke Swamp rapidly approaching my windshield. In an aircraft not built for supersonic speeds, some strange things began to happen. Being a test pilot, I was supposed to observe all phenomenon calmly and objectively. However, when the wings on the jet began to twist and bend slightly under the pressure, my eyes got a little wider.

I heard creaks and groans from the aircraft's framework that I'd never heard before. Then I *"punched through"* and the feeling was unbelievable. Not so much because I'd broken through the sound barrier, but because I could now plant my feet firmly on the console and yank back on the stick to pull out of my nose dive. What a *thrill!*

The *high-performance process* is not about winning or being number one. It's about running the good race and pursuing a personal best. However, life is a series of ups and downs. No one lives on a perpetual high *(although some work hard at maintaining a perpetual low)*. Anyone determined to focus on negativity has an addiction to life-strangling habits that block personal productivity.

Those with a solid grip on reality accept that times are sometimes tough and results often fall short of expectations. That's okay to a high-performance person. High-performance people don't congratulate themselves for just taking a stab at something. Making an effort is not on face value worthy of reward. When a person makes the best effort s/he is capable of making, rewards are due—whether or not the goal is achieved. Too often, too many folks settle for too little effort. Never the high-performance person who is *"on the grow"*.

Natural vs. self-imposed barriers

To best illustrate what personal high performance is, it's important to first understand where and how all of us tend to fall short of our potential. Self-imposed barriers take over where natural barriers leave off. Most people never know the difference between the two and, therefore, erroneously assume that their lack of achievement is someone else's fault.

Self-imposed barriers get higher and wider when individuals focus on their own weaknesses as pointed out to them by friends, employers, teachers, parents, conventional wisdom, etc. Shifting focus to developing strengths immediately weakens self-imposed barriers.

An example of a *natural* barrier is my career in the NBA. I have no career in the National Basketball Association and I have no reason to be ashamed of my inability to play professional basketball in the United States. At five-feet-five-inches and 50-plus years of age, there is a natural barrier between my abilities and the job requirements of guarding Michael Jordan. Even those few five-foot-six miracle players who *do* play professional basketball will be retired long before they're 50.

Physical challenges are the most obvious of the natural barriers and it's important to be realistic about them. Mental challenges are more insidious and less well-defined. In most cases where someone is not performing up to his or her ability, it's a direct result of a self-imposed psychological barrier. A self-imposed barrier is not a wall in life, it's simply the *margin* where nothing has yet been written—yet.

If you're frustrated and wonder why you aren't getting any further in life, you're undoubtedly looking at that margin as if it were a wall. Many people feel as if they've *maxed out* and simply can't do any more or any better than they've done to date. Most of us get our cues from our parents and feel deep inside that we can't rise any further professionally, make any more money or perform at a higher level than our parents did. Until we make a more informed decision of our own, that is.

Such people haven't seen themselves glow in the dark. They haven't looked at their lives through different eyes that see beyond what is—to what they're capable of. As years go by, the wall tends to get thicker, higher and more difficult to see over. Yet, what we can build out of self-doubt and ignorance, we can also disassemble. If a barrier is truly self-imposed, it can be self-deposed.

Increasing personal productivity and the overall productivity of an entire organization depends upon how much potential is developed in each individual. Even though an organization can't rise above the quality of its leadership, it's possible for people at every level to improve their lot through a commitment to personal productivity and exert a strong influence on the organization through their higher performance.

Drawing a picture

Peter F. Drucker said that *"Strong people have strong weaknesses."* What often appears to be a glaring personality deficit is more likely to be an unresolved personal challenge. Answers to personal challenges are just as likely to be found in the reservoir of undeveloped strengths stored between self-imposed barriers and the full extent of personal potential (See Fig. 0-1).

Personal self-esteem is defined by self-imposed barriers. Locate your barrier and you've measured the range of your self-esteem. Whether self-esteem defines the location of self-imposed barriers or vice versa is a chicken-and-egg debate. It's far more important to discover your reservoir of undeveloped strengths.

Once you begin developing previously undeveloped strengths, self-esteem improves and productivity increases. Once you look at

Where You are Now

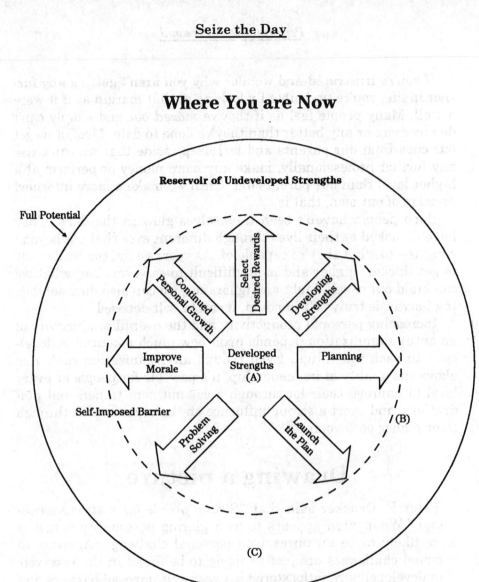

Figure 0.1

Developed strengths (A) are inside self-imposed barriers (B).
Your personal reservoir of undeveloped strengths (C) resides
outside of your self-imposed barriers.

yourself through different eyes and see your undeveloped strengths, full of promise and potential, you can't help but become more enthusiastic. In the same manner, leaders who are responsible for the development of others need to see members of the organization not only for what they have accomplished in the past, but also in light of their undeveloped strengths.

Another way to illustrate the difference between developed and undeveloped potential is to visualize a thermometer. (See Fig. 0-2) The mercury level represents your current level of developed potential. The top of the thermometer represents the full range of your potential. The exercise involves identifying and resolving the issues that cause the mercury level to stay below what you're capable of.

How likely you are to achieve your full potential depends upon how hot or cold you're running. Obviously, whatever fires your boilers becomes the key ingredient to fuel the development of undeveloped strengths. Ask yourself:

"Where do I see myself on my thermometer?"

"Where do I want to be on the thermometer next year?"

"What's my action plan for getting there?"

Seven steps of the high-performance process

The following chapters are devoted to methods and techniques of expanding the circle of self-imposed barriers as more and more strengths are developed. As undeveloped strengths are developed through the *high-performance process* (See Fig. 0-3), personal performance increases and life changes. The heat that causes the mercury to rise in the personal potential thermometer comes from the same energy source that heats the center of the circle of self-imposed barriers.

Think of the arrows that push the circle of self-imposed barriers outward as radiating heat. The heat is produced by burning *desire.* The desire to earn more, to live and work happier, to

Your Thermometer of Personal Potential

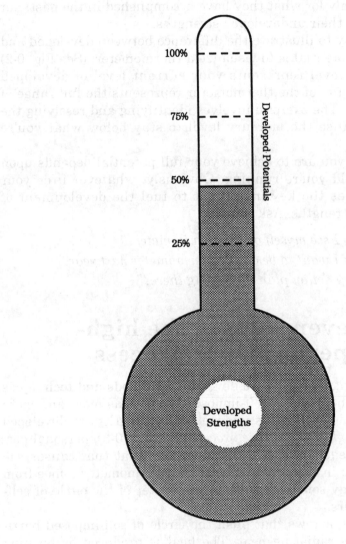

100%

75%

Developed Potentials

50%

25%

Developed
Strengths

Figure 0.2

Where You Want To Be

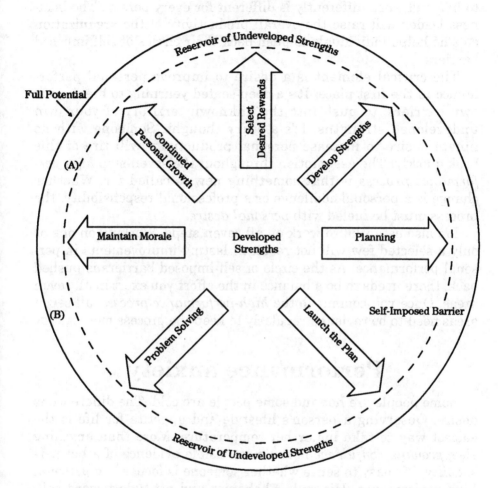

Figure 0.3

As you execute the seven steps of the *high-performance process*,
self-imposed barriers (A) are pushed back as undeveloped strengths
become developed strengths and you edge increasingly closer to
your full potential (B).

accomplish more meaningful tasks and/or to achieve a more desirable lifestyle are just a few examples of fuel for the fire. The desire to live and work differently is different for every person. The business leader will raise the overall productivity of the organization as s/he helps individuals to push back their circles of self-imposed barriers.

The critical element is a desire to improve personal performance in the first place. It's a deep-seated yearning to break your own barriers, to push into the unknown territory of your own undeveloped strengths. It's a scary thought. Someone with no innate desire to increase personal productivity will tire of this book quickly. The assumption throughout the seven-step *high-performance process* is that something new is called for. Whether change is a personal challenge or a professional responsibility, the process must be fueled with *personal desire.*

It's also essential to work on all seven steps. Working on one or only a selected few will not result in lasting improvements in personal performance. As the circle of self-imposed barriers is pushed back, there needs to be a balance in the effort you exert in all seven areas. Once you commit to the *high-performance process,* all seven areas need to be revisited regularly to keep the process moving.

Performance anxiety

Some people are hot and some people are cold. The difference is desire. Observing a person's lifestyle and appetite for life is the easiest way to take his or her temperature. More than anything else, *growing confidence* is the most visible evidence of a hot personality. It's easy to sense whether someone is focused on personal high performance. His or her behavior and attitude toward self, others and the circumstances will reflect the necessary personal commitment.

Nobody can see the future any clearer than the next person. However, the high-performance person is excited about the potential of the future just the same. The lukewarm or cold personality would rather stay wrapped in the comfort of the familiar. Change *when + why did I start evading commitment in the guise of "flexibility?" Actually it is a pathological refusal to place myself in a s...*

means uncertainty and uncertainty can cut both ways. Although the new lifestyle might be better, chances are that it might be worse. Hence the strong affinity for the familiar.

One of the primary reasons people *avoid* developing their previously undeveloped strengths is fear of the imminent life changes that an increase in personal performance will require. Higher performance leads to higher expectations.

> *"If my performance stays where it is,"* their reasoning goes, *"then I won't run the risk of disappointing myself or others."*

The bad news is that they won't make themselves or others very happy either. This timid, failure-avoidance approach leads to repetition in personal and professional behavior. Repeating yesterday is a time-honored technique for getting from the cradle to the grave without experiencing anything really bad, or *really good*. In today's fast-paced business world, there's no future in that kind of thinking.

Repeating yesterday

Repeating yesterday can be a self-hypnotic behavior. Most people do it so regularly and effortlessly that they don't give it a thought. When I ask people if they regularly repeat yesterday, they usually reply, *"Gee, I never thought about it."* As soon as they think about it for a moment, they invariably admit that they habitually follow the same routines and patterns day-in and day-out.

The trance-like tendency to repeat yesterday produces a comforting feeling of *"the familiar."* That's why people look at you funny when you suggest doing something a bit unorthodox or somehow differently than it's been done before. It never ceases to amaze me that the rationale given most frequently for why something is done in a particular way is, "Because that's how we've always done it." You'd think that people would be ashamed to admit that such a reason is the best they can offer. Just the same, that's the answer I hear time and time again.

mation where any degree of "performance" is required or one?

If a person doesn't think s/he is repeating yesterday, then s/he probably is. The 19th-century author and great thinker Elbert Hubbard said that stagnation is evident when the past seems bigger and more important than the future. In other words, if you're consciously attempting to approach each day in a fresh, new, innovative way, then you're certainly not repeating yesterday. Focusing on the future is a guaranteed method of breaking the cycle of stagnation and the habitual ritual of repeating yesterday.

Stagnation = when the past seems bigger than the future.

Substance abuse

Because repeating yesterday is a way to stay in comfortable, familiar territory, and venturing into the reservoir of undeveloped strengths guarantees that things are going to change in life, it becomes easier to understand why we all have a natural inclination to remain in nonthreatening patterns. It makes as much sense as peeling a banana, eating the peel and throwing the banana away. If personal undeveloped strengths can be considered part of our essential substance, then repeating yesterday must be considered substance abuse.

People who repeat yesterday are in motion but not in *direction*. A strong sense that you're pedaling hard but going nowhere is a prime indication of cyclical repetition in your life. If you don't know where you're headed, but feel you are making good time, you've been on the treadmill too long. Effort needs to be associated with progress or hypnosis begins. Ask yourself throughout the day:

"Am I in direction right now or just in motion?"

Doing what doesn't work

A frighteningly common way that we repeat yesterday is by continuing to do what we already know doesn't work. It's fascinating to interrupt people who are about to do something for the umpteenth time and ask them point blank if they think their task is going to produce positive results. They usually give you that same funny look as before and shake their heads, "no." Once again, they are repeating behavior that they consciously know isn't getting them anywhere but do it anyway as a means of preserving the status quo. *Did I allow my problems with Karen to be used as an excuse for not pushing forward? When really the underlying problem was that I had insufficient passion for what I was doing (EA2 LL2) for the flames of enthusiasm to drive me beyond the problems the pretended self welled up with?*

Problems anyone?

During my tenure as a district sales manager for a large corporation, I counseled many team members about problems they encountered. One man had been selected as one of our top 10 rookies. It's not unusual for some people to get a fast start out of the blocks. However, the following year, the same man's production was near zero—not that unusual either.

When the two of us discussed his rapid decline, it became obvious that his job wasn't fun anymore. His fire had gone out. Under close examination, we discovered that, somewhere along the line, he had begun to see his customer transactions as problems. As a result, he developed the habit of carrying out 90 percent of his responsibilities by rote and stopping short of the critical 10 percent necessary to finish the job.

By unconsciously sabotaging the successful completion of his tasks he was *"avoiding"* problems. In reality, he was creating bigger problems. When I asked him if he realistically expected to execute his job without encountering problems, he admitted that he could not. Moreover, when he consciously prepared himself for the problems he knew were sure to come, he wasn't afraid of them at all.

He realized that his desire had been stifled by a natural but counterproductive defense mechanism against encountering the unexpected. Once he committed to stoking the furnace of desire again, problems became little more than part of the landscape and he went on to exceed even his previous performance.

Low performers don't tend to leave organizations as often as high performers. One of the myths business executives tend to believe is that high performers are content and confident. The fact is that more high performers hop from organization to organization than low performers. That's why business executives sometimes look around their organization and scratch their heads when they only see mediocre performers. Low performers tend to accumulate. High performers move on. Why?

High performers, feeling pressured to maintain their level of productivity, often move to new organizations so they can use the move as an excuse for ~~not maintaining the same high performance two years in a row.~~ *maintaining direction & not just motion –*

The *personal high-performance process* allows an individual to be credited for developing personal potential over time and diminishes unreasonable expectations. Managers who understand the *personal high-performance process* will keep their high performers and simultaneously raise the performance levels of everyone else in the organization at the same time.

When problems are dragged out and exposed to the light of day, they become less intimidating. Once you are liberated from fear of encountering problems, personal performance will start to climb.

Procrastination

Gathering information or learning something new tends to wake us from repetitious slumber. Those who would rather snooze become information *deflectors* rather than information gatherers. In much the same way, when we constantly promise that we'll get to something but never seem to, we're helping to preserve the past by postponing the present.

"*As long as change is in the future,*" their subconscious minds conclude, "*nothing's going to catch me unprepared today.*"

People who claim that they'll get down to business "*someday*" are forgetting that "*someday*" includes "*today*" as much as it includes any other day. The old saying that goes, "*Someday never comes*" really means that people who use "*someday*" as their deadline are really using "*never*" as their schedule for action. To high-performance people, "*someday*" means "*some now*".

At least people who pledge to act in the future are bringing a tacit indictment upon themselves for being aware that, at the very least, something needs to be done that's not being done now. The greatest

(postponing the present)
Someday must mean SOME NOW !

tragedy in repeating yesterday is that, by not looking enthusiastically toward the future, we admit that the high point of our lives is in the past, not in the future. That's not a very hopeful thought.

The new road

The only way to guarantee that tomorrow can be more exciting than yesterday is to embark on an action plan to set, pursue and achieve new goals. No new goals means old ones are being recycled. If getting up in the morning is difficult and there is little or no enthusiasm for the day ahead, there's no doubt that it's the old road that lies ahead, not a new one.

Repeating yesterday causes what former Disney executive Mike Vance, calls *"psychosclerosis"* or *"hardening of the mind."* Repeating yesterday can also be characterized as freezing at a single rung on life's ladder. It doesn't mean that no climbing has ever been done. It means that progress has stopped.

When past accomplishments occupy more daydreams than future visions, chances are good that every day starts back in the same old spot. No one in history was ever honored for how well they repeated yesterday. As a rule, honors are preserved for those who break new ground.

> *"Life is a lively process of becoming. If you haven't added to your interests during the past year; if you are thinking the same thoughts, relating the same personal experiences, having the same predictable reactions—rigor mortis of the personality has set in."*
> —General Douglas MacArthur

Exercise your potential

It only takes a couple of questions to determine where you stand in terms of current performance vs. potential performance. The exercise to determine the presence of untapped potential goes like this:

1. What am I currently earning? (Other types of accomplish- *NIL* ment or milestones can be substituted for earnings.)
2. Do I know what I would have to do to earn more? *YES*
3. What could I earn if I had more training or knowledge? *Dont have time now, have to use what I know.*

There once was a man who hung by his fingertips from the window ledge all night long only to discover at first light that his feet were only a few inches off the ground. I've never known anyone who completed this exercise without realizing how close s/he was to significant increases in performance and the rewards that go with it. It's a real eye opener, and a little embarrassing to acknowledge that the answers to improving performance have always been so close at hand.

The mentor's eye

The best view of ourselves is usually through someone else's objective eyes. That's why mentors are invaluable. Not only do people who we respect and who respect us offer nuggets of knowledge and wisdom, they can also provide priceless powers of observation. Peers with varied agenda and loyalties are hardly a reliable source of feedback. Not that the reactions of others aren't important, all input goes in to the mix of self-assessment. However, mentors have a genuine desire to see their charges grow and develop, and they don't spare the rod or sugar-coat the truth in their effort to help.

Let me be your mentor for a moment and I'll give you some high-performance characteristics that need to be developed in healthy doses if you intend to increase personal performance and keep it high. Studying people is something I do constantly and I recommend that you make it a habit, too. My personal library at home is filled with thousands of volumes that chronicle the achievements of great men and women through the centuries. My wife and I invest every moment we can on whatever continent is necessary to spend time with people of accomplishment. I just can't get enough of these people's thoughts and actions.

Learn, do, develop

Mentors don't have to know you. They don't even have to be alive. Studying and learning from the writings of great people are activities that we can do on our own time and at our own speed. Books are chunks of people's lives that anyone can experience. There are so many men and women who have blazed trails before us that we have no excuse for thinking we're encountering problems and challenges no one has ever seen before. We can take the time to figure out what others have *already* figured out or visit the public library and tap into the experiences of those who have gone before.

There are three actions that must accompany the seven-step high-performance process if there's to be a lasting commitment to becoming a high-performance person:

1. *Learn* and *visualize* how high-performance people, past and present, *think* and *act*. This is where the diligent study of successful people comes in.
2. *Do* what high-performance people *do*.
3. *Develop* the personal characteristics of high-performance people.

1. Learn

It's important to learn and visualize how high-performance people think and act because nobody has a crystal ball with which to predict the future. If the psychics we see on television or read about in the newspaper could *really* access the future, they would rule the world instead of doing psychic readings or writing syndicated columns for a living.

Pretend for a moment that you *can* reach out five years into the future and pull back a copy of the yellow pages, your company newspaper, *The Wall Street Journal,* your tax return or some other record of who's who and what's what. If you knew five years ago what you know now, chances are good that you'd be far better off than you are. But we can't predict the future. Neither could the successful people throughout history.

Repeating yesterday = Frozen on a step/Rung of Lifes ladder

One of the first things you learn in studying the lives of high-performance people is that they didn't plan every step on their road to success. However, each and every one of them had a strong sense of who they were and what their mission in life was. High-performance people think in high-performance terms and act accordingly. They can't predict what they will encounter along life's road, but they respond to their circumstances in ways that produce positive results.

Around the turn of the century, Orison Swett Marden said:

> *"Make every occasion a great occasion for you cannot tell when fate is testing you for something greater."*

Looking back five years into your past, how different would your life be now, both personally and professionally, if you had thought and acted in high-performance terms when you encountered the challenges and opportunities that came your way? I've got a news flash for you. Today and every day for the rest of your life there will be challenges and opportunities that can benefit you and those around you in a more meaningful and positive way *if you resolve to think and act like a high-performance person.*

2. Do

It's possible to have all the knowledge in the world and still repeat yesterday. Learning and visualizing what high-performance people think and do will not have any effect on your future until you begin to *do* what high-performance people *do*. Even if you begin in a limited, nonthreatening way, it's critical that you begin to *act*. If you learn something and don't act on it within 72 hours, all of the time, money and energy in learning it is wasted.

Throughout my many travels and extensive interaction with business people, I find that there is a tremendous gap that exists between how people do their jobs and *how they know how to do their jobs*. There isn't a person alive who isn't aware of how s/he could do what s/he does even better. The earlier three-question exercise on current performance vs. potential performance proves that you're among those who are a hair's breadth away from

I am a 'high performance people',
I have just lost the High Performance Sea
I was doing HP swimming in. Need a vehicle

breaking through in one or more areas in your life. In our effort to maintain the comfortable *familiar* we don't even do the things we *already know* would elevate us to the next performance level. Everyone commits self-sabotage in some way.

I've never met a person who couldn't come up with at least one idea or technique that would improve performance. Without engaging in the study and observation of high-performance people, past and present, every one of us already knows how to improve our personal performance. Therefore, think of how much farther and faster you would go if you spent some time learning and then *applying* what you've learned through *action.*

I used to think that the *Nike* shoes slogan, *"Just Do It,"* was a bit naive because it didn't explain exactly what it was that we were supposed to *"just do."* Then I remembered that we all know at least *one thing* that would boost our personal performance if we *"just did it."* Don't be intimidated by thinking that you have to mimic every behavior of every high-performance person you ever knew or studied. Start with one behavior and go from there.

My all-time pet peeve is someone explaining someone else's success by saying that s/he was/is a *"natural-born high achiever."* Not true. I've written in the past about the myth of the natural-born leader and the same is true of high-performance people. There is no such thing as a "natural-born" high-performance person. A high-performance person makes a specific decision to stop repeating yesterday and, in doing so, is fully aware of the conscious decision to elevate personal performance.

The decision to become a high-performance person is like getting a new birthday. In truth, our high-performance birthdays should be honored more than our chronological ones. Your actual date of birth has little or nothing to do with the decisions you make later that shape and determine your life.

It's true that childhood experiences, role models, social pressures and other factors will alter your appetite for work and accomplishment. However, a commitment to learn the things that must be learned and do the things that must be done to increase personal performance is a highly individual and completely informed decision. It doesn't happen unconsciously or by some kind of osmosis. No one is *born* with a personal commitment to high performance.

[handwritten: How did my commitment to Personal High Performance get smothered?]

3. Develop

Learning and launching into action what we've learned leads to the internalization of the ideas and principles involved. Learning and applying what's been learned are conscious and willful acts. Over time, the more we learn and the more action we take leads to the unconscious adoption of ideas and principles as our own. When I talk about developing the personal characteristics of high-performance people, I'm talking about the natural internalization of what we consciously commit ourselves to doing in the *learn* and *do* stages.

The experience of truly becoming a high-performance person includes the literal adoption of personal and professional principles that inform the way we think and act. The cycle is complete when the thoughts and actions of high-performance people become *our own* thoughts and actions.

Remembering that what's true in your personal life is true in your professional life, it's time to build consistency into your guiding principles. If you have constant conflict between the ethical construct or lifestyle requirements of your professional position and who you choose to be in your private moments, a career change might be in order. These personality traits are present in high performers that I've observed and studied over two decades and are the key ingredients of any high-performance personality. Think what high performers think and you'll find yourself doing what high-performance people do. Do what high performers do and you'll find yourself thinking the way high performers think.

My good friend Jim Rohn advises poor people to take rich people out to lunch and *listen*. Most poor people would reason that the person with all the money should buy *them* lunch. According to Jim, the poor person fails to understand that most rich people were poor at one time or another and have nothing to learn from someone who hasn't been able to overcome his or her poverty. It's the poor folks whose lives can be changed by learning from more successful people and adopting their thoughts and behavior.

[handwritten left margin: Think what they think & you's do what they do]

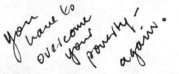

[handwritten: you have to overcome your poverty! again.]

Critical characteristics

I've observed that the people I respect most each have a *uncompromising integrity*. Don't ask them to bend the rules, leave work early or pad their paycheck with a little creative accounting. These people understand the reasons behind rules and regulations. They are not dedicated to strict codes of conduct for the sake of militaristic uniformity. They are interested in the long-term impact of their behavior and appreciate how their consistency in the present will benefit them and their organization down the road. Uncompromising integrity makes no sense unless you are looking at the larger, long-range picture.

High-performance people are *high-energy people* who refuse to get bogged down in unimportant matters. Knowing the difference between important and interesting can shape up your day considerably. The tendency for those who repeat yesterday to distract high-performance people is epidemic. As one of my mentors once told me: *"Don't walk away from negative people...run!"*

People who worry about the size of their paycheck more than the significance of their accomplishments instinctively try and turn the high-performance person's eyes away from important goals and entangle them in pettiness and counterproductive concerns. No one who is focused on the long-term best interests of the organization and the individuals within the organization will have time to waste on negativity and generally selfish matters.

There are big games and there are little games. High-performance people play at big games. One way to gauge whether you're on the road to higher personal performance is to take note of whether you're dealing with bigger issues or smaller issues than you were a year ago, a month ago or even a week ago.

One of the test pilots in the motion picture "The Right Stuff" had a terrific line. He said, *"You never know how far you can go until you've gone too far."* Are you holding yourself back because you're afraid of going too far? The truth is, nature has ways of telling us when we're going too far and we can adjust accordingly. There are natural barriers that define real limits. Our self-imposed barriers will never allow us to know the full range of our possibili-

Working Priorities — when each item gets to the top of the list it gets full energy as if it was first!

ties—unless we push our self-imposed barriers back. We never know the real meaning of the word _"yes"_ until we encounter the word _"no."_ It's the word _"stop"_ that gives meaning to the word _"go."_

High-performance people are _tough-minded problem-solvers_ who are stable under pressure. They're confidence is boosted by their commitment to keep their lives moving forward. High-performance people know how to _work priorities._ Simply making lists and assigning priorities isn't enough. Anybody can do that. In fact, most people who make priority lists turn right around and ignore them.

Every one of us has made a priority list, ranking tasks from most important to least important and then jumped into the list somewhere in the middle. _Working priorities_ means the top item on the list gets full energy until it's finished. As soon as that task is accomplished, the next item moves to the top of the list and gets the same treatment until every item gets its turn as the number-one item on the list. High-performance people never treat minor tasks as unimportant because they started at the bottom of a list. At some point in time, every item has its turn at the top of the list.

High-performance people are _courageous._ Safe plodders seldom end up at the head of the pack. High-performance people are not afraid to put the other foot down. Someone who leaves one foot dangling up in the air is waiting for everything to be right before s/he proceeds. Another news flash. If everything is right, if all conditions are perfect (which they never are), it would only be for a moment. By the time your foot hit the pavement, something, somewhere along the line would have changed.

In other words, waiting for everything to be right before proceeding means that you'll never get started, which is exactly _why_ the repeating-yesterday crowd does it. None of the famous inventors, explorers, leaders, scientists, change agents of any kind would be household words if they hadn't had the courage to take risks. If fear calls the shots in your life, your life will be spent in hiding. High-performance people make a point to do the things that they fear.

Have you ever done something that you feared, and survived to tell about it? If you have, I don't have to describe the feeling of exhilaration that goes along with it. Why not get that feeling on a regular basis. It's like waking up your taste buds with a wonderful delicacy. It never ceases to feel great. The more the circle of self-imposed barriers is pushed back, the more your sense of pleasure and reward comes back to life.

I've seen employees literally resurrected from emotional death by intentionally stepping out of their comfort zone. Good things can still happen to you when fear is in charge of your life. Taking the initiative to *make things happen* is evidence that you've taken command over your fear. Fear and confidence are mutually exclusive. Either you or your fear is in charge of your personal and professional lives.

High-performance people are *committed* and *dedicated hard workers.* These people are the first in the office and the last to leave. They love what they do and can't get enough of it. Don't confuse workaholism, which serves to avoid personal responsibilities, with genuine enthusiasm. People don't die from hard work in a job they love. However, workaholism can kill. I believe that work is a basic human need and we can't be fulfilled unless we are committed to some type of task.

High-performance people are *unorthodox* and have an *urge to create.* Leaders who want to have a record-breaking, pace-setting organization will choose an unorthodox and creative person over the safe, compliant bureaucrat every time. I've had people work for me that absolutely drove me up a wall. I'm not talking about loose cannons, but rather dedicated people who aren't afraid to try the unusual without permission and ask forgiveness later.

Many managers act as if unorthodox people are somehow threatening their precious authority. Forget it. Any leader worth his or her salt knows that his or her own success will be enhanced by the enthusiastic creativity and drive of unorthodox and creative people. It might take some getting used to at first, but the payoff is tremendous.

To increase your personal performance by acting more unorthodox and creative, you must help out those around you by being understanding and sensitive to the fact that your change will take some getting used to by others. It's unreasonable to expect everyone you live with or work with to immediately accept your new image. When they do though, you'll be happier and they'll be more excited and entertained by the relationship.

Perfect failures are more palatable than *screw ups* and less likely to impede future efforts. Learning from failed efforts means that the effort was not a total failure. What we customarily consider to be wasted effort isn't wasted at all if it provides us with knowledge of what not to do and, therefore, helps streamline the future.

High-performance people have the *goal orientation* to face tough decisions. Being able to focus on the goal is essential to keeping all energies flowing toward it. As always, the high-performance person will be tempted by distractions from those who find it easier and more comfortable to avoid goals. Many people willfully avoid setting goals and focusing their energies because they want to avoid accepting responsibility for the outcome, good or bad, at all costs. If the going is tough, staying focused on the goal will always bring the exercise to a faster conclusion and diminish the discomfort you may experience along the way.

On the surface, refusing to accept responsibility for how good we can become doesn't make much sense. Dig a little deeper and it becomes apparent that these people are not avoiding how good they can become as much as they're avoiding the perceived obligation to keep getting better once they begin to improve. They know that staying in a rut is a way to maintain control in life despite the knowledge that a better life is outside of the rut. At least the rut is certain, familiar and predictable.

Goals need to precede self-discipline, not the other way around. Many people use the excuse that they're not ready for goals because they lack structure in their lives. Goals and the need to focus on something beyond yourself are invaluable to creating and maintaining structure and order. You're not going to arrive at your destination safely if you drive with your eyes fixed on the rear-view mirror. You might as well not have a destination at all.

High-performance people have *inspired enthusiasm*. This isn't the first time I've mentioned enthusiasm. Yet it's important enough to have its own mention. Enthusiasm, whether it's present or absent, is *contagious*. People around you get what you've got.

That's what determines whether people want to be around you or want to avoid you.

Fall back on your own experience to confirm this one. Who do you want to be around and who do you prefer to avoid? You might not enjoy being in the presence of a screaming maniac who is spewing so much enthusiasm that you come away with stains on your clothes, but genuinely enthusiastic people are fun to be around. Genuinely lethargic or downright negative people are not much fun to be around. The choice is yours.

High-performance people are *realistic* and can organize turbulent situations. All of the enthusiasm and energy I've been describing doesn't mean that high-performance people have their heads in the clouds. These people are not likely to sit around and cry over spilled milk. Neither do they cling to the sordid details of a recent episode in their lives and bore you to tears as they recite them.

To the high-performance person, all of the characteristics I've listed are grounded in *reality*. It would be nice if people, left to their own devices, were always kind and generous with one another or sought to build one another up at every opportunity. Unfortunately, only a few people are like that. It would also be nice if money and creature comforts didn't take precedence over the needs of others in most people's lives. Wouldn't it be great if all people wanted desperately to work and grow in their personal and professional lives, and were willing to invest themselves in a career, starting at the bottom?

The list could go on and on. The point is that, although many things *would be nice,* they simply aren't realistic. High-performance people always strive toward benefiting the most people most of the time. However, they're realistic enough to acknowledge the difference between the exception and the rule. In doing so, high-performance people are much better equipped to achieve meaningful accomplishments and not waste their time on Pollyanna pursuits that ultimately benefit no one.

High-performance people know that mistakes happen. They're aware that people frequently fail to do what they say they'll do. They understand that circumstances change and that life is not always fair. Nevertheless, they accept those things that can't be changed and move forward in spite of them. Life may not be perfect, but human beings, guided by immutable principles, have a tremendous capacity to adap in an ever-changing environment.

Finally, high-performance people have a *desire to help others grow*. I don't think it's possible for someone to truly be committed to the high-performance process without helping others do the same thing. Except in the rarest of circumstances, we don't live and work in isolation. There is always someone, at some level, to interact with.

Synergy can only occur when there are multiple parties to contend with. Anyone with management experience knows that a group of people can have a collective negative energy or a collective positive energy. The negative energy is produced by self-absorption, invariably modeled by leadership. Positive energy is produced by team members making a concerted effort to help those around them—internal and external customers. Like the negative environment, the *positive* energy must be modeled and encouraged by the people in the visible, leadership roles.

When people are wandering aimlessly and don't know what to focus on, my first advice is to *find someone to help*. In the absence of any other specific directive, helping someone else grow and succeed is, in and of itself, an effective and life-changing goal that will produce structure and direction to end the drifting.

It makes a difference

Striving to improve personal performance is like running a race with no finish line. The process never ends as long as the high-performance person is alive. Bob Hope, Dr. Norman Vincent Peale, Mother Teresa, Norman Rockwell and Grandma Moses are only a few examples of people who have demonstrated no desire to ever stop getting better at what they do. Every one of them has or had a never-ending dedication to the principles I've just described.

The high-performance person won't accept 99.9 percent as *"good enough."* Natalie Gabal listed a series of effects that accepting 99.9 percent would have on our lives:

1. Two million documents would be lost this year by the IRS.
2. 811,000 faulty rolls of 35mm film would be loaded into cameras this year.
3. 22,000 checks would be deducted from the wrong bank account in the next 60 minutes.
4. 12 babies would be given to the wrong parents each day.
5. 268,500 defective tires would be shipped this year.
6. 2,488,200 books would be shipped this year with the wrong covers.
7. Two airliner landings each day at O'Hare Airport would be unsafe.
8. 3,056 copies of tomorrow's edition of *The Wall Street Journal* would be missing three sections.
9. 18,322 pieces of mail would be mishandled in the next hour.
10. 291 pacemaker operations will be performed incorrectly this year.

A way of life

Dedicating yourself to the *high-performance process* means committing your talents and energies to an ongoing agenda. It's not something you do from nine to five and then leave at the office. Becoming a high-performance person is more than a way of working, it's a way of living.

To summarize this overview, I can't improve on the words of Phillips Brooks, so I'll just pass them on:

"Once you discover that you've only been living half a life, the other half will haunt you until you develop it."

STEP ONE
Your Moment of Truth: Selecting the Desired Rewards

"The bravest are surely those who have the clearest vision of what is before them, glory and danger alike, and yet notwithstanding, go out to meet it."

—*Thucydides*

The quality of our lives is a direct result of the choices we make. That makes how we go about making choices very important. Having those *different kind of eyes* I mentioned earlier becomes increasingly valuable as we attempt to peer into the future. We can't of course. Peer into the future, that is. We can only *predict* what we *think* the future might bring, based upon our present knowledge and experience.

Stunt man/filmmaker Hal Needham decided to jump a California river bed with a rocket-powered pick-up truck. This kind of stunt was not unusual for Hal. However, it was one of his more dangerous endeavors. I asked him if he was ever bothered by his mortality. I wondered if he ever considered the fact that this kind of behavior could cost him his life.

When I confronted him with the fact that he was playing a high-stakes, life-and-death game, he calmly replied, *"If I'm killed doing one of these stunts, I'll have the comfort of knowing that I died doing exactly what I wanted to be doing."* Hal is still alive. He's been mighty banged-up over the years, but he's still around, doing exactly what he loves to do.

Weighing the pros and cons of your actions in terms of future consequences is a constant challenge. If your eyes are fixed on what lies ahead of you, then you're at least pointed in the right direction. One of the reasons so many people fixate on the past and literally back into the future is to avoid facing the dreaded *"moment of truth."*

In our moment of truth or turning point, each of us must call upon our life experience and accumulated knowledge as well as our best instincts to make decisions. What scares most folks is that they must also bear responsibility for the wisdom or folly of their decisions. In not turning around and looking squarely into the potential positive *and* negative consequences of their decisions, some people feel as if they can avoid responsibility for the outcome.

Unfortunately for them, there's no way to avoid responsibility, regardless of the outcome. The axiom, *"Not to decide is to decide,"* is so common it's almost a cliché. Nevertheless, for many people, it's somehow emotionally less threatening to passively allow the future to take its course without making any effort to set the stage for it.

Going through life without facing moments of truth is like piloting a rudderless ship. If ending up wherever the wind and current take you is preferable to accepting responsibility for plotting your own course, you're not ready for the *high-performance process.* High-performance people are people who have definite intentions about life and how they want to live it. They weren't necessarily born that way, but somewhere along the line they decided to take charge of their lives.

The courage of a 5-year-old

Children often cut to the chase much more fearlessly than adults do. Observing children reveals much about human character that adults have become too adept at hiding. Predicting the potential cost of our decisions is relative to what we value most. Our decision-making courage or cowardice is measured by the potential downside consequences of our decisions. When I observe someone add up the positives and negatives, contemplate the consequences and then boldly make a decision, I'm impressed. I'm impressed by people who aren't afraid to ask the *hard questions.*

My grandson Rex was in kindergarten when he caught a case of spring fever. It hadn't been too long before in his young life that he had the freedom to come and go with his mother as their schedules allowed. So he probably thought he had a good chance of convincing his mom to play hooky with him for a day.

Living in Southern California, Rex was well aware of the many diversions that would make excellent alternatives to a day in the classroom.

"Mom, it's too beautiful today to go to school. Can we go to the beach?" He asked.

"No, honey," his mom replied. *"You have to go to school today."*

Rex figured that the destination he had suggested wasn't enticing enough to gain his mother's compliance.

"Then how about Disneyland? Think of the fun we could have there," the little salesman continued.

"No, Rex," his mother countered, hip to his trick, *"you have to go to school today."*

Rex was en route to a moment of truth, his own turning point you might say.

"Why?" Rex was taking the argument to a new level.

Facing her own moment of truth, she decided to appeal to her son's sympathies.

"Because if you don't go to school, they could put me in jail."

He looked at her for about two seconds, put his hands on his hips, cocked his head to one side and asked,

"For how long?"

My daughter was correct in thinking that she had steered her son to his own moment of truth. However, she didn't realize that he hadn't *quite* arrived. As far as he was concerned all options weren't exhausted yet. In short, the potential negative consequences of *his* decision grew out of a different set of priorities. She had hoped to make the decision for him by placing him in an untenable position. But, as she turned more cards over on the table, he simply asked to see the next card.

None of us can claim to have truly experienced a moment of truth until we have looked at all the cards. Only looking at the good cards or the bad cards means we aren't fully accepting the challenge to make the best-informed decision possible.

Selecting desired rewards

To this point I've attempted to heighten your awareness of how much your personal success depends upon your total commitment. As we each stand at our personal turning point, each one of us determines where it is we want to go and what we want when we get there. Recognizing that nothing worth having comes easy and the good always comes with some measure of the bad, we nevertheless set a course and lay out our flight plan accordingly.

We have much more control over our destinations, or rewards if you prefer, than we do the route to achieving them. Once in a while we might get lucky and negotiate our plotted course flawlessly. It's more likely, however, that we'll need to alter our course many times along the way to accommodate uncharted obstacles and other variables beyond our control.

What keeps us returning to the stated goal is whatever we feel makes the new effort worthwhile. Like my grandson Rex demonstrated, it's not the reward we seek that drives us forward as much as how badly we desire it. We might have to alter course many times or even plot one or more *new* courses in the pursuit of out desired rewards. A high-performance person might also put it this way: *"Many roads lead to the goal."* You must be looking forward to keep your eyes on the prize.

Butt snappers

As jet fighters were being introduced to the Air Force, a problem arose with ejection seats. Jets flew faster and higher than their propeller predecessors and pilot ejection in cases of emergency became a more sophisticated and dangerous predicament. Ejection seats were separated from the cockpit by an explosive charge equal to a 35mm artillery shell to insure that the pilot cleared the aircraft before the parachute deployed.

The pilot simply needed to roll forward out of the seat once clear of the aircraft and the parachute would be free to open. Unfortunately, a common problem started to pop up (no pun intended) in some ejections. Some pilots would pull up both arm rests exposing the ejection seat triggers, squeeze the triggers detonating the explosive that launched the pilot and seat 150 to 175 feet above the aircraft.

Then, instead of letting go, some pilots kept a death grip on the seat handles, reluctant to separate themselves from the last tangible piece of the airplane that had, until then, always been a safe place. As long as the pilot remained in the ejection seat, the parachute remained trapped against the seat back, unable to open. Striking the ground at 200 miles-per-hour, still sitting in an ejection seat with an unopened parachute *will* ruin your whole day!

The Air Force went back to the ejection seat manufacturers with the problem and the government contractors returned with a solution. The new design called for a two-inch webbed strap that attached to the front edge of the seat, under the pilot and behind him, and attached to an electronic take-up reel behind the head rest. Two seconds after ejection, the electronic take-up reel would immediately take up the slack, forcing the pilot forward out of the seat thus freeing the parachute to open. The pilot was *"butt-snapped"* to safety.

A body in motion tends to remain in motion and a body at rest tends to remain at rest until acted upon by an external force. Dr. Alexis Carrel used this definition of inertia in a sentence:

"Life leaps like a geyser for those who drill through the rock of inertia."

In a seminar, I once quoted Dr. Carrel and gave a lengthy dissertation on the role of external forces to overcoming inertia. After I had finished, one of those in attendance came up to me and winked.

"I know what you're trying to say about overcoming inertia," the man said. *"What you mean to say is that we need butt snappers on every chair around the office."*

A *butt snapper,* as he described it, is something akin to a spring-loaded *whoopee cushion.* The bottom line is that, when detonated, it launches your rear end out of the chair. So, if words like *"external forces overcoming inertia"* leave you uninspired, think about what *butt snappers* on everyone's chairs would do to productivity around the office. Think about how much a *butt snapper* on your own chair would do to your personal productivity.

The tough road

A man I'm proud to call my friend had a troubled childhood. So troubled, in fact, that he graduated from not one, but *two* reform schools. Later in his life he went on to make two multi-million-dollar fortunes in separate fields. He told me once that he made the second fortune just to prove to himself that the first one wasn't luck. I like his spirit.

When I asked him how he did it he told me that he asked himself four questions. But unlike most people, he *listened* to his answers. Until he pointed it out, I hadn't realized how often we ask ourselves probing questions without listening to the answers. The answers are always there when we engage in self-inventory. Unfortunately, we simply ignore them most of the time or note only the portions that don't present a major personal threat. The questions always seem harmless enough, it's the *answers* that are scary.

It's time to turn off the easy road to nowhere and take the harder road to where you can genuinely feel happy and satisfied. Truthful answers to tough questions become landmarks along your journey. If you question your own candor, just imagine that you've been shot with sodium pentothal (truth serum) and have no choice but to answer truthfully.

I've kept on doing what I can do instead of what I want to do. (With the exception

Question one: What do I really want?

of writing that is, which domestic issues white anted)

There has to be some reason for all the hard work you do. We never do anything for *no reason*. If it seems that way at times, it's because we're in such an ingrained pattern that we're functioning in a trance. How many times has someone startled you awake by asking, *"what are you doing?"* Whatever it was that you were doing, you were doing it in a trance.

Why were you doing something so familiar and redundant that you were in a trance? Why had that activity become such a habit that you could do it while semi-conscious? Ultimately there was a reason. And so it is with everything we do. Whether we do it in a trance or with hyper-focus, there's a conscious or unconscious reason for everything we do.

If someday you look back down your life's course and say, *"That's what I proudly did with my life,"* what landmarks would you be looking at? A friend and mentor of mine once asked me, *"Wouldn't it be Hell if someday God showed you what you could have done with your life?"* Since then I've often wondered if I would want to sit down some day after I've graduated to the other side and watch *"The Life And Times Of Danny Cox—As They Should Have Been."* Would you want to watch your movie?

You propel yourself closer to your selected rewards when you make conscious choices to do what you do for *good* reasons. If the reason behind every action is well thought out, then each action works in concert with every other action to keep things moving toward your desired rewards. Identifying what you want and making sure that everything you do moves you closer to that goal takes much of the chance out of your personal success equation.

Question two: What does it cost?

Talk about mitigating factors. If defining desired rewards is important to motivation, then evaluating potential costs is important to avoiding *demotivation*. As my grandson Rex figured out, there is a line that needs to be drawn that establishes when the desired reward is no longer desirable because the cost is too high.

Cost evaluation is often improperly used as an excuse for not boldly trying something new. While it's irresponsible to set goals without considering the negative implications, it's just as irresponsible to misrepresent the potential liabilities of positive action. As with so many things in life, it's appropriate to strike a healthy balance between courage and caution.

A bang-up lesson

Teaching people about costs is a powerful behavior modification tool, just like rewards are. While getting rewards for appropriate behavior is always more pleasant than receiving some form of punishment, the two influences have been known to shape what we do. I had a radar observer I'll call *Gibs (that's fighter-pilot lingo for "guy in back seat")* who flew in the rear seat of my F-101 fighter during my Air Force days. Gibs was a good example of how costs can influence behavior.

Gibs and I were on alert status during a war games exercise at an Air Force base outside of Tucson, Arizona. Alert status means that you've got to be ready to go at the sound of an alarm. It doesn't matter if you're sound asleep. When the alarm sounds, the pilot and radar observer have to go from a sound sleep to being airborne in under five minutes. Stopping to shower, shave and read the newspaper was out.

Obviously there is a great amount of training, preparation and coordination between flight crew and ground crew involved. Gibs and I had rehearsed the exercise thousands of times. Everything from our flight suits to the seat belt harnesses in the cockpit were precisely preset to maximize efficiency of movement when the time came to *scramble*.

It was a regular ballet. No wasted motion could be tolerated. Every detail of the preflight and take-off process had been memorized and rehearsed until it was second nature. One hand was starting engines and adjusting throttles while the other hand was buckling belts and moving on to another hundred small-but-critical tasks—all without stopping to think about it. Ultimately, the idea was to get off the ground and engage the enemy before the enemy catches you on the ground.

The Air Force brass wasn't at all happy with poor performance in the war games that measured our country's military preparedness. The positive rewards we received for superior performance were decorations and honors for our outfit. However, among the costs of poor performance was a concentrated dose of what was already grueling training.

Gibs and I were sleeping in the alert barn located near the end of the runway where the fighters were poised for immediate departure when the "scramble" horn went off. Instantly we were in our flight suits and climbing into the cockpit. Literally within moments I was swinging the fighter onto the runway in a rolling takeoff. When I lit both afterburners it felt like we had been rear-ended. Within 13 seconds we went from 0 to 200 miles per hour.

The ballet seemed flawless with each movement becoming more like instinct than learned behavior. So it was not unnatural to be instantly aware of any deviation in the pattern. But deviation there was. Almost the moment we became airborne I noticed a loud banging. It was not like any sound I had heard before. It sounded like somebody was outside the aircraft using a jackhammer on the fuselage.

The canopy was closed and there was no way to confirm visually or with instruments what was causing the banging. I requested a fly-by so the crew in the control tower could examine the exterior of the aircraft. The tower reported seeing nothing unusual. About then Gibs informed me that, in the haste of our departure, he had forgotten to fasten his shoulder harness. The big metal buckles were dangling outside the canopy where they had been preset for quick attachment as he got settled into his seat. Now they were banging against the metal skin of the aircraft. At speeds of several hundred miles per hour the buckles were banging pretty hard. I immediately decided to abort the flight and land the aircraft. There was no telling how much damage those buckles could do.

Gibs sheepishly admitted that he forgot to fasten his seat belt, too. Maybe to redeem himself he offered to cut the straps loose. I instantly had a vision of the big metal buckles getting sucked into the air intake of the left engine. That would have been sure disaster. I instructed Gibs to leave the straps where they were and I landed the aircraft with the straps hanging on either side of the cockpit.

It seemed like the entire United States Air Force was waiting for us when we taxied in. As we taxied, Gibs said, *"I think I'm in trouble.* I replied, *"I know you're in trouble.* As you can imagine, we had not been a shining example of American military preparedness that day and we had brought embarrassment upon our outfit in front of the combat readiness inspection team from headquarters. Our local commanders were not pleased.

Gibs and I went through an interrogation the likes of which I had never seen before. All Gibs had done was forget to fasten his shoulder harness. Yet it had nearly brought down our aircraft. After we had been grilled by our commanding officers, Gibs was sent out to pay the price for his oversight and the cost *was* high.

Carrying a 65-pound ladder and wearing his crash helmet and parachute, he had to do a complete cockpit preflight preparation in every one of the 18 fighters in our group—by himself. In the 110-degree Tucson sun, Gibs got so hot that his body stopped perspiring. It doggone near killed the man, but the brass had a point to make and Gibs had a lesson to learn. Gibs was practically staggering when he reported back to the commander who asked him, *"Do you have any questions about how to set up the cockpit of an F-101?"*

About a year later, in a similar exercise near Nellis Air Force Base outside of Las Vegas, Gibs and I heard a slow thumping while in flight. Almost before I could ask Gibs if he heard the thumping, he shouted, *"It's not my shoulder straps."* Gibs had learned the cost of not fastening his shoulder harness and there was no other malfunction at that moment that posed as much of a threat to him as the cost of not flawlessly executing his preflight exercise. The thumping was caused this time by a mechanical malfunction that was later corrected.

Rewards are great motivators, but sometimes so are the potential costs. Never take the costs too lightly. They're always an important part of the decision-making equation.

Question three: Am I willing to pay the price?

Before my grandson Rex was willing to answer question three, he wanted a precise assessment of the price to be paid. After his torture in the hot Arizona sun, Gibs didn't need much reminding that the price for negligence during war games was too high to consider for any reason. To Rex, the price of his mother spending some time behind bars might have been worth a day at *Disneyland,* providing the sentence wasn't too long. Of course it wasn't a price that he had to pay *directly* either.

There will always be a price to pay for a worthwhile goal. Achieving our desired rewards, whether they be personal, social or professional, will cost us something. Time, effort and the opportunity to be doing something else are all things that we potentially give up in pursuing our goals.

Too high a price

Another of my less humorous Air Force experiences illustrates what can happen when the price is too high and the person faced with paying it is unwilling. I was stationed in the Philippine Islands and running intercepts on a simulated target aircraft the day I witnessed a mid-air collision between two Philippines Air Force (PAF) fighters.

There were lots of scattered clouds that day and the Filipino pilots were also running air intercept exercises. With jet aircraft zipping in and out of the clouds at several hundred miles per hour, there's a heightened need for care and vigilance. It was also a mountainous region and, as the saying goes in the Air Force, some of the lower clouds have "rocks" in them.

I was on my way to intercept my target when I noticed the two PAF aircraft coming dangerously close to each other. I assumed they would break away to avoid each other as I momentarily lost sight of them in a cloud. Philippine and United States military operations were separate and I had no radio contact. It became apparent that they had collided when I saw a puff of black smoke and one of the fighters spiraling out of the cloud toward the earth. The other airplane had apparently disintegrated.

As I spotted the Philippine fighter going in, the aircraft didn't appear to be unflyable. I decided to abort my intercept and dove down to catch up with the earth-bound pilot. As I caught up with him, the pilot didn't appear to be unconscious. His head was erect and he appeared to be looking forward. I rolled my aircraft in front of him to make sure he could see me. He didn't respond. I tried calling him on the emergency frequency and even used hand signals to get his attention, all to no avail.

I got an eerie feeling on top of the adrenaline rush of the crisis. I knew he could see me but he wouldn't respond. I was there to be whatever help I could be. I tried giving him more hand signals to eject or pull out of his spiral. Still no response. I was convinced he knew exactly what I was doing. He was simply seized up by panic, or "clanked" as we called it in the Air Force.

It was downright creepy watching another fighter pilot disappear into the clouds still at the controls of his fighter. He simply didn't want to be helped. An investigation of the wreckage a few days later revealed that he never did try to eject. As it turned out, he was the only Filipino pilot I knew personally. Neither he nor I recognized each other in those frenzied few moments as anything other than fellow pilots.

In the Air Force, a "graveyard spiral" is like being in a rut with a sudden stop at the end. My Filipino friend apparently rode his graveyard spiral all the way to the ground because he was not willing to pay what, to him, was too high a cost for the chance to survive the mid-air collision. In his mind, culture and world view, the price he paid with his life cost him less than the alternative of survival. Although this example is admittedly extreme, the point is well-taken. In the Filipino pilot's moment of truth, he asked himself whether he was willing to pay the price. I witnessed his answer through confused and helpless eyes.

Question four: When is the best time to start paying the price?

Now. Stop and think about it. If you've decided that you're willing to pay the price to achieve your desired rewards, then what could possibly make delay worthwhile? The future is nothing more than a series of *nows* approaching you, all in a row. Sure, if you miss the present *now,* there will be another one right behind it.

The future is nothing more than a series of NOWS, approaching you, all in a row.

But what's the point of letting any of them go by without enriching them with positive, progressive action?

By the time you reach the end of this sentence, someone, somewhere will have taken a positive, progressive action. It happens just that quickly. Because each positive, progressive action propels you closer to achieving your desired rewards, seizing the first available moment makes sense. Our parents and grandparents used to say, *"Never leave until tomorrow what can be done today."* British author and flamboyant personality Quentin Crisp said:

> *"Don't take too long to decide. You can become what you don't want to be."*

You already know from personal experience how good it feels to wake up knowing that an important project or a series of smaller but equally vital tasks are behind you and not still waiting to be done. The future becomes the past the instant that it passes the control point known as *now*. I call *now* the *control point* because neither the future nor the past can be controlled. The only place we can influence what happens to us is in the present.

Boeing Aircraft Corporation came out with some great advertisements several years ago. The advertisements featured a beautiful blue sky with the caption, *"Tomorrow you can be anywhere."* Below the photograph the copy continued:

> *"All of us have dreams of going off someday to a special someplace, to a lonely beach, to an historic city, back home."*

Another ad featured a couple walking along a white, sandy beach with the surf rolling in. The copy read:

> *"Someday we'll take off, just the two of us. No kids, no pets, no worries. We'll lay on a lonely beach and plan another hundred years together."*

Then came the challenge:

> *"Remember the first time you mentioned going away? How many somedays ago was that? Is your warm and wonderful someday every really going to happen?"*

The final advertisement in the three-part series featured Venice, Italy, at sunset with romantic gondolas gliding by in the foreground. The message read:

> *"Someday we're going to see the other side of the world. As soon as the kids are grown...or after retirement...or maybe after that."*

What's after *that?* It's *now* that makes all the difference. The only place we can act is in the *now*. If the price is worth paying, it's worth paying *now*. Even though it sounds so simple it's still hard to get moving. There is something inherently scary about making that step or taking that leap. I've already explained how accepting responsibility for our actions is often a frightening thought that freezes us up. The only place we can freeze up is *now*.

Types of goals

When setting out to identify what it is you truly *want,* it's crucial to understand what type of goal you're dealing with. There are basically three types of goals:

1. Financial Goals
2. Lifestyle Goals
3. Personal Growth Goals

Financial goals are most often what people consider first. There's nothing wrong in that. Financial resources seem to represent a sort of universal language. British author and playwright Somerset Maugham, said it this way:

> *"Money is like a sixth sense. Without it you can not fully appreciate the other five."*

The lifestyle goal deals with how you want to live. It's one thing to have financial resources. It's something altogether different to decide what exactly you're going to do with your money. My grandson Rex, was contemplating how to spend his mother's money and freedom in light of a lifestyle choice.

The questions of where to live and how to live
son to the question, *"What should I live for?"*
personal growth. It's possible, even commonplac
consumed with the acquisition and alloca
resources without ever considering *who you are* as a human
Yet it's an unwritten law that we must grow personally if we're to
continue making bigger and better things happen in our lives.

All goals, whether they be *financial, lifestyle or personal
growth,* must also be *realistic, measurable, challenging* and, therefore, *exciting.* How, or why for that matter, would you want to
invest the energy to break through that rock of inertia if the goal
you seek isn't exciting?

When I asked my friend who had graduated from two different
reform schools how *big* my goals should be, he answered, *"Big
enough to turn you on."* If you're feeling a little depressed, unmotivated or uninspired, you obviously don't have any goals that *turn
you on.* Each one of us has the ability to set goals that excite us.
The secret to what excites each of us is found within our personal
compositions. The terrific promise in your moment of truth is that
what you elect to pursue can and should stimulate you.

FiRST GOAL: CUT FUTURE LOOSE FROM

Present problems and their relationship to goal-setting

Anchors of the PAST.

Goal-setting and problem-solving are so similar that they are
often scarcely distinguishable. Goals should be more than new outcomes somewhere in the future. Goals should also be a commitment to solve problems of the past that continue to contaminate
the present. Many people tell me that they tried goal-setting in
the past and it didn't work.

They say it felt like their feet were nailed to the floor and they
just couldn't get anywhere no matter how much energy they exert-
ed. When people share these experiences with me I immediately
suspect that there are unresolved past problems acting like an
anchor. That's why your *first goal* must be the solution of whatever is weighing you down. Cutting your future loose from anchors
of the past is essential to goal attainment.

Executive insomnia

I love all of the programs I conduct on personal high performance, leadership and customer service. However, I get particular satisfaction out of a three-hour program I do for senior executives at large corporations. I was once a senior executive for one of the nation's largest firms and I know where the skeletons are hidden. In learning how not to rock the boat, I learned what *rocks* the boat. Moreover, I've now spent the better part of 20 years conducting seminars for and consulting with businesses large and small. My finger is on the proverbial pulse.

It's my personal mission to keep these top executives awake not only for the three hours of the seminar, but for many nights thereafter. I want to rattle as many cages as I can. I want to stomp on their mental toes. I now live for the once-repressed freedom to speak out and tackle the difficult issues and ask the hard questions for which I would have been ostracized when I was on the corporate payroll.

You can imagine how much I enjoy being invited to address the folks at the top. Let me describe the scene. These upper-level seminars are held, of course, in the *upper room* somewhere in the *ivory tower*. Like the problems that most large companies like to keep hidden, the boardroom is a very private place known as the *sanctum sanctorum,* truly the *holy of holys*.

There is always a breathtaking conference table featuring inlaid, exotic, imported woods or marble. The executives take their appointed places around this corporate *altar* and watch the next person up the food chain for cues on when to speak and when to remain silent. I now stand in front of richly paneled walls recalling how intimidating this whole scene was back when the person at the head of the table signed my paycheck and I had to keep a sharp eye on the person up the food chain as well as the next person down the food chain.

Even though, as a consultant, the same person still pays my fee, I now get my fee up front. The head honcho expects me to come in and shape up the staff, not the president or the CEO. Wrong. I stand knee-deep in plush carpet, no longer intimidated as I was as an employee, but bursting with excitement about the journey I'm about to launch these people on. Little do they know that the president and/or CEO will be in the bow of the boat. These conferences are fun for me because I take no prisoners. I grant these highly paid executives no quarter.

As soon as the bell sounds for round one (usually a droll introduction by a starchy CEO), I turn to the highest-ranking executive in the room and ask, *"Do you have problem-solving meetings at this company?"* The answer comes back as if it were recorded on a wire. "We most certainly do." The explanation usually goes something like this:

> *"Every week we meet in this very room and I personally conduct the problem-solving meeting. The executive vice president, the senior vice president, the first vice president, the human resources director, the training director and every other key player are present."*

At this point I ask if there is anyone else present at the meetings. The president or CEO thinks for a moment and appears to be stumped. I prompt the executive a little.

"How about your secretary?"

"Of course," comes the reply. *"Someone has to take notes and distribute them."*

I play dumb.

"Then everyone here has the minutes from last week's problem-solving meeting?"

"Of course we do," comes the confident reply once more. *"We have them in our offices, on the shelf in silk-screened three-ring binders, filed by week, month and year."*

Then I make my move.

"Then what I would like everyone to do is get up right now, go back to your offices and come back with last week's problem-solving meeting notes."

They start to get up, a little annoyed that they weren't told in advance to bring the notes with them. I stop them before they get out of their chairs.

"Wait a minute, there's more." I continue. *"Also bring some meeting notes from six months ago, one year ago, two years ago and three years ago."*

By now they begin sinking back into their seats. Someone nervously says, *"Let's do that later. Right now let's just go on with the seminar."*

"This is the seminar." I insist, knowing full well that they don't want to fetch their notes because I'm going to point out that the same problems have remained unsolved for six months, one year, 18 months or more. I'll save you, the reader, the cost of an upper-level executive seminar by simply asking, *"How long have you been working on the same list of problems?"*

The longer the period of time that you've been working on the same set of problems, the more comfortable your set of problems must be. People laugh nervously when I say that in my seminars. It's a disturbing notion to many to think that problems can be *"comfortable."* But they are and that's why we tend to keep them around like a favorite old sweater.

If I could just snap my fingers and solve the problems that have been holding you back, most people would panic and begin to hyperventilate. They would feel naked.

"What would I do at work tomorrow?" They would ask.

"How about make progress?" I would calmly respond. *"What had you planned to work on tomorrow?"*

Most people don't realize that they purposefully keep their desk piled high with problems so that they have something to worry and stew about from morning till night. Is that you? Do you have a Ph.D. in worrying and stewing? Your assignment is to identify which problems should be at the top of your goals list.

Top the list

The sodium pentothal is still flowing through your veins, you cannot avoid the truth. You must answer honestly. The first question to ask in identifying the problem(s) that are holding you back:

What is my biggest unresolved problem?

Answer carefully. The problem that pops into your head may not be the correct answer. Remember that we play all sorts of conscious and unconscious mental tricks on ourselves in order to maintain a comfortable and familiar security zone around us. What your mind offers up as a major problem might be a diversion. The one true test that reveals what your biggest unresolved problem really is comes in the answer to this question:

What do I spend most of my day dealing with?

Behavior speaks louder than words. What we say and what we do are often two different things. Our stated intentions might be very admirable. However, it's what we actually *do* that reveals our real priorities. If you log a week of your life, it will become apparent where your priorities are.

I don't mean look at your calendar alone and note what you intend to do. Calendar entries account for very little of the actual time we spend on this planet. Logging your day means actually stopping periodically and spending a few minutes noting what you've been spending your time doing. Many people avoid the task of logging their day because they truly don't want to know what they spend their time doing.

It might sound like I'm accusing every human being of avoiding the truth. The truth is, I think we *all* tend to focus on what preserves the familiar status quo and avoid making ourselves aware of the things that present personal challenges. It's a conscious and willful choice to become a high-performance person. Becoming a high-performance person and expanding the horizons of personal achievement is an unnatural decision that leads to extraordinary achievement.

If you feel like all of this questioning and personal reflection is leading you to the very extremes of your comfort zone, then it's *working*. Stay with it. Change is seldom comfortable, especially if it's taking you into unfamiliar territory. However, it is always exciting. Like my reform school-graduate friend says, if it's not stimulating and exciting, what's the point?

So find out what you do all day long and therein will be the real answer to the question, *"What's my biggest unresolved problem?"*

Now that you're aware that your biggest unresolved problem is probably serving to keep you going around in circles, you simply need to spot the circles. Find the biggest circle and you've found the biggest problem.

Once you've identified what your biggest unresolved problem is and you have it at the top of your goals list, the next question becomes: What am I doing about it?

This question has pretty much been answered already. Nevertheless, it's important to ask. If nothing else, the process of answering this question might help highlight the absurdity in how we deal with problems. For example, if the problem has been keeping you occupied as I've already pointed out, then the fact is that you've probably been investing energy in keeping the problem around, *not in solving it.*

If the problem is big, comfortable and familiar, then it's incumbent upon you to change your attitude about whether your life is better served by what's comfortable or by what's challenging, exciting and stimulating. Answering the second question, in turn, gives you a head start on question number three:

"If I'm not doing anything to solve the problem, why am I not doing anything to solve the problem?"

The interesting revelation here is that companies tend to have the same problems that people do. Why? Because they're made up of people. A company doesn't desire a big comfort zone, protected and padded with old, familiar problems, the way people do. However, when you pile a whole bunch of people into an organization, their collective comfort zones add up to one enormous problem-avoiding mechanism for the company.

Avoiding effort

One reason that personal problems or the problems of an entire organization go unresolved is because problem-resolution requires effort. Exerting effort, of course, is never as comfortable as coasting. If a problem is of any appreciable size, effort will always be required to resolve it. The only problems that require no effort to resolve are problems not worth worrying about.

I never fail to ask company leaders what their company's biggest unresolved problem is. Every one of them quickly gives me some kind of answer. Sometimes it's efficiency within the organization. Other times it's massive turnover in the sales department or difficulty holding on to talented people in other departments. No matter what the unresolved problem is, I follow up by asking *who* has been assigned the task of solving the problem.

It's amazing how many companies don't have anybody assigned to tackle their largest unresolved problems—or any major problems for that matter. Sometimes the company head will sheepishly acknowledge that there once was someone assigned to the problem, but that person quit and wasn't replaced. You would think that keeping big problems around is more important to some organizations than keeping good people.

As I mentioned, these company heads can identify their number-one problem. They usually admit to having a meeting sometime back where the biggest problems facing the company were identified and ranked in priority. When I ask what problem the company is currently working on, if any, I'm often told that they're working on number 10 or 12. I ask what's going on with 1 through 9 only to find out that they're being avoided, ostensibly because they require too much effort to deal with.

Selling sonic booms

Those who have been in my seminars, heard me speak in other situations or read my first book already know that I was the first *"sonic boom salesperson"* in the United States Air Force. The title and the activity itself emerged from my answer to the question, *"What's the biggest unresolved problem in your fighter squadron?"*

With the advent of supersonic fighters, pilots like me were dragging sonic booms all over the countryside and annoying just about everybody who heard them. People didn't like being awakened at 4 a.m. by plaster falling in their face or by their windows being broken. Farmers were convinced that their chickens would not lay eggs and their cows wouldn't give milk because of the noise. Exaggerated claims that sonic booms caused everything from headaches to infertility kept an angry public up in arms.

Although sonic booms were our number-one problem in a peacetime Air Force, at least for those of us who had to live around the folks with broken windows and cracked ceiling plaster, I was embarrassed to admit that we were making no effort to resolve the problem. I felt a twinge of guilt as I told the fellow who had asked the question that we were trying to *learn to live with the problem.*

How many times have you said that to yourself in the course of your personal and/or professional affairs? Learning to live with it is a copout if their ever was one. It's ridiculous. So I went out and spoke to hostile audiences as a representative of the United States Air Force, explaining why sonic booms were our edge against communist aggression and other threats to our national security. I called my 30-minute speech, "Better Boomed Than Bombed."

I created the job and filled the vacancy. The Air Force was only too happy for me to help get angry citizens off its back. The base switchboards had been lit up almost constantly since supersonic testing had begun. In a lesson that would help me become a successful corporate leader in the years that followed, I learned to turn adversity into opportunity.

My speaking challenges were opportunities for creativity. I would dress up in my "go-fast" suit with all of my medals proudly displayed across my chest. They were E.G.O. medals (In Air Force lingo, E.G.O. means "everybody got one." But civilians didn't know that.) If you thought that you've sold a product or service with a high objection factor, you've never tried to sell broken glass and cracked plaster. Whereas I could dazzle my audiences in the beginning, they started to realize about halfway through my presentation that the sonic boom salesperson on the platform in front of them was also a sonic boom *distributor.*

When I saw the countenance of the audience begin to change, I shifted gears and appealed to their patriotism and sympathy by describing how I took my little body, strapped it into a 70-foot-long, 22-and-one-half-ton jet fighter, lined up that aircraft on a windswept, ice-slicked runway in the middle of the night with less than one-sixteenth mile visibility, jammed the throttles forward, lit both afterburners and felt 79,000 horsepower and 39,000 pounds of thrust flatten me against the seat back, rocketing down the runway from 0 to 200 miles per hour in 13 seconds, climbing from sea level to 35,000 feet in 92 seconds traveling 1,200 miles per hour, 20 miles per minute, flying that aircraft to the ragged edge of uncertainty, staring across that chasm into the face of the grim reaper and laughing defiantly because I knew that I was helping to make the world safe for democracy.

That got them on their feet. For a moment, the farmer forgot about his chickens and the homemaker forgot about sweeping up broken glass and fallen plaster. Of course I knew the rest of the story that they didn't know. As I accepted their thunderous applause, I knew about my instructions to my radar observer in the rear seat before every take off when I would say, *"If you ever hear me give the order to eject, don't say, 'huh?' because you'll be talking to yourself."*

The moral to my story is that working on your biggest unresolved problem can, and usually does, demand creativity and innovation. When people access their creative and innovate juices, they become energized. A burst of creative and innovative energy is the best butt snapper I've ever seen. Now that you know that taking on your biggest unresolved problem can be your biggest opportunity, you can stop avoiding it.

When folks refuse to tackle their biggest unresolved problems because the effort required seems too high of a price to pay, I often ask them what it is they're saving their precious effort for. None of us carry over unused effort from one day to the next. On the other hand, we can make tomorrow more effortless by working hard and smart *today*. Thomas Edison put it like this:

> *"The reason a lot of people do not recognize opportunity is because it usually goes around wearing overalls looking like hard work."*

Well said.

Get after it

If you are frustrated because you think you've engaged in problem-solving and no solutions are forthcoming, it's probably because you're wasting time looking for a *no-effort* solution. When you bear down and get after a problem, no matter how large, you're going to make progress. The satisfaction that comes from moving a mountain, even just a little, is far superior to the frustration of still scratching your head, some time later, in search of the mythical *effortless way*.

Caution!

Many people say to me, *"Danny, you just don't understand."* They go on to explain that they've never been any good at goal-setting—that it's never worked for them. These people are caught in their own trap. The fact is, they *are* setting goals. Worry itself is a goal-setting process. It's the ability to create vivid mental pictures of things *not wanted* but will no doubt be achieved because of misguided concentration.

In other words, what we vividly picture in our minds is what our energies are ultimately committed to achieving. Our minds are essentially saying to us, *"You've been spending so much time thinking about this it must be important, so here it is for real. You've got it."*

Obviously, visualizing a positive goal, the way things *should* be in the best of all possible worlds, dedicates your natural energies to making that image a reality. I don't mean to reduce the entire concept of positive thinking to a couple a paragraphs, but the fact is that it's pretty simple. If you're thinking about anything at all, it's got to be something you want or something you don't want. Make it your personal rule to concentrate on what you *want*. Focus on the positive.

Much of the goal-achievement process depends upon the developed powers of concentration. Therefore, the high-performance person lives *intensely in the present*. These people's lights are on and they're *home*. Spending the majority of your time in the past or the future distracts you from the effort that's required right now to resolve problems and clear the decks for better things to come.

People who dwell on the future might consider themselves visionaries. But they'd better have some dutiful and energized folks around them to deal with the *now* if they ever expect to reach the future, much less influence it. The excellence of our efforts in the present sets the stage and the tone for the future. After a seminar for hotel executives, Joe Topper of Red Lion Inns came up to me and said that he is committed to being an "island of excellence" in the pursuit of his career goals. What a great picture he drew. Being an island of excellence in the past or somewhere in the future has nothing to do with *now*.

Excellence is only effective in the present. All the goals in the world are meaningless unless you're living fully in the *now*. Deciding *not* to have a specific goal *right now* is a specific goal. If your goal is to not have a specific goal, then you've achieved it. You might feel empty and listless, but you've achieved your goals.

Breaking through

All of the pep talk and methodology in the world won't move you an inch until you invest the energy. I've described how making the solution of your biggest problem your number-one goal will energize you. I've thrown out some probing questions designed to bring you face-to-face with your true wants and desires as well as the courage of your convictions.

You can read through this stuff and nod your head as you turn the pages. You can feel yourself swell up with resolve to use this information and *get after it* like never before. You can put this book down and forget about everything you read within 30 minutes. Unfortunately, the latter is the most common course among those who give lip service to change.

To experience the exhilaration of *breaking through* your self-imposed barriers and experiencing life from the other side, you must dedicate yourself to a high-performance lifestyle not once, but every day and, often, numerous times throughout the day. As a final example of how you can emerge from your moment of truth and realistically expect to achieve all that you're capable of, I give you Mary Lawrence.

The Mary Lawrence story

Of the many people I'm proud to call my friends, my former employee Mary Lawrence is among the most inspiring. The description of her turning point might be more vividly definable than yours, but it was no less critical to the impressive achievements in her life than your turning point or moment of truth will be to the quality of your life from this moment on.

Long before I met her, Mary was no stranger to tragedy. By her own admission, the five years following her husband's death had been a time of existing with little real direction in her life. She was a lonely and discouraged lady the night a driver ran a stop sign and left Mary's body tangled in the twisted rubble that was once two automobiles.

When the police and ambulances arrived, they discovered her motionless form. She later learned the ambulance attendant who found her said, *"Get the rest of them first, she's already dead."* By Mary's own account, an unconscious will to live was already building within her. In her unconscious state, she was facing a moment of truth—the first of many turning points to come.

In the ambulance, one of the attendants detected a faint pulse. No one's really sure why the attendant checked her, but her heart was refusing to quit. When doctors examined her at the hospital, they offered no hope for her survival through the night, much less any type of recovery. They felt that her facial and head injuries were too massive. What they didn't realize was that her unconscious will to live was becoming massive as well. Her spirit hadn't received a *scratch*.

With each passing day, Mary became stronger—not appreciably stronger, but stronger just the same. She knew what her biggest unresolved problem was and every ounce of energy she had was dedicated to living. She maintained her resolve in light of the fact that nobody predicted that her life, if she survived at all, would be anything more than a vegetative existence with tremendously impaired mental functioning.

Her facial bones and jaws remained wired together for months as she existed on a liquid diet. Doctors explained to her that, if she were to recover, they would have to perform two major reconstructive operations on her face, neither one of which could be done with the aid of anesthetics. Mary's reply to their warning was, *"Let's get started."*

During the protracted surgical experience, which included 15 root canals in addition to the reconstructive surgery, she learned more about the limits of human endurance than most people could ever know. During the long, painful months of recovery, Mary adopted the motto *"I can"* as the most basic tasks became monumental for her broken body.

Emerging from the hospital one year later, she began to fully understand how different her life would be from then on. People she knew well couldn't recognize her face, still swollen a year after the accident. Some simply turned away, unable to look at her. But what caused Mary the most alarm was her loss of memory. She could no longer command her brain to remember names or thoughts. Somehow she heard that studying for a real estate license was extremely difficult and required detailed memory work.

Anyone who knows Mary Lawrence isn't surprised to hear that the next thing she did was begin studying for a real estate license. She chose the hardest path available, not the easiest. She purposefully chose an activity that required an excessive amount of effort. Mary had to read each page of the complex text 50, 60 even 70 times just to reach a normal retention level. She made it her goal to solve the biggest problem confronting her and succeeded not only in passing her licensing exam, but passed *on the first try*.

Mary came into my life after she had worked briefly for a couple of real estate offices without much success. It seems that working with the public was a bigger challenge than even getting her real estate license. The first two offices she worked for weren't able to provide her with the support or encouragement she needed to get a foothold in the business. Bosses told her again and again she couldn't cut it.

When she called me, she had already been through numerous moments of truth and each time refused to turn away from her goal. I'm sure that every time she "failed" in a new office, every instinct within her must have said, *"Quit. Why put yourself through any more of this?"* Nevertheless, she called because she heard that my company was opening a new office and she wanted to try again.

Her deliberate manner of speaking, necessitated by her memory problem was what first *appealed* to me over the telephone. We brought her on board and it quickly became obvious that Mary had learned much from her previous experiences. We put her in our sales training class and within months she became one of our outstanding first-year salespeople.

I thought Mary had climbed her mountain as she was recognized as one of the top 10 rookies of the year. As I presented her award at the annual awards dinner, she said to me, *"Danny, save a place for me. I'll be back for an award again next year as a member of the Million Dollar Club."* Even for someone without the setbacks that she had faced, entering the elite Million Dollar Club was an ambitious goal to say the least.

The next morning, Mary bought a beautiful pink evening gown to wear a year later at the next awards dinner and hung it in the center of her closet. She set a goal to maintain or even exceed her performance level for an entire year. Seeing the pink gown in her closet every day helped Mary visualize wearing it as she walked on stage the following year to accept her award. One of the greatest lessons Mary had learned was that she faced her personal turning point *every single day*.

Most people would have resolved to repeat a good performance in the exhilaration of the awards dinner only to drift away from the commitment as daily problems came up and obstacles got in the way. Not Mary. She faced a personal moment of truth every day and decided all over again to take the hard road to success. She knew that what she had almost lost was more than just being alive. What she had almost lost the night of her near-fatal accident was the *opportunity for self-determination*.

Needless to say that one of the proudest moments of my life came a year later when I introduced the members of the Million Dollar Club. In the year that had transpired, I learned for the first time the *full story* of what Mary had gone through. Mary was not only a new member of our company's Million Dollar Club, but was our office's sales leader in all four categories.

Mary came on stage to accept her award wearing the beautiful evening gown she had looked at in her closet every morning for a year. She seemed to float across the enormous dance floor at the Disneyland Hotel amidst a standing ovation. "Climb Every Mountain" from "The Sound of Music" was playing and there wasn't a dry eye in the house. When I handed her that big trophy, she leaned over to me and said, *"I told you I'd be back."*

Spotlight on you

As the old sayings go, *"You don't know what you've got until it's gone." "You never appreciate what you have until it's taken away."* Etc. How can those of us who have not faced the loss of everything worldly, as Mary did, know how valuable our life and its potential can be? I don't recommend going out and having a near-death experience. The most effective method is to continue taking fearless personal inventories. That means more questions.

Questions are only as useful as you are committed to answering honestly and reflecting on those answers. I suggest that you pause and *write down* the answers to the following questions and any other self-examination questions you read in this book. It's too easy to give a flip answer, flip the page and keep reading. It's not the following sleepless-night questions that will disturb your sleep. It's the *answers*. These are not questions to ask yourself some night when you have insomnia. These are questions to ask *tonight* to give yourself insomnia. If you ask yourself these questions, answer them, and then doze off, you didn't answer honestly. The first step to giving these issues focus in your life is to write them down. Etch them into your brain and begin developing a new context for the way you spend each day.

Sleepless-night questions

1. If I had to describe myself in three sentences, what would I say?
2. Each person I meet today takes my measure but, more importantly, how do I measure myself?
3. How much of my potential have I developed?

4. How much more of my potential will I have developed a year from today?

5. What's my plan for making that happen?

6. What extra effort am I willing to make today to launch my plan?

7. Will I make the effort?

8. What *mind games* do I play to convince myself that today does not matter and I can do today over again?

9. Is the high point of my life a past event or something I have carefully planned for the future?

10. Do I spend more time thinking about the past than I do planning my future?

11. The quality of my future lifestyle depends upon my current time habits. What can I expect from my future lifestyle?

12. I'm living my life in 24-hour segments. Which of my accomplishments of the past 24 hours am I most proud of?

13. Do I really believe that my success depends totally on me?

14. When I feel a rumble, even thunder in my heart, what am I willing to do to keep it there?

15. Will I do all that I am able to do to insure the achievement of my desired rewards?

I constantly ask myself, *"Will I be like Mary Lawrence? Will I face my own personal moment of truth each and every day? Will I set goals? Will I keep my goals in sight every day? Will everything I do today improve tomorrow?"* I know *I can* if I will:

1. Accept responsibility for how good I can really be.

2. See my goals as attainable.

3. Visualize the personal benefits that extra effort will bring.

4. Remain flexible and embrace change.

5. Anticipate success rather than fear it.

6. Identify what I really want.

7. Identify the *cost*.

8. Be willing to pay the price.

9. Start paying the price *now*.

10. Separate my goals into *financial, lifestyle* and *personal growth*.

11. Make my goals *realistic, measurable, challenging* and therefore *achievable*.
12. Make my first goal the solution to my biggest unresolved problem.
13. Concentrate on the positive results I seek.
14. Live intensely in the present.
15. Commit myself to a goal.

High-performance people see the future almost as clearly as they see the present moment. Their energy level is high because anticipation is the appetizer for accomplishment. It was Elbert Hubbard who said, *"We can achieve what we can conceive."* The same 19th-century author also said, *"Success is the realization of the estimate you place upon yourself."* I would go on to add that you place a value on yourself and your potential in your moment of truth.

STEP TWO
Developing Strengths

"To be nobody but yourself in a world which is doing its best, night and day to make you everybody else means to fight the hardest battle any human being can fight and never stop fighting."

—*e.e. cummings*

Many an author, lecturer and/or business consultant has trumpeted the virtues of goal-setting without providing the rest of the story. Many an individual comes out of a seminar or closes a book feeling as if setting a goal and realizing its accomplishment are one in the same. Many an individual is disappointed when s/he learns that setting goals and reaching goals are two entirely different processes.

In the *high-performance process,* goal-setting is one of the easier tasks, even though no task is fairly described as *easy* when we set out to change our behavior patterns. Yet one of the most common experiences nearly all human beings share is the experience of setting and *not* actively pursuing goals. We are all eager believers in the mythology of miracle cures. Even when we know better, we would still *like* to believe.

As much as we would like to believe that the mere act of setting goals will somehow guarantee that the goals will be attained, it doesn't work that way. That's probably why most diets fail. It's not the intention to do, but the doing itself that gets the job done. Intending is always easier than doing. Just willing something to get done won't budge the real world one inch.

Emerging from your personal moment of truth with realistic, measurable, challenging and exciting goals in the financial, lifestyle and personal growth categories simply means that you've set the stage for the next step in your personal *high-performance process*. The next component you need is a realistic inventory of your strengths. Everyone has strengths. Are you familiar with yours?

Out of the fire

Just like the blacksmith strengthens iron by repeatedly heating it and pounding it on the anvil, so too are human beings strengthened by the fire of adversity. Few concepts are more universally accepted among the many races, creeds and cultures around the world. Somerset Maugham said it this way: *"Adversity puts iron in your flesh."*

Primitive tribes have historically made their prospective warriors endure tremendously difficult (and usually painful) rites of passage to prove their mettle. Initiation rituals for all manner of society and organization are designed to prove worthiness through the ability to successfully negotiate rigid tests of spirit and will.

Christian scripture in both the Old and New Testaments is replete with examples of how individuals become stronger and refined through adversity. To one degree or another, everyone has been tested by some sort of struggle in life. Although none of us looks forward to adversity, 99 times out of 100, every one of us is emotionally stronger for it in the end.

It's also healthy to get right down to business in our lives with the understanding that it ain't gonna be easy. Like Fred Allen says, *"The world is a grindstone. Life is your nose."* There are no teacher's pets in the classroom of experience. Comedian Louie Anderson once said, *"Anybody who's had an easy life doesn't have anything to say that I want to hear."*

No matter who says it or how, the point is always the same. The school of hard knocks will turn out students better prepared to succeed than the school of comfort and charm. Those with character strengthened by adversity will be able to penetrate and/or overcome obstacles that those with easier lives will bounce off of.

There is always luck to contend with. Just don't count on it. Like J. Paul Getty's formula for success:

1. Rise Early
2. Work Hard
3. Strike Oil

When you are committed to the *high-performance process,* you'll be extra appreciative when luck pays a visit. If you rely on luck or someone else's efforts to get you somewhere, you'll be bitter and resentful when either or both are in short supply. It's not so much about being lucky as it is about being in the right spot when luck arrives—and being in the right spot has nothing to do with luck.

If you want to calculate the riches of your life, don't recount every time you got lucky or that somebody bailed you out. Look back on times of adversity and challenge because those were the times when your strengths were being developed and refined. To inventory the areas in which you're truly skilled, look to your *experience.* Even more than training, it's experience that makes you good.

What you have when you have nothing

One of the finest speakers on the circuit these days is Charlie Plumb. Charlie was a prisoner of war in North Vietnam. When Charlie comes on stage, he puts two chairs a couple of feet apart and paces silently between them. The audience is riveted by his solemn, rhythmic pacing. Finally he speaks and explains that for over six years, he paced in a North Vietnamese cell, less than three feet wide.

On the day he was shot down, he had left the world he knew behind on the aircraft carrier and entered the prison with only his tattered flight suit. He had nothing. Or did he? With the audience's help, he begins to list what he had with him as he was captured. His ability to think, to remember, to reason. He had skills and knowledge. He had courage, creativity and imagination.

As the list gets longer, it's increasingly apparent that Charlie had a lot more than his tattered flight suit when he entered that prison cell. So it is with your strengths. There is a lot more there than meets the eye. When you feel like you have nothing to offer yourself or anyone else, you're just not looking deep enough.

It's in there

When people come up to me and say that they're facing what seems to be an insurmountable problem, I ask them if the current problem is the biggest or toughest one they've ever faced. *"Oh, no,"* they reply. *"This one is nothing compared to that problem."* These folks soon learn that if they treat their current problem with the same perspective that their larger problem required, the current problem suddenly seems far less ominous and foreboding. The net result is that these people instantly unleash problem-solving energies that they weren't aware they possessed.

You and every person around you have problem-solving skills and energies that are directly proportionate to the amount of adversity each has experienced. Not that everyone exploits or is even aware of those hidden resources by any means. That's why it's imperative at this stage of your personal *high-performance process* to call up those strengths and put them to use.

There's a *Broom Hilda* cartoon hanging on the wall above my desk. The cartoon, featuring the comical little witch, impressed me so much that I spent $50 to have it custom-framed. The whole Sunday paper only cost a buck. Actually, Broom Hilda herself is not featured in this particular cartoon. Instead, her troll-like, naive, innocent little friend Irwin puts on a long-tailed formal tuxedo jacket, picks up a conductor's baton and walks into the woods alone.

Irwin steps up on a fallen tree trunk and begins to wave his arms as if to conduct. There are no musicians, only rocks, trees and flowers. Soon, musical notes pour from the rocks, trees and flowers and fill the panel. Finally, Irwin turns and confidently says to the reader, *"It's all in there, you just have to work at getting it out."*

The problem word once again seems to be "work." I swear there would be more people praying if they could only find a softer place to kneel. I meet a lot of people who are all set to hitch their wagon to a star—just as soon as someone hands them a star. Once each of us accepts that problem-solving, goal-achieving energy and talent exists within us, all that's left is the "work" required to get it out.

It doesn't happen automatically. As always, traveling the hard road requires a conscious, informed choice. The decision to travel down easy street tends to come more easily and effortlessly. Unfortunately, easy street doesn't go anywhere and you always end up no farther than where you started. Except in the rarest of circumstances, those whose success you admire only got there through tremendous, conscious effort.

Undeveloped strengths

In the overview of this book, we talked about how exercising previously undeveloped strengths pushes back self-limiting boundaries in your life. You're now learning where to find and how to identify those hidden strengths. Now that you know they're there, you can get past the wondering stage and expect to find substance within.

Take time to reflect on your life and its most challenging problems, even from your youth. How did you overcome those problems? Did you overcome them or did you just learn to *avoid* them? What problems have you successfully resolved? What's the biggest one? What types of problems can you solve well and often? The answers to these questions will serve as a window into your untapped reservoir of undeveloped strengths.

Your personal charter at this point is to do the very best that you can with the strengths available to you. Anything less is unacceptable.

"Few people during their lifetime come anywhere near exhausting the resources dwelling within them. There are deep wells of strength that are never used."
— *Rear Admiral Richard Byrd*

There's no excuse for not realizing your full potential once you've discovered the secret cavern in which all of your undeveloped strengths are hidden. The business you need to be about is the development of your undeveloped potential.

Returning for a moment to that personal-potential thermometer we talked about in the overview, it's important to understand that the fuel you have to burn in order to make that temperature go up is your woodpile of undeveloped strengths. If you have honestly answered the questions, *"Where is the mercury in my thermometer?"* and *"Where do I want the mercury level to be a year from now?"* what's left is the task of heating up the mercury using your undeveloped strengths as your source of energy.

If the mercury level a year from now is the same as it is today, then it's safe to say that you've not put any of your undeveloped strengths to work. I've already covered many of the reasons why we often avoid stepping up the development of personal potential. Knowing what you know now, you can no longer claim that you don't know where your strength is going to come from. Your stash of undeveloped strengths has been found.

Recipe for failure and frustration

Undeveloped strengths mixed with laziness. That's it. When we refuse to exert the energy to drag wood from the woodpile to the stove, the stove goes cold. Knowing that we're frustrated and unsatisfied with a cold stove, you might wonder why we sometimes let the fire go out. Laziness. A cold stove, as useless as it is, is sometimes preferable to the cost of stoking the fire. Preferable in terms of our anti-work, lazy side, that is. Letting the fire go out is never preferable in the long run.

No one can guarantee success. However, no effort to determine or develop personal strengths, usually out of laziness and/or lack of motivation, will virtually guarantee failure and frustration. A

2 Coins and a fountain

Desire
Fear
Desire
Laziness

man recently won a bunch of money on a $1 lottery ticket. This was a poor man. He was so poor, you have to spell "poor" with four or five "o's" to get the picture. And he won a *bunch* of money. Bunch with a capital "B."

This man quickly squandered his winnings on gambling and fast women. A curious journalist asked him why he spent all of his new-found wealth so quickly. The reporter wanted to know what was so attractive about poverty that made him want to return to it as soon as possible. The man simply replied that, because the small fortune he won only cost him one dollar, he didn't feel it was worth any more than one dollar.

Strange thinking when it's put that way. But we all have our moments when we apply some of the screwiest logic to the most straightforward situations. The man who won the lottery didn't search for the inner strengths that might have changed his life for the better. He relied upon the outside phenomenon of free money to improve his life. He took the easiest road and the lack of substance eventually caught up with him. He left his strengths undeveloped and wound up frustrated.

The mountaintop interlude

The mountaintop interlude is simply my name for the time you set aside for doing the reflecting I've been talking about. It could be the "creek through the pasture interlude" or the "day at the beach interlude." It really doesn't matter. I'm a great believer that, if we're going to learn anything about ourselves, we must spend some time alone, away from the distractions of others, including family. We're all too willing to be distracted by others when we need to focus on our own issues.

When I faced some of the most critical situations in my career, I went to the beach. There was an instinct that urged me to just dig in and work harder. Fortunately, I knew by then that just doing more of the same old stuff that got me in trouble to begin with would only dig me in deeper.

The best definition of insanity I've ever heard is, *"Doing the same wrong thing over and over, and expecting a different result each time."* I can't tell you how many times I've acted insane and I'll bet you've done the same thing a few times yourself. The crazy part is that we all go back and do it again—something that we already know doesn't work. A sign of real growth and maturity is developing the ability to catch yourself and change course before going down that same old road for yet another time.

> *"Everybody is a damn fool for fifteen minutes every day. The trick is to not exceed your limit."*
> —*Elbert Hubbard*

My search for sanity through those mountaintop interludes is strictly a solo affair. My family doesn't go with me. Solitary thinking and reflection means *alone.* By going away from the problem and not getting buried deeper underneath it, I was better able to draw a perspective that helped me *solve* it. Most important of all is the fact that genuine solitude allows me to clear the decks and go below to see what's in my personal hold.

It's the application of your undeveloped resources to the problem at hand that will produce the solution. Only when you can get an uninterrupted view of yourself can you properly scrutinize your undeveloped resources. Unleashing that untapped energy and creativity can't be done when your focus is on other people and other things.

I'm not suggesting that you retreat to some desolate place and contemplate your navel for the rest of your life. Getting alone and reflecting honestly and thoroughly on the experiences in your life that have strengthened you is only appropriate when you intend to move above and beyond where you are at the moment. It doesn't require a crisis. Tapping your own hidden resources is a means of self-empowerment that leaves you with a desire for more, and what you uncover and develop can help in most any aspect of your life.

Insight produces a change in self-expectation. Self-expectation is not limited to any singular situation, although it might start somewhere or be inspired by something specific. With elevated self-expectation will come a new perspective on everything you do. Peter F. Drucker said, "When you focus on a strength, it puts a demand on performance."

I need the real me back, hardworking, dynamic, successful, inspirational

Curiosity and courage are the batteries that power your inner searchlight. Curiosity asks, "What have I not yet developed about myself that would benefit me?" Courage empowers you to use your new information once it's discovered. The following list suggests some of the discoveries you can expect to make during your own mountaintop interlude. The list with your name on it is as long and complex as your experiences have been to this point in your life.

Personal discoveries

I chose to begin the *strengths* section of this book with the e.e. cummings quote about individualism because strengths are highly personal. As I've already described, it's what's inside of you that determines your potential. In a world that throws images before us of what culture, commercialism or conventional wisdom regards as desirable, it's difficult to know where our own uniqueness stops and where the synthetic image begins.

For example, why do you want to be what you claim you want to be? Is it because that's where your unique strengths lead you or is it because you've been indoctrinated with what the media and social norms have preached as appropriate? There's nothing wrong with being a chicken farmer if you're good with chickens. If you're happier working on the farm, why are you pushing paper in the World Trade Center?

I'm not suggesting that everyone who reads this book drop his or her career and responsibilities cold and move to Newfoundland to write poetry. However, it's important that you be able to discriminate between what is in your personal arsenal of strengths and what's not. Time and time again, I meet people who tell me how frustrated and/or unsatisfied they are with their current job. They often feel stuck and unable to get ahead.

When I hear such complaints, it's a sure bet that these folks haven't engaged in sufficient self-discovery to appreciate their personal career composition. They haven't yet found out what they're uniquely good at or what their personal experience has prepared them to do best. Once you discover your strengths, don't be surprised to find out that the source of your greatest frustrations is

Am I frustrated because I fear I might not be uniquely good at writing which may be (subconsciously) the laziest way I think I can make big money?

found in your attempt to work in areas other than where your strengths are.

The following list of probable discoveries is by no means complete. It's simply a guide as you conduct your own self-inventory. The items I've listed will suit some better than others. The goal is to find what strengths are uniquely yours so you can use that information to sketch your own game plan for the future. Seek and ye will probably find:

1. Great storehouse of *tools* in the form of *talents, knowledge* and *personal experiences.*

Philip!

"what are you uniquely good at & what was your personal experience best prepared you for?"

Talent

Each of us was born with certain talents. Although practice and refinement are required to maximize what might be called "*natural*" talents, each individual seems to be naturally inclined toward certain activities from earliest childhood. Some people are better with their hands while others are better with their minds. Some people become painters and sculptors while others become poets and composers. Some people are creative and expressive thinkers while others are intensely analytical and number-oriented. Some people are talkers and some are quiet.

There comes a point at which acquired knowledge begins to shape, and possibly distort, natural talents and inclinations. However, I refer to the tendencies people have from birth as their natural talents. The knowledge I refer to is the accumulation of what you've been taught by *others*.

Knowledge

Of the three, *talent, knowledge* and *experience*, knowledge is the most suspect because it's what *someone else* thinks. Children are less equipped to discriminate between what's right thinking and what's distorted thinking. To the child, any adult has a certain credibility simply because that person is an adult.

Now that we're adults, we would hardly recommend to all children that they accept and adopt what any adult thinks merely on the basis of their being an adult. One of the signs of maturity is the ability to sift through the maze of contradictory thinking and develop a personal world view and set of priorities. This is one of the reasons that I urge people to read and study as much as possible.

Reading and studying what others think is a terrific way to challenge your own thinking and also learn what thoughts are behind the great accomplishments you admire most in others. The key to your self-discovery process, as far as thinking is concerned, is to recognize which thoughts are truly yours as opposed to thoughts that you might have blindly accepted along the way, perhaps in your youth.

Many of the self-imposed barriers we face are constructed from thoughts and ways of thinking that are not helpful or that might even be negative or damaging. Just because someone else thinks something doesn't mean it's correct. Not all knowledge that we acquire though the years is helpful. Much of the knowledge we acquire needs to be dumped like ballast to lighten our load.

We have enough to deal with in life without adopting someone else's negative thoughts as our own. By the same token, much of the knowledge we can acquire by studying the thoughts of great and successful people can accelerate our quest for excellence. Talent refers to natural gifts, knowledge refers to acquired thoughts and both are filtered through personal *experience*.

Experience

Experience is the best measure of who you are. It's not the situations you find yourself in as much as it's what you choose to *do* in those situations that tells you what you're made of. Of course you're made of your talents and your thinking. However, it's how you *behave* in life that reveals to what degree you've allowed thinking to stifle talent or vice versa.

Experience is where the rubber meets the road in life. You can talk all you want about how you think and where you feel your talents lie, but I'll watch what you *do* if I want to get to know you. It's what you *do* and not what you *say* that opens the book on who you really are. If what you think and say you want in life is distinctly different than what you do, your self-examination isn't over yet.

Experience shapes and molds you according to how open you are to *learning*. To repeat yesterday and continue going down the same road-to-nowhere day-in and day-out is a sure-fire indication that you're not learning much from experience. For experience to be a positive tool in your life, you must learn from it and accept what your behavior says about your true intentions in life.

As my friend and creative thinking mentor said:

> *"We do what we are, we are what we think. What we think is determined by what we learn and what we learn is determined by what we experience.*
>
> *"What we experience is determined by what we expose ourselves to and what we do with that experience."*

We all begin life with little or no control over our experiences. As we grow older, we gradually develop the capacity to get outside of ourselves and our circumstances and learn from them. Just like talent and knowledge, experience becomes a tremendous tool once you begin to learn from it and apply the lessons to your own *high-performance process.*

2.   As enthusiasm builds, procrastination gives way to initiative.

Dam Busters

One of the most important reasons why goals need to be *exciting* is to invoke the positive benefits of enthusiasm. Where there is a lack of enthusiasm, all of your best-laid plans will get all

dammed-up behind the slightest obstacle. Enthusiasm is the dyna-
mite that blows up the logjam and gets you moving again.

Procrastination itself is the foreign object that blocks your flow.
Whatever empowers an obstacle to bottle up your initiative is sure
to be one of the many faces of procrastination. Usually it's fear
that the successful outcome of some effort will make more
demands on you than just leaving things the way they are.

Enthusiasm carries with it a healthy dissatisfaction with the
way things are. That's why enthusiasm tends to keep things in
motion and won't tolerate anything that bogs down the process.
An office full of enthusiastic people is like a beehive. You don't
need *butt snappers* because nobody stays in their seat for very
long. Everybody is in high gear getting after something or other.

You get enthusiasm by witnessing the accomplishment of your
daily goals, which are part of a larger plan. Notice I didn't say the
accomplishment of your daily tasks but daily goals. When you're
accomplishing daily goals, you're doing something new and not
repeating another yesterday. When you're doing that, you can't
help but be excited and enthusiastic.

Walk into an office without any enthusiasm and you're not
going to see much movement. You can look at it the other way, too.
Next time you walk into an office without much movement, note
how much enthusiasm you can detect among the folks working
there. I guarantee that you won't find much. Enthusiasm is the
antidote for procrastination.

desire ?

3.   Control over attitude.

In your intense self-evaluation you're going to discover something that surprises most people. Specifically, you have a great
amount of control over how you *feel.* Attitude is the leading edge of
how effective you are in life. If your attitude is such that you
blame everyone and everything else for what happens to you,
you're destined to fly in circles for the rest of your life.

Depending on the frustration level you feel as a result of the
cumulative imbalance between *talent, knowledge* and *experience,*
your attitude might be only slightly out of adjustment or in self-
destruct mode. In the early days of my business career, I could

have made you a list of how everyone around me was contributing to my lousy attitude. How about you?

Are you still laboring under the misconception that others determine your attitude? There's nothing like a time of solitude and self-examination to reveal that each one of us is in full control over our attitude. Other people can do many things to you, but they're powerless to determine how you're going to *feel* about it.

In the days when I would have rattled off a long list of names to describe who was in charge of my attitude, there would have always been one name conspicuous by its absence from every list—*mine*. Even if you're not willing to fully let go of the notion that others control your attitude, at least put your own name at the top of the list to give credit where it's due.

That way, you can focus all the blame you want on everyone else on your list after you've dealt with yourself. I don't think you'll find any need to waste your time blaming others for your attitude once you've confronted yourself. Regardless of your circumstances, it's your choice and your choice *alone* how you're going to feel about it. Once I learned that, I knew that a lousy attitude was only holding me back from enjoying my own *high-performance process*.

4. As performance increases, energy and morale stay high.

What has self-examination got to do with increasing performance? Everything. You wouldn't be this far into the book if you didn't feel a real need to increase your personal effectiveness. The common belief is that energy and morale proceed high performance. The fact is that increasing performance pumps up energy and morale. They go hand in hand over time, but increases in performance will always result in increased satisfaction and enthusiasm.

There seems to be a natural connection between approaching the limits of your personal potential and happiness. People seem to be the least happy when they're nowhere near their potential. I've never seen a sad person succeeding at something that requires use of his or her natural talents.

Self-reflection will no doubt bear out that the times when you felt happiest and fulfilled were the times when you had your natural talents, your knowledge and your background all lined up. If you're not sure of your natural talents, your acquired knowledge and your library of experience, go to the times when you felt satisfied and excited about what you were doing. That was a time when your personal and unique combination of talent, knowledge and experience was in alignment.

Upon reflection, it might seem as if such times of happiness and satisfaction happened purely by accident. They probably did. If you haven't before sought to identify your own unique composition, how could you have planned to match your activities with your personality? After spending time in self-examination, enthusiastic pursuit of what interests you most will never again be an accident.

Coming down from the mountaintop

Time in solitude, self-examination and recharged batteries all prepare you for the next chapter in your life. As you come down from the mountains, home from the beach or back from wherever you've gone to reflect, you bring with you a precious new understanding. You now know that it's not what you're doing that makes you miserable, it's not investing enough of *you* that makes whatever you're doing unattractive.

The whole point of learning who you are is to make it easier to inject more of what is uniquely you into your life. As I mentioned earlier, the commercial culture in which we live, critical parents and a host of other influences have probably distorted your self-image, if not completely annihilated it. Are you in a career that *somebody else* has convinced you to pursue?

Are you doing what you're doing because it's the only way you can afford to live in the house, drive the car, wear the clothes or generally live the life that *somebody else* has convinced you is proper? If everything you do leads to the lifestyle that genuinely pleases you, you've somehow managed to align the talents, knowledge and experience that you went up the mountain to get in touch with.

The last thing I want to do is encourage you to become one of those *"touchy-feely"* creatures who can't make up their mind about anything until someone else gives them permission. But unless you discover who you truly are and what makes you tick, how can you make an informed decision to make anything truly *yours?* Increasing your level of sensitivity is valuable because your job as well as your life in general won't become truly *yours* until you discover and develop your unique strengths.

When you bring more of *you* to anything you do, you earn respect and admiration from others around you. When you see someone who's truly dedicated and passionate, you don't even have to agree with what they do to acknowledge that they at least deserve your respect for *fighting the good fight.*

You were built to be an original. Other influences have conspired since you were born to transform you into someone who was defined by what others think—usually for commercial purposes. Regardless of *why* others have felt compelled to shape your life, it's high time you take it back. In the end, it's not other peoples' attempts to shape your life that matters as much as how much you buy into it.

Don't take this as an invitation to act irresponsibly.

If you're over 50 and 5'4" tall, don't fight against your natural barriers and try to land that NBA contract. Self-examination is not intended to lead you into a useless battle against your natural limitations. In fact, quality self-examination will take you in the opposite direction.

Knowing who you are and what you're made of will serve to focus your energies more effectively on those things that you do best. Becoming a high-performance person means expending your energies in a *more efficient* manner than ever before. You can't do that by watering the milk or trying to make water flow uphill.

Creative people are unorthodox

Creativity is the opposite of conformity. There is a time for both. However, spending more time in conformity makes a dull boy. Spending 100 percent of your time being creative-but-irresponsible might land you in jail or, at least, make you wind up liv-

Dont know what to do, Too many things
Creative - but - irresponsible pulling me apart.

ing behind a dumpster. Whatever responsible balance you achieve, weight it on the side of creativity. If for no other reason, being creative and a bit unorthodox will make you a more entertaining and fun person for the rest of us to be around.

Creativity is an indispensable component of the high-performance lifestyle. Creativity is defined in the dictionary as originality of thought and action. That's exactly what the *mountaintop* self-discoveries had in common. You are an original, unique in your thoughts and actions. To be a high-performance person, you can't escape creativity. It has to part of your unique and original composition as a human being.

The sucker hole

As I said, conformity has its place in a civilized society. In many ways, there is no more civilized society than the Air Force. The Air Force is certainly well-ordered if not civilized. Nevertheless, I probably survived the Air Force because I never completely lost my uniqueness and the ability to break formation when the alternative was to become a smoking hole in the ground.

I once had a commanding officer who preached precision formation flying with a passion that was something to behold. He hammered and hammered us with the concept of holding formation and following the lead of the formation leader no matter what. We were to do what the *lead* did without question. Responding to every move the *lead* made in flight had to become an instinct, not a choice.

I recall a classroom situation in which a young pilot asked the instructor, *"What if the lead flies into a mountain?"* The instructor thought for a moment and then turned to the young pilot. *"I would want to see four equally-spaced holes along the cliff."*

We're talking discipline here, folks. The young pilot as well as the rest of us got the message. And that message as well as countless hours of training in precision formation flying was etched into my brain one day when I was the third fighter in a three-aircraft echelon or *fingertip* formation. In a fingertip formation, a second airplane follows the lead plane to one side with less than six feet separating their overlapped wing tips. I was in the third plane and less than six feet separated my left wing tip from the right wing tip on the middle aircraft.

We were returning to base through some pretty stormy weather, maintaining our delicate spacing through severe turbulence at speeds around 500 miles per hour. I was paying attention. Our *lead* spotted a hole in the clouds below us and began a rapid descent. He was confident the worst weather was behind us and he called the control center to cancel our instrument flight plan.

When flying under instrument rules (IFR), aircraft are directed by the air traffic controller who monitors the aircraft on radar. Canceling IFR means that you convert to visual flight rules (VFR) and the controller no longer provides separation and directional guidance. In short, you're on your own. As soon as our lead canceled IFR, we were eye-balling it by the seat of our pants.

Our lead, a very proud Air Force officer, fully expected to break out of the cloud cover as soon as we descended through the hole and make a VFR landing. He must have been surprised to find that the hole was a *"sucker hole"*, meaning that what looked like our ticket to clear sailing was merely a passage to even more severe weather below. Indeed, the storm at the lower altitude was more violent than the one we just descended from. At moments like this I, the fighter pilot, used to reconsider the old adage, *"If God had wanted us to fly, he would have given us feathers."*

Trying to maintain formation, we were in the soup, flying blind with no air traffic assistance, getting knocked around as if we were in a cocktail shaker. I lost sight of the other two aircraft as we darted into thicker clouds. It was limited vision one instant and complete white-out the next. Still our wing tips were only feet apart. Precision flying at all costs.

Then I lost sight of them again. The next thing I saw was the lead fighter and the number-two aircraft flying canopy to canopy with their canopies about six feet apart. If this wasn't going to be a mid-air collision, it was going to miss a whale of chance. As we said back in the Ozarks of Southern Illinois, "It's better to say this is where he turned and ran rather than this is where he died."

I decided to become a nonconformist and do my world-famous *"let's get the heck out of here"* maneuver. I pulled the nose of my

I described earlier the need for two "C" batteries to power your inner searchlight. *Courage* was one battery, *curiosity* was the other. Without curiosity, what's going to inspire your search for hidden strengths and abilities? Without curiosity, what will motivate you to look beyond your present circumstances for any reason? Thank heavens people like Alexander Graham Bell, Madame Curie, Thomas Edison, Benjamin Franklin, Walt Disney, George Washington Carver and so many others were *curious* people with a childlike sense of wonder.

If you've allowed yourself to become cynical and closed off over the years, it's time to re-stimulate your curiosity factor. Reading more, traveling, initiating discussions with interesting people you admire and purposefully getting involved in new and unusual activities and hobbies are just a few ways to get your inquisitive juices flowing again.

Peter F. Drucker once suggested that you walk away from your situation, bend over and look back between your legs. He contends that once you look at a situation backwards and upside down, you'll have a more functional perspective. I can't think of one person or business that ever suffered from gaining a broader and more creative perspective. Besides, bending over and looking through your legs beats by a long shot *eyeballing it* and *flying by the seat of your pants*.

2.   Creative people are open to as many alternatives as possible.

People who are closed off to new ideas and suggestions don't make many friends. They also don't make good bosses, employees, spouses, parents, teachers, etc. High-performance people are never threatened by new ideas. On the contrary, they encourage new ideas and outlooks. A high-performance person appropriates time to hear and absorb new and off-beat solutions.

Listening and considering the new and unorthodox doesn't mean that you must act irresponsibly and do weird things just to call yourself creative and inquisitive. You might end up adopting very little of what you hear and learn. However, being open to the earth-shattering proposal when and if it comes is how you *make your own luck.* As you know, people can't actually manufacture luck. Making your own luck refers to a manner of living that remains open and ready to great new ideas when they emerge. Being vigilant and prepared is impossible when your eyes, ears and mind are closed.

3. Creative people constantly search for alternatives.

A creative person won't get trapped in narrow thinking. Sometimes we hear a new idea and jump on the bandwagon. That's good to a point. What if the new idea is not the best alternative? You have to be willing to consider other ideas. The fact that you backed a new idea to begin with is evidence that you're not afraid of change. So don't limit yourself. If one new idea is worth considering, then others are worth considering too.

There was once a pottery manufacturer in Ohio who realized he had a real bottleneck at the packing stage of his operation. He went into the plant to look things over for himself and discovered that the pottery was being packed in newspapers. It immediately became clear to him that there's a natural tendency when working with printed material to *read* what's on the paper.

His people weren't sitting around reading newspapers instead of packing pottery. But they were sufficiently distracted now and then to slow the process down. Used newspapers were still the least expensive packing material he could get his hands on and he didn't want to buy more expensive packing materials, thereby adding costs to the operation.

He thought to himself, I wish these people could be blindfolded. So he did the next best thing. His solution: acquire *foreign language* newspapers that his people couldn't read. That's what he did and the packing operation returned to full speed. He looked for alternatives and found a good one.

4. A creative person is eager to test new ideas.

Even before a new idea is completely finished, refined, formulated, etc., it can be put before others for feedback and evaluation. A creative person does this because the input of others will no doubt have a beneficial effect on the quality of the idea as it reaches maturity. Keeping a new idea under wraps until it is unveiled as a new policy excludes most of what's good about the creative process.

Not only do people resent new ideas being forced upon them without the opportunity to participate in the development of the idea, it's possible that there was a better idea available that nobody got the opportunity to promote. Perhaps the new idea, once it's launched, proves to be a failure. The liabilities and vulnerabilities of the new idea could have been exposed in a less embarrassing development process that encouraged input from others. Creative people put new ideas out for maximum scrutiny as soon as possible in order to tune up the program.

5. Creative people develop comparisons to illustrate points.

It's not enough to simply speak in terms of numbers when portraying the probable outcome of a new idea. There's always more to an outcome than numbers. A creative person will adopt a metaphor or two to help others best get the complete picture. An increase of 100 percent, for example, is like doubling the sales. Doubling the sales is like shoving the throttle forward. Shoving the throttle forward places a bigger demand on manufacturing. Etc.

In personal terms, learning a new word every day and using it in a sentence three or more times is like earning an advanced degree in semantics. Studying a new language means introducing an entirely new nation and society to your life. The creative person finds lots of comparisons and similarities to use in communicating ideas.

6. Creative people stay flexible at all times.

As I mentioned earlier, new ideas sometimes need to change direction, shape, size and composition along their developmental path. None of that upsets the creative person. Although it's more convenient for new ideas to work perfectly the moment they're conceived, that rarely happens. A creative person will nurse a new idea along and make whatever investment in it that's required.

Part of remaining flexible is the willingness to abandon an idea if it proves unworthy of further development. Forcing a square peg through a round hole for the sake of pride is not the kind of attitude you'll find in a truly creative person. Creative people don't think in terms of failure, but in terms of learning from every experience. To the creative person a failed idea represents knowledge gained.

Becoming more creative

For those who don't feel creative at all and want to, as well as those who want to stimulate even more creativity in their lives, there are a few steps that will help. You should be noticing by now that the ideas I'm setting before you all dovetail into one another. Once you're committed to the *high-performance process,* these ideas become second nature to you and feel natural.

For starters, the first step to becoming more creative is to *spend more time alone.* As I described in the section on solitude and self-examination, spending time alone is the best way to distance yourself from the contamination of interruption and distraction. You have enough of this every day, you receive extra points for trying to be creative in the middle of chaos, even though it never hurts.

Step two is to *dream with a purpose* during the day. It's possible to be too focused on your work and stifle any creative thoughts that might come your way. Notice I didn't say *daydream.* Clearly, it would be irresponsible to waste valuable time keeping your mind completely free for any errant idea that might pop into your head. The key to keeping your mind open and available to wander where your creative spirit leads is to identify times throughout the day when you can afford to dream of new high-performance ideas. A survey that appeared in the 1993 summer issue of *Exec* magazine revealed that 71 percent of the office workers surveyed reported they had, over the previous year, made at least one dream that occurred during the day become a reality.

Driving, walking or getting a cup of coffee or a sandwich are all times when you can knowingly let your mind wander a little. Just sitting and staring out the window for a few minutes at various times of the day is well worth the time spent if you knowingly keep your mind available to new thoughts and information. There's no vice in letting your thoughts wander freely in the context of a productive day.

Step three is to *be gullible*. Be willing to stay with each new idea until you have a good, solid reason to reject it. Too many people choke the life out their own creativity by discounting new thoughts and ideas too soon. To reject something out of hand just because it doesn't make *complete* sense at the moment is to potentially forfeit what might materialize into a tremendously beneficial concept if given sufficient time to ferment.

Step four is to *allow yourself emotional conflict*. Emotional conflict or uncertainty is the genesis of creativity. If an idea seems unsettling to you, there might be a good reason. If a new thought shifts your load a little, chances are good that you're really on to something. When something makes you uneasy, it's time to do something about it, not ignore it.

The truly creative person lives to challenge old, staid beliefs and attitudes. If something pops into your head that makes you a little nervous, check it out. Grant yourself some creative free time to dig deeper and see what's going on. You could be missing a breakthrough idea by dismissing it simply because it makes you feel uncomfortable.

> *"Only those who attempt the absurd will achieve the impossible."*
> —*Albert Einstein*

Step five is to *assume that illogical thoughts have credibility*. To dismiss new thoughts just because they might not seem logical at first blush is to run the risk of throwing out the baby with the bath water. The fact is that you simply might not be prepared to receive the information. Who knows what mode your mind might be in when a stray thought happens by?

If you're busy working out of your analytical/linear left brain when a artful/aesthetic thought occurs, the new thought won't compute. That doesn't mean that the idea lacks value. When this occurs, jot the new idea down so that you can revisit it later when your more creatively right-brain oriented. The once illogical thought might suddenly make all the sense in the world. I'm convinced that many terrific solutions to personal and professional problems are lost because they're not digestible the moment they arrive.

> *"Some of our best ideas have come from letting our engineers wander where angels fear to tread."*
>
> —*Henry Ford*

The creative environment

What Henry Ford was talking about isn't as simple as it might seem. To this day, it's a rare company that makes a conscious and concerted effort to establish and nurture a creative environment. Why else would they send their executives away from the company campus to some resort setting to be *"creative"*? Creativity needs to be part of everyone's diet, every day. A high-performance person doesn't wait for a management retreat to be creative. S/he is creative day-in and day-out, awake or asleep. Creativity should be a way of life.

Business managers, employees, salespeople, teachers, parents and anyone who can benefit from personal growth and the growth of others can't ignore their personal responsibility to encourage and support the creative process. The primary manner in which creativity can be encouraged and supported is to create and sustain an environment were creativity is applauded and rewarded instead of discouraged.

It's all too common for creative impulses to be criticized and even punished. The pattern often begins at home in early childhood and then continues through school and into the workplace. As I mentioned, there are times to conform and times to be creative. However, the balance between creativity and conformity can be tilted too far in favor of conformity if the parent, teacher or business manager seeks to *maintain order* at all costs.

Sam Walter Foss, who died in 1911, penned a rambling rhyme that truly captures the essence of mindless conformity:

One day, through the primeval wood,
A calf walked home, as good calves should;
But made a trail all bent askew,
A crooked trail as all calves do.
Since then two hundred years have fled,
And, I infer, the calf is dead.
But still he left behind his trail,
And thereby hangs my moral tale.
The trail was taken up next day
By a lone dog that passed that way;
And then a wise bellwether sheep
Pursued the trail o'er vale and steep,
And drew the flock behind him too,
As good bellwethers always do.
And from that day, o'er hill and glade,
Through those old woods a path was made;
And many men wound in and out,
And dodged, and turned, and bent about
And uttered words of righteous wrath
Because 'twas such a crooked path.
But still they followed—do not laugh—
The first migrations of the calf,
And through his winding wood-way stalked,
Because he wobbled when he walked.
This forest path became a lane,
That bent, and turned, and turned again;
This crooked lane became a road,
Where many a poor horse with his load
Toiled underneath the burning sun,
And traveled some three miles in one,
And thus a century and a half
They trod the footsteps of that calf.
The years passed on in swiftness fleet,
The road became a village street;
And this, before men were aware,
A city's crowded thoroughfare;
And soon the central street was this
Of a renowned metropolis;

And men two centuries and a half
Trod in the footsteps of that calf.
Each day a hundred thousand rout
Followed the zig-zag calf about;
And o'er this crooked journey went
The traffic of a continent.
A hundred thousand men were led
By one calf near three centuries dead.
They followed still his crooked way,
At least one hundred years a day;
For thus such reverence is lent
To well-established precedent.

A moral lesson this might teach,
Were I ordained and called to preach;
For men are prone to go it blind
Along the calf-paths of the mind,
And work away from sun to sun
To do what other men have done.
They followed in the beaten track,
And out and in and forth and back,
And still their devious course pursue,
To keep the path that others do.
But how the wise old wood-gods laugh,
Who saw that first primeval calf!
Ah! Many things this tale might teach,
But I am not ordained to preach.

We would do our children, our fellow human beings, our students, our employees *and ourselves* a better service if we acknowledged the value of creativity and invested the extra effort to make room for creativity in our day-to-day lives. For example, children should be rewarded when they discover a new and better way of solving a problem or accomplishing a task.

That might sound easy, but what usually happens is that parents and teachers reward children for falling into the line of conformity, even when they've been creative. To a child, discovering that s/he can do something that s/he could never have done before is an act of creativity. In fact, *new and never done before* is a good definition for creativity.

Learning the roles and rules of civilized people is important, but it takes some extra effort to make people of any age feel as if their productive behavior is part of their uniqueness and not a function of becoming like everyone else. In other words, even though we all do many of the same things, each of us has a unique way of going about it. That's the point we want to encourage in others and in ourselves.

By creating an environment that encourages and supports uniqueness, creativity becomes part of our lifestyle—at home, at school, at work and at play. The high-performance person seeks to maintain a creative flow in his or her life at all times. When creativity is part and parcel of your everyday affairs, life is never dull and it's usually much more productive. Creativity fuels performance by drawing constantly on that reservoir of undeveloped strengths that each of has within us.

Creativity flourishes in an environment of:

1. Experimentation
2. Playfulness
3. Spontaneous behavior

Experimentation

When people try something that doesn't work, do you tell them that they screwed up? Do you say that to yourself? How many times have you heard a parent say to a child, *"That was dumb"*? It doesn't take a whole lot of effort to say *"That didn't work. It's time to try something else."* The latter comment carries an entirely different message.

The first comment means, "Don't try things that might not work or your intelligence will be questioned." Not many people are going to try new things when they can expect criticism. The second comment doesn't cast aspersions at the person who tried something new, it merely acknowledges that the experiment didn't produce the desired results. Such acknowledgment doesn't discourage another try.

In the classroom, the home or the office, if experimentation is openly encouraged, there will be more experimentation.

Remember, behavior that's rewarded tends to be repeated. You can post notes on the refrigerator or the bulletin board that detail the problems that certain people are working on. Such a display of experimentation underway is a clear signal that experimentation is encouraged.

Your discussions should include mention of experimentation that you're involved in. Sharing ideas with others is always good practice. Discourse about experimentation is another way to send the message that creativity is a worthwhile and desirable part of day-to-day living. Both words and actions should be purposefully used to encourage experimentation.

Playfulness

That might sound childish at first, but remember that it's valuable to maintain a *childlike sense of wonder* about things. Someone who is constantly serious, with nose to the grindstone might *look* like the picture of dedication. In truth that person might be missing a great many creative solutions. Encouraging and maintaining an atmosphere of playfulness isn't difficult when dealing with children. With adults, it's a bigger challenge because so many people have been led to believe that playfulness is childish and immature. Some of the most productive offices I've ever seen go out of their way to make sure that the mood stays light and that there's humor everywhere.

Humor is one of the best ways to keep a healthy and productive perspective on things. Humor and playfulness go hand in hand. When the parent, teacher or boss is a stoic old grouch, nobody else has permission to be funny. As with all things, there can be too much emphasis on humor at the expense of productivity. On the other hand, a lack of humor and lighthearted spirit will also have a detrimental effect on productivity. Keeping everybody around the office solemnly towing the line doesn't necessarily result in maximum performance. An environment of laughter adds a lot.

Spontaneous behavior

Rules and regulations should only exist to keep everyone in the organization pulling their oars in the same direction. *How* each person pulls his or her oar should be left to the individual as much as possible. As I've already discussed, the more uniqueness a person can bring to his or her tasks, the more personal energy will be invested.

No matter how many rigid rules and procedures an organization adopts, real life doesn't obey strict rules and regulations. I've seen companies that are so regulated that they begin to demand that their customers follow *company rules*. Real life doesn't work that way and companies that try and impose their rigidity on the general public ultimately become flexible or go out of business.

People are spontaneous creatures by nature. Only when the spontaneity has been snuffed out by an inflexible environment do people become dull. I've found that, even the most bland personality has a lot of spunk if you coax it out. Maintaining a healthy balance of appropriate behavior at home, in school or at the office is important. That means that spontaneous behavior should not only be allowed but actually encouraged.

Let the spirit move you and those around you. When a great idea hits, don't waste time getting some feedback on it. When you see someone trying something risky, let that person know that you appreciate it. When someone's efforts don't produce desired results, go ahead and let that person know how much you appreciate the *effort*.

Give yourself all of this encouragement as well. When it seems like a good day to send the entire office to the beach, do it. Being spontaneous is a hedge against losing good ideas and emotional momentum. If someone in the office has a burning desire to work on this or that problem today, bend the schedule, change a few appointments and do whatever is necessary to exploit whatever creative burst of energy is taking place.

The same goes for you. When *you* feel like being spontaneous, there's generally a reason. It's probably your creative control center telling you that a solution is at hand and all you have to do is follow your creative impulses to access the desired results. You might not even know what the problem is when the solution pops out at you, but your spontaneous impulses will let you know that what you're coming up with is important.

The kaleidoscope approach

Like Peter F. Drucker's earlier suggestion to bend over and look at things from a backwards and upside-down perspective, the *kaleidoscope technique* is a way of changing how things appear. Looking at life, problems and day-to-day activities as if they were tumbling in a kaleidoscope can present an endless parade of possible solutions. Make it a point to consider things from every angle you can think of, then turn the whole thing upside-down and repeat the process. Granted, most of the new patterns and arrangements won't result in higher performance. But it only takes one good solution to turn around a bogged-down operation or speed up a good one. Who cares how many times you tumble the kaleidoscope! The point is to *do it.*

What makes a new idea successful

How do you know when a new idea is destined to be successful? There's nothing that beats experience to confirm the validity of a new idea. However, you can't try *every* new idea you come up with. There just isn't time. Spending all of your time testing new ideas would throw your productivity out of balance. You need to put new ideas through a screening process.

I've found that a simple, three-step examination that Walt Disney used is all you need to indicate whether a new idea should be taken to the next level. The three criteria are:

1.   A successful idea must be unique.

If a new idea isn't sufficiently different than what you're currently doing, then the idea is probably a rehash of present policy.

Doing more of the same is hardly a way to inject new thinking and enthusiasm into the process. The element of uniqueness stimulates a natural curiosity and heightened sense of anticipation to those involved with its implementation.

2. A successful idea must have an element of proprietary interest.

When people take a special interest in something, it become proprietary, or a part of them. When someone recommends a book, a movie or a restaurant it's because that person has taken a personal interest in it.

Word-of-mouth recommendations are called the best possible type of advertising because a personal recommendation is genuine and not a ploy for commercial gain. When a new idea gains the proprietary recommendation of those involved with its implementation, it's because those people feel the idea will work in their best interest. If your interests are consistent with theirs, then a highly-endorsed idea should move to the top of your list.

3. A successful idea must have a flair factor. If it's worth doing, it's worth doing *big,* it's worth doing *right* and it's worth doing *with class.*

A successful new idea deserves to be celebrated. After all, a good new idea will increase personal and organizational performance. If the new idea doesn't seem as if it's worth any fuss or special attention, perhaps it's not worth the effort. If the new idea is worth celebrating, the attention it's given will help promote it and get more people on the band wagon sooner. A good new idea should excite everybody involved in its implementation.

The creativity process

There are four steps to the *creativity process.* As with any developmental process, it's important not to skip over any of the steps in the creative process. Failing to give new ideas sufficient scrutiny will likely result in premature implementation or premature abandonment. In either case, the new idea wasn't given the opportunity to increase performance.

Step one: Preparation

If you're intent on solving a problem, you must prepare. Unless you make an attempt to learn what others before you have tried, you're doomed to cover the same ground they did. Thomas Edison was a good example. He spent a great deal of time studying what others had done with a concept before he would begin his own experimentation. He saw no value in repeating mistakes that others had made before. Edison saw more value in making new and creative mistakes that brought him closer to success.

Preparation means research. Another type of research is soliciting opinions on how a problem should be defined and how others think it would be best resolved. If there is consensus on certain unsatisfactory outcomes, then why waste time going down those roads? In the end, the net result of preparation is that the ultimate solution you devise will probably be largely comprised of elements that nobody had thought of before.

Preparation will get you closer to those undiscovered elements faster by saving the time and energy that would have otherwise been wasted retracing old efforts. This doesn't mean ignoring the findings of others. Certain components of the experimentation others have done might fit well into your puzzle.

Step two: Incubation

Individual items in a delicious stew, if eaten raw, wouldn't have the same flavor or texture. Raw carrots, potatoes, celery, beans and pieces of beef wouldn't be very appealing if they were mixed together but not cooked. The same is true of ideas. Good ideas are usually made up of smaller ideas that need to be "cooked" before they represent the usable idea—not to water them down or dilute them but to add synergy.

The incubation phase of the creative process is a time for patience as you observe how the various elements react to one another when combined at certain temperatures and in various proportions. If all the pieces seem to be there but they haven't jelled yet, you probably need to let them simmer a little longer.

When I'm in a problem-solving mode and run into a dead end, I back off and let things steep. Usually, I'm awakened in the middle of the night with the answer. When you see a high-performance person rush into the office early in the morning, s/he has probably been awakened in the middle of the night with a possible solution to that problem that was incubating. Believe me, when a solution is ready to emerge from a short, medium or long incubation phase, it will let you know.

Step three: Insight

After the idea has emerged from the incubation phase, everything looks much clearer to you. That's insight. When the answer looms vividly before you, don't get suckered into thinking that the creative process is completed. The clearly identified solution is now ready for the fourth phase of the process. Although the idea might appear to be a flawless solution, watch out. Looks can be deceiving.

Step four: Verification

Is the idea really as good as you think it is? When we give birth to a new idea, we're naturally protective of it. After all, it's proprietary. Be careful not to put up a fence around your new idea and defend it to the death. For starters, if you act like that, others will withhold valuable feedback from you. Who wants to comment on a new idea if they're going to get their head bitten off?

When you're all pumped up about a new idea, the temptation is great to say, *"Let's go with this immediately."* Even when fast action is called for, a verification process is still a good safeguard against premature implementation and, possibly, the wasting of a good idea. The four-step verification process, outlined below, can be done quickly. However, the important questions it raises shouldn't be taken lightly.

1. Suitability. Will the new idea remedy the problem, be a *stop-gap,* or a permanent solution?
2. Feasibility. Is it affordable and practical?
3. Acceptability. Will management and/or the customers go along with it? What positive and negative things will *each* of these groups have to say about it?
4. Improvability. The idea might be good now, but how will customers demand improvement over time? How can the idea serve as a springboard for improvements after being put into practice?

These questions all need to be answered on paper. You should always get input on these questions from a variety of sources to promote objectivity. Consider defining management and customers to best represent your situations. For example, to a teacher, management might be the school principal or the school board. Customers might be students and/or parents. Hearing negative feedback should be considered beneficial. Negative feedback gives you information that will help you *tune* the idea before it's put into motion.

Roadblocks to creativity

It should be obvious by now that creativity is a process. New ideas need to evolve. During the time that new ideas need to evolve, problems can arise that block the development. Some of the roadblocks are unpredictable and need to be dealt with as they arise. Other blockages are caused by pre-existing conditions that can be addressed ahead of time.

Like barriers to personal growth and development, barriers to the creative process can be either natural or self-imposed. Besides the roadblocks that are beyond your control, the creative process can be encumbered by roadblocks that you erect yourself. Self-imposed barriers to the creative process can be conscious or unconscious, intentional or unintentional.

The following list of four primary roadblocks to creativity contains self-imposed barriers because those are the ones that you can minimize or completely eliminate through modification of your existing thoughts and behavior. It's not easy changing thoughts and behavior. You've been thinking the way you think and acting the way you act for a lot longer than you've been interested in creativity.

Roadblock 1: Habit

"But we've always done it this way." This is still the mission statement of too many organizations that ought to know better. Saying that you've always done something a certain way is not the same as asking, *"If it ain't broke, why fix it?"* I'm not a big fan of the latter comment either. But at least it acknowledges that something is working.

I frequently hear people defend traditional and time-honored methods *even when the methods don't work!* Habit and ritual seem to have a strangle hold on the productivity of many individuals and organizations. As I discussed earlier, human beings are creatures of comfort and comfort can be found in what's *familiar*. One of the main obstacles to the high-performance process is the desire to be comfortable at the expense of productivity.

Roadblock 2: Fear

Fear and creativity are mutually exclusive terms. They cannot exist in the same space. Fear is a real emotion and no one can make fear go away completely. However, fear should serve as the springboard to launch a search for solutions, not as the driving force. Where fear is left in charge, everything everyone does becomes avoidance. People's energies are used in *not* rocking the boat instead of moving the boat forward. I've seen people balk, saying, *"The competition wouldn't like it."* Can you think of a better reason to go ahead and do something?

You need to acknowledge those things that make you afraid. If you've done some honest self-inspection, you'll be aware of the things you fear and why. The good news is that fear, when brought out into the light of day, tends to dissipate. Only when fears are kept under pressure in dark, secret caverns deep within you do they have such powerful influence over your thoughts and actions.

Where the development of new ideas is concerned, the poison gases that fear gives off can suffocate an idea before it's had a chance to mature. Fear avoidance is one of the human race's most ardent pastimes. Like the actor Glenn Ford told me, either you do the things you fear or fear is in charge. The high-performance person knows how important it is to get fear under control so that fear itself doesn't take control.

Roadblock 3: Prejudice

One of my biggest frustrations as I travel back and forth across America working with corporations is hearing the same response to new ideas over and over again. *"That idea sounds great, Danny,"* they tell me, *"but it would never work here at our company."* Prejudice. The prejudging of ideas without considering their individual merit.

Rigid and inflexible thinking, designed to preserve the established order of things, is prejudicial thinking. Prejudice has roots in habit, but more so in fear. People fear what they don't know much about. Yet, instead of reaching out and learning more to counteract their ignorance, they avoid it even more. It's a shame, but it happens all of the time. A high-performance person has no time or energy to waste on prejudice, jut as s/he has no time or energy to waste on unimportant and petty considerations.

Roadblock 4: Inertia

When people ask, *"What's wrong with the way we're doing it now?"* What they're really asking is why they should start moving when they've been motionless for so long, or why they should chart a new course after so much time on their old course. An individual or an organization that makes daily sacrifices to the status quo is fighting nature. A good rule of thumb: *If it's been done one way for two years, there's an 80-percent chance there's a better way of doing it.*

You can't expect to get anywhere by repeating yesterday in a world that doesn't. The world of business in particular is increasingly intolerant of sluggish performance and resistance to change. Fortunes are being lost or, more appropriately, swept away by a flood of new thinking and initiative. The old maxim, *"S/he who hesitates is lost"* has taken on renewed meaning.

I did a program for a major industrial association not long ago and the national president made a comment during his speech that really struck home with me. He said that there has been more change in that industry over the past five years than in all the time before. I had already heard that the human race has acquired more knowledge since 1960 than from 1960 back to the beginning of recorded history.

There is simply no way that a person who seeks the benefits of the *high-performance process* can stay out of the information current. The constant flow of new information isn't going to slow down any time soon. In fact, it appears to be accelerating. The application of new information, guided by timeless truths, demands constant motion and defies stagnation.

Slaying the "idea killer"

Even when you get a new idea through the verification process, there might be some who will ask you to soft-pedal it. No matter how good an idea is, there will always be someone in the organization who insists on smothering it under a bureaucratic blanket. It might be professional jealousy or any number of other unfortunate reasons. But it happens. What can you do?

The answer is: turn the idea *killer* into a valuable *devil's advocate*. Take up the idea with its principal detractor and ask what points about the idea the person likes. Try to get at least two or three positive comments. Then ask what the detractor *doesn't* like about the idea. Now acting as a helpful critic, the idea killer will highlight weaknesses in the idea that you need to address.

Once a person has said one or two positive things about an idea, the negative comments will be more objective and helpful. The comments that your chief detractor makes should focus your thinking on how to make your idea even more effective. Turning negatives into positives is a significant feature of a high-performance person. There is always some positive energy in negativism. The challenge is extracting it.

Maximizing a new idea

Even as new ideas are being developed, their horizons should be stretched. The world is full of useful products that resulted from attempts to solve problems that had nothing to do with the idea's ultimate application. Part of remaining open to new ideas is to remain open to new applications. In finding broader or different applications for new ideas, you can also recruit support from other sectors that wouldn't have had any previous reason to be involved.

Can the idea be put to uses other than the use it was originally deigned for?

Can the idea be modified in any way?

Can the idea be reduced in scale or expanded?

Can the idea be upgraded?

Can the idea be substituted?

Can the idea be rearranged?

Can the idea be reversed?

Can the idea be combined with another idea?

The following questions are a helpful final guide to making a go or no go decision on a new idea.

Does the new idea make better use of most peoples' time, talent and energy?

Does the idea improve operations or product quality?

Does the new idea cut waste or unnecessary work?

Does the new idea improve working conditions and customer service?

Does the new idea represent the goals of the high-performance process?

A new idea doesn't have to solve the problems of the world to be worth a shot. As long as a creative new concept meets the criteria set forth, it's a valuable addition to your life. You will always have to use your best judgment and exercise discrimination. That's simply part of being a responsible person.

Creativity is critical to the *high-performance process* because it is the most effective mechanism to access your unique talents and abilities. Nothing is more central to the discovery and development of your undeveloped strengths than creativity. As Thomas Edison said, *"The answer is out there. Find it."* I say there's a great deal more inside of you than you're aware of. Find it.

Good news and bad news

Adversity lies ahead for anyone who wants to commit themselves to the self-discovery and strength development that the *high-performance process* requires. If it was easy, everybody would be a high-performance person and the world would be unrecognizable. It's a nice thought, but highly unlikely.

Even though every human being has undeveloped strengths and unrealized potential, high-performance people are few and far between. But that's an even greater motivation to become one. Unclaimed opportunity is waiting for the few men and women who are willing to make the sacrifices the *high-performance process* requires. The effort necessary to develop your undeveloped strengths pales in comparison to the excitement of learning and understanding more about *yourself*.

Becoming a high-performance person and engaging in the strength-development that the process calls for means that you must seize on the best aspects of your character and build upon them. The balance in your life will shift away from negativism and toward a brighter, more positive outlook.

You will feel young again. It's true. One of the personal characteristics we most mourn the loss of is the optimism and upbeat, never-say-die attitude of youth. If you feel increasingly cynical about life as you grow older, it's because you've grown tired of the bumps and snags. It's easier to build up a callous around your heart than to continue risking rejection for the sake of some elusive goal.

Once you realize that the goal is inside of you in the form of undeveloped potential—completely under your control—attaining it becomes less threatening. How can anyone stomp out your desire to know yourself better and mine the vein of precious undeveloped personal strengths? How many of your hidden strengths ever see the light of day is up to nobody but *you*.

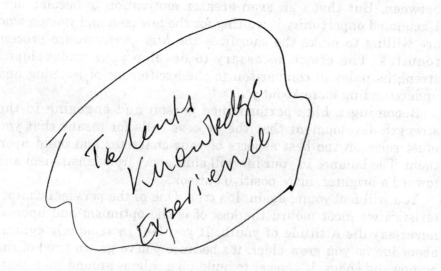

STEP THREE
Planning for Performance

"Many people fail in life, not for lack of ability or brains or even courage, but simply because they have never organized their energies around a goal."

—*Elbert Hubbard*

Selecting desired rewards and setting goals establishes a target. Discovering and developing hidden strengths provides the tools for making the goal a reality. Planning for performance means setting a *strategy*. The plan you establish to reach your goals will serve as a road map that leads from where you are now to your desired rewards, using existing and newly-developed personal strengths.

Like goal-setting, planning requires focusing on the future. My good friend and mentor James Newton had the privilege of knowing Thomas Edison, Henry Ford, Harvey Firestone, Alexis Carrel and Charles Lindbergh, all of whom were mentors to him. Jim Newton is a brilliantly successful entrepreneur and thinker. One of the characteristics that he recalls most fondly about his five famous friends is the way *they* were always thinking ahead. In his book, *Uncommon Friends,* Jim describes how his mentors always focused on the future. Until the time of their deaths, they never ceased planning for accomplishment.

As with goal-setting and self-examination, planning can also become an endless treadmill used to avoid increasing personal performance. Planning needs to be used in concert with the first two steps in the high-performance process to keep you in motion rather than to provide you with another way to get sidetracked. The excitement of becoming more uniquely you is key to keeping the planning phase in perspective.

With excitement and anticipation comes increased energy. Elbert Hubbard's quote at the beginning of this chapter well describes the value of focusing energy. In achieving goals, a wide variety of existing and newly developed strengths must be employed. Despite the best-laid plans, there are sure to be many twists and turns, victories and setbacks along the way. Focused energy will keep the ball rolling and your plan will be the focus of your energies.

Unimportant work

Many people do unimportant work very efficiently. Are you such a person? In the overview I listed 10 characteristics of high-performance people. The second characteristic is *high energy in an absence of pettiness*. Pettiness is mentioned in the same breath as high energy because unimportant things are the enemy of focused, productive energy.

High-performance people know the difference between what's truly *important* and merely *interesting*. I've always liked the analogy of rearranging deck chairs on the *Titanic, after* it had been struck by the iceberg. It seems to be a waste of time to any rational person. Nevertheless, in virtually every company and organization in America, somebody is intensely rearranging the deck chairs, seemingly completely oblivious to the more pressing issues at hand.

Getting caught up in minor, inconsequential stuff makes it *appear* as if we're engaged in work of tremendous importance when in fact we're merely busying ourselves with low-risk activities. Low risk because, the more inconsequential the issue, the less anyone really cares about the outcome. Rearranging deck chairs on a sinking ship is easy because the chairs are floating. In the same way, lining up paper clips in a failing business is easy because nobody cares about paper clips.

Expending energy on unimportant things is just our old nemesis *procrastination* popping up in another disguise. When we procrastinate, we're avoiding responsibility for *succeeding*. Making something happen is to run the risk that things could improve. Making sure that you're not involved in anything of consequence guarantees that nothing will change—for the better.

Unfortunately, those who seek to distract themselves from productive work also tend to distract others from productive work. The unproductive person is setting up an alibi to explain or justify low productivity. The fact that others are recruited into his or her scheme is part of the rationalizing or justification process.

Planning failure

I had a salesperson working for me once who had a cynical, sarcastic sense of humor that humored no one in the office but him. He was a *bubble-popper*. He lived to burst other people's balloons. The time and energy he wasn't spending on his own success, he eagerly spent on spoiling the success of others. His exploits were intended to take the focus off of his own marginal performance.

Turning around this person's attitude was no easy task. After all of my conventional coaching had failed to make a dent in his attitude, I finally asked him to make a written list of everything that didn't work in our business. *"Do you mean make a list of all the ways to not make money here?"* He asked. I nodded my head. *"Well I can do that,"* he continued confidently, *"I do that every day."*

I proceeded to wipe the smile off his face by asking him, in light of his last comment, what he had planned for the next day. The light bulb went on above his head. He looked me straight in the eye and, in a more serious tone, said, *"My God, I've never stopped to think about that."* He suddenly realized that he makes a plan every day to not succeed.

In how many aspects of your life do you make a plan to not succeed? How much energy do you spend every day executing such

I am planning and living failure every DAY, waiting for

plans? You don't have to have an irritatingly bad attitude to fall victim to this elaborate procrastination scheme. The fact that people who aren't very visible don't get shot at very much encourages us to lay low.

What better way to lay low than to make sure we never rise very far on the wings of success? Planning for failure is surprisingly more common than you might think. The more comfortable folks become with complacency, the more likely they will operate not in the absence of a plan, but with an actual plan to repeat the things that are known to fail.

The cynical man who worked for me turned his thinking around 180 degrees, and his personal performance broke out of its slump. He resolved to discontinue repeating what he knew didn't work. It is easier said than done. But just acknowledging the existence of such a practice is unsettling enough to keep you on your toes. Refusing to repeat failures takes courage because it elevates the very expectations you've been trying to avoid.

I believe that most people want to be productive. Put another way, I believe most people want the rewards of productivity without the risk. Once the rewards seem more attainable and the risks are exposed as essentially inconsequential, productivity will naturally increase. My salesperson realized that he was causing his own misery, which he gladly exchanged for the possible misery of increasing his personal performance.

He found out that there was no misery in increasing his personal performance. Instead, there was a great deal of support and encouragement from those around him, which pleased him to no end. When you give up your plan for failure and replace it with a plan to increase personal performance, the payoff far exceeds the misery of occupying yourself with unimportant matters.

Many people who repeat what they know doesn't work do so in only certain aspects of their lives and work. You don't have to be a complete screw-up to be guilty of petty distraction. It's possible to have success in a variety of ways and to also sabotage your complete victory by holding back certain key components needed to bring everything to completion.

I've seen countless people make incredible strides to increase personal performance only to stumble just short of the finish line. Every time, I'm surprised and scratch my head. I just want to believe that, once someone gets past the first few major roadblocks to higher productivity, s/he will overcome every obstacle, internal or external.

If every one of us took the time to honestly evaluate our work on a daily basis, we would no doubt turn up a number of things that are productivity-blocking repeated failures. When a plan has been established for increasing productivity, it's easier to flag out nonproductive behavior. All you have to do is hold up your daily activities against the backdrop of the plan and evaluate which tasks and activities did not promote progress.

Goals vs. fantasies

In effective planning, it's important to know the difference between what is a legitimate goal and what's not. A fantasy is not a goal. By definition a fantasy is imagination unrestrained by reality. A goal is a fantasy with a concrete, measurable, realizable plan for achievement. If you don't know specifically what you have to do to on a daily basis, in addition to your customary activities, you don't have a real goal.

It's the combination of desired rewards *and* a plan to achieve them that makes a goal worth your energy and attention. Some public speakers make a lot of money by getting up in front of audiences flailing their arms and jumping up and down until the audience is doing the same thing. They do it in the name of *enthusiasm*. These motivational speakers do in fact inspire enthusiasm in their audiences—for the moment.

A purely motivational presentation without redeeming substance will wear off by the time most people get to the cars in the parking lot and certainly by the time the audience wakes up the next morning. As I discussed earlier, each of us faces a moment of truth each and every day. Our inspired enthusiasm comes from rededicating ourselves to the *high-performance process* that brings more of our unique strengths to the surface.

As long as an intended goal remains a fantasy, excitement and enthusiasm will turn into frustration and disappointment. Hanging a picture of the expensive car, sailboat, dream house, secluded beach or other material goal on your refrigerator or office wall—without a concrete plan for achievement—will ultimately produce resentment when you discover that you're not getting any closer to living your fantasy.

Looking at a picture is not the same thing as taking action to identify and do those things that you know will bring reality closer to imagination. I've seen people in companies across America who have pictures of all sorts of things on their office walls. Sadly, the pictures are often old and yellowed with age because they've hung there so long.

One fellow had a picture of a Rolls Royce above his desk. It was so old, the edges were cracked, taped together and cracked again. I asked that man about the picture and he confirmed that it was his goal to own a Rolls Royce. I asked how long he had been pursuing that goal and he confirmed that it had been a long time, many years in fact.

I next asked the man what he was doing over and above his regular daily activities to get his hands on a Rolls Royce. He was stumped. He went on to tell me that all he was told to do was hang the picture up where he could see it every day and one day he would find it in his driveway. Even though his life experience confirmed it, he was surprised to hear me say that simply doing what he ordinarily does day-in and day-out wouldn't get him any more than he already had.

Breathtaking moments

Mary Lawrence, the woman who nearly lost her life in an automobile accident and went on to be a record-breaking real estate salesperson, hung her pink dress in the closet where she would see it every day. Mary knew exactly what she needed to do on a daily basis to make that dream come true. In a personal moment of truth, she stood at her own crossroads each day and made a decision. The realization of her goal was the net result of the decisions she made day after day. She was visually reminded of her goal each day, but she also had a plan in place to guide her actions toward the meeting of imagination and reality in her life. She executed her plan.

When I presented her with the trophy for being the number-one salesperson, the award she had predicted winning a year before, I was reminded of an expression I had once heard. After Mary had glided toward the podium to accept the award amidst a standing ovation, I told the audience that *we shouldn't measure life by how many breaths we take, but by how many breathtaking moments we experience.* The number of breathtaking moments we experience is directly proportional to the amount of effort we invest in our plans for achievement.

Time divisions for better planning

Just as goals are subdivided into three categories, *financial, lifestyle* and *personal growth,* so, too, is planning divided into three categories for the purpose of identifying length of execution. The three categories are:

1. Short-term *(up to one year)*
2. Medium-term (one to five years)
3. Long-term (over five years)

The length of time you allow yourself to realize a goal should be determined by a realistic time table more than on the intensity of your desire to reach the goal. A young couple without any savings might *want* to buy an expensive house in one year, but it's not realistic. Without any financial assistance, their goal might be better served by setting up some intermediate steps such as saving the money for a down payment on a more affordable home in 12 months and then moving up to a more expensive home in five years or so.

Remember that a goal needs to be *attainable.* If a plan is not given sufficient time to be properly executed, it's doomed. Plans of any length need to be thought of in daily increments. If adding up the daily efforts puts you somewhere between one and five years, you've got yourself a medium-term goal.

Don't fall into the trap of thinking that you can simply double or triple your daily effort and speed up the realization of your goal. It might simply be unrealistic to expect so much of yourself. Nobody is super-human. Everyone has required regular tasks to do in order to provide food, clothing and shelter for the household. How much *additional* effort can you and *will* you put forth *each day* to attain your goal?

Goals that relate to home purchases, home improvements, education, career and family all need to be planned in reference to the length of time needed to properly accomplish the required tasks. Logging daily efforts toward goal attainment requires dedicated discipline. Keeping the *big picture* in perspective requires vision. Dedication, discipline and vision must all work harmoniously if you expect successful goal attainment.

Small bites

The good news about breaking down goals into daily efforts is that the effort you face each day is far less overwhelming than the overall process. When I think about writing a *book,* I see images of that enormous, 300-page manuscript sitting on my desk. It's intimidating. But when I chart a goal of 10 to 15 pages per day, suddenly the task is reasonable. When the enormity of an entire project starts to make your knees weak, immediately focus on your much more manageable daily task.

Small bites are never as intimidating as the thought of swallowing the entire thing whole. Caution. Just because you've broken down your plan into small, digestible portions, don't take the daily tasks so lightly that you begin to slack off. When writing a book, I can imagine how easy it would be to skip a day here and a day there until I'm faced with writing 50 pages per day to keep pace with my deadline.

Looking at 50 pages instead of my usual 10 to 15 is a great reminder that *"a stitch in time saves nine."* To help emphasize the importance of keeping pace with your plan, you should celebrate the accomplishment of each day's tasks. I don't celebrate the writing of 15 pages the same way that I celebrate the book after it's completed.

However, I do acknowledge my daily accomplishment by writing the new page count on a post-it note and sticking it to the edge of the computer screen. When you're working on a project with a specified time allocation for completion, you often get into a *"zone"* when the daily extra effort comes automatically. That can be a trap too. But over time, dedication to daily tasks actually forms a positive habit and the progress seems to accelerate.

The planning process

You need to *write each goal down*. Holding your dreams in your head doesn't count. Writing down the goal gives it greater focus and commitment. Included in the first draft of your goal must be the time division I just discussed. How long do you predict it will take to reach your goal—short-term, medium-term or long-term? Listing your goals on paper, including estimated time of execution, focuses your thinking on the tasks required for goal attainment rather than on the intimidating big picture. It's okay to post a picture of your desired reward as long as your written goal and its timetable are posted right next to it.

Next, *establish a timetable* by breaking down the short-term, medium-term or long-term time division into daily increments. If the daily steps seem too large and unreasonable, you need to move into a longer overall time division. You can always add more time to goal attainment if you fall short of your mark. Just remember that every time you fall short, you build disappointment and make it harder on yourself the next time. So be as realistic as possible the first time.

Concentrate on results. From the outset, achievement of the daily goals must be considered part of the overall mission. You're doing whatever it is you're doing for a reason. You want something. That's why you set out in the first place. Your efforts should produce the type of enthusiasm that you felt when you committed to the goal in the first place.

Be aware that the desired outcome can become *too consuming* and obliterate the daily tasks required. Results in daily terms and in longer time division terms go hand in hand. At the planning stage, you need to include some method of monitoring progress.

Get started and stick with it. Winston Churchill said, *"Never, never, never give up."* Unless there is some material change in your desired rewards, there's probably no reason to stop other than fatigue or fear of success. Neither fatigue nor fear of success are acceptable outcomes to your goal-achievement process.

High-performance people know that they need to plan for the temptation to quit. It's going to come. Even though you start with all the conviction of Winston Churchill, you might turn into W.C. Fields without realizing it. Bulldog-like Churchill said to never quit. W.C. Fields said, *"If at first you don't succeed, try again. Then quit, there's no use being a damn fool about it."* When the inevitable temptation to quit arrives, back off at your own peril. Do you want others to see you as Churchill or W.C. Fields?

Celebrate the achievement of a goal and immediately replace it with a new goal. As mentioned, appropriate celebrations along the way are merely a prelude to the big party you should throw when the overriding goal is achieved. All celebrations are important when kept in context. But intermediary celebrations need to include a look ahead to what's left and major celebrations must be the launching pads for bigger and better things to come.

Don't miss your own victory party by immediately diving into a new major task. Instead, acknowledge that what's just been accomplished can and will be followed by equal or greater accomplishments. The establishment of a new goal should be part of the celebration. As soon as it's practical draft a new vision, complete with a plan for accomplishment.

Establishment of a new goal is critical to your ongoing success because you will feel an inevitable letdown following the accomplishment of the previous goal. That's why we suffer from the *"post-holiday blues/blahs/depression."* Without something to look forward to, there isn't much to be excited about. When there's not much to be excited about, nothing seems very exciting.

In goal achievement, like in any much-anticipated event or celebration, the buildup and anticipation is most of the fun. That's why a realistic, manageable timetable is critical. You need to feel that the accomplishment is possible. Holidays always come every year. They're on the calendar. The achievement of your goals should be as dependable.

In developing your plan, account for the post-accomplishment letdown by planning for the establishment of a new goal. You know how your emotional calendar works, so plan accordingly. I did a program in Hawaii shortly after the new year. I asked the audience, who had come from the mainland for the conference, if they ever felt post-holiday depression. Virtually every hand went up.

I asked how many of them had experienced their usual post-holiday letdown after Christmas a few weeks earlier. No hands went up. Why? All of them were anticipating their trip to Hawaii in early January. Their much-anticipated celebration of Christmas and New Years was immediately followed by the anticipation of a new celebration.

I remember having new-car fever in the worst way. When I bought my *Porsche* I got over it. For the first few weeks after the purchase, I used to get up in the middle of the night and go down to the garage and look at it. Standing there in my pajamas, admiring my car, the celebration continued. Now, I sleep through the night and find the car waiting for me in the morning. I still love it, but the anticipation has evaporated.

Some of the *NASA* astronauts who went to the moon suffered terrible post-mission depression after they returned. When you work so hard, for so long on achieving a goal like going to the moon, how do you follow that up? You and I can always say that, when we've done everything there is to do on this planet, we still have the moon to look forward to.

Finally, *evaluate your progress each year on your birthday.* Birthdays are intensely personal mile markers on life's journey. Regardless of how many goals you've planned in whatever time divisions, your birthday is a great opportunity to check progress. I challenge you to write yourself a letter, seal it in an envelope and open it on your next birthday.

In the letter, tell yourself what you plan to have accomplished by that time. If just thinking about writing that letter is making you sweat, you're normal. A letter to yourself with a commitment to accomplish certain things proves the power of writing down goals. Documented goals can't be ignored with good conscience. Courage is one of the personal characteristics I listed for high-performance people. You'll need courage to write that letter every year. Keeping your promises to yourself might be a feeling you've rarely felt before.

Recapping the planning process:

1. Make a written list of your goals, including time divisions.
2. Break down the timetable into manageable tasks and deadlines.
3. Concentrate on results.
4. Get started and stick with it.
5. Celebrate when a goal is achieved and simultaneously replace it with a new goal.
6. Evaluate your progress each year on your birthday.

Making it happen: six thoughts

"I don't mind taking chances, but I never leave anything to chance."

—*Charles Lindbergh*

Lindbergh's comment does not contradict itself. The *high-performance process* requires you to step out of your comfort zone and experience new things. Because venturing into uncharted territory is uncomfortable, you're bound to feel anxious and hesitant. As Lindbergh lifted off on his solo flight across the Atlantic Ocean he must have felt every bit as anxious as you and I will ever feel.

The best way to minimize anxiety when boldly taking your life to another level is to do your homework. Be prepared. Expecting the unexpected makes the unexpected less of an unsettling surprise when it occurs. Chance is unavoidable when you endeavor to push back your horizons. However, preparation reduces the risk.

Lindbergh's point is to be a *smart* adventurer. Life without adventure is a boring existence. Your commitment to becoming a high-performance person will bring you as much adventure as you can handle. Like Lindbergh, your journey will be more productive and lastingly beneficial when you bring knowledge and skill to the process, leaving as little to chance as possible.

Lindbergh's solo flight across the Atlantic was measured in hours. Preparation for the flight took *years*. Whether you're aware of it or not, your life to this point has been preparation for the decisions you're about to make. The planning phase of the *high-performance process* is the formal, structured processing of what you've learned and experienced.

Thought one: Organization

Organization means different things to different people. What it must mean to you is the ability to look at your resources as they relate to your stated goals. Whatever you have learned and experienced needs to be inventoried as it relates to your intention to become a high-performance person. As I've mentioned, you are a store house of valuable talents, information and experience.

Continuing the idea that Elbert Hubbard set forth about organizing your energies around a goal, your stated objectives become the focal point of all that you've accumulated in your storehouse. That's organization. Merely keeping copious notes and well-documented files on all manner of information doesn't necessarily identify the ultimate purpose that the well-organized information serves.

Thought two: Planning

Proper prior planning positively prevents poor performances

Back home in the coal-mining country of Southern Illinois they used to say it like this, *"It's okay to have a tiger by the tail—if you know what to do next!"* I learned this lesson flying supersonic fighters in air shows. When I was flying 25 feet above the concrete runway at 700 miles-per-hour, it was a thrill to watch people, trees and buildings shoot past my wing tips.

After I swung out into a big teardrop-shaped turn and came back past the crowd, I was flying 100 miles-per-hour slower, *upside-down.* The concrete runway flashed by 25 feet below my canopy at 600 miles-per-hour. One word I never wanted to hear myself utter during an air show was, *"Oops."* Flying as close to the edge as I did, that would have been the *last* word I would have uttered.

It was countless hours of training and preparation that taught me to climb before I made my teardrop-shaped turn. Striking a wing tip while rolling into a 700 mile-per-hour turn at 25 feet would have produced a 700 mile-per-hour cartwheel. The crowd might have loved it and I probably would have made the evening news, but it would have been my first and final performance.

Likewise, it was exhaustive preparation that helped me to remember, while flying upside-down, hanging from my straps, that my controls were *reversed.* Had I lapsed for a moment and pulled back on the stick to climb out, I would have buried my nose in the pavement at 600 miles-per-hour without time to note my error and correct it.

The unexpected will come, but it will be expected. I mean that to be a contradiction. Proper planning will bring you through the predictable, leaving you the flexibility to deal with the unexpected—precisely because you anticipated the unexpected. When you're unprepared, anything that comes along can untrack you. When you're prepared, it takes a catastrophe to knock you off balance. And even then preparation accelerates recovery.

Thought three: Less time and more action

There's a term in the business world that I hear with increasing regularity. It's called *sprinting.* Apparently business people are beginning to realize that there is a natural human tendency to make a job last as long as it's given time to be accomplished. As a result, many people take eight hours to do what could be done in four. But, if four hours of work is all that's required of them in an eight-hour day, the four-hour job will take eight.

Clearly, I'm not describing high-performance people. Yet, all of us tend to drag things out if we're not paying attention. To concentrate action and get a job done in the optimum amount of time gives the opportunity to relax and reflect a bit before charging into your next event. People who appear calm and organized around the office are the people who know how to get things done efficiently and swiftly.

The people who look as if they're on the brink of disaster at all times are probably the ones who take too long to get started on tasks, take too long to accomplish them and are therefore in a constant state of catchup. The person who chooses to focus energy around goals and concentrate action for rapid results is far more likely to lead a low-stress life than someone who is always behind.

Poor planning and inefficient use of time lead to disorganization and frustration. Proper planning and emphasis on action lead to a richer existence. The net result of proper planning is to add more life to your years, not more years to your life. Being finished with an important task feels good. Being buried in work with no relief in sight feels hopeless.

Thought four: Change the present and change the future

You have no control over the past. You have no control over the future. You only have control over the present. People hear me say that and disagree saying, *"But, Danny, isn't everything we do supposed to control the future?"* Unfortunately, we have no control over whether there even is a future. That possibility is in the hands of a power much bigger than us.

Realistically, all we can do in the present is to set the stage for what happens in the future. However, not taking charge of our lives in the *"now"* cuts our future adrift. Just bobbing in the waves now, without any attempt to power or steer your ship, means that you'll still be drifting aimlessly tomorrow, no matter what the future brings.

What you establish today by concentrating your energies around a goal makes tomorrow a better-defined opportunity, even though you won't be able to influence tomorrow until it arrives. By planning and committing yourself to the *high-performance process* now, your course is charted and the resources are made ready for the decisions you make while standing at tomorrow's crossroads.

The fellow with the picture of the Rolls Royce on his office wall wasn't actively engaged in any organized effort to do the things *today* that would influence his future. Somehow he thought that by merely picturing a future the way he would like it to be, he was going to exert some cosmic energy to create future change. He, like the rest of us, only has the *now* to work with.

As I pointed out to him, the change he needed to be concerned with should have been in the present, not the future. It's what you do *today and every day* that determines, to the greatest possible degree, the quality of your future. It might be exciting to dream and fantasize about the future and all of the potential it holds, but it's a lot *more* exciting to realize that you can plant seeds today that will bloom tomorrow.

Thought five: Time to be creative, relax and live

One way that working intelligently and effectively in the present will improve the quality of your future is by clearing away worries and responsibilities that would otherwise be carried forward and added to your future burdens. Creativity, an essential element of the *high-performance process,* requires some space.

Although the future is not under your control, you can do yourself a favor by dispensing with as much clutter as possible now to be ready when the time and opportunity arises for creative thought. I'm referring to the reflective, stream of consciousness type of creative thinking, not the creative outlook that you should bring to everything you do.

Rest and relaxation are important to recharging your batteries. All work and no play, over time, makes you an increasingly unproductive individual. Some people feel too guilty to relax. Don't confuse emotionally driven workaholism with high performance. Bringing more of yourself to the work you do makes the work more satisfying and fulfilling. Bringing more of your uniqueness to your play strikes a better balance between work and relaxation.

In total, the quality of your life is determined by how much of your unique identity is reflected in your work, play and lifestyle in general. Good planning is critical to keeping these things in proper

*I do know
that running a
big business brings the best out in me,*

balance and perspective. The *high-performance process* is a method of encouraging crosspollination between the various aspects of your life. By bringing the elements into balance and harmony, the whole becomes a more fertile environment for doing what makes you happiest.

Thought six: "Live life, don't portray it"

Somerset Maugham said that. Maugham's imperative brings the planning of time and resources into alignment with the basic theme of the *high-performance process*. That is the understanding that your talents, knowledge and experience combine to form a truly unique creature. The closer you get to living in a way that reflects your uniqueness, the more your productivity increases.

Proper planning of your time and resources is the antidote for stress. When you're trying to portray an image that someone else thinks you should portray, you're not functioning in your strongest state. That's not good for you and that's not good for the people who rely on you. The greatest stress you can encounter is to try and conform to an image that you're not prepared or equipped to handle.

Planning is the focusing of *your* energies around a goal, not someone else's energy. To have maximum control over your life as it should be defined, that is in terms of your personal talents, knowledge and experience, you must develop a strategy that reflects what you bring to the situation. When that's accomplished, you're living your life and not play-acting in a miscast role. Living life on your terms means maximizing your personal performance potential, which is the lowest-stress environment.

*e.g. acting like some of the GM
bricks at Marmon*

Reasons people don't plan their time

We've all done it. Caught ourselves unprepared and overwhelmed with work or other obligations that could have been easily managed with a little planning. It's in those moments that we berate ourselves and wonder why we don't do what we know we should do—plan the use of our time. It doesn't matter whether we ask ourselves or if someone else asks us, the pat answers always seem to come out of the same script.

Each of the common answers that follow are undefendable in light of what we already know about the *high-performance process.* Nevertheless, such excuses pop out of our mouths from time to time, given sufficient frustration. Once you've enrolled yourself in the *high-performance process,* at least you can dismiss such foolishness as soon as it appears.

For example, one of the most common excuses for not planning time better is, *"It would limit my freedom."* High-performance people know that proper planning increases personal freedom. Greater control over the positive and negative aspects of your day-to-day activities results in maximizing what you want and minimizing what you don't want.

Those with the most freedom are those with effective control over their lives. Those with effective control over their lives are high performers who understand the process of planning and executing the tasks and activities that fill the day. Lack of planning makes you a victim of other people's agendas. With proper planning, *you* set more of your own agenda. That sounds like freedom to me.

Another excuse offered for not planning is, *"Things are just too unpredictable."* The statement that things are unpredictable is basically true. The implied futility of planning isn't. While it's true that we can't predict the future and lots of things can and will happen that are beyond our control, it still doesn't make sense to abandon the very thing that offers us hope.

Why should athletes practice for the big game if they can't predict exactly what's going to happen? Why do pilots and astronauts prepare so meticulously for their missions if they might encounter the unpredictable?

Why do financial institutions make such a big deal about investing for retirement? You never know what might happen between now and then. Even though time can't be socked away in an individual retirement account or in a coffee can buried in the back yard, the disciplined habits you acquire today insure that whatever you encounter in the future won't be as threatening or potentially devastating as it would be to an unprepared person.

136

Saying that an unpredictable future makes planning moot is like saying that doctors shouldn't bother studying so hard in medical school. Would you look up from the operating table and say, *"I don't blame you for skipping most of your medical classes, Doc. When you get into these surgery situations, who knows what's going to happen?"*

I think you would prefer that the surgeon with the scalpel be as well prepared as possible with lots of thought invested in the surgical strategy. Aren't you operating on your life every day? Shouldn't you invest in your future by giving ample thought to planning your personal surgical strategy? It's precisely *because* the future is unpredictable that you're better off being prepared.

How about this one? *"I just don't have time to plan my time."* Somebody switch on a light. Time is the critical commodity here. Trying to save time by not planning how your time is going to be best used makes no sense. All you're doing by ignoring time planning is to guarantee that most of your time will be used very inefficiently.

You already know the frustrating liabilities of being on someone else's schedule. Yet that's exactly what you do if you don't chart your path in advance. Sure, unpredictable obstacles will leap into your path. Others will make demands on your time. However, these distractions and disruptions are far more manageable when you've thought ahead and prepared your own agenda, complete with the flexible anticipation of interruptions.

At the bottom line, high-performance people know that proper planning *increases freedom, makes life more predictable* and *clears more time* to be used at your personal discretion. The use of excuses usually means that someone is not yet comfortable with moving their life to the next performance level. By evading increased productivity with excuses, they're giving tacit confirmation that planning *does* make a difference.

Don't try and convince Mary Lawrence that she would sacrifice her freedom, that the economy, the customers and the market are too unpredictable or that she is wasting valuable time when she takes time to plan her strategy for success. She's living proof that planning pays off. You can't tell me that intricate planning and preparation didn't save my life a thousand times, both figuratively and literally during my years as a supersonic fighter pilot and a business executive.

Don't claim that you don't have enough information to plan with. All *anybody* can do is plan with the information they've got. If it's fear that's driving your unwillingness to predict the future, you need to remember actor, Glenn Ford's, admonition that either you or fear will be in charge. You know that planning will make demands on your performance. If that's a frightening thought, find out why.

Controlling your time: three steps

You might be among the people who has all the best intentions about increasing your personal productivity but feels as if time is your worst enemy. Other than the fact that you've probably adopted some of the time-wasting habits I just outlined, you no doubt feel as if time controls you and not the other way around. High-performance people know and accept that they can't alter the passing of time. Instead, they sharpen their skills at managing their time allotment. Proper planning and management of your available time will provide you with the maximum control possible. Peter Drucker says it takes three steps to manage time.

Time management step 1: Record your time

Most people claim they're aware of how they spend their time. Almost without exception, they're wrong. Your memory is a horrible liar when it comes to accounting for your time. You would think that keeping track of time is somehow related to keeping track of calories on a diet. It never ceases to amaze me how I can keep gaining weight when I'm sure my caloric intake is going down. At least as far as my *memory* serves I'm eating less.

Even though time seems like an elusive commodity and you're always a day late, your memory will probably still tell you that you're putting every available second to the best use possible. To get an accurate picture of how conscious you really are when it comes to time, keep a log of how you spend your waking hours. I guarantee that you'll be surprised.

It's physically easy to do. The avoidant part of you will procrastinate. Once you break through your procrastination, simply sit down with your daily planner at the end of each day, for three days, and record how you time was spent. Be specific. If a one-hour block has a meeting noted, think back to whether the meeting actually took place.

You might have only spent part of that hour in a meeting. How was the rest of the hour spent? Traveling to and from the meeting? Talking on the telephone or to someone at the coffee machine? Were the conversations personal or business-related? You can immediately see that a three-day accounting for your time—morning, noon and night—will bring you face to face with the realities of your personal productivity. I predict you'll appreciate the urgent need for time management—*now!*

Time management step 2: Manage your time

"Until we can manage time, we can manage nothing else."

—*Peter F. Drucker*

You can't manage time itself in the sense of speeding it up, slowing it down or otherwise altering it. Time is like the ocean. We're all in the same sea and nobody can realistically change the volume of water. The only decision left is whether to sink or swim in it. There is more to come shortly on the specifics of time management. For now, just etch into the inside of your forehead the fact that managing time means swimming in it and not managing time means sinking in it.

Time management step 3: Consolidate your time

As a prelude to a full-scale organizational effort, it's important to begin looking for tasks and chores that can be grouped together in more efficient units. A phrase I like to use is, *"Don't just plan your time, time your plan."* In other words, you can very deliberately schedule time for even the most minuscule task without considering how the grouping of specific tasks can add a great deal to the time efficiency of your day.

You can group chores together because they are geographically compatible, because they call for similar tools, because they call for the same mode of thinking and operating, or for any other reason that eliminates an unnecessary duplication of effort. Your goal in grouping tasks together is to avoid covering the same ground more often than is absolutely necessary.

Reevaluating your time for increased earnings

Perhaps more than anyone else, salespeople understand and appreciate the direct link between time and money. If a salesperson is working on a commission basis, any time not spent in the pursuit of a sale is nonproductive time. In the business world the same is true of everybody. It's just harder to see. Everybody in a for-profit or not-for-profit enterprise is there to ultimately serve a customer.

Sometimes customers are internal to the organization in the form of co-workers. At other times the customer is someone outside of the organization who wants and/or needs the product or service that the organization exists to provide. Most of the time, people serve both internal and external customers. As such everyone's time is tied to the quality of service and performance of the organization as a whole.

The example I'm about to use will focus on earnings as they're tied to commissioned sales. However, the analogy holds for every type of vocational or avocational assignment. No matter what you do, the relationship between executing your regular activities and how you use your time is the same. You can break down whatever process you're involved with into time-related components.

First, *decide what you want to earn in a year*. In broader terms, what do you want to accomplish in a year? Using the time division method I described earlier, use a 12-month track that's appropriate and realistic for a short-term goal. Make sure that you're not selling your talents, knowledge and experience short. The target you choose should reflect what you are capable of and have good reason to expect of yourself.

Second, *divide that goal into 50 weekly goals.* (I'm assuming that you'll allow yourself a two-week vacation.) If the annual goal is an earnings figure, then it's easy to divide that figure by 50. If your goal is subject to seasonal influences, take that into account as you break down the larger goal into its more attainable and digestible smaller parts.

Third, *divide your weekly target by the number or hours you work in a week.* This is where the time-planning process rubber meets the road. How many hours are you willing and able to work week-in and week-out to reach your goal? Most people stumble here because they bite off more than they can chew in a day. Planning to work on your goal eight hours a day, six days a week might seem doable when you're drafting your plan, but it's not. Trust me.

Someone once told me that it's impossible to lead a successful life. It's only possible to lead a successful *day.* If you already completed the exercise of logging how efficiently you use your daily time allotment, you already know that a day is filled with distractions, disruptions and altered plans. You must account for how much of your day you can realistically expect to devote to accomplishing your plan.

Fourth, *divide your hourly projection by four.* Now you have a 15-minute segment of one year's worth of effort. Now you can ask yourself throughout the day, *"What was my last 15 minutes worth?"* Time is rushing past you nonstop. The only time you can work with it is in the moment that it passes through you. At that moment, your future becomes your past. The value of your past, relative to your future, is determined in the *"now."*

For example, if you want to earn $50,000 in the next 12 months, that's $1,000 per week. (I'd try and factor in your tax burden, but by the time this book goes to press it will be higher.) Divide $1,000 per week by 40 hours, to get $25. Then, $25 per hour divided into 15-minute segments is $6.25. Is every 15-minute segment of your workday worth $6.25?

If your 15-minute segments are not being used efficiently enough to bring in $6.25, then the $50,000 annual figure is unrealistic. Rather than give up on the annual figure, wouldn't it make more sense to increase your performance in the 15-minute segments of your day? Get into the habit of evaluating your productivity in 15-minute intervals.

"What was the value of my last 15 minutes?" That question should be tattooed on the back of your hand. It should be displayed on the back of the nameplate on your desk. It should be stickered on the cradle of the biggest time-waster of them all, your telephone. It's *important* to be as conscious of your time as possible.

Don't waste your time worrying about larger time increments. You have no control over the larger time segments except for what you're doing in the present moment. By focusing on the efficient and effective use of the present moment, you are establishing the value and quality of your future. There will always be the unexpected to contend with, but you're filling in as much of the painting as you can—the way you want it to look when you get there.

Once you're aware of how your time is spent throughout the day, you'll be able to write yourself a mental check at the end of each day for what you feel the day was worth. Did you exchange each hour of your time that day for $25? Was it less? Was it more? Don't be lulled into complacency by a big day. Unusually productive days are something to feel good about, but they can tempt you to slack off as well.

Checking up on your productivity every 15 minutes doesn't mean you shouldn't take breaks and stop for lunch. Rest and relaxation are important to your ongoing productivity. The high-performance person appreciates how recharging his or her batteries affects overall performance. Being vigilant about how effectively your time is being used provides helpful insight into how valuable the time is that you spend resting, having lunch and/or conversing with customers and colleagues.

Once, when Thomas Edison was called upon to deliver a message to a graduating class, the prolific American inventor said:

> *"Always be interested in whatever you're doing at the time and think only of that thing in all its bearings and mastery. Don't mind the clock, but keep at it and let nature indicate the necessity of rest. After resting, go after the work again with the same interest. The world pays big prices for [those] who know the values and satisfactions of persistent hard work."*

Identify time wasters

There are certain criteria that you can use as a template or time-waste screening device. There will always be occasions when you won't know that time and effort have been wasted until it's too late. But in most cases you can screen out time wasters in advance, if you know what to look for. Your 15-minute productivity reviews will show much better results if you scrape some of these time-wasting barnacles off the hull of your ship.

1. Doing something with no return
2. Doing something that keeps you from a higher priority task
3. Attempting too much at once
4. Poor time scheduling
5. Procrastination
6. Not listening
7. Not saying "no"
8. Doing instead of delegating
9. Personal disorganization
10. Snap decisions
11. Inefficient telephone use
12. Imitating the way an inefficient person carries out his or her day

Back when I was a salesperson, just out of the Air Force, I had a boss who would come by my desk and ask, *"What are you doing there, Danny?"* Depending on how I answered him, he would usually follow with the question, *"How is that putting money in your pocket—right now?"* If I had to admit that what I was doing wasn't putting money in my pocket at the moment, he would keep after me.

"How is what you're doing now going to put money into your pocket a month from now or three months from now?" I caught his drift pretty quickly and changed the way I thought about using my time. There are quite a few things that are fun to do, but bring no return. I'm not suggesting that you shouldn't have fun. Just put it in perspective regarding the value of your time.

First 15 mins of the day, write a plan, including e-mail time.

Seize the Day

Favorite activities will usually wind up as misplaced priorities. Will a close examination of your recent history reveal that you spend a disproportionate amount of time on personal rather than professional activities? Fortunately for you, the *high-performance process* brings personal and professional interests into alignment.

It's also important to realistically assess your activities in light of your documented priorities. All too often, we go for the easiest thing to do at the moments, figuring that we'll shoot all the slow rabbits first and then have time for the more important tasks. Somehow it never works out that way. That's why prioritizing is so critical.

Never dive into your list at number two, three, four or below. Never be caught working on your number-two, three or four priority while the big number one is still sitting up there at the top of the list. When the number-one item is dispatched, then number two becomes the new number one. That way, you're never making a second- or third-priority effort. You'll always be working on your top priority.

Attempting too much at once is a sure way to waste time. More than that, adding one too many things to your plate means you'll probably do an inferior job on everything. If your eyes are bigger than your ability, you're setting yourself up to be chump instead of the hero. Not only will you do a poor job, you'll probably dam up your own progress and the efficiency of the organization by having to go back and cover the same ground all over again.

As I've just detailed, poor time scheduling will rob you of your opportunity to excel. The breakdown of your time allotment into daily, hourly and 15-minute segments keeps the value of your time in the front of your mind and makes poor or inefficient time planning a repugnant thought. Once you're aware of how valuable your time is, I doubt that you will give a low priority in your planning process.

Procrastination rears its ugly head once again on this list of time wasters because it's so common. Procrastination is a subtle enemy that sneaks up on you in a variety of insidious ways. You won't usually realize that you're procrastinating until you do your 15-minute check up and/or check to see if in fact you're busily working on priority number one.

Not listening is an incredibly obnoxious time waster. When I was an executive, I adopted the policy that I only explained things once. That might sound cruel and unusual, but it was a matter of survival. Too many people would be told what the plan was only to come back and waste their time and my time asking me to tell them all over again. As soon as I started allowing them to twist in the wind if they didn't get it the first time, my staff's hearing and retention made a remarkable improvement.

Because of the inevitable relational dynamics that exist in the workplace, it's highly probable that somebody is going to foist some work off on you that they should rightfully be doing. You must be able to say "no." This doesn't mean that you cease being a team player and barricade yourself in your office. High-performance people know how essential it is to draw appropriate responsibility boundaries with others in the organization. Invariably, the most respected workers are those who have a helpful spirit, but do not allow themselves to be exploited.

Your ability to delegate comes with rank and skill. You must have the right to delegate, based upon your standing in the organization. But more than that, you must have the planning and people skills to spread the workload fairly. Doing things that someone else in the group is better-suited for or can do with less drain on the organization's resources is selfish at best and ultimately unfair to everyone in the company.

Personal disorganization that results from your refusal to properly plan your time and resources will kill any hope you might have of using your time effectively. If your plan is to remain as ineffective as possible, staying personally disorganized is a sure way to do it. What many people don't understand is that their personal organizational habits have a profound impact on the effectiveness of the organization as a whole.

Making snap decisions without properly thinking through the benefits and potential liabilities will come back to haunt you in the form of time wasted undoing your work. Once in awhile you might get lucky and score with a seat-of-the-pants call, but I wouldn't bet the farm on it—if you want to keep the farm.

Folklore might be filled with the heroics of risk-takers, but nobody I know wants to fly with a seat-of-the-pants pilot. I'd rather fly with Charles Lindbergh who leaves nothing to chance. When you think about it, just working through the *high-performance process* itself will provide all the challenge a sane person needs.

The telephone can murder your time. I always recommend that, if your phone system doesn't display how long a call has been in progress, you jot down the time that a phone call starts, whether you placed it or it was incoming. It's too easy to chat away valuable time and think that you're accomplishing something. Chatting on the telephone is a favorite distraction for most people who find it entertaining.

Use the telephone wisely. When the phone rings or when you place a call, don't look at the upcoming conversation as an opportunity to get in touch with the world that you've sealed yourself off from. The more you have your nose buried in solitary work, the more likely you'll seize the opportunity to make your telephone conversations *social contacts* that fill your need to interact with someone. Instead, plan to meet your interaction requirements during your breaks or lunch hour. Use the telephone as a business tool.

The grass is always greener on the other side of the fence. It's not unusual to see someone who seems to be having more fun with what they're doing than you are. Of course, once you've brought as much of your unique talents, knowledge and experience to the job as possible through the *high-performance process,* imitating the low performers' behavior will cease to be a temptation.

Suffice to say that you might at times be tempted to imitate someone who has a less responsible, more casual attitude (and performance) about them and gives the *appearance* of enjoying himself or herself more than you do. The way that you increase the level of satisfaction you feel is to be more like *you,* not more like somebody else.

Always when you are working hard + someone near you complains about what a lousy life you have it can detail,

Getting organized

Using your documented goals as the spine, build an organizational skeleton. Organizing your talents, knowledge and experience around a goal means that the goal must remain central to your organizational efforts. You can do all of the things I'm about to suggest without having a purpose beyond putting things around you in order.

You can have a well-ordered life without having accomplishing anything. The commonly uttered phrase, *"I've got to get organized"* is a bit misleading. The thought that merely getting organized will put your life back on track is a myth. You can have the most elaborate filing and time-accountability system in the world and still go nowhere.

I've found myself from time to time organizing my heart out only to discover that I'm really procrastinating. One of the most popular methods to avoid tackling truly important tasks is to *"straighten up"* around the home or office. It seems like the more imposing the assignment, the more important it is to have all of your pencils sharpened, all of your paper clips sorted by size and color, and the desk must be dusted.

Before you get started, you'll want to answer that mail that's been sitting there for six months and you haven't even *begun* to clean out your drawers. There are people who have spotless offices where everything in the world is neatly filed alphabetically, chronologically and geographically. When you ask them what they do with all their data, they give you a blank stare. They're ready for anything, they just don't know what it is yet.

Organization is critical to the *high-performance process.* However, any attempt at organization must be anchored to a goal or set of goals if the organization is to be meaningful. Form must follow function. Organize because your continued growth and success depend on it. *Organize with a purpose!*

Here are some tips:

1. **Purchase a large week-at-a-glance daily planner.**

I talk to people all the time who claim they plan their time and then take out a tiny pocket calendar to prove it. Not only is it too small to use for detailed time planning, it's usually a *month-at-a-glance* calendar. With one half-inch square for each day, you could write in *"pick up laundry"* and it would look like you have a big day planned.

A time-planning aid must have each day broken down into the 15-minute segments I described earlier. As you fill in each line, you're not trying to kill time, you're trying to *fill* time. Each 15-minute segment is important. Each 15-minute segment must be spent on an activity that moves you closer to your stated objective.

There are a variety of good time systems available on the market. Each one has an elaborate planner and provides training in various methods of time efficiency. No matter how sophisticated or expensive your time-planning system is, the bottom line is still how effectively you organize around your documented goals.

2. Organize your physical environment.

Despite what I said a few paragraphs ago about avoiding responsibility by over-organizing, it's still important to be physically organized. If you're dying to clear away clutter, here's your chance. Take an evening, early morning or weekend to organize your office, briefcase or car (if that's your office).

The goal in ordering your physical environment is to remove obstructions to progress. What good are having tools and resources if you don't have ready access to them? You don't want to plan efficient use of your time only to be thrown off-schedule looking for the items you need to conduct your daily activities.

Be merciless in throwing things away. If you haven't used something in a year, chances are good that the item is not essential to your ongoing activities. Clutter accumulates when you stash something away for that fantasy project, novel or other low-priority use that has nothing to do with your ongoing activities.

If you must store low-priority items, establish an archive somewhere away from your place of business. If something is to die for, archive it where your grandchildren will find it someday. Otherwise, *throw it away!* Forego sentiment whenever possible and cut off as much ballast as you can.

There are very few articles or other published resources that couldn't be found through your local library if you really needed them. If you're a pack rat with an enormous accumulation of stuff, chances are good that you're not stockpiling resources for a well-focused project, but rather a wide variety of nonrelated material in case any of it ever interests you enough to pursue someday.

Put the things you use most frequently closest to you, in a top drawer or your briefcase. People often put things they *intend* to use nearby and then have to dig through those items to get to what they *really* need to use. You must be realistic about what you do and how you spend your time to properly organize yourself.

Set up a filing system so that you can find what you need in a hurry. Anything that's important enough to store is important enough to have access to. A filing system simply refers to a systematic storage strategy with a simple, efficient and easy to understand retrieval capability.

Time-lapse motion picture photography studies have revealed that people spend a great deal of time reaching for files or objects that could have been stored closer at hand. According to Stephanie Winston, business managers can spend upwards of 150 hours per year just looking for things. To get into economy of motion issues is pretty sophisticated, but the point is relevant to anyone who can benefit from a more efficient physical arrangement.

Have an 'intend to use' maybe will one day use area which is away from those you really do use

3. **Divide your job into parts.**

Determine which elements of your job require the most organization and which elements are less important. Don't waste your time on that proverbial paper-clip sorting when you could be setting up a tickler file for following up with clients.

Don't base your decision of what to organize on what's the most disorganized. The least organized aspect of your job might not be the most vital aspect of your job. Priorities matter in organizing as much as being organized.

4. Make sure that you set a deadline for your organizing efforts.

Even if you're not using the organization process to procrastinate about other things, it's possible to drag out the process to the point that it's more of a liability than a benefit. Each step of your organizational plan should be ranked by priority.

5.   Get started.

The *intent* to organize your life is different than actually doing it. Intent has no positive benefits. If organizing your resources, affairs, etc., is going to help you increase your personal productivity, it makes no sense to delay. High-performance people don't think in terms of delaying the start of something beneficial.

Priority lists

One of the things that Stephanie Winston stresses in her great book, *The Organized Executive,* is the importance of having one master "to do" list. Everything that you know you have to do should be on that list. From the most important task you face, to filling the car with gas on the way home, everything should be on that list. Everything from getting a college degree to getting a new pair of shoes should be listed.

Stephanie further suggests that you visit that list each day and pull out the things that need to be accomplished in the next 24 hours. Even so, there will be a disparity between high-priority and low-priority items. Incidently, getting a number of low-priority tasks accomplished and out of the way can give you a tremendously liberated feeling. It's important to clear away the stubble as it were. Even so, it's the big tasks that receive your primary attention.

The psychological benefit from crossing items off a list is obvious. When an item is completed and crossed off, a burden has been lifted from your shoulders. After crossing a number of items off the list, what remains shows clearly what still needs to be done. In other words, a list—even a partially completed list—will give you your current bearings.

Because the *high-performance process* has a time component, working a priority list helps keep you on schedule. You have a sense about the amount of time each task requires for completion.

What remains to be done on your list is also an estimate of your time frame. Working your priority list will require some flexibility. You will have to make decisions along the way to decide which items should be grouped together and in what order should they be executed.

One of the most frustrating feelings I've ever experienced is to know that there's much to be done but not have an inventory in front of me. High-performance people always have their priority list close at hand and use it constantly to ensure the most effective use of their time. The more often you refer to the list, the more information you retain in your head, giving you an ongoing sense of where you are in your plan for the day.

Setting up a priority system

It's possible to be efficient without being effective. Like the person who organizes without a purpose, you can dispatch tasks, large and small, without much consideration for how those tasks are affecting goal accomplishment. Busying yourself with task after task without regard for how those activities propel you toward the accomplishment of your documented goals is like rowing a boat with one oar. You can keep yourself mighty busy just going around in circles.

> *"It's more important to do the right thing than to do things right."*
>
> —*Peter F. Drucker*

Don't overkill low priorities with excessive planning and energy. You don't need a sledge hammer to kill gnats. The amount of planning and energy you invest in an activity should be directly proportionate to the value of the outcome. Even though you want to pick up your laundry on the way home better than anyone else picks up their laundry—particularly because that's now the number-one priority on your list—it doesn't require quite as much pomp and circumstance as the presentation to the chairman of the board earlier that day.

Make sure that your first consideration is getting the right things done. After that, concentrate on how efficiently you're doing them. Row with both oars in the water. The difference between a failure and a success is two well-planned hours per day. Two well-planned hours out of 24 is not very much.

I've worked with many high achievers and *wanna-be* high achievers who dedicate themselves to time-planning only to sit down and plan a series of days that Superman, Captain Marvel and Hopalong Cassidy couldn't pull off together. The eager over-achievers hit the bricks running and look terrific until, somewhere in the middle of the day, they burp.

The burp wasn't on their three-day plan and throws them so far behind schedule that they can't catch up. I advise people to start by planning two blockbuster hours a day. Over time you'll get more proficient and be able to plan half of the day with tightly scheduled activities. Work up to it and you won't be disillusioned that you can't become a miracle worker overnight.

I've never met a person who can effectively schedule more than 90 percent of his or her day. No matter how good you get to be at drafting and working priority lists, there will always be influences beyond your control. Stay flexible and you will spend less of your energy being frustrated and disappointed. High-performance people learn quickly that much of the day will be spent operating in the *"margins"* of their schedule.

"I always say to myself: What is the most important thing we can t'link about at this extraordinary moment?"

—*Buckminster Fuller*

The T-R-A-F formula

In helping executives organize their activities for increased efficiency, Stephanie Winston also suggests that every item that comes over the transom be handled in one of four ways: *Trash,*

Refer, Action or File. High-performance people learn quickly that some items are simply not worth their time. These things have to be thrown out.

This doesn't mean throwing things away because you don't *want* to deal with them. To *trash* something because it helps you avoid responsibility is wrong. Something is eligible for the circular file only when the time and effort it requires don't move you closer to attaining any of your documented goals. In other words, when the item requires you to waste time, it's not worth pursuing. Develop the ability to discern quickly.

Referring or delegating an assignment to someone else is appropriate when the time and effort required are not worthy of your time according to the priority list you've established. What is down the list for you might be a noble cause for someone with less authority or less responsibility. Any efficient organization understands that items with varying priorities should be handled at different levels of the operation.

Action in Winston's model stands for things that *you* should do yourself. Items could include calls *you* should return, letters *you* should write or visits *you* should make in person. When the items facing you represent top priorities for the accomplishment of your goals, there is nobody more appropriate than you to take care of them. *Action* means *you.*

Filing means storing information that you think might be helpful down the road. Filing something that will cause your plans to suffer if not attended to isn't wise. Only bits of information that don't require any immediate or even pending action on your part should be filed. Be careful that filing doesn't become a method of delaying action on something that you merely want to avoid or postpone.

Stephanie Winston's *T-R-A-F* model is helpful because nothing you encounter requires anything other than one of the four treatments. Nothing should remain on your desk without receiving one of the four treatments. The high-performance person will do something with everything that comes his or her way without delay. That's how you can keep your decks cleared and ready for action at all times. The last thing you want to do is leave something critical undone because you're buried under unimportant matters.

The thing TRAF doesn't cover is the Necessity to GET things (Routine things) that should be done DONE and quickly out of the way!

Laying out a daily plan

1. **The first thing to do in laying out a daily plan is to consider priorities. Distinguish between urgent and unimportant tasks.**

Dwight Eisenhower said, "Urgent things are seldom important and important things are seldom urgent." Urgent tasks require immediate attention, but have little or no impact on the achievement of long-term goals. Important tasks are valuable in reaching the all-important long-term goals.

2. **When laying out your daily plan, allow 10 percent more time for each task than you initially estimate it will take.**

Allowing for the margins of your day gives you flexibility to adjust to the pace of the day. As I've mentioned, there will always be unexpected distractions and intrusions on your time. You want to avoid adding pressure to your day by scheduling your priority items too close together and forcing yourself to be constantly behind and playing catch up.

3. **Strive to make the first hour of your day the most satisfying. Do the three things you want to do the least in your first hour.**

It's better to get unpleasant tasks out of the way early so they don't hang over your head all day long. Having unpleasant things ahead of you tends to tarnish everything else you attempt. When the least pleasant tasks are dispatched early in the morning, the rest of the day will be a happier experience, no matter what you do.

Whether you're a *morning* or an *afternoon* person, you'll never have more natural energy throughout the day than you do in the morning. Many people feel as if they can't get going in the morning. Unfortunately, these folks are allowing the time when their minds and bodies are the most rested to be wasted. I suggest that you rise a half-hour early if you're a slow starter and go for a brisk walk before your morning shower. That way you'll be able to devote the most energized hours of your day to accomplishing difficult tasks that would be even more overwhelming later in the day.

4. Schedule your most important creative work during your personal best time of the day.

Despite the fact that your mind and body are most rested in the hours after you first wake up, every one has a different internal clock when it comes to the part of the day when s/he is most productive and creative. Call it your own personal *zone* if you wish. You ought to know by now what the most productive part of the day is for you. If not, pay attention to when you seem to get the most accomplished when you're not consciously thinking about it. When you're cranking out work a mile a minute and it doesn't even occur to you until you look back and say to yourself, "Wow, I don't remember doing all of that." For different folks that period of tremendous efficiency represents the best part of the day for creativity. It's a period when it just sort of all "happens" for you—a time when you're at your personal best. It occurs during the same part of the day, every day.

5. When a problem pops up, step back.

The natural inclination when an obstacle appears is to bull ahead with greater velocity. We all have a natural tendency to bear down harder on the square peg when it won't slip easily through the round hole. The truth is that a square peg shouldn't slip through a round hole unless somebody fiddled with the laws of physics while we weren't looking.

When a problem pops up and impedes our progress, there might be a good reason. Just pushing and pounding harder won't promote understanding and enlightenment. By stepping back from the problem, taking a longer view of it—grading its parts and priorities, you can move back in and start to solve the problem.

I learned about backing off from problems and letting naturally corrective forces take over when I was in the Air Force. The 22-ton fighter I was flying had a slight design flaw. If the aircraft reached a certain angle of climb, it was subject to a *"pitch-up"*. A pitch-up meant losing control of the aircraft and possibly entering an uncontrollable tumble to the ground.

The Air Force had already told me not to worry about pitch-ups. There were systems designed into the aircraft to safeguard against the problem. I had learned early on that when the Air Force said not to worry about something, it was worth worrying about. Sure enough, I was doing practice target runs at a simulated high-flying intruder when my fighter went into a pitch-up. The systems meant to safeguard against such things failed.

I began to tumble out of the sky. The aircraft rolled so violently that the inside of the plexiglass canopy was torn up by my crash helmet beating against it and had to be replaced. I tumbled out of control for over 30,000 feet or more than six miles. I was fighting like mad to pull the aircraft out of the tumble.

It felt like every drop of blood I had in my body was in my head. The negative "G's" inside the cockpit were so intense that all of the blood vessels in my eyes ruptured. This was more than the average problem that pops up around the office on a typical day. However, the principle that saved my life that day applies to the office as well as the physics of flight.

I finally figured out that bearing down harder on my problem and trying to force the controls of the aircraft wasn't going to work. Only three out of nine pilots who had experienced pitch-ups before me had survived. I didn't want to be doing whatever it was the six unlucky guys were doing when they hit the ground.

I neutralized the controls and released, popped the drag chute and lowered the landing gear. Suddenly the air began flowing over the wings again and the fighter stabilized all by itself. After all, those things are built to *fly*. I saved my life and several million in taxpayers' dollars by backing off, just when my instincts drove me to press the situation harder.

So next time you feel like you're tumbling out of control, especially in a debate with someone else, back off the controls, pop your drag chute and let some natural stabilizing effects occur. If the best possible thing is to hammer harder, you can always do that later. For starters, make it your policy to step back and gain a broader and clearer perspective on the problem *first*.

6. Prior to each task, take a 30-second test.

The following questions only take a few moments to ask and answer. However, they will provide you with keen insight into how appropriate it is for *you* to be doing that particular task at that time. It might seem like I propose asking a great many questions and it's not hard to understand that concern. The value of putting things under the microscope as much as possible is not found in the questions, but rather in the *answers*.

The better-informed you are, the more likely your decisions are going to bring lasting benefits. That's why you want to take the time to evaluate your activities with the following inquisition:

1. Why is this task being done?
2. Can it be eliminated?
3. How is this task helping me achieve my goals?
4. Based upon what I've scheduled myself to earn (accomplish) this month, am I the one who should be doing this task?
5. Based on my established priorities, is this the most important task for me to be working on right now?
6. Is their a better way to do this task? How can I improve on the traditional method?

The time spent qualifying the things you do will result in freeing up more time for higher-priority tasks by shifting time away from tasks that are better done by others or not done at all. Figure 3-1 shows how this short question-answer process can liberate you to move to your next task at the first *"yes"* answer.

7. Never commit to a future assignment unless you have time for it now.

For some reason, the future always seems full of potential to do things that we just can't seem to accomplish now. In the correct context, that thought probably has some merit. Yet, the most common myth we buy into is that we will magically have some capability and/or capacity in the future that we don't presently possess. My friend Jim Newton comically refers to his future as *"spotless."* In truth our futures are spotless, but that's only because we haven't been there yet. Unless you are doing something specific now, over and above what you ordinarily do, to make your methods more time-efficient, why would you think that you'll have more time in the future than you have right now?

Can you look back over the past few years and spot big holes where you had too little to do? Unless you have a history of encountering slow periods when you can take on extra projects and responsibilities, there's no reason to believe that you'll be able to in the next week, month or year. The *high-performance process* will make you more efficient over time, but your future commitments should always be based on your present capabilities.

Learn to say *"no"* and mean it. It's more disrespectful to others to make promises you can't keep than it is to be honest up front. The desire to possess supernatural abilities is natural, but it's also a fantasy. No manager worth his or her salt expects you to work beyond your natural capacity. If you don't have time for a project now, you won't have time for it later. Trust me on that. Gauge future commitments on your present capacity to handle your work load.

8. Don't beat yourself up for not completing your priority list each day.

You can only do what your natural talents, knowledge, experience and circumstances allow. High-performance people know that working a priority list correctly means that their energies are always being spent on the *number-one* priority. Because of that, they're always filled with confidence knowing their efforts would not have been better allocated elsewhere.

If you're working your priority list correctly and have put each task to the 30-second test I described earlier, there are no items more important than the items you're working on. If anything needs to be left undone or pushed farther down the schedule, it should be the lower priority items.

You always want to finish every item on your list, but it's more important to focus on your priorities than the number of tasks you can scratch off. Many people procrastinate and avoid important,

Task-Evaluation Sequence

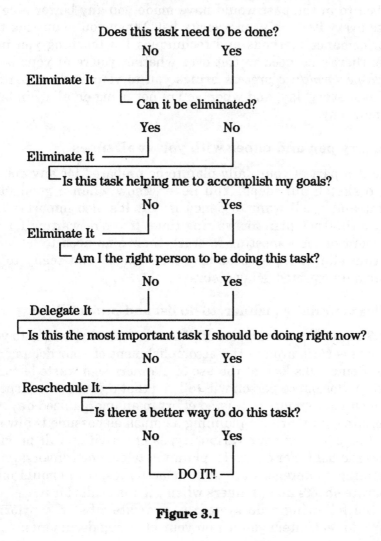

Does this task need to be done?

No   Yes

Eliminate It

Can it be eliminated?

Yes   No

Eliminate It

Is this task helping me to accomplish my goals?

No   Yes

Eliminate It

Am I the right person to be doing this task?

No   Yes

Delegate It

Is this the most important task I should be doing right now?

No   Yes

Reschedule It

Is there a better way to do this task?

No   Yes

DO IT!

Figure 3.1

high-priority items by busying themselves completing all sorts of less-important tasks. They appear to be constantly busy, and indeed they are. The high-performance person is constantly busy as well, but the value of his or her labors is far different.

If you're committed to the *high-performance process,* you're already aware that no other method of operation you might have subscribed to in the past would have made you any better able to complete every item on your priority list. When you're putting the high-performance methods and techniques I'm teaching you into practice, there's no need to fret over whether you're at your best. The *high-performance process* brings you to your highest performance level every day, and when you're not firing on all cylinders, you'll know why.

9. Carry pen and paper with you at all times.

Make it a part of your daily plan to be prepared for any opportunity to sketch out ideas. You never know when a good idea might hit and you'll want to pencil it out. It's also important to have a contingency plan for waiting time. If you're waiting for an appointment or for a meeting to start, there's no need to let your momentum slip. Have a secondary task staged and ready to go when some unexpected delay occurs.

10. Use your daily planner, to-do list and project sheet.

Figures 3-2 and 3-3 are samples of planning tools that will help you focus your energies around the accomplishment of your documented goals. Some folks look at the use of planners as a waste of time. Any high-performance person will tell you that a few minutes spent planning will save hours in wasted effort in an unorganized day.

Combining your written planning as much as possible is always helpful, but planning your various types of activities will provide more specific help. For example, planning telephone conversations and planning conferences are similar activities. You should only use separate sheets and planners when the task calls for it.

Use the following code system to indicate what the priority ranking is for each item you list on your planning documents:

Project Sheet

Project	Date Assigned	Deadline	Date Completed

Figure 3.2

Meeting Planner

Date _____

NAME	NAME	NAME
NAME	NAME	NAME
NAME	NAME	NAME
		NAME
NAME	NAME	NAME
		NAME

Figure 3.3

1. Do immediately
2. Do by the end of the day
3. Do today if possible
4. Delegate

How to handle interruptions

Interruptions are inevitable but not unmanageable. One of the primary reasons for scheduling margins in your day of 10 percent or more is to accommodate unscheduled activities. One of the most common mistakes among people who have a busy agenda is to focus too much attention on what happens to fall in front of them or whoever might drop in or call.

These types of interruptions contaminate your time because they are instigated by others. When other people determine how your time is spent, you lose control. More than that, when other people are allowed to dictate how you spend your time, they, and not you, are establishing your priorities. High-performance people accept that interruptions are bound to occur and they anticipate them. However, high-performance people have a plan to keep interruptions from stealing or undermining their control.

Step one in handling interruptions is to *rearrange your office* by relocating your desk where you will no longer be in the line of sight of those passing by. It's too easy for people to make eye contact with you as they pass by in the hall and simply walk in to socialize. As soon as that happens, you're confronted with the distracting and time-consuming task of politely excusing yourself so that you can return to work.

There's nothing wrong with social interaction during the day—in fact a healthy rapport with your associates is valuable. However, socializing must be kept in perspective and always on your terms according to the priorities and schedule *you've* established. There are times when higher-ups will make social demands on your time and you'll be hard-pressed to maneuver your way around them. But that's where your personal talent, knowledge and experience come in handy. People use the discussion of all sorts of ostensive business problems as excuses to kill time, theirs and yours. Procrastination loves company. You don't want to be that company.

Reduce the number of chairs in your office and keep the remaining ones as far from your desk as possible. Don't create an appealing nuisance by fashioning a conversation pit right in front of you. A cozy conversation area is another incentive to socialize. When you do elect to take time to carry on a discussion with a visitor, get up from behind your desk and move around to one of the chairs yourself.

If the discussion is important enough for you to leave your desk and focus all of your attention on your guest, it must be a high-priority task. If it's not important enough for you to move, it's probably a discussion that's robbing a high-priority task of your attention. It's easy to talk and talk and talk, hoping to cover some important ground somewhere in the conversation. The high-performance person knows where the important ground is and goes there immediately or, realizing the lack of value in a conversation, excuses himself or herself quickly.

When you are in conversation with someone in your office, relocate the clock relative to the chairs so that both you and the other party can see it. A casual glance at the clock is a subtle reminder that valuable time is passing. More than one glance at the clock is a pretty unmistakable cue that it's time to move on.

If the other person doesn't take the hint, no matter how obvious, look at the clock and say, *"I see it's time that I get back to work on my priority job for the day,"* or something to that effect. Then *stand up and move back to your desk*. Your movement is a physical gesture to support your verbal comment about getting back to work.

If necessary, complete the conversation while walking the visitor back to the reception area or back to his or her desk. In this way, *you* become the person with the prerogative to leave when you so choose, which will be promptly. Never sit and wonder to yourself, *"When is this person ever going to let me get back to work?"* You determine when you go back to work.

Step two in handling interruptions is to *keep an interruption log* for one week. (Fig. 3-4) I know that it's another time-consuming bother, but the educational value can be tremendous. This isn't something to do constantly. The point is to illustrate the impact interruptions are having on your time. Once you've seen on paper the scope of your interruptions, it's easier to get fired up about eliminating or minimizing their debilitating effect on your performance.

Step three in handling interruptions is to *establish a quiet hour* when you will not be interrupted, no matter what. I've found that during a quiet hour, I can get the equivalent of two or three hours of work done. Having a quiet hour set aside during the day will provide you with a boost if you feel your productivity lagging behind.

Step four in handling interruptions is to *say "no" when someone asks if you have a minute.* This doesn't mean cut yourself off from other people or be rude. However, it's important to establish with your fellow workers the necessity to plan ahead. If someone needs some help or information, they will be willing to come back at the top of the hour or whenever you're at a logical stopping place. When s/he returns at the designated time, deal with the issue s/he originally came to you about and deal with nothing else.

Step five in handling interruptions is to *reverse the tide.* When someone has a habit of coming into your office, seeking advice or help, look up and ask him or her what s/he thinks is best. If it sounds feasible, offer affirmation and encouragement and then drop your head and get back to work. Again, this is not permission to be rude, but a way to quickly dismiss an invitation to waste valuable time.

Step six in handling interruptions is to avoid being a part of the problem. Some "problems" are not only unimportant, they're much less of a problem than you might think, given the number of people dropping everything to work on it. High-performance people know how to apply the 30-second test to a problem and quickly determine whether it's worth their time and attention. When a problem is not worth getting entangled in, or it's really not a problem at all, you must have the ability to concentrate and not be distracted by all the clamor going on around you.

Project Sheet
Interruption Log

Inter-ruption	Description	Time Begin/End	# of Minutes	Preventive Action to be Taken
1				
2				
3				
4				
5				
6				
7				
8				
9				
10				
11				
12				
13				
14				

Figure 3.4

Getting off the telephone . . . fast

You already know that one of the biggest time-wasters in your life is the telephone. Here are some ways to consciously control the time you spend on the telephone, based on these techniques originally developed by Stephanie Winston:

1. Preset the time limit. When someone calls to talk about an issue, immediately tell that person how much time you can spend in telephone conversation. This means that you need to determine quickly how much time you feel is appropriate for that subject in light of your priorities.

    Once you've determined the appropriate amount of time, say something like, *"Yes, I can spend three minutes with you on that."* As soon as you've designated a specific time frame for the conversation, the caller must focus on the issue and not babble aimlessly.

2. Foreshadow endings. When someone calls you on the telephone and takes a long time getting to the point, a little reminder that your time is limited might help him or her focus. For example, as you notice that the caller is not focusing, you might say, *"Before we hang up I want to be sure I've answered the question you called about."*

    Your comment communicates your sincere attempt to be helpful while, at the same time, making it clear that the conversation is not open-ended and will soon be over. It's a courteous method of drawing the telephone conversation to an end.

3. Use *their* time. Whenever someone is being especially talkative on the telephone and doesn't seem to be getting the message that your time is valuable, tell the person that you're in the middle of an urgent project and ask if you can call back.

    When you call back, make sure it's just before that person's quitting time. That way s/he will place a value on the matter relative to his or her desire to get out of the office. In the vast majority of cases, I believe you'll find the matter wasn't all that important to begin with.

4. Use the other person's estimate. When someone calls and asks if you have time to discuss something, immediately ask how long you think the discussion will require and then suggest less time. If someone says they think it will take 10 minutes to discuss something, say, *"Let's try to do it in five."*

Once again, you're not refusing to spend time helping the caller. You're just establishing parameters on how much time you're willing to invest. In the long run you're not only protecting your own valuable time, but also helping the other party focus his or her energies.

5. Change focus. If it appears that your time is being wasted on unimportant matters and the other caller is difficult to reason with, steer the conversation toward your own problems. Ask questions that the caller can't answer.

The purpose of shifting focus from the caller's problems to your own is to take the fun out of it for the caller. When a person is going on and on about his or her own issues, it can be an extremely narcissistic episode. One thing a narcissist never wants to do is share the spotlight.

6. Get help. If you can't get someone off of the phone easily or if the person is too important to risk offending in any way, have your secretary or someone working close to you call you on another extension, giving you an excuse to terminate the first call.

7. Use your conference planner. When you're the one initiating the call, don't fall into the same time-wasting traps that others subject you to. Plan your calls before you make them. Note what you want to discuss and how long you realistically feel it should take. Out of respect for your own time and others' time, stick to your plan as closely as possible.

Learning from emergencies

There once was a man who drank liquor to excess and was booted out of the local tavern every night at closing time. As a shortcut home, he staggered through the village graveyard in the dark.

Although he knew his way among the grave stones fairly well, he wasn't aware one night that a fresh open grave had been dug earlier that afternoon in preparation for a funeral the following day. He fell into the hole.

The inebriated man tried and tried again to scale the vertical walls of the grave with no success. Finally accepting the futility of his situation, he sat down in a corner of the pit and decided to sleep until morning when someone would surely discover him.

Later that night a traveler who had lost his bearings wandered into the same cemetery and promptly fell into the same open grave. In the pitch blackness, the traveler wasn't aware of his drunken companion sleeping it off in the corner.

As the traveler tried again and again to scale the sheer walls of the neatly dug grave without success, the drinker woke up and noticed that someone else was in a similar predicament to his.

Unfamiliar with his surroundings, the traveler called out for help several times. There was no response. Slumping into an opposite corner of the grave, he felt alone, helpless and scared.

Wanting to comfort the new arrival, the drinker spoke up. "It's no use, you can't get out." An instant later the inebriated man was alone again in the grave.

Just when you think there is no faster way to get a job done, an emergency will arise and somehow, some way, you'll get it done much faster. How could that be? It's the same task and you're the same person. Although every situation is different, the lesson to be learned is that virtually anything can be done by virtually anyone in a state of emergency faster than it would be done under normal circumstances.

I'm not suggesting that you pull a fire alarm every time production slows down. A high-performance person is aware of how much his or her capabilities seem to increase under pressure and has that increased capacity in the back of his or her mind at all times. It can be a confidence-building technique, knowing that you can do a great deal more if need be. It also keeps you aware that you might be doing less than you could be in a normal operating environment.

How would you be doing your job if a medical problem arose and forced you to cut your workday by half? If you had no other choice but to try and salvage as much of your productivity as possible under altered conditions, how would you go about it? The answers to these questions will tell you a great deal about your present working habits.

Would there be parts of your job that you would drop completely without diminishing the end result? Which tasks would you delegate to others so that the end result is not diminished? Which people would you avoid because the drain they place on your time would detract from the precious little time you have left? I've never met anyone who couldn't shed some dead weight off of his or her routine and maintain—if not improve—productivity.

Reading faster

Reading, as important as it is, can slow you down if you don't do it with the same intensity and purpose that you use to execute your other responsibilities. The way you approach work-related reading is quite different from the way you read for pleasure. Work-related reading is a search for relevant and useful information as quickly as possible.

Speed reading experts say to move your finger or a pencil under the words as fast as you can and force your eye to keep up with it. Your brain can input visual data much faster than you would customarily ask it to. Bear in mind that you're searching for ideas, not individual words. Moving your finger or a pencil under the words will have the immediate effect of doubling your reading rate. If you practice this method with your daily reading, you will soon be able to jump your finger or pencil down the page.

You can begin picking up entire ideas that the writer has formed using words and sentences without poring over the words and sentences themselves. The more you use speed-reading techniques, the more proficient you will become and the more information you will retain.

Handling paperwork

Keeping your desk and mind clear for the high-priority tasks is an integral part of your planning process. You won't keep your decks cleared by accident. If you find yourself bogged down by telephone calls, handling the mail or paperwork in general, it's because methods and techniques for steering clear of these distractions were not given their rightful place in your high-performance strategy.

There are new beliefs you need to adopt as well as new habits and behaviors. The following list applies to handling paperwork:

1. You don't have to read everything that comes across your desk or arrives in the mail.

This piece of news sounds astonishing to many people who feel as if they're somehow obligated to examine everything that someone mailed to them or routed in their direction. You can live very well without the vast majority of correspondence that flows through your life.

Develop the habit of scanning things very quickly to determine if the correspondence is something related to a current project, generated by someone important to your objectives or of some potential future value to your documented goals. In the latter case, you'll probably visit your files of delayed correspondence from time to time and pitch most of them when you realize they didn't have much value after all.

By quickly filing the correspondence for later review in the first place, you saved yourself the wasted time of contemplating the possible relevance of the information when you had higher-priority fish to fry. Like the telephone, meticulously scrutinizing the mail and every item in your in box can be a time-wasting tool for procrastinators. *No, this is wrong*

2. Preview materials for key words and phrases.

Even faster than speed reading, this technique helps you make a virtually instantaneous appraisal of the document and its value to you and your objectives. If you spot something that's relevant, go back and give it a closer skimming using the speed-reading techniques I described earlier. As always, your goal is to make a rapid determination of how the document fits into your current high-performance strategy.

3. Organize your paper work according to priority.

As you determine what items you're going to deal with yourself, delegate to others, etc., spread them out according to the priority ranking you've assigned them. Processing the material that comes across your desk without organizing it in an accessible fashion means that you'll duplicate part of your effort later when you go digging to see what needs to be attended to.

4. Never pick up a piece of paper unless you intend to do something with it.

If you don't resolve that you're going to take action on something before you pick it up, you're wasting your time looking at it. If you catch yourself reaching for something on your desk, quickly ask yourself if you have the time and inclination right then to do whatever will be required to dispatch that item and move on to something else. If you don't, then don't pick it up. It's just that simple.

If the doubting voice in your head is saying, *"How am I going to know if it's important?"*, you haven't prioritized your paper flow the way I suggested in the previous items. If it's on your desk at all, you've already determined that it's a priority and you have a sense of what level of effort will be required to handle it.

Therefore, if you reach for it, you must be prepared to deal with it. Otherwise you're just piddling around. When you reach for an item, you're triggering your focus mechanism. By virtue of the fact you've selected that item to deal with, you've ranked it as your number-one priority at that moment and it deserves your complete attention and energy.

Realistically, not every task can be completed in one effort before going on to the next. If that's the case, put a red dot in the upper right-hand corner of the paper each time you set it down. The red dots will give you an instant assessment of how often you're returning to that task to make progress. It's good information to know in case you're spending more time and effort on the issue than it deserves.

5. Plan your response method.

My favorite method of responding to someone's communication is to write my comments right on the original document and send it back. I also make a copy and file it in order to keep a record of the written exchange. In other cases, I'll have a form response prepared for items that appear frequently and require a stock reply.

I prefer the former method because writing on someone's original document gives the impression that you've seen it, handled it and that it got your attention. If you're concerned that folks might feel you didn't care enough to draft a letter or memo to respond to *their* letter or memo, have a rubber stamp made that says, *"Hand-written reply for immediate response. Copy on file."* If the originator of the document wants to call and discuss the matter further, s/he knows that you have both a copy of the original and your response on file.

Using the form letter or paragraph to respond is definitely less personal and, as such, can be appropriate when the correspondence you're responding to is annoying or trivial. Much of your mail is unnecessary and tedious. In such cases, when the tedious material arrives regularly, a form response will save you time and convey your opinion of the matter's urgency or value.

Be considerate of others' time

To some folks, the methods and techniques I recommend that you include in your planning process for minimizing distractions, interruptions and saving time seem impersonal. To the contrary, I've found in my career that people appreciate brevity and straightforward behavior. I certainly carry out my tasks in a respectful and friendly manner.

Just because you plan time-saving efficiency techniques into the execution of your responsibilities doesn't mean that you have to be abrasive. In my experience, most of the abrasive and rude people I encounter are precisely that ones who *need* to adopt some time-saving techniques. It's usually those who are overwhelmed by the unnecessary pressures brought on by chaos and disorganization who tend to bite your head off.

Brevity is the essence of good communications. If someone is a busy, hard-working person, s/he will appreciate your brevity. Try and boil your ideas and comments down to less than a minute if possible. Someone once told me to, "Speak in headlines. If the listener wants to hear more, give 'em the text." If an idea that you want to communicate is well thought-out, you will have already formed headlines.

In the same way that you scan printed information for the larger ideas and concepts, you should communicate with others by beginning with the overview and stating the central message clearly and succinctly. Even if your time is not limited, making your basic point quick and easy to grasp makes your message easier to follow. Nobody enjoys being confused.

An *"interruptee"* can also become an *"interrupter."* Are you part of the problem? When someone interrupts you, it's possible to ignore the time-efficiency techniques you've learned and drag the conversation down all kinds of meaningless avenues. If someone agrees to abide by the time restrictions you request of them when you're interrupted, do you turn around and violate their time by not listening effectively and hogging the conversation?

Be prompt. Don't keep people waiting. Being respectful of other people's time will always be appreciated. If you've agreed to see someone and deal with issues s/he brings to your attention, don't delay. Show the other person respect by honoring his or her commitment to see you and respect your own time by handling the issue as expeditiously as possible. Because promptness is as much a benefit to you as it is to the other party, it makes sense to be prompt with anyone, not just those people you feel are important. Any behavior that's worth making an extra effort for should be part of your regular routine. Wouldn't you want to be known as a person who is prompt, courteous and respectful of others?

Your personal time effectiveness affects the productivity of others. That's true even if no one else reports to you. How efficient you are with your time has a profound impact on everyone around you. It's a good idea to periodically ask people under your supervision how you can do more to help their time efficiency. Ask them, *"What do I do that consumes your time without contributing to your effectiveness?"* Then change accordingly.

How to recharge your enthusiasm

It's important that your planning process include provisions for the inevitable drain on your enthusiasm. You know that any major effort will require energy, and periods of intense focus on an issue will take something out of you. Don't think that you can simply bull your way through one task and move directly to another without any loss in enthusiasm or energy.

Plan some quiet time alone. Make it part of your overall strategy. Know going in that, after you've given your best effort to a task, you will have a period of peace and quiet to reflect on what you just did, to ponder what lies ahead or to not think of anything at all. Having your rejuvenation included in your plan makes the effort seem less overwhelming.

Break a job down. By taking a big task and breaking it down into smaller tasks you automatically engage a sense of accomplishment at the completion of each smaller task instead of staying frustrated at the enormity of the overall challenge. Being happier along the way keeps your enthusiasm and energies up. Keeping your enthusiasm and energies up will speed the accomplishment of the bigger chore.

Reward yourself for completing tough jobs. By building the reward into your original plan, you will have a constant sense of what the job is worth to you on a personal level. Too often you can appreciate the professional accomplishment without personalizing any unique benefit. Knowing there is a carrot out there that's been budgeted as part of the process helps the medicine of hard work go down easier.

Take a break. Plan to pause at midday or other appropriate time to let your body and brain load up on oxygen again. If your refreshment breaks are not included in your original plan, it will feel like even going to the restroom means falling behind. Breaks are inevitable. You'll take some whether you plan them or not. You might as well plan on them to have better control and to properly exploit the benefits of periodic rests.

Plan where you will go and when. Going to lunch or walking in the park have different effects on different people. Which is better for you in light of the task you face? Knowing in advance that you're going to pause in your effort helps you come back to the job with renewed vigor. Your thoughts during a planned time off tend to be creative, free-flowing concepts that might contribute much to the task at hand.

Make somebody else happy. In the play *Cheaper By The Dozen,* the father calculated that most people are awake 16 hours per day. Out of that 960 minutes, 1 percent should be spent making someone else happy. There's nothing like getting outside of yourself to recharge your batteries. When all of your focus remains inward, it's easy to lose perspective and think that the problems of the world are greater than they really are. Planning to spend some time, even a small amount of time, brightening someone else's day will help you keep your task in perspective and improve your personal performance.

Know when to stop for the day

If stopping places are part of your strategy, you will not debate in your own mind whether to press on a little further. On a job that requires an extended amount of time to complete, you know that you'll have to stop each day anyway. So plan your stopping places in advance and avoid the problems of deciding how far to go.

Just as breaking a large job down into smaller parts gives you more chances to experience a feeling of accomplishment, granting yourself advance permission to end each day at a reasonable hour tends to alleviate guilt. The close of a workday will begin to feel like an accomplishment because you've structured your progress in appropriate segments.

When you've stopped at a preplanned spot, you'll return the next day with increased energy, eager to take on the job once again, knowing that you'll feel good at the end of another productive day. When it's not possible to predict where you'll be at the end of each day, make sure that you choose to end on a high note. A good feeling as you leave the job sets the stage for good feelings as you return. Note the specific phrase or calculation that you'll begin with upon your return.

If you are forced to stop when you're stalled on an unresolved problem, take a moment to write the problem out in simple, clear-cut terms. By focusing both your creative right brain and your linear (writing) left brain on the problem before you break, you will unleash creative powers in your unconscious that will work on the problem even when you're not consciously thinking about it.

I suggested earlier in the section to have pen and paper with you at all times. Be prepared to write down creative solutions that might come to you at any time. When your unconscious mind is searching for solutions, you never know when they'll come or what they'll be. The worst thing you can do is stimulate your creativity to find an answer only to forget it shortly after it pops into your head.

Finally, clear your desk every night, leaving only one high-priority item waiting for you when you return. While you might have a number of high-priority tasks ahead of you, having them all greet you first thing in the morning can be a disincentive. You can only effectively work on one at a time anyway. So pick your most pressing chore and get after it with all the energy and vitality you bring with you at the start of the new day.

The same technique holds true for lunch breaks. Before you go to lunch, clear away everything except that one big job that you want to jump into with both feet as soon as you return. The point is to get those high-priority jobs out of the way as soon as possible. Identifying them before you break means the most energized moments upon your return will be spent solving the problem, not deciding which problem to solve.

STEP FOUR
Launching
the Plan

*"All things come to those who wait provided
they hustle while they wait."*
—Thomas A. Edison

M y wife and I were passengers in a hot air balloon early
one African morning. As the balloon rose gracefully,
we saw a herd of wildebeest running frantically across
the vast expanse below us. The herd stopped suddenly
and began looking around as if they were confused. We asked our
pilot/guide why the herd had stopped so suddenly and what they
were looking for.

He told us that the wildebeest, which migrate by the millions
across grassy African plains, are not good learners. An entire herd
will take flight at the slightest indication of danger. They will run
wildly for a short time and then stop, forgetting why they began
running in the first place.

According to our local expert, the lions, who are good learners,
simply follow the stampeding wildebeest herd at a leisurely pace
and wait for them to stop. When the wildebeest forget why the
herd was running, it's dinner time for the lions. Our guide said
that wildebeest are so memory-challenged that they will even
walk up to a sleeping lion and sniff at it. The lion wakes up and
has breakfast in bed.

The wildebeest remind me of people who lose focus and/or lose direction by not following their plan. These folks remember that they had a plan once, but can't remember what it was or why it was important. As you launch your plan into action, the plan must remain your central focus and purpose. Only then will all of your hustle and energy be concentrated on achieving your documented goals. The subject is action.

Anticipation without action breeds frustration. Frustration breeds disillusionment.

The reason I set this statement apart is to demonstrate that launching a plan is a critical link in the *high-performance process.* Many people give up on planning, not because they have any problems completing that phase of the process, but because they can't seem to get started on the *action* phase. As a result, their plans, which produce great anticipation, never see the light of day and the net result is frustration.

The more frustrated you get, the more disillusioned you become. The more disillusioned you become, the more powerless and less motivated you feel. In the end, it doesn't make sense to plan any more if you can't expect to see any results. All of this is under your control, of course. That's why it's important to devote a section to *launching your plan.*

Sweaty palms

Someone once advised me to live every day as if it were my last day on earth because one day I would be right. Wouldn't it be a shame to get to the last day you have on earth and say, *"Wait a minute, I never did any of those things I planned to do."* By then it's too late. Launching the plan means transforming *thinking* into *action.*

Thinking and planning are one thing, but actually getting up and *doing* is something else. There is little threat of anything changing in your life if all you do is sit around and think about things. The thought of actually taking initiative to make things happen is enough to give you sweaty palms. As I've mentioned before, your actions speak with a louder and more credible voice than do your thoughts and words.

When you take the initiative to make something happen by putting your plans into action, things will change. It's impossible for your life to stay the same while you exert effort toward the attainment of a goal. If you *think* you're working toward a goal and nothing is changing, you're probably doing a lot more *thinking* than *acting*.

Loren Janes is the stunt person who doubled for the actress playing the role of Jill Kinmont in the film *The Other Side of the Mountain*. In shorthand that means he took a 50-foot fall on skis, off the side of a mountain, on purpose, to simulate the accident that left Jill partially paralyzed. He fell and the cameras rolled.

I asked Loren if he still gets sweaty palms before he does a major "gag" (movie-biz lingo for a stunt). *"Danny,"* he replied, *"if I don't get sweaty palms, I don't do the gag."* At first blush, that sounds like you should only do things that make you nervous. That's partially what Loren meant. If you're not doing something that makes your palms sweat, you're not stretching yourself very far.

On the other hand, you can attempt something outrageous and even dangerous and convince yourself that it's really not a big deal. If Loren steps up to do a challenging stunt with dry palms, he knows right away that he's not mentally prepared and he backs off lest he blow the attempt and/or injure himself. The same goes for you and me. When *thinking* becomes *doing*, sweaty palms indicate that we're embarking on a true adventure—and in touch with reality.

"Life is either a daring adventure or nothing."
—*Helen Keller*

Those are profound words from a woman who was rendered deaf, dumb and blind by a serious illness in her infancy. Helen Keller was never expected to develop the ability to communicate with others, much less become an inspiration to the world. Nevertheless she did. Thank goodness someone who was never expected to understand life as a normal human being was able to get the message to us that, as a rule, we take life's opportunities too lightly.

Helen Keller's message is that life can either be an adventure or it can be a holding pattern until death. The choice belongs to each one of us. Creativity expert and author Roger von Oech uses a tombstone as an illustration in his book, *A Whack On The Side Of The Head*. The tombstone bears the inscription:

> *Here lies So-and-So.*
> *Died at the age of 30.*
> *Buried at the age of 70.*

Helen Keller was so grateful for the opportunity to live fully that she savored every moment and didn't let precious time slide by uneventfully. That meant she had to be an *active* person. Von Oech is telling us the same thing. Once you stop being active, you're as good as dead, even if you don't physically expire for another 40 years.

How many people do you know who are walking zombies? Are *you* a walking zombie? I'm convinced that zombies can actually be great planners. They simply stop at the planning stage and never do anything that would initiate change in their lives. Without change there can be no adventure outside of the terror you feel while being swept away by circumstance beyond your control.

The emotional death that von Oech refers to is insidious. It creeps up on you so slowly that you don't even realize you're dead. It's complacency that kills you. A nonadventurous, passive existence will suffocate whatever spark you once had inside. For most adults, all you have to do is ask what's the difference between how they feel about life now and how they remember feeling about life in their early 20s.

During early adulthood, life was constantly changing. Everything you did was a challenge. Change and activity stimulated your creativity and zest for life. People who stay excited about life and passionate about what they do right into their senior years are *active* people. They're *doers*. Those are not the folks watching the parade go by, they *are* the parade.

Before you write this off to hype and motivation, think of the practical application of this knowledge. I have already established that it's your uniqueness that brings meaning to your personal and professional lives. More than meaning, your unique talents, knowledge and experiences are what fuel excellence in everything you do.

As you stand at your personal crossroads in your personal moment of truth, can you honestly say that you don't want to be a mover and a shaker? If you told the truth, the whole truth and nothing but the truth, so help you God, would you say, *"I really don't want to be in the parade. I'd rather just watch, thank you."*

Do you really expect to be given a more powerful and influential position based upon your *lack* of initiative? Should your employer or customers realistically give you more money for *doing less?* Just because the federal government can get away with that doesn't mean you should aspire to such contradictory standards. If you're not in a government job, you'd better become an adventure-seeker if you want to thrive and prosper.

Self-talk

Both low achievers and high achievers talk to themselves. The difference is what they say. Low achievers and high achievers have both discussed at length with themselves how quickly they each adapt to a new idea and how well they perform their daily tasks. Therein lies the problem or the progress. What does your self-talk do for you?

For starters, your internal dialogue has shaped your self-image. Your self-image controls your performance level—that is, how well you do your job. It's a cycle. (See Fig. 4-1) Self-talk informs self-image and self-image dictates performance. As a child, did you ever spin the little merry-go-round at the park as fast as you could and then try to jump on?

That's much the same challenge as breaking into the self-talk cycle. It's hard to break into. But break in you must if you're to exert any control over your productivity, much less change it. A high-performance person knows that it's not *how* you break into the cycle, but *where* you break in that matters. Many people expend a great deal of energy trying to hop on the merry-go-round at the self-image or productivity stages.

Self-Talk Cycle

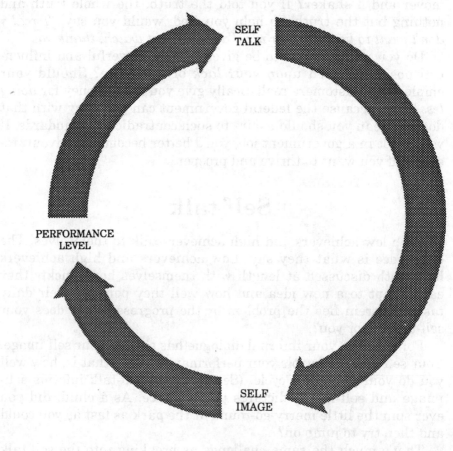

SELF
TALK

PERFORMANCE
LEVEL

SELF
IMAGE

Figure 4.1

If you've tried to improve your self-image or increase your productivity without lasting success, it's probably because you didn't break into your cycle at the self-talk stage. The self-talk stage is where it all begins and that's the only place that you can influence self-image or personal performance. You know what you're saying to yourself day-in and day-out. In fact you're the only one who can hear it.

Others can observe your productivity and sense your self-image, but you're the only one who can hear the internal dialogue. You're also the only person who can change the dialogue. Encouraging yourself rather than beating yourself up will produce remarkable results as far as self-image and personal productivity are concerned. Sincere encouragement peps anybody up. Why would you be any different?

If you're not familiar with your internal dialogue, *listen.* You speak out loud in a clear, articulate voice in your head. You don't speak a foreign language (unless you're trying to be cute) and you don't speak in code. There's no excuse for not hearing what you say to yourself unless you're avoiding the subject. Make a note on your daily planner to listen to yourself.

Make a note at various times throughout the day to pause for a moment, just a moment, and hear the words. You might be amazed. At times when you're under tremendous pressure, listen to yourself. At times when you score a victory, listen to yourself. Just after someone really ticks you off or when you really do something stupid, listen to yourself.

If what you hear is negative, tell your internal voice that negativity isn't going to make anything better. Put in an encouraging word and get back to work. Have you ever seen a professional athlete, Olympic figure skater or gymnast put in a good performance while screaming at himself or herself?

The first thing trainers encourage their performers to do when negative thoughts emerge is to *"shake them off"* and once again visualize the positive images of attaining the desired rewards. Nobody knows better than superstar performers that self-talk is the control point for performance.

Understanding motivation

Motivation is probably the most corrupted word in the English language. Motivation is so overused and improperly used that it's become synonymous with hype. I agree that much of what's passed off as motivation these days *is* little more than *hype*. When I talk about motivation, I'm talking about the no-monkey-business, honest-to-goodness, dictionary definition.

. To motivate is to provide with a motive—a *reason* to do something. Motivation is the byproduct of desire. Desire and motivation are joined at the hip. Neither can exist in the absence of the other. They exist at the same level. No matter what your job responsibilities are, your desire for the rewards for a job well-done will be an exact match for your motivation level to do the job well.

The next time someone tells you that they want this or that so badly they can taste it, ask that person what it will take to get the object of his or her desire. If s/he knows what's required, ask if s/he is willing to do what it takes. It doesn't take much to figure out that we all do what's necessary to get whatever we want, provided we truly want it badly enough. If we don't have what we want, it's probably because, in reality, we don't want it as badly as we say we do.

Actions speak louder than words. If you want to know what's most important to someone, watch what s/he does. *If it's important to know someone's* real motivation, watch his or her behavior. Where his or her motivation is, so too will his or her desire be found. Have you fallen into the trap of saying, *"I've been planning to do this or that for the longest time?"*

The stepping-off place between planning and launching your plan into action is at your motivation level. A plan that remains indefinitely on the launching pad isn't within the planner's sincere desire. Any attempt to verbally convince you otherwise is just talk. The planner's energy would be better spent in constructive self-talk than in trying to convince someone else that s/he really wants that thing for which s/he hasn't seen fit to invest the necessary effort.

Levels of motivation

There are four levels to motivation. (See Fig. 4-2) You're at one of the levels. If you have people working for you, everyone of them is at one of the levels. Every human being in control of his or her faculties is at one of the levels. Each level represents a motive for action, ranging from the least encouraging motivation (level one) to the highest level of encouragement.

Level one (lowest): Compliance

Do it or else. Few people enjoy working under these conditions. Nevertheless, the most frequently invoked management imperative is to do what you're told. Maybe that's because one of the most frequently invoked parental imperative is, *"Do it because I told you to."* The timeless logic to back that one up is the equally infamous, *"Because I said so, that's why."*

When you join the military, you're temporarily placing your other levels of motivation on the shelf, at least initially. In an organization that demands ultimate compliance, regimen and cloning in the name of efficiency, that's where you always begin. When the mongrel hordes are descending upon you with death in their eyes, it's not a good time for management to form a task force to study the problem.

In civilian, that is to say *civilized,* society, compliance is the least productive form of motivation and the most resented. Why? Because it forbids the injection of your unique self into the equation. If bringing your unique talents, knowledge and experience to the job leads to the highest possible productivity, keeping your unique qualities under lock and key is destined to result in the worst productivity.

In a word, compliance, as a means of providing motive, is counterproductive. The first major office I managed as a civilian after leaving the Air Force was nearly destroyed by you-know-who. I managed to take my company's leading sales office, full of leading salespeople, and bring it down to number 36 out of 36 offices in

Motivation Levels
and Mental Mood Chart

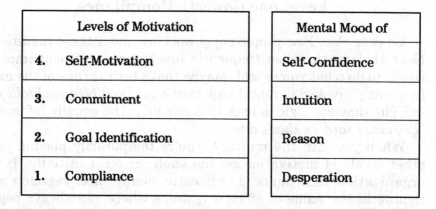

Levels of Motivation		Mental Mood of
4.	Self-Motivation	Self-Confidence
3.	Commitment	Intuition
2.	Goal Identification	Reason
1.	Compliance	Desperation

Figure 4.2

three months. I had a knack for de-motivating people and I worked it to perfection.

What was my secret? *Compliance. "Say it the way I say it, do it the way I do it and we'll all get along just fine."* Believe it or not, little Napoleonic autocrats like I was in those days don't demand conformity solely out of a need for power. There is seemingly sound logic behind cloning everyone in the organization after your own image.

I figured that if I could get everyone to think and behave just like me, they wouldn't bring me any problems that I hadn't already learned how to solve. Moreover, if I was so terrific that the company wanted me to manage the top office, then I must be doing things right. Right? If my behavior pleases the company brass, then what could be better than cloning everybody in the office to think and act exactly like me?

Character is not built at the compliance level. However, resentment flourishes. As parents we know that the sooner a child is brought into the decision-making process, the greater his or her compliance will become. The longer a child is told to blindly comply with orders, the greater his or her resistance becomes. Adults are like that, too. Except that adults are less forgiving than children.

If an adolescent is told to move a box in the garage three feet, s/he will ask "why?" If the answer is, "Because I told you so," you'll be amazed at how much damage a box can sustain being moved only three feet. Actually the box is only getting the treatment you would get if the kid could get away with it. And you wonder why people at work are not more careful and conscientious with company property.

Level two: Goal identification

If you want to generate animosity and resentment, operate on level one and demand compliance. If you want to begin building character, move up to level two where the objective is identification with the goal. That's all the adolescent is asking for when s/he asks *why* the box needs to be moved.

You're the one assigning the task. Therefore, you're the one who must provide the motive. You should know that people have a natural desire to identify with the goal and a natural resistance to being told to *do it or else.* All you have to do is monitor your own feelings. *You* can feel the difference between being ordered to comply and being included in the reasoning behind an instruction— why should anyone else be different?

This is easy stuff. If you hate operating under compliance, you'd better believe everyone else does too. If you feel better about following instructions if you're informed about the objective, everyone else does too. You will put a plan into action with much more energy and enthusiasm if you identify with the goal. Even if you don't *agree* with the goal, knowing the desired outcome makes any task easier to deal with.

If you don't *want* to know the reasoning behind an assignment because you strongly disagree with the outcome, then you have an ethical dilemma that needs to be addressed. Why are you engaged in something that contradicts your beliefs in the first place? If you face such a challenge, it's time to return to your moment of truth and ask the hard questions.

Even if there's no direct benefit to you, it's still important to identify with the goal. At a core level, simply *agreeing* with the wisdom behind what's to be accomplished will heighten your motivation. It's hard to find a worthwhile task that doesn't, in some way, benefit everyone involved. When the adolescent understands that a clean garage contributes to the efficiency of the household and an efficient household has more time for fun things, goal identification becomes *personal.*

If you're the one providing motive to others, make sure that if you predict benefits from completed tasks, those benefits are realized. If you sell a lot of blue sky and don't deliver, you're doing nothing more than manipulating others and soon you won't have any alternative but to try and enforce compliance. When people feel exploited, their performance is bound to be *worse* than unmotivated.

In the same way that the box was damaged by a resentful helper, a person motivated by goal identification will not only move it, but dust it off to boot. Despite bearing the brunt of countless jokes in our day, Napoleon was a great leader in *his* day. He embraced and employed the concept of goal identification as he led thousands of troops on his military campaigns.

Napoleon said, *"A great leader is a merchant of hope."* Isn't the same thing true of parents? How about teachers? Anyone who successfully provides motive to others is a merchant of hope who communicates to others that their labors really do pay off after all. People naturally hope that they will have some personal investment in anything they're involved in. The desire to have your natural talents, knowledge and experience recognized as part of the big picture is a tremendous motivator.

Level three: Commitment

The only way personal motive can become stronger than identifying with a goal is to *internalize* the goal. In the same way that your personal talents, knowledge and experience make anything you do more exciting, a goal is never more enthusiastically pursued than when it becomes part of you. Your level of personal investment is at its peak when you're genuinely committed to achieving your desired rewards.

High-performance people operate at level three and four. When folks are motivated by personal commitment, you'd best step out of their way unless you want footprints running up your back and down your front. The *high-performance* process of bringing as much of your talents, knowledge and personal experience to the job as possible plops you right in the highest levels of motivation.

When you commit to a goal by internalizing it, you commit your strengths to the task. You bring all that's the best of *you* to the table. The adolescent who is motivated by identification with the goal of having more time for the family to do fun things can be bumped up to the top motivation levels by personalizing the task. After you've explained *why* the box should be moved and the benefits that will result, tell the adolescent why you think *s/he* can do a good job of it.

As always, call on your own experience. How well do you do a job when you receive recognition for your skill and effort? Personalization is the essence of excellence. People who feel truly appreciated for their personal contributions will not only move boxes better than anyone ever moved boxes before and dust them off to boot, they'll be back looking for more boxes to move.

When you focus on strengths in yourself and others, you strike internal chords that reverberate far beyond where you happen to be standing at the time. The influence you create by focusing on individual strengths has far-reaching and long-lasting effects. Peter F. Drucker told us that focusing on strengths places a demand on performance. I say high-performance people *live* on their strengths and therefore create a constant environment of excellence.

Level four (highest): Self-motivation

The only way to top the commitment of internalization is to have the motivation originate and emanate from *inside of you*. If the adolescent decides to straighten out the garage for some reason all his or her own, you can bet s/he will do the best job possible. The more you subscribe to the *high-performance process,* the more initiative you're bound to see emerge from your natural talents, knowledge and experience.

If you're responsible for the performance of others as well as yourself, the same principles apply. The highest level of motivation will always result from self-initiative. Encouraging self-initiative takes skill as a leader, but it's well worth the effort. Once I learned from my sales mentor that my labors were tied directly to my lifestyle, my efforts started coming from within instead of needing to be associated with outside rewards.

Mental moods

Each of the four levels of motivation has an accompanying *mental mood.* Similar to the merry-go-round of *self-talk, self-image* and *productivity,* your *state of mind* is a primary determinant in your level of motivation. At the same time, your level of motivation will fuel your state of mind. Your *mental mood* and your level of motivation dance together so closely that it's difficult to determine which one is leading.

Level one mental mood: Despair

When you're operating at the compliance level of motivation, you quickly begin to feel the frustration and futility of repeating yesterday over and over again. You tend to feel helpless or powerless. The resulting emotion is *despair*. The desperation you feel clouds any vision you might have of breaking the cycle, getting out of your rut and changing your life.

Without vision, there can be no goals. It's impossible to move up to the *goal identification* level without visualizing desired rewards. So your desperation tends to become a self-fulfilling prophesy. People who struggle in level one are aware of their despair, but they rarely have the vision to see any way out of it.

Level two mental mood: Reason

When you identify with a goal, it's possible to consider your desired rewards in realistic terms. Attaining what you want becomes more believable and justifiable. Applying yourself toward a goal makes sense when you identify with the anticipated outcome. At level two the process of goal attainment becomes more logical and easier to follow.

Your resistance to doing something will naturally diminish if the task makes sense to you. How reluctant would you be to do something if you had no idea what would happen as a result of your effort? If you don't have any reason to expect a profitable outcome for someone, even if that someone is not you, it's not likely that you'll be able to function at the second motivation level. Unless your mind can *reason* with the task, your mental involvement can't be expected to exceed unthinking compliance.

Level three mental mood: Intuition

At the commitment level of motivation, your logical mind gives way to the subconscious. When you've truly internalized a goal, the goal becomes part of you and you become part of the goal. You become so familiar with the desired rewards that attaining them seems like second nature to you. When a problem pops up, you correct it as if by instinct.

Other people observing you might comment that you seem to know just what to do without thinking. You're *always* thinking of course, but when you reach the intuitive stage, much of your mental processing goes on auto pilot. When you're focused on an internalized goal, you can handle a much bigger load than you can at level one or two. With much of your thinking on auto pilot, your mind is free to be more aggressive.

The subconscious engages when you've committed your talents, knowledge and experience. In other words, when your strengths are brought to bear on a task, every dimension of your personality becomes involved. When you observe someone who seems to be working intuitively, you can bet your bottom dollar that they're at the commitment level of motivation.

Level four mental mood: Self-confidence

When the impulse for action comes from within you, it is the product of your self-confidence. Doing something that comes from your heart means maximum inspiration. There's no need to convince yourself of the goal's merits or identify with the goal when your motivation is truly instinctive. You can't operate out of a more confident emotional position than to be self-motivated.

Befriending an unpopular fellow

When I first got into sales, just out of the Air Force, there was a guy in the office that nobody liked. There probably wasn't a single soul in that office who didn't pull me aside as a newcomer and say, *"Stay away from that guy."* When I asked why, I was told that he hated all other salespeople, but especially *new* salespeople. As I was warned about this fellow again and again, I couldn't help but keep an eye on him and my curiosity grew.

It seemed strange to me that this much-maligned salesperson was also the one with the most trophies, plaques and awards for top sales performance. Something didn't quite add up. So I made it my mission to get to know this guy and solve the mystery. I found out that even though professional jealousy cost him popularity in the office, he was popular with his *customers*.

I learned more from that guy than from anyone else in the organization. One day the two of us went out to prospect for new home listings. I *should* say that he convinced me to join him as *he* went out to prospect. As usual I was too busy planning to launch my plan into action. He helped me see the error in my ways. The first thing I felt was a slap on the back as I sat at my desk.

He said, *"Let's go out and do some door-knocking, Danny."* I replied that I had too much to do at the office to get out and solicit new business that day. As usual he asked me a question I couldn't answer, "What have you got to do in the office that's more important than drumming up new business." I wasn't sure how to answer him, but I knew that I didn't want to go out and bang on doors.

He got impatient with me. "What could you possibly do here at the office that's more important than to go out and find somebody who needs our help and is willing to pay well for it?" I had to admit there wasn't anything more important than that. He said, "Then let's go," and we launched out the door. Truthfully, he practically dragged me out to his big Cadillac.

He deposited me in the passenger seat and got in himself. As he started the engine I noticed he was impeccably well-dressed in an Italian silk suit with a white-on-white shirt. He looked the part of a successful person.

In stark contrast to his confident poise, I was slumped in the right front seat, an unwilling passenger. I felt like a hostage being driven away from the safety of my desk against my will. I liked planning as long as I never had to launch the plan. But here I was, too embarrassed to ask him to take me back. It was a good thing I was too meek to protest.

That man taught me one of the most important lessons of my life. As we drove I looked over at this man that I hated and loved at the same time and asked, *"Have you ever not wanted to go out and prospect?"* I wondered if he had ever in his life felt the way I was feeling at that moment. I had flown high-performance jet fighters to the very doorstep of disaster and yet I was afraid of talking to a few prospects.

He told me that he'd felt the same thing. He even went on to describe the queasy feeling I had in my stomach. He accurately recounted the whim-whams I felt all over my body. He could see the perspiration across my upper lip, but when he told me my tongue was stuck to the roof of my mouth I thought he was clairvoyant. Amazed, I asked, *"How did you know that?"*

He said, *"I felt that way 20 minutes ago."* I thought he was pulling my leg. That got my back up a little and I cautioned him not mess with my head because I was on the verge of throwing in the towel and looking for another line of work. He reaffirmed that he had really faced trepidation similar to mine less than a half-hour earlier.

Seeing an opportunity I said, "Let's go back to the office. Neither one of us has any business out here bothering these folks when we both feel the same way." He told me that he didn't feel fear anymore. It was hard for me to imagine that, once someone felt fear, they could get to a point of not feeling it. I asked him what his secret was, half believing it was still impossible.

That's when the lesson began. He asked me, "Danny, if I were to hand you a thousand dollars, what would you do with it?" I told him that I would pay some bills. "Wrong." He said it so fast it frightened me. I knew I hadn't given him the right answer. You know the feeling when you give the wrong answer and still have no clue as to the right answer. I took a stab and said, "Okay, if you gave me a thousand dollars I'd have some fun with it."

He wanted specifics. "What *exactly* would you do with it?" He persisted and I resisted. Finally, I told him that the Reno air races were coming up in a few months and I had always dreamed of going. I'd been to Reno before and loved it, but I always wanted to see the air races. He said that sounded good and asked me for some details about the weekend event.

I proceeded to tell him all about what I had read and learned about the three separate classes of swift and powerful planes. For anyone with any flying blood in them at all, watching those planes zoom past the crowd at full throttle, 40 feet off the ground was supposed to send chills up your spine. I said, "That's what I would do with that thousand dollars."

He wasn't through with me yet. He asked where my wife and I would stay. He asked me to describe my favorite Reno restaurant. My descriptions were becoming increasingly detailed and exciting. A public relations/advertising firm couldn't have described a more incredibly delectable scene, right down to the steak dinner with twice-baked potato and homemade bread.

Still a little slow at the switch. I finished telling him how I would spend the money and then said, "Why do you ask?" "Why don't you figure up your side of the commission when we get a new listing today and sell the house?" In those days, it was $1,000. He knew what he was working for that day. I was going out to see if I could get lucky. He was going out with a purpose.

About then he lit in to me something awful. "You were willing to forfeit your dream trip to Reno just so you could sit at the office and push papers around today then go home to tell your wife and kids how hard you worked at the office all day." I thought for a minute and said, "Would you drive a little faster?" When we hit that neighborhood, I was out of the car before he rolled to a stop.

I hit the ground running. Knocking on door after door, we stayed at it. An hour later I hopped back into his car with a big smile on my face and a listing appointment for that evening. We got the listing, sold the house and I went to the Reno air races for the first of 11 years in a row. The lesson I learned that day made my career the success that it was more than anything I learned in the corporate training materials.

Strangely, when he got back in the car that day, he had a grim look on his face. I was grinning from ear to ear and he was glaring at me. I asked him what was wrong. After all we had just set a listing appointment (and got two more leads that we later turned into listings and sales). From the look on his face I began to think that maybe the folks in the office were right about him.

In the aftermath of our successful prospecting that afternoon, he solemnly said, "I'm going to tell you something and don't ever forget it. Never work hard to pay bills. Work hard to have fun with the money. Otherwise, you won't have enough to do either one." I realized at that moment that I had been working hard to pay bills with the money. He was right. I didn't have enough to pay all my bills or have fun with the money.

The two things I despised the most, paying bills and knocking on doors went hand in hand. I *had* no idea that I was operating at the lowest level of motivation and felt desperate. I had to do something I didn't like in order to do something else I didn't like. What a life! My sales mentor walked me right up the motivation ladder that day, from compliance to goal identification to commitment. From despair to reason to intuition.

Since that day, I've never worked to pay bills and my life has been filled with fun. Sure, I've had struggles along the way, but from the plains of Africa to the glaciers of Alaska, my wife and I have experienced adventure after adventure, filling our years with the most fascinating people and exotic places. The entire nature of work changes when you operate on the commitment level of motivation. Launching a plan into action at any other motivation level will compromise the outcome.

> *In a nutshell, the lesson I learned from my mentor, Jim Raco, in the sales business was: As the "want" gets stronger, the "how" gets easier.*

Laziness

When launching your plan into action, it's important not to forget about that old, insidious enemy, *procrastination.* Although procrastination can rear its ugly head at any stage of the *high-performance process,* it's most likely to appear when you put your thoughts into action. Risks are greater at the action stage because actions commit you more than words.

For that reason, you seldom procrastinate when talking. However, all sorts of things will creep up out of nowhere to keep you from *acting.* Of course these impediments to action usually come from within or are at least sanctioned by your own unconscious mind. Genuine roadblocks to your productivity that pop into your path are not part of a procrastination conspiracy.

In case you sometimes feel as if you're wasting a lot of time on a mediocre career, laziness is not a cause of reduced productivity, but a *symptom*. There are some people who are so genuinely lazy they don't know what to do when a holiday comes along. You know the kind who are born tired and then have a relapse. The type who don't want to work between meals.

However, the real reason we all tend to procrastinate can be broken down into three parts:

1. The inner fear of making a mistake.
2. Reluctance to shoulder an obligation.
3. The desire to avoid criticism.

Mistakes

Somewhere in our childhood, each of us learned that mistakes get frowns while victories get smiles of approval. Reacclimating ourselves as adults to believe that mistakes are not terrible, but in fact represent honest efforts and lessons learned is difficult but oh, so important to the *high-performance process*. If you go through life trying to avoid frowns, you'll never try anything. If you never try anything, the only *big* mistake you'll make will be not to try anything.

It sounds a little weird, but most high-performance people I've known in my life seem to seek out situations that have a high risk and a high probability for mistakes. That's where the prize is usually hidden. If the prize were laying in the middle of the street for everyone to reach down and pick up, everybody would be rich and/or successful.

Obligations

The high-performance people I know are quick to shoulder obligations as long as the obligation is necessary for the attainment of a worthwhile goal. High-performance people have no desire to shoulder the problems of the world. Just heaping responsibility upon yourself for no reason doesn't make sense. Yet some people feel guilty unless they're absolutely buried under more responsibility than they can possibly deal with.

Making a commitment means to accept responsibility for the outcome. It makes sense that someone who is afraid of making a mistake doesn't want to be held responsible for any sort of obligation. If you're the one responsible, you're the one who gets frowned at when things don't work out correctly. As long as you can avoid obligations, you can avoid mistakes. As long as you can avoid mistakes, you won't be criticized.

"Is it that I have had so much pain from when I commit I'm too scared to commit to anything again?"

Criticism

Nobody likes to be criticized. The frown that we worked so hard to avoid as children can take on harsher and more pungent characteristics in adult life. Unfortunately, many of the firms I consult with owe a great deal of their productivity problems to an atmosphere of criticism. It takes a rare individual to plow ahead and take risks in a critical environment.

Nevertheless, high-performance people know that risking mistakes for the sake of breaking new and productive ground is well worth the potential penalty in criticism. If the great inventors and artists whose work has enhanced the quality of our lives over the centuries had allowed themselves to be stifled by criticism, our lives would be much poorer for it.

Criticism is a fact of life, like death and taxes. It's unfortunate—it seldom, if ever, helps anybody do anything better. But there it is, waiting for you around every bend. You can even watch low achievers and productivity saboteurs at meetings rubbing their hands together when others accept high-risk assignments.

Like vultures circling above a dying person in the desert, these buzzards of the business world hope others will make mistakes so that they can swoop down and pick the poor soul's bones clean. The desire to avoid having your bones picked clean is natural. To high-performance people, the desire to attain the rewards available only to risk-takers is stronger.

High-performance people know that criticism is not likely to come from the mouths of enlightened people. Part of the valuable respect for others that I described in the Overview means being a problem-solver rather than a people-basher. If you're willing to take risks for the sake of personal high-performance and excellence, you must be willing to take the heat.

It's somewhat comforting to know that only people who are *not* willing to take risks criticize others. Those who have experienced the slings and arrows of trying, failing and trying again aren't prone to criticize the courageous endeavors of other risk-takers. Noting who around you is quick to criticize and who is quick to encourage is a fast way to separate low achievers from high-performance people. High-performance people never allow laziness to take root in the fertile soil of procrastination.

A realistic look at fear

When you start talking about transforming thoughts and words into action, fear enters the picture. Fear is the driving force behind your old enemy procrastination. If you can successfully deal with fear, you can successfully deal with procrastination. Since fear is an inescapable part of life, it's best to do what Glenn Ford recommended and intentionally do the things that you're afraid of, thus keep fear from taking charge of your life.

Some people have suggested to me that fear can be a positive influence in life and that my crusade against it is overstated. While I agree that fear is natural and it's always best to admit its presence and not deny it, I find little positive about fear. Even though it's good to pay attention to emotions because they're constantly telling you things about yourself that you might not otherwise be aware of, letting emotions govern your behavior is wrong.

Ask yourself how many good things fear has done for you. The answer is *"Not very many."* Fear influences your life to be sure, but the greater the influence fear plays in your life, the more it costs you in personal performance. The mental and physical exhaustion from battling fear alone can be overwhelming. Other than informing you how a situation affects you emotionally, fear has no other value.

Ask yourself if self-confidence does more for you than fear and the answer will be, *"Yes."* Your self-confidence does far more to promote positive results in your life than fear ever will. How self-confident your self-image is determines how productive you are. Following the self-talk merry-go-round, your self-image is determined by your internal dialogue.

That leads to the next question, *"Which voice am I listening to right now, fear or self-confidence?"* The answer to that question is critical to your personal performance. As you think about what you're going to do next, both fear and self-confidence will have something to say about it. Which is speaking louder? Which are you going to listen to?

Usually, fear speaks with a louder voice than self-confidence. That's because fear has become a habit. Listening to self-confidence can become a habit too, if you work at it hard enough. Fear seems to come by its loud voice naturally. Self-confidence can only be amplified through your conscious effort. Self-confidence can be given a representative voice in your self-talk, and your self-image and productivity will be much the better for it.

Four commitments for launching your plan

1. Honesty
2. Courage
3. Determination
4. Conviction

Honesty with yourself means taking initiative to look at things realistically. All the best-laid plans in the world aren't going to make me a player on a National Basketball Association team. I'm older now than I was when I started this book and I haven't grown an inch. You must be honest about what you're capable of *and* what you're willing to invest of yourself in the *high-performance process.*

It takes *courage* to set goals realistically high. Just because you can't do everything your heart can dream of doesn't mean you shouldn't try *anything.* Goals need to be realistic. But, if goals are to move you to a higher level of living, your targets need to be

Goals

increasingly higher. That takes courage because the higher you reach, the farther you have to fall. Courage is more than a buzz word when it comes to launching a plan into action.

Determination to put the plan into action is fueled by desire. Because motivation is a byproduct of desire, all three, *determination, motivation* and *desire,* work in concert with one another to transform thoughts and words into action. Determination must be more than grim resolve and willpower.

There may be times when you need to give a push. However, identifying your true desires and level of motivation will have the effect of *drawing* the plan into motion rather than forcing it like the square peg through the round hole. Committing yourself to determination means committing yourself to giving the plan a push if necessary.

Conviction that goals can be reached means believing that success is attainable. Your firm belief that your desired rewards are within reach is essential to your success. Without that belief, you won't have the resolve to keep investing when the going gets rough. There will be times when you begin to doubt and consider giving up on the plan.

It's in those moments that the strength of your conviction will either mean the salvation or abandonment of your actions. The stronger your conviction, the more likely you will be to deal in terms of *when* rather than *if.* Without a strong belief that your goals are attainable, you'll be prone to say, *"If I go ahead and do such and such..."* all the while straddling the fence in case the whole thing turns sour. A strong conviction sounds more like, *"When I do such and such..."*

The difference between thinking in *if* terms and *when* terms is the difference between *trying* and *intending* to do something. I know that many of us say that we intend to do something and then never do. The reason I mention a difference here is to illustrate how action varies from words. Look back on something you've done recently and ask yourself if you *intended to do it* or just whimsically *gave it a try.*

Sometimes we surprise ourselves and do worthwhile things without really trying. But it's never a way of life. If someone says to you, *"I'll try and call this week"* or *"I'll try to squeeze you in for lunch,"* I doubt if you would clear your calendar in anticipation. Instead, if that person said, *"I intend to call you Monday because we're going to have lunch before Friday,"* you'd get out your pencil and planner and ask, *"What day looks good for you?"*

Learn to talk to yourself in definitive action terms. Make *honesty, courage, determination* and *conviction* part of your daily language of higher productivity. When you break into the self-talk merry-go-round at the self-talk phase, those are the type of terms you want to add to your internal vocabulary. It doesn't do you any good to speak profoundly to others if you're not speaking profoundly to yourself.

> *"I'll take adventure before security, freedom before popularity and conviction before influence."*
> —*Charles Lindbergh*

That quotation is attributed to Charles Lindbergh by my friend, Jim Newton, who knew Lindbergh personally. Nobody can question the courage of the first man to cross the Atlantic in an airplane. When Jim was at the Smithsonian for the filming of a television documentary on Lindbergh, he turned to astronaut Neil Armstrong, who was also part of the film, and asked if he would have attempted the solo transatlantic flight.

Jim was a little surprised to hear one of America's greatest space heroes say, *"no."* Armstrong went on to explain that his mission to the moon was heavily researched, funded and planned by teams of scientists who collectively knew about everything there was to know about space travel. The astronaut then pointed out that, while his Apollo mission had a supporting cast of a million, Lindbergh flew off alone with no radio, no radar, no lights, no high-tech amenities. It was just one man up there, alone at the controls of a flying gasoline tank.

How do you spell relief?

Some people keep a little energy or effort in reserve as a bromide for their *anticipated* failures. When these folks try something new, they're so confident in their own failure that they give it less than they've got. Holding something back is a way of preserving an *out* more than a way to preserve energy. If their attempt falls short, they can always tell associates, friends and family that they didn't give it their best shot. The implication is that their best shot would have assuredly succeeded.

Not every adventure you and I embark upon has the history-making potential of what Charles Lindbergh accomplished. However, whenever you or I break new ground in our lives and go places and do things we've never done before, the same principles apply. We need to call upon our own *honesty, courage, determination* and *conviction.*

Life where you are, doing whatever you do must be played by the same rules if you're going to reap the rewards of the *high-performance process.* Lindbergh is a good example of how critical it is to launch your plan into action. Had his plans to cross the Atlantic ocean in a single-engine airplane remained plans, it would have been up to someone else to accomplish the feat.

There were no doubt many people who dreamed of and planned to cross the Atlantic as Lindbergh did. The difference between Charles Lindbergh being heralded as the world's greatest aviator and the other would-be Atlantic crossers was the fact that he, quite literally, launched his plan (and his plane) into action.

For some reason, many people would rather be able to make that excuse than to say that they gave it everything they had and it didn't fly. Contrary to popular opinion, the latter attitude of confession leads to success nine times out of 10, while the former attitude leads to success one time out of 10. It's not a matter of statistical probability as much as it is common sense. If somebody's trying with all they've got, it's perfectly natural to assume they will succeed more than someone who's not.

If you're going to fall, fall *toward your goal.* Big effort will beat small effort over time. Ask any athletic coach or player if withholding talent, knowledge and experience will lead to a starting spot on the team or cheers from the fans. Falling down or not falling down doesn't make you a hero. It's how and how often you get up and dust yourself off that brings the crowd to its feet.

When to expect results after a change of habit

When a group of people tries a new behavior day after day, approximately 20 percent of them will show tangible results within 30 days. The remainder usually meet expectations within 90 to 120 days if they keep at it. Do you have the patience to develop a new habit? The key is sticking to it. Successfully launching a plan into action requires *patience* and *persistence*.

Your forward motion will be faster at some times and slower at other times. The most important factor is your direction. As long as you're moving forward, you're sticking to your plan. Every moment you spend moving forward, you're adopting new and positive habits. That's what launching your plan means in behavioral terms—changing behavior for the better.

If life is to be an adventure, you must move forward. If you're a growing person, your largest adventures are ahead of you, not in your past. Monitor your motivation and mental moods to see if you need to move yourself up a notch. Deal realistically with fear and procrastination. Most of all, act. High-performance people know that *actions* and not mere words, are what increases personal performance and improve the quality of your life. Real change comes from *doing*.

If you think there's no real need to launch your plan into action, consider what humorist George Ade said:

"Anyone can win, provided there's no second entry."

STEP FIVE
Problem-Solving: Expecting the Unexpected

"If a problem has no solution, it is not a problem but a fact of life like any other. If a problem has a solution, it is not a problem either. The problem is the strength of will and determination to adopt the solution."
— *Richard Needham*

Wﾠhen inventor Thomas Edison first tried to record the human voice on a piece of tin foil with a crude device he had assembled in his research lab, *it worked.* According to biographer Jim Newton, a personal friend of Edison's for many years, the inventor never trusted his voice-recording invention for the simple reason that it worked the first time he tried it.

Of the thousands of inventions Edison brought into our world, he fully expected to fail numerous times before he made any progress. He was a visionary who anticipated a difficult process every time. In other words, Edison knew that problems were part of life—and especially part of the creative process. If a great inventor like Edison could accept that, can it be that hard for us to learn?

Once, in his laboratory, Edison tried an experiment for the thousandth time. It failed. According to Newton, Edison turned to the researcher next to him and said, *"We're making real progress. We now know 1,000 ways it can't be done."* That's not only a positive attitude that all of us should strive to emulate, but also a great testament to learning.

"Fate seems to work with dice rather than a T-square."
—*George Ade*

Experience is another word for mistakes. Edison credited himself for failing more often than anyone else on earth. Of course, he was *trying more new things* more often than anyone else on earth. That's why he believed so strongly that the answer is always out there if only you work to find it. Experience is not only the best teacher in the world, but the most expensive. Once an answer is found, though, improvement and refinement come quickly.

Edison, best-known for inventing the light bulb, had to patent more than 300 other inventions before he could install electricity in the Lower East Side of New York City. Before he could put the light bulb to practical use, he had to invent electrical wiring, meters, switches and so on. The birth of a new idea might come slowly, but growing up is fast.

Even Alexander Graham Bell, who invented the telephone, couldn't put his revolutionary invention into application until Edison invented the carbon transmitter that allowed communities to finally enjoy the miracle of electronic communications. Bell's telephone was a great discovery, but its signal was too weak to be put to general use. The telephone, as great a discovery as it was, raised even greater and more profound problems by its very existence. Edison was instrumental in solving the problems posed by Bell's progress.

What Edison possessed in creative skills he lacked in negotiating skills. Jim Newton recounts the story about Edison's invention of the carbon transmitter for the telephone. When the organization developing the telephone asked how much he wanted for inventing the device, Edison thought of a price range in his head. It was $3,000 to $5,000 (a great deal of money in those days).

Not sure of himself as a negotiator, Edison replied, *"What will you give me for it?"* He was offered $25,000, which he promptly accepted. Afterwards, he told the men representing the early telephone company that he had a much lower figure in mind and, if they had held out, they could have got the transmitter for $5,000. They replied that, if *Edison* had held out, they were prepared to give him *$50,000.* (Perhaps Edison's later invention of the motion picture camera was indirectly responsible for the evolution of the Hollywood agent.)

Today, we can't turn on an electrical appliance, launch a rocket into space, listen to a recording or see a movie without owing something to Thomas Edison. He had made 1,000 short films before the first film was ever shot in Hollywood.

Virtually everything worth having in life comes with problems attached. Your progress and personal growth will never come without the need to resolve problems along the way.

Old you meets new you: shadow vs. light

As you discover and develop your potential, the new problems encountered are nothing more than the expanding *shadow* of your personal growth. The *new you* can solve problems that the *old you* couldn't. Once you successfully unleash your talents, knowledge and experience, you're essentially a new person. Realistically, you're more of who you always had the potential to be rather than a new creation.

Leonardo da Vinci said, *"Shadows do not exist without their opposite light."* Robert H. Schuller said, *"If you're seeing only shadows, you're looking in the wrong direction."* When I began my career as a lecturer and consultant, I saw many problems. I was worried about who was going to pick me up at the airport in the cities where I was scheduled to speak. How was I going to get around? Who was going to make sure I had the right hotel and all of the equipment I needed to make my presentation?

There were shadows everywhere. Then it occurred to me that I needed to book an engagement before any of my imagined problems would even apply. As my speaking career grew and prospered, I grew and prospered as a human being. Accordingly, I faced many problems along the way. That was the ever-expanding shadow of my personal growth. My real growth began as soon as I turned and looked toward the light and stopped focusing on the shadows.

As far as the way you handle your life, you might as well be a new person. If problems have eyes, they won't recognize you as a high-performance person after knowing your old self. As you approach problems more aggressively, they'll appear far less intimidating. If you've delayed taking on an important task because you're hesitant to confront the inescapable problems that are bound to arise, you have allowed yourself to get seized up by fear—you've become problem-phobic.

Preparation for problem-solving

Before I describe the concise problem-solving process, it's important for you to know how to prepare yourself and keep yourself prepared for problem-solving, from beginning to end. The steps in the problem-solving process seem simple and easy to execute. Indeed they will be more manageable if you use this preparation process to make sure your head's on right when you take on inevitable problems.

1. Stay calm and keep the problem in perspective.

It's easy to say that in a noncrisis atmosphere. Remembering to tell yourself to stay calm in a crisis will be more difficult. High-performance people know that those two key words, *"Stay calm,"* can make all the difference in the world when it comes to defeating a problem or allowing the problem to defeat you. All of your problem-solving skills become useless the moment you lose control.

When a problem pops up, whether it's a surprise or not, remaining calm needs to be your *first* priority. Memorizing those

Commitment: I have not (recently) been committed enough to anything to — Maintain momentum when I hit a program two words is a good place to start. Have them so ingrained in your mind that when other people are saying, *"Holy cow! What am I going to do?"* You'll be saying, *"Stay calm."* If that's your knee-jerk reaction to a surprise problem, you'll be establishing an atmosphere for problem-solving while others are still trying to decide whether to run and hide.

2. Be aware of your self-confidence.

"You can tell the character of the person by the choices made under pressure."
—*Winston Churchill*

The late Dr. Norman Vincent Peale said, *"You're only as big as the problem that stops you."* Think about the last time a problem stopped you in your tracks and you decided to abandon your efforts. Can you recall how pumped up you were initially about reaching that goal and collecting your desired rewards? What happened? Did you change your mind?

You probably didn't change your mind about how valuable your goal was. Instead, a problem probably came up that made the desired rewards look less desirable than the amount of effort required to solve the problem. That's not a change of perspective as far as the goal is concerned. It's more likely to be a distortion created by your own problem-phobia.

In hindsight, I doubt if you can find many instances in your life when abandoning the goal was a suitable tradeoff compared to any threat the problem might have presented. How much further along in your career would you be if you had gone ahead and faced down that problem and then, having overcome it, continued on your charted course?

Knowing that you have talents, knowledge and experience (in this case *especially* experience), you must ask the question that calls out your self-confidence for inspection. Right after you say to yourself, *"Stay calm,"* ask yourself, *"Is this problem more than I can handle?"* In the past, have you ever solved problems that are similar or even larger? Probably.

→ !?. I haven't cared enough about anything to maintain enthusiasm.

What's the worst that can happen if you forge ahead? Will somebody yell at you? Will it cost you a great deal of money? Will it cost you your job? Worst of all, will people expect more of you in the future if you succeed? That last one stops more folks than any of the other questions. If you have the confidence that you can overcome the problem, then get started. If you don't feel you have the confidence, get started anyway. Every step you take toward solving the problem will increase your confidence.

3. De-confuse the problem. Define and break it down to its component parts on paper.

A big, intimidating challenge is really just a collection of smaller, less-intimidating challenges. When a problem hits, it's natural to experience confusion. Problems don't present themselves in neat, easy-to-understand packages. It's not unusual to feel disoriented. Just because you can see the front end of a problem doesn't mean you can see the back end or even the middle. How do you know that's the front end you're looking at anyway?

You've told yourself to *stay calm* and you've decided that there's enough *self-confidence* in your tank to take this thing on. Now calmly begin dismantling the problem before it dismantles you. Writing things on paper engages the linear lobe of your brain where logic is the order of the day. Trying to sort things out in your head means you will be using, at least partially, the spatial lobe of your brain where your imagination can run wild.

Your right brain will come into play soon enough. There's nothing like imagination to feed the creativity you need to solve the problem. First, you have to know what it is you're trying to solve. As logic and reason kick in from your linear/logical brain lobe, you will begin to feel an increasing sense of control. A model will begin to emerge from your list of the problem's component parts.

When the problem has been sketched out, it will no longer seem confusing or intimidating. In fact, you're now setting the stage for the fun part of problem-solving. Because of the focus problems require, they can contribute beneficial refinement to your goal-attainment process. Problems often act as stones that wear away the rough edges of your plan rather than as roadblocks.

4. Use creativity, personal experience and/or the experience of others to solve the puzzle from start to finish, from finish to start, or begin in the middle.

Out of conflict comes creativity. You've stayed calm, called out your self-confidence and sketched out a profile of the problem on paper. Now you've got the problem right where you want it. The problem now becomes a vehicle to bring out all that's best in you. Moreover, you can have fun in the process. Consider the problem as a unique challenge that your talents and abilities will ultimately resolve, possibly with the help of solutions suggested by others.

Orison Swett Marden, a great thinker and author chronicled the lives of great people who left their marks on the world. The people he studied and wrote about didn't become well-known because they didn't have problems. Great people become known for the way they managed to deal with problems—and even turned problems into opportunities.

Marden was the original founder of *Success* magazine and continually urged his readers to *"ride on the shoulders of giants."* His contention, and the basis for the early magazine, was that time you spend covering the same territory that someone else has covered is time wasted. He might have even been the one who coined the phrase about reinventing the wheel.

Your personal knowledge and experience are very important, but should be used as a supplement to what you can learn from the experience of others. Once again, reading, attending seminars and studying audio and video materials can enrich your talents and save you tremendous time as you go about the business of problem-solving. You can start at the public library.

If you're unclear about where to start on a problem, try visualizing the final solution and work backwards from there. If you know where you want to go or can picture the desired outcome, it becomes easier to backtrack and apply some reverse engineering to build the bridge you need. Sometimes the view is clearer from some point other than the front end.

You might as well have fun solving your problems. That's where much of your time's going to be spent. Frank A. Clark said, *"The next best thing to solving a problem is finding some humor in it."* I say that finding humor in the problem-solving process will speed up the solutions. It's not necessarily true that, if you can smile when things go wrong, it's because you've got someone else in mind to blame. On the other hand, if someone says, *"This is as bad as it can get,"* don't count on it.

5. Use relentless, dogged determination until the solution is in action.

Problem-solving, like planning, doesn't begin to benefit anyone until ideas are implemented. You need a Ph.D. in *stickology*. Remember how I like to shake up boardrooms full of top executives by having them review their meeting notes from past problem-solving sessions? The ugly truth I bring them face-to-face with is their own lack of action. They talk about their problems, even come up with good solutions, but seldom do they boldly put those solutions into action.

Solutions really aren't solutions until they're in action. Up to that point, they're just thoughts and talk. One of the reasons that solutions aren't implemented is because they're too simple. For some reason people tend to believe that a solution has to be complex and profound to be useful. Thomas Edison himself would argue that solutions don't have to be fancy to be good solutions.

The problem-solving process

Against the backdrop of your mental preparation for problem-solving, the following steps give you a practical blueprint for taking on any problem that pops up as you carry out your plan:

1. *Identify the problem.* How will you know where you're going if you don't first figure out where you are? Being clear about what the problem *is* and what the problem *is not* will save you time and energy as you seek solutions.

For example, it's often thought that *people* are problems and roadblocks when it's a misunderstanding or communication disruption. The people don't need to be fixed; the communication does. Separating people from problems is almost always a good first step.

2. *Gather all relevant information.* It's imperative that you know as much about the problem as possible. By this I'm not suggesting that you spend an inordinate amount of time on negative issues. The point is to understand the nature of what you're up against.

   If you're not sure if your problem is a result of implementation or planning, where are you going to begin? The more information you have, the more quickly you'll be able to diagnose what you're up against.

3. *List all possible solutions.* This one helps build self-confidence right off the bat. As your list of possible solutions grows, the problem becomes less menacing. When you've got your mind engaged in problem-solving, it's neither fair nor smart to try and keep lists in your head.

   By having a list of all possible solutions nearby, you can quickly scan to see if what you're doing could be enhanced by incorporating a component of another solution. When the solution you're trying doesn't bear fruit, a list will speed you on to the next try.

4. *Test possible solutions.* In prioritizing the list of solutions you come up with, it may be difficult to determine with any certainty which solutions are the most promising. In that case, testing solutions will help make that determination.

   Again I urge you not to spend needless time testing every solution that comes to mind. Instead, only test those that hold the most promise and can't be clearly eliminated by pondering. Testing or trial runs will help you correctly prioritize the top few solutions on your list.

5. *Select the best solution.* Sounds easy, doesn't it? You'll be glad you took time to test your top choices when it comes time to throw all of your energy and effort behind the best possible solution.

You want to be as sure as you can be, but even when you've still got some doubt about which solution is absolutely best, you will have to make a choice. Whatever solution you choose, make sure you go with it 100 percent.

6. *Get the solution into action.* I might sound like a broken record on this point but it's the most important. Just like launching your plan was the key step in the *high-performance process,* implementing your solution is the key step in the problem-solving process.

   People are hesitant to implement solutions in the problem-solving process for many of the same reasons they hesitate when launching their plans. There is an element of risk. Go back and dig into some of the courage, determination and conviction I talked about in step five and *do it!*

The art of persuasion

Sometimes your problem is convincing others to adopt your point of view. The *high-performance communication system* (see Fig. 5-1) is based on a process that former Disney executive Mike Vance explained to me many years ago. When adopting a new solution, you might have to *"sell"* others on the plan or possibly even a definition of the problem.

To overcome resistance, you must, first of all, accept that the other person might be looking at the same wall you are, but from the opposite side. A curved wall might be convex from your perspective, but *concave* from the opposite perspective. In the Figure 5-1 illustration, person A must take a trip around to view the wall from the perspective of person B.

Person A must ask as many questions as possible while standing in person B's position. Person A must list every possible objection person B might articulate based on his or her perspective. If, after examining things from all relevant sides, person A has not improved upon or come up with a better solution, it's time to talk.

Discussing a problem after you've taken the time to ingest what the other party might think based on his or her perspective puts you light years closer to arriving at a consensus. You won't be

The High-Performance Communication System

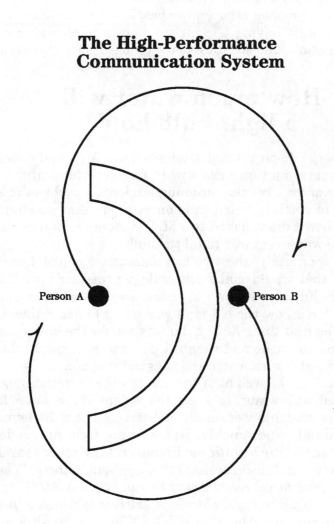

Figure 5.1

tempted to force your perspective on the other person once you've seen theirs. The whole dialogue will begin and proceed on common ground, which makes agreement much more likely.

Remember, a problem between two people is not solved until there is agreement. Just having a great solution in mind isn't enough. Effective communication is critical to the problem-solving process.

How much water will a light bulb hold?

Every year, Edison invited students from MIT and other top schools to assist and observe in his research laboratory. The renowned inventor gave the incoming students a problem to solve as a means of getting their heads on straight. Jim Newton tells the story of how Edison asked two MIT students to determine the weight of the water required to fill the bulb.

Working separately, the two ran exhaustive calculations and calibrations that would make any college professor proud. They came back to Edison with two different answers and everyone in the lab wondered how the old man was going to determine which was right. The first thing Edison did was ask for the bulb back. He then put it on the scale and weighed it. Next he removed the end of the bulb, filled it with water and weighed it again.

By subtracting the weight of the empty bulb from the weight of the bulb filled with water, he knew the weight of the water filling the bulb. The students were a bit embarrassed that he found his answer so simply and quickly. But, coming from an academic, and—shall I say—*bureaucratic* environment, they never considered his direct approach. Edison realized this and said to them, *"There is your answer. Now forget everything they taught you at MIT."*

Edison also liked to say, *"There's no extreme to which a [person] won't go to avoid the labor of thinking."* When you're all wrapped up in finding a solution to a problem, you might think you're thinking. It's more likely that you're avoiding the clear thinking that will bring a simple and direct solution to mind. When the simple and direct solution hits, what excuse do you have for not taking action?

Harvey S. Firestone, another long-time friend of Jim Newton's, got successful enough to eventually need an engineering department. Nothing was as much fun after that for the entrepreneurial Firestone. As the story goes, the Firestone company developed a brake lining powder and the product development folks brought it, all neatly packaged, to Harvey.

The company founder asked if the package would withstand shipping. His employees looked at each other and decided to take the problem to engineering to determine if the packaging could withstand shipping. Firestone stopped them, took the package and shook it hard. It broke open, spilling the powder all over his office. He handed the package back to one of his people and said, *"It won't withstand shipping."*

Henry Ford was another character who could cut through the cackle and get to the corn. Jim Newton recalls an incident that involved Ford's engineering department and a no-nonsense boss. Henry ordered a design change on the fender of his early automobiles. He gave the design idea to engineering and then checked back about a week later.

The engineers told him that they needed a few more days and Ford checked in with them *again*. The company founder was again told that engineering needed a few more days. Ford went straight from engineering to the factory floor where the old fenders were still being stamped out. He ordered the stamping machines stopped and had the fender molds removed and placed in the middle of the floor.

He then had the biggest worker he could find take a sledge hammer and break each mold in the middle. The man who developed the assembly line brought his own plant to a dead stop in order to light a fire under his engineering department who had decided to make a career out of solving one design problem. The new fender design was not only completed but *on-line* very quickly.

Problems due to error

We create some problems for ourselves. Any problem that's due to an error should only appear once. If the same problem appears again, the lesson of the first problem was never learned. Peter F. Drucker says, *"A crisis must never be experienced for the second time."* *Planning, judgment* and *implementation,* in that order, should be your plan for trouble-shooting a problem that's caused by your own efforts. If the problem you're faced with is due to an error, immediately check your planning to determine where and how you set yourself up for the problem.

Review your judgment. Perhaps it was your thinking that allowed the problem to occur. Everyone can always learn to make better judgments. I don't feel comfortable turning a project over to a person who thinks s/he knows it all. Someone who is always open to learning and improving his or her own judgment will do a better job by allowing for more possibilities.

Maybe your plan was fine and you didn't err in your judgment. It's possible that the solution was implemented improperly. Getting thoughts into action is important, but getting them into action *correctly* is even more important. If the problem is due to an error in implementation, you then know where to take corrective action.

Mary Lawrence, the problem-solver

After her near-fatal automobile accident, Mary Lawrence had many problems to deal with, any one of which would put a lesser person on public assistance. She was a great one for finding a practical, no-nonsense solution and putting it into action. One of her biggest problems was her lack of memory. The accident left her so impaired that she had a difficult time remembering how she began a sentence by the time she ended it.

That's why she spoke so deliberately on the telephone. She had to concentrate on every word. Passing her licensing exam was a result of endless hours of literally memorizing the codes and regulations. When it came to speaking with customers on the telephone and in person, she carried a small tape recorder. She repeated everything someone said to her on the phone about what they wanted in a home.

Mary didn't have shorthand skills and wasn't able to take notes that would make any sense to her after she hung up the telephone. By then all recollection of the call would be lost. She didn't break the law by recording someone over the telephone, instead she told them she was writing down the information. In reality, she was taping her end of the conversation, which she referred to over and over as she made her notes.

When she showed a house, Mary spoke into the recorder to store valuable information about her clients' needs and desires, explaining to the clients that she was keeping a detailed file on them back at the office—which she was. In virtually every case the clients were impressed that she would work so hard to keep tabs on what they wanted. Mary had problems and Mary found solutions. Most of all, Mary stayed in action. Today she's a millionaire property owner, proving that even the most difficult problems can be solved.

The not-so-helpful helper

I know a fellow who would give you the shirt off of his back if you needed it. He's truly one of the most unselfish people on the face of the earth. He told me about an experience he once had helping out a fellow traveler. It was a hot and humid summer day as my friend was driving between Chicago and Detroit. About an hour and a half west of Detroit, he was driving along in the air-conditioned comfort of his car when he spotted a man beside the road.

One glance told him that the man was hot and exhausted. The man's tie was loosened and his collar was open. There was a gasoline can sitting beside the man who had his thumb up in the air and a *"I know you're not going to stop either"* look on his face. Dick, being the good Samaritan that he is, pulled over. The man ran up to the car with new-found energy.

The man was exceedingly grateful and told my friend that he was beginning to believe no one was going to give him a ride. The gasoline can had no lid so they decided to wedge it between some suitcases in the trunk rather than risk spilling it in the car. With the gasoline can secured they were off. On the way, the poor traveler told my friend about how he had walked 20 miles in just over four hours to get to the gas station and spent almost another two hours trying to thumb a ride.

My friend told me later that he never felt more alive than when he was helping this stranger solve his problem. Apparently hundreds of cars had gone by and no one stopped. Now they were on their 20-mile journey back to where the man's car had run out of fuel. My friend pulled over and let the exceedingly grateful man out.

As my friend pulled away he was bursting with satisfaction at his good deed. He gave the man a salute in the rear-view mirror and drove the remaining 90 miles to Detroit. As he opened his trunk to unload his luggage, *there sat the man's gasoline can.* True story. My friend still has nightmares about what that man must have felt as he realized my friend wasn't coming back.

The moral of this story is:

> *"Don't forget the person you've decided to help"*—or—
> *"Don't get so wrapped up in the excitement and satisfaction of problem-solving that you forget to solve the problem."*

Always remember the same adversity that causes some people to break causes others to break records. As Confucius said, *"The gem cannot be polished without friction, nor [people] perfected without trials."* Make problems a tool as you engineer your success. Problems won't go away. If they're not working for you, they're working against you.

STEP SIX
Keeping Morale High

"Keep away from people who try to belittle your ambition. Small people always do that, but the really great people make you feel that you, too, can become great."
—*Mark Twain*

Whenever you venture out and attempt the new and different, your personal morale will be tested. Through the planning and launching phases of the *high-performance process* your morale and motivation tend to peak with anticipation. As the problems arise and you reach the bleak mid-winter of your process, your morale will come under assault.

As a high-performance person, you need to understand how your personal growth and increased productivity are tied to morale. If morale is not given sufficient consideration, you will unwittingly sabotage your efforts. Major stumbling blocks and other obstacles to your progress are obvious and are overcome with head-on confrontation or clever manipulation.

The erosion of your morale is something altogether different. Loss of morale is an insidious, creeping menace that will quietly eat at you like cancer. It sneaks up on you like termites eating away the floorboards in your house. You might not know that you have a morale problem until you fall into the basement one day. You'll probably sit there on the basement floor and scratch your head saying, *"I think I have a morale problem."* The fact is you had one long before you fell through the floor.

Don't wait until it's too late to deal with morale issues. By the time they become apparent, it might be too late to save the structure. Morale is an issue that requires attention every day.

A. M. Maslow, who documented the hierarchy of needs, also developed the *four levels of learning.* I've added a fifth level:

Level one: Unconscious incompetence

Down in southern Illinois where I come from, *unconscious incompetence* would be described as *messing something up without even knowing you're messing it up.* Of course you're not happy once you begin to pay the penalty for what you've screwed up. It's only for the moment that you're doing it that ignorance is bliss.

Level two: Conscious incompetence

When you become aware that you don't know what you're doing, you've graduated to Maslow's second level of learning. Operating on learning level two does not produce loads of self-confidence. People usually engage in activities they're not prepared for because they want the rewards anyway. Pride also encourages us not to admit when we're not sufficiently trained for something. In short, we don't want to look stupid.

At other times, knowing that you're operating outside of your expertise is helpful in not taking on tasks or assignments at which you might fail. You can use the awareness of your own incompetence as a guide to what you're prepared to do and what you're not prepared to do. At the same time, you don't want to restrict yourself from trying new things and growing simply because you're being called upon or challenged to do something new. Knowing your limitations will help you to handle your new endeavor more responsibly.

Level three: Conscious competence

Conscious competence means you can do something correctly as long as you think about what you're doing. As a pilot, I'm sure that anyone riding with me as a passenger wanted me operating on level three. Any time you enter the operating room at the hospital, you'll want the surgeon and the attending staff to be operating at a conscious level of competence.

Operating at level three requires intense focus on your project. You have the training, the natural talent, knowledge and experience to do something, but you can't apply those resources lightly. Level three can be the most exciting level in which to function. When you're keenly conscious of your skills, you tend to appreciate them more. It's not uncommon to feel proud when you're doing something well for the first time—or doing something exceedingly well.

Do you remember the first time you drove an automobile on your own? You had studied and been taught about driving, but it felt very different to do it yourself. Your first driving experiences were no doubt emotionally stimulating, even exhilarating. Then came a time that you drove all the way across town, making numerous stops and turns.

Level four: Unconscious competence

When you first parked your car, got out and began to walk away without thinking about what you had just done, you had crossed the line into level four, *unconscious competence*. Driving had become second nature to you. It no longer required intense focus nor produced a feeling of accomplishment.

You've probably experienced the same transition in a job. What might have begun as a stimulating challenge, with a rewarding sense of accomplishment, eventually became mundane. You might have changed jobs in the past because the job ceased to be a challenge. People tell me all the time that they want a change of scenery in their professional lives. They say that they need a new challenge to stimulate them.

I'm not recommending that you change career paths any time you become extremely competent at what you're doing. There are many ways to increase challenges within the scope of your present responsibilities. The first place to look is a part of your job you *don't* do particularly well. What are the things you *avoid doing* because they don't come as easily or effortlessly?

You can lead yourself right back through the emotionally-invigorating *conscious competence stage* by developing a new skill or venturing into an area that has made you nervous in the past. That's why I added the fifth level of learning, *conscious of unconscious competence.* By being conscious of your unconscious competence, you are aware of your situation and can avoid its perils.

Level five: Conscious of unconscious competence

You can put the spring back in your step by making efforts similar to the ones I just described to find new challenges and new responsibilities. I don't mean jump ship and replicate what you've done in one place in another place. That's not personal growth. Increasing personal productivity through the *high-performance process* always means you'll be conscious of emotionally stimulating efforts to push back your threshold of undeveloped strengths.

Becoming conscious of your unconscious competence brings you full-circle back to your personal moment of truth. If you're in a career position that has ceased to challenge you, the question becomes, *"Do I want to stay here and grow or go somewhere else and do what I did here?"* That's a more provocative question than it might seem at first blush.

If you stay and make what you're doing more challenging and fulfilling, you have no choice but to grow as a human being and increase your personal productivity. To move laterally to another position means you can keep doing the same old stuff over and over. The only difference is the scenery. You've probably already found out that even new scenery becomes old over time.

Job hopping, career hopping, marriage hopping and geography hopping all tend to seduce you for a short time and convince you that the future will be different. But that's seldom if ever the case.

If you aren't growing as a person and pushing back your threshold of undeveloped strengths, you're bound to eventually stagnate anywhere you go.

Taking whatever challenges you the most about your job, and bringing that challenge into level three, the exciting time of *conscious competence,* will spice up your life wherever you are. It could be improving organization skills, communication skills, becoming more involved with others, taking on a new and dynamic assignment or any number of things.

How about just increasing your level of personal productivity? There's no one alive who has maxed out his or her productivity potential. The more you learn, the more you become aware of how much you *don't* know. Consider the cliché, *"A little knowledge is a dangerous thing."* How many times have you seen the havoc wrought by someone who *thought* s/he knew a lot but didn't?

A little knowledge is not in and of itself dangerous. Someone operating well outside of his or her universe of competence can be *exceedingly* dangerous. The ideal level of operation remains level three, *conscious competence.* It's true that having skills and talents so ingrained that they become second nature will elevate your skill level. However, you still want to be keenly aware of what you're doing and be excited about it.

I'll use my surgeon simile again. If you came out from under you anesthesia for some reason right in the middle of an operation, would you rather hear your surgeon talking about his golf game the day before or how marvelously the operation is proceeding? Think about it. You might say you want a surgeon who is so skilled, s/he can successfully remove organs without even thinking about it. On the other hand, you darn well want him or her *thinking about it* while s/he's doing it.

Unconscious competence is terrific as long as you are functioning in an energized state of *conscious competence.* If you're aware of your *unconscious competence* and still don't feel compelled to read, study, attend seminars or consult with a mentor, why not? Are you that content where you are? Have you become complacent? Maybe you've simply not been doing what you're doing long enough. Trust me, without investing in your personal growth, you're going to sink into a hypnotic rut.

Someone once said, *"You don't grow old. You become old by not growing."* Is that ever true! Haven't you noticed that the great artists, entertainers, scientists, authors, thinkers all seem to be somehow timeless? They can be 80 or 90 years old and they're still as enchanted by new and innovative things as they ever were.

People like Thomas Edison, Bob Hope, Norman Vincent Peale, Mother Teresa, Grandma Moses, Norman Rockwell and others are known for their longevity. Or are they really known for ongoing activity throughout their lives? Lots of people live to be 80, 90 or more than 100 years old. How come they're not all famous if the number of years you live is the only criteria?

As I mentioned earlier, whoever first said, *"It's the amount of life in your years, not the number of years in your life that counts,"* had a valuable and timeless message for every man, woman and child who ever lived. Growing as a human being keeps your morale high. There's nothing else like it. If you wonder where the vigor of your youth has gone, it's fallen victim to stagnation. To get it back you must do what you did when you were young and invigorated—grow.

Feelings as habits change

You can see in Figure 6-1 the four progressive emotional levels that accompany the acquisition of new skills and the development of new strengths. Part of understanding the vital role of morale in your personal development is to accept that it's going to change as you change. For every improvement in your emotional state, there is a potential trap door you might fall through if you're not aware and vigilant.

Level one: Guilt and shame

When you first try something, it's likely that you'll set yourself up for some disappointing results. Unrealistic expectations are common to new efforts. When I first entered the sales business right out of the Air Force I still had my gung-ho, fly boy confidence. I told the other salespeople in my office that I didn't need to prospect for new business, I just sold off inventory.

Feelings (and Trap Doors)
During Change of Habits

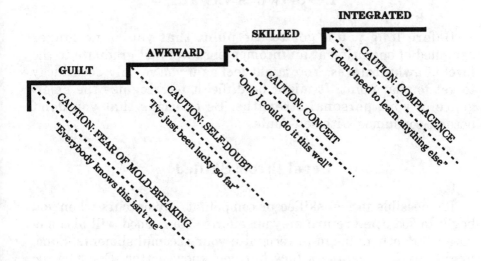

Figure 6.1

Before long I was a more humble sales professional out prospecting. How did I feel? Guilty. You might say to yourself, *"Everybody knows this isn't really me doing this."* Unfortunately, it is you, and you don't feel very good about it. At this level you're very aware of your incompetence. Beware that you don't develop a fear of mold-breaking. Sometimes you have to break the mold if it's not productive or realistic.

Level two: Awkward

Before long you'll get to the point that you're no longer ashamed of operating at an incompetent level and graduate to the level of awkwardness. You might feel as if you've only been lucky to get to that point. It might be difficult to recognize the emergence of your personal strengths. Be cautious that you don't become consumed with self-doubt.

Level three: Skilled

It's possible to feel skilled or competent. This occurs when you begin to see some return on your efforts. Your mood will also elevate when others begin to recognize your accomplishments. Some might say it's *beginners luck* but you know better. Don't be too quick to over-congratulate yourself, though. Conceit at the *"skilled"* level could mean trouble as in *"a little knowledge..."* You're never the *only* person who can do well and other people don't appreciate being told that you are.

Level four: Integrated

The change of habit or new behavior becomes part of how you go about your business. You feel the most confident at the integration level. What was once embarrassing, became awkward and then skilled, and is now a developed strength. Now it's part of you. It's second nature. You can comfortably rely on what you're now capable of doing.

Your self-confidence bolsters your morale. The only caution here is to not feel as if you can stop growing and be satisfied. You already know better than that. Part of keeping morale high is remembering where you came from and how much progress you've made. Knowing that, if you made the journey once, you'll be able to make it again, is a morale booster.

Survival training

I flew single-engine jet fighters over some of the most rugged mountain country in the United States, the Philippines, China, the South Pacific and points in between. The key term in the previous sentence is *"single-engine"* jet fighters. When your one and only engine decides to quit, you stand the chance of going from *king of the sky* to becoming an *unwanted guest in hostile territory* in a matter of moments. I wanted to be as prepared as possible.

I attended every survival school I could locate. Everything sounded good in the classroom because we always broke for lunch. But on a survival trek, alone in the wilderness, I once lost 18 pounds in seven days. Dirt and bark don't have a high calorie content. It's difficult to appreciate the amount and variety of food you take for granted until you spend a week away from it.

The classroom instructor for military survival training is always the same *character*—different people, but the same character. I swear they must go to Central Casting to find these guys. They're always craggy-faced, old, rugged, gruff, with pants tucked into highly-polished boots and stripes from cuff to shoulder. They were the forerunners of today's motivational speakers.

The survival instructors got me so pumped up about the adventure of survival in the wilderness that I used to dream about one day punching out of my aircraft just to prove I could survive out there. These guys would pace back and forth in front of the class and point at us as they lectured:

> *"I'll tell you what's going to happen to you, Captain. One day you're going to be sitting up there in that multi-million dollar jet and it's going to have a serious case of the 'come-aparts' on you.*

231

"Then you're going to decide to get out of there and the ejection seat will lift you out of any situation you determine is intolerable. That 35mm cannon shell under your seat will lift you 150 to 175 feet above the aircraft and you're going to parachute down somewhere in the wilderness.

"You'll be out in that wilderness for two, three, four days or more before we find you and, when we do find you, you'll be dead, graveyard dead, unless you..."

I decided to make a special note of whatever he was going to say next. I imagined that he might say something like, *"...unless you parachute into a McDonalds restaurant, a cornfield or a high school reunion picnic."* He didn't say any of those things. What he said caught me off guard. He said:

"You'll be dead unless you have a feeling of accomplishment on a daily basis."

"Huh?" Just as I was all set to write down something about how to find food, the instructor takes a sharp turn and starts talking about *emotional health.* He was serious as he went on to explain that, unless you have a feeling of accomplishment on a daily basis, your deteriorating morale will kill you faster than the wilderness will.

15 steps for keeping morale high

I offer you yet another list to consolidate some of the many activities you can engage in to boost your morale and keep it high regardless of your circumstances. I do all of these things. Some may appeal to you more than others, but they all have value. If you gave it enough thought, you could assemble your own list of things that you do, even without thinking about them, that brighten your mood.

1.   Lay out a new list of goals.

Doesn't that sound like a lot of fun? I didn't think so. I've heaped a ton of goal-setting and morale-building thoughts on you in this book. You've been buried under this list and that list. Why would you want to make another?

Remember what the survival instructor said about feeling a sense of accomplishment on a daily basis. Laying out a new goals list on a regular basis, especially a list of goals for the next 24 hours, sets you up for accomplishing a few things. The fact that you *listed* your goals makes you all the more aware of their accomplishment.

Improving your situation on a daily basis gives you the *feeling of accomplishment* necessary to sustain life. You don't want someone to find you dead in your office. Dwelling on the past (over which you have no influence) and worrying about the future (over which you have no influence) will kill you, or at least make you wish you were dead.

Operating in the *conscious competence* of the moment, where you can influence your destiny, will produce the sense of hopefulness to sustain you.

2. Go for a walk.

A solo stroll in the park, on the beach or in the mountains will have a rejuvenating effect on your psyche. Incidental pauses and repose from your workload give your spirits a lift by momentarily lifting the load. When you have your nose to the grindstone, you're forcing all of your energies through a pretty narrow corridor. Giving your mind an opportunity to wander in wide open spaces, *away from your principle place of business,* will help restore morale.

3. Buy (and read) several books on various topics.

Even if you're not an avid reader, force yourself to read a book or two from time to time. Don't, however, force yourself to read only on topics of success or increasing your personal performance. Read fiction or whatever. The act of reading is what will exercise atrophied parts of your brain that otherwise might be ignored.

4. Get away for a weekend to a luxury hotel or spa.

Definitions of what's luxurious vary from person to person. The important factor here is to be pampered. If you're used to working and driving hard, why not let someone wait on you for a couple of days? Again, it breaks the routine, changes the focus and gives your emotional batteries an opportunity to recharge.

You may personally prefer a weekend camping in the mountains or by the seashore. If your weekend is an extension of the well-ordered, matter-of-fact way that you work, you're not gaining much. Avoid skipping weekend opportunities figuring you'll take one or two extended vacations per year. I have nothing against extended vacations, but once your batteries are dead, they're dead until you recharge them. That suggests to me that mini-vacations on a regular basis are important.

5. Get in better physical condition.

How you feel physically has a profound effect on how you feel emotionally. The reverse is also true. The higher your morale is, the better you will feel physically. Absenteeism in a high-morale environment is only a fraction of what it is in a low-morale environment. All of these suggestions are tips on pumping up your personal morale. Walk, swim and/or join a health club and exercise on a *regular basis.* Your peak physical conditioning is another way to feel a sense of accomplishment.

6. Buy something you've always wanted.

If you're the kind of person who shops incessantly as a way of soothing anxiety, this isn't a good suggestion for you. The point of buying something you've always wanted is to combine personal reward with personal effort. That way, planning for, saving for (if necessary) and purchasing something that's been on your wish list for a long time produces yet another feeling of accomplishment.

7. Invite interesting people over for dinner.

Author James Newton got to know Thomas Edison, Henry Ford, Dr. Alexis Carrel, Harvey Firestone and Charles Lindbergh mostly by sharing meals and nonworking hours with them. Sharing relaxing, nonwork time with stimulating people, especially those who are not in the same field you are, is another way to open up parts of your brain that otherwise tend to stay locked up. Hearing other people's perspectives can't help but to widen yours.

8. Listen to good music.

Like reading a variety of books, music calls out certain brain functions that you probably don't exercise on a regular basis. It doesn't matter if you and your spouse or family agree on what "good" music is. You need to listen to something that pumps you up. If there are lyrics, sing along, preferably at the top of your lungs. Again, you're accessing parts of your brain that aren't given much exercise in your day to day affairs in order to elevate your mood.

Someone suggested to me that I listen to classical music to calm my mind. I had never listened to classical music before. Now I listen to classical music constantly. I even carry a portable cassette player with headphones when I travel. Taking your mind in a direction it wouldn't ordinarily go has an incredible calming and rejuvenating effect.

9. Organize your home and office.

When your home and office are cluttered, you feel as if you're out of control. Many people blame a sloppy office or home on being creative. I think that's an excuse for not taking control of their lives. Being in control, even of just your personal environment, means taking responsibility for it. I've already discussed why some folks avoid that. But ordering your personal environment is a sign of control and adds to your sense of accomplishment, thus propping up your personal mood.

10. Go see a funny movie or comedian.

In other words, *laugh*. There's nothing like laughter to remind you that life isn't to be taken too seriously. When you lose perspective, it's usually because you're giving too much consideration to something that would be better off with a more balanced approach. I don't mean to imply there are no topics that require serious consideration. Making a conscious choice to include laughter in your life will help you strike the appropriate balance and boost your morale at the same time.

11. List your assets and achievements.

Don't stage an elaborate episode of "This Is Your Life." Just take time periodically to list accomplishments so that you log them in. Many people, and you might be one of them, are very slow to appreciate their own achievements. Kept in proper perspective, a healthy consciousness of what you've accomplished and accumulated in terms of rewards over the years helps you to feel more confident about what you're capable of achieving today.

12. Talk to someone who always makes you feel good.

Preferably someone outside of your field. That might be your spouse, a close friend or family member, possibly a mentor. There is usually someone or several people in your life who have an uplifting effect on you. They're probably individuals with high self-esteem who respect and encourage you. Too many people are hesitant to ask for help. I know that has been one of my biggest problems over the years. The sooner you learn that asking for help with your morale is as important as asking for help on a project, the sooner your morale will improve.

13.   Develop a hobby.

This might sound trite, but it's yet another way for you to expand your thinking. When your mental faculties are devoted to a narrow range of endeavors, you tend to quickly exhaust your capacity for thinking while wasting much of the broad range of interests your talents, knowledge and experiences will support. This doesn't mean carrying on multiple careers simultaneously. Your career path should be well-focused. But give other talents and abilities their moment in the sun to add new ways of sensing accomplishment.

When I first hit the speaking circuit I used to hit a hotel room after a long flight and lay wide awake. I couldn't put my mind on hold long enough to sleep. Everything I did was so narrowly focused that I began to *lose focus*. In the middle of a seminar, I couldn't remember what city I was in.

As soon as I took up collecting and reading old and rare books, my mental prowess changed dramatically. Initially, I resisted the notion of developing a hobby. But since I picked up a mental diversion, I can sleep more soundly, wake up more refreshed and be far more alert when I'm doing my job. Now I spend my spare time in strange cities browsing through used book stores and I spend much of my time on airplanes (I fly an average of 1,000 miles per day) reading what fascinating people have written.

14.   Give help to someone who needs it.

There's no more effective way to climb out of your personal emotional rut than to get outside of yourself and help somebody else. Helping others in your working environment should always be a major priority. However, finding someone less fortunate than you (there are always people less fortunate than you) and giving them a hand on a regular basis (not just at holidays) helps to keep your life in perspective and exercises a nurturing side of your personality that's too easily ignored in your fast-paced world.

15.   Make someone else happy.

This is different than helping someone else succeed or merely survive. It means spending just 10 minutes per day cheering people up. One person or several, it doesn't matter. If you make a concerted effort to cheer up someone else, you can't avoid boosting your own morale. It takes a surprisingly short time.

"There are some days when I think I'm going to die from an overdose of satisfaction."
—Salvador Dali

"Mirth is God's medicine; everybody ought to bathe in it. Contentment is the fountain of youth."
—Oliver Wendell Holmes

"I've found there is very little success where there is little laughter."
—Andrew Carnegie

"Wisdom is to know that rest is rust and that real life is in love, laughter and work."
—Elbert Hubbard

What more can I say?

STEP SEVEN
Your Personal Plan
for Growth

Jim Newton, Henry Ford and Harvey Firestone stood staring up Madison Avenue through the large bay window of Firestone's apartment at the old Ritz Carlton in New York City. As the three men watched in silence, the street lights went out. Section by section across town, the city fell dark. The glittering lights of Broadway were turned off and the torch on the Statue of Liberty blinked out.

It was the night of October 21, 1931, and all across the United States the lights were being switched off for two minutes to mark the death of Thomas Edison. Few mortal men had influenced life on earth more positively than Edison. In one lifetime, this prolific inventor had been granted 1,093 patents, one patent for every 10 to 12 days of his adult life.

Edison had invented *more* than 1,093 patented objects. He simply gave away his medical inventions in hopes they would be put into practice far and wide. As Henry Ford gazed out of Firestone's window at the darkening city that autumn night, he must have thought about how, as a young entrepreneur and visionary, Thomas Edison had taken the time to encourage him.

Jim Newton describes that evening as one of those breathtaking moments in life. I can't think of a better way to begin this final chapter on personal growth. The *high-performance process* is intended to increase your personal productivity. But why? Why invest so much in yourself and why stay with it for the rest of your life?

Inward focus for outward results

You must find what timeless contribution you can make to the human race and keep that contribution in sight at all times. Few people will ever affect life on this planet as profoundly as Thomas Edison. Some will—and maybe you're one of those people. But, even if you're not, timelessness should still be part of your plan for personal growth.

Elbert Hubbard said:
"We were not put here to keep things the same, but to make things better."

That's a pretty straightforward philosophy. If what you're doing isn't making things better, then what are you doing it for? I'm not saying that you need to drop what you're doing and become Mother Teresa or devote your entire life to a high-profile humanitarian endeavor. But what you choose to do with your life, both professionally and personally, is either outward-focused or inward-focused.

Even if your outward focus doesn't extend beyond your spouse and family, it's still outside of *you*. As my wife and I rode on camels past the great Egyptian pyramids, I wondered if what I was doing was outward-focused. I wondered what monument, either physical or emotional, I would leave behind for my children and grandchildren. At the bottom line, your personal growth is tied to how outwardly focused you are.

This is not a bunch of motivational hype. This is *your life*. The issue of your personal growth and how profound your impact will be on the world around you only becomes irrelevant when it's blown out of perspective. The way you help make your organization a more pleasant and productive place to work is at stake more than whether someone will write your biography someday. So keep the issue of your personal growth in focus.

After reading everything in this book to this point, you're still in your moment of truth. You still need to make hard decisions and embark on new directions. The difference between you *now* and the way you were before you picked up this book is how much you know about your personal value in the scheme of things. You now know that the secret to becoming a high-performance person is to tap your own unique talents, knowledge and experience.

Hopefully, you're through trying to be what other people think you should be. The tool chest of methods and techniques I've now equipped you with only works on you. You can always use these tools to be more understanding and helpful to others, but you can't change anybody but *you*. That means *you're* the one on the hot seat.

What's in your hyphen?

A tombstone bears the date of when a life began and the date it ended. A simple hyphen stands for the rest of it. You can look at the *high-performance process* as a way to pack more into your hyphen. Years from now, how will you be remembered? What you choose to do today has everything to do with what will be said about you in the years to come.

Figure 7-1 illustrates what happens during your hyphen, depending upon the choices you make. The curving lines influence each other as time passes. For example, the *health and well-being* line absolutely begins at birth and ends at death. However, your goals line will either hasten your demise or prolong your life. As the goals line descends, initiative and desire fall off, too.

When initiative and desire fall off, your health and well-being tend to disintegrate. The faster your initiative and desire fall off, the more rapidly your health and well-being decline. In the United States, the average time between retirement and death is only a

Personal Growth's "Moments of Truth"

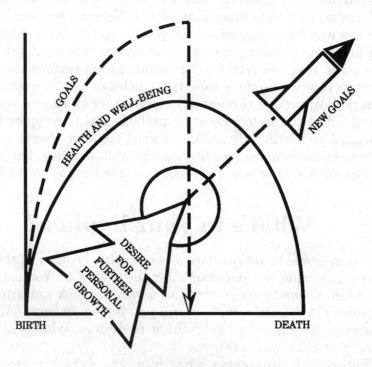

GOALS

HEALTH AND WELL-BEING

NEW GOALS

DESIRE FOR FURTHER PERSONAL GROWTH

BIRTH

DEATH

Figure 7.1

few years. Retirement for many is so short that some insurance experts recommend that, after retirement, you might as well go lay in the box and wait. L.L. Taylor wrote:

> *"When you get that gold watch after 35 years of dedicated service, take that gold watch and drive directly to the undertaker. You've got just enough time to make a down payment."*

The difference between work being a goal in itself and goals being a reflection of your desired rewards is personal choice. Either you make your own goals or someone else will make them for you. I watched a 78-year-old executive give a talk a few years ago. Few people are as full of life at any age as this guy was at 78. What he said really rang my bell.

His message was that, when you hit the age of 50, you don't make shorter plans, you make *longer* plans. He went on to say that if you have no further goals, you're telling your body that it's all right to begin the death process. Make no mistake about it, *death is a process.* Unlike the *high-performance process* that requires focus and effort on your part, death will slowly and insidiously overtake you if you have no goals leading you away from it.

As the illustration indicates, a powerful force called *desire for further personal growth* can enter the picture and make that rapidly deteriorating goals curve take off again. It can happen at most any time. As long as you're not in the ground yet, a renewed desire for further personal growth can revive you. The earlier in your life you commit to personal growth, the more fulfilled years you will enjoy.

As the saying goes, youth is wasted on the young. Unless you know the value of strength and energy, you'll probably waste it. When the force of your desire for further personal growth bangs up against the descending goals line, the goals line takes off again, often faster, higher, stronger and farther than it's ever gone. The older you are, the more dramatic the change.

Colonel Sanders didn't begin his fried chicken empire until he was 65 years old. George Burns had a career comeback like few have ever seen, winning his first Academy Award in his 80s. Burns was speaking to a college audience recently and a young person asked him what the secret to great acting was. Without a second thought, Burns shot back, *"Honesty. If you can fake that, you've got it made."*

Despite his age, Burns is getting faster, not slower. Another student asked him if he ever worries about dying. Without hesitation, Burns replied, *"I'm booked."* He's too busy looking ahead at his upcoming engagements to worry about anything as unproductive as death. Jim Newton, who had the close friendships with the great men I've previously mentioned, had to start over from scratch at the age of 68.

He had endured a financial collapse but resolved that he wasn't going to quit. How many people do you know who will refuse to quit in their late 60s? How many people do you know who quit long before that? Newton was so broke, he set up a desk in the lobby of a Florida hotel where he was living and published the number of the lobby pay telephone as his business number. Ten years later, his company had 15 offices going full force. He was nearly 80 when he sold his company for a substantial sum.

After he sold his company, I asked Jim Newton if he might retire. The man bubbled over with energy as he told me that his greatest work is still in front of him. How's that for an attitude? My wife and I still spend as much time with Jim and Ellie Newton as we can, hoping some of his vigor and enthusiasm will rub off on us. Jim Newton was 20 years old when he was building Edison park in Fort Myers, Florida. A lifetime later, Newton is contributing to the health and well-being of those around him more than ever.

More questions

As a good mentor, it's incumbent upon me to stimulate your thinking. That's what Jim Newton has done, and continues to do for me. It was on a trip to Florida to visit Jim that my wife and I formulated these last questions to help you focus on your further personal growth:

1. If you could spend 10 days alone asking questions of 10 great
    people, living or dead (one person per day), who would they be?

Heroes can be great historical figures or anyone from whom you can learn—it's up to you. The reason you feel you can learn something from the people you list is because you sense your strengths and beliefs somehow line up with theirs.

2. If you could spend 10 days alone asking questions of people who are living only (no duplications from the first list), which 10 would you pick?

    These questions reveal who your living heroes are. You now have a list of 20 guideposts for your customized training program.

3. In one sentence, which facets of each listed person's personality or accomplishments do you find most attractive?

    For example, I put Winston Churchill on my list because he had a gift and passion for oratory. He was not only a great thinker and writer, he was a master at inspiring an audience with his words. (The fact that he flunked English as a schoolboy is an interesting aside.) This list helps you focus your training from these great people's lives.

4. Why would any one of these 20 people enjoy spending a day in isolation with you?

    My wife answered the last question brilliantly. She said since she didn't know who her listed people's best friends were (or are), there was no reason she couldn't feel comfortable imagining herself as their best friend. Fame was not a requirement to be their friend. Furthermore, she felt they would enjoy spending a day with her because she is so anxious to learn—*about them.*

5. If you were given 28 hours per day for the rest of your life instead of the 24 you now have, what would you do with the four extra hours?

I gave these questions to another friend of mine, Og Mandino. Og is the author of the best seller, *The Greatest Salesman In The World* and a great thinker in his own right. After studying the questions, he immediately commented on how the answers speak volumes about your personal values. Your personal values are the life blood of your personality as defined by your natural talents, knowledge and experience.

How else are you going to discover, cultivate and stay true to your uniqueness as a human being if you don't have a fix on your personal value barometer? How better to explain why trying to be what others want you to be is such a frustrating and ultimately futile effort. As the character Felix said in the Neil Simon play, *The Odd Couple, "We are who we are."*

Can we get better? Of course. But the goal is not to pretend you're someone other than yourself, but to get better at discovering and developing your own personal strengths. These final questions will serve you as a navigational device if you take a few moments to answer them honestly and thoughtfully. Then use what you learn as you work through the *high-performance process*.

The first two questions provide you with a path for your own learning by focusing on who represents the most admirable and attractive components of human behavior. Question three specifies what you value most about each person. The fourth question speaks directly to your sense of self-value as you relate to the people you listed. Finally, question five exposes how you value your time resources.

Incidentally, the time-planning component of the *high-performance process* can open up four or more extra hours per day through more efficient time-use habits. You can't get away with saying that you could accomplish great things if only you had a few more hours in the day. Great football and basketball coaches don't say there wasn't enough time to win the game when the final gun or buzzer cuts short the big come-from-behind rally. More effective use of regulation time would have made the difference between victory and defeat.

And so...

I want you to use the *high-performance process* to be the best you can possibly be. That way you'll always know you did the best you possibly could for yourself and everyone around you. It's safer to have an enemy, confident in his or her true identity than to have a friend who doesn't know who s/he is. Never approach a bull from the front, a horse from the rear or a fool from any direction and always ride on the high side when the folks around you refuse to declare their intentions.

As your potential turns to performance on the pathway to power, always remember this:

Seize the Day! The best is on its way!

For more information on Danny Cox's speaking programs (live or recorded) contact:

Danny Cox
Acceleration Unlimited
17381 Bonner Drive, Suite 101
Tustin, California 92680
(714)838-3030

Index